SPACE LINE

BY

MARVIN E. FOX

© Feb. 9, 2012 Registration Number TXu 1-798-324
ISBN-13: 978-0-9896905-0-8

TABLE OF CONTENTS

CHAPTER	TITLE	PAGE NUMBER
1	THE EARTH LINE	3
2	THE GALACTIC FORUM MEETING	27
3	THE LAST TRY QUEST	63
4	TRIUMPHANT RETURN TO ARGA	76
5	CARGO SHIP OR HOLE IN THE GROUND	78
6	THREE CARGO SHIPS	84
7	THE FRIENDLY SPACE LINE	86
8	EGRIN AND BUST	93
9	NOT SO PEACEFUL IKLUG	105
10	THE VEOLSH PLANET	113
11	THE SAVE SUPEK OPERATION	122
12	THE CHOKNG FOUILD, KURSIT BALT PROBLEM	129
13	THE ASTOLIAN EMPIRE CRISIS	132
14	THE ARGAN WOMEN ATTACK CHOKNG AND KURSIT	156
	THE END	174

SPACE LINE BY MARIVIN E. FOX

1
THE EARTH LINE

Jeonk and Shok had been talking about running a cargo line from Arga to Earth for several years. Their plan had finally jelled into an accomplishable project. They expected to be surprised by a few problems with the project but they felt they had a handle on the surprises. Their engineers had solved all of the technical problems. The money and the markets were where they liked them on both ends. Good quality merchandise was available for customers on Earth and Arga. Cargo ship commanders were waiting to be hired and crews were available. Ports of entry were no problem at the Arga end; they could use the same ones they always used. The deals with the Earth nations for ports of entry were solid. Jeonk and Shok thought they were sitting pretty high except for one more little problem. They had to fly the cargo ships through hostile space to get to Earth.

The one little problem had more than on head but they thought they could handle all of the heads the same easy way. The first part of the problem was the route to Earth. Their cargo ships would have to fly close to the planet Prssk whose dictatorial government refers to itself as Prssk Command. Prssk Command, itself, doesn't engage in piracy or interplanetary illegal activities except on special occasions. If there happens to be more than the usual amount of money to be made, they want a part of it bad enough to dirty their hands.

Prssk's specialty is providing hideouts, bases of operation or holes in the ground for anyone from any part of the galaxy who is trying to get away from, or prey on, someone else. It doesn't matter what kind of crooked business they are into; they can pay Prssk Command for the privilege of going unnoticed in as grand a lifestyle as the payer can afford.

Arga's Space Command had raided Prssk on some occasions. It still maintains spies there to keep Space Command informed of the various types of criminals Prssk Command is providing a cover for at any given moment. A cargo line flying anywhere near Prssk can expect the pirates, smugglers and thieves based at Prssk to be a major problem.

Another head of the problem is Gamac. A planet of rust colored people nearly the same size as Earth people. The Gamacs are ruthless, strong and brutal. Their skin looks like skin stretched over large seashells of some kind instead of muscles. The Gamac's can be counted on to impress an illegal element on any problem. They operate from the planets Prssk or Gamac with equal illegal ferocity. Gamac is involved in piracy, slavery, smuggling, high dollar kidnapping, gun running and everything else that turns into quick money.

Gamac is the nearest planet to Prssk. The galactic class outlaw kings from those two planets are guardedly friendly with each other. The cargo ships can avoid what Gamac considers to be its own space but avoiding both planets would make an already long route too long.

Gamac is a dusty, mountainous planet with a minimum of water and a maximum of trouble. People need to be tough to survive on the unfriendly planet. Most Gamacs pass the toughness test easily. Their only good feature is their ability to determine when they are outmatched. When that happens, they leave in a hurry. Quick footwork is a part of the Gamac survival instinct.

The most dangerous head sticking up in the problem is a remnant of the Veolsh Empire. Arga had recently beaten the Veolsh in Galactic War 1. In that war the Veolsh tried to conquer Arga as a prelude to conquering the entire galaxy. Some of the defeated Veolsh escaped as the war ended, but the escapees are unwelcome on most of the other planets and wanted by the law on their home planet. The left over galaxy conquering Imperialists are making friends with anyone who doesn't want to put them in prison for past crimes. The highest hope of the Veolsh tyrants is to find a return path to the galactic empire game.

Before GW1 (Galactic War One) began, the Veolsh regime hired the Gamacs and the Prsskians to provide them with slave laborers. Jeonk and Shok are sure they will find the leftover Veolsh tyrants among the Prsskian and Gamac pirates they have to get rid of.

Not long after the Galactic War ended, the Argans discovered the Veolsh who escaped the war had hidden thirty imperial war cruisers. The survivors of the defeated Veolsh space armada were commanding the cruisers. Those commanders have a special hatred for Jeonk and Shok. They, correctly, believe the two engineered the demise of the Veolsh regime. Most of the Veolsh's personal wealth and power was lost when the old regime was ousted. The Veolsh survivors with thirty powerful imperial cruisers still had enough leftover wealth to cause a lot of trouble. They won't be satisfied until the wealth and power they have left is used to spill the blood of King Jeonk and Admiral Shok.

The two new cargo line owners decided their first problem solving effort would begin on Prssk. Jeonk and Shok left Arga on a course for Prssk in a souped up spacecraft, called a corsair, they had captured in a little war with the planet Krex. Prssk is nearly always the starting point for any mischief going on or about to start in this part of the galaxy.

Going to Prssk in an Argan cruiser or fighter was out of the question. If Prssk Command's scanners picked up a cruiser, the Prsskians would shut every thing down and go into hiding. It would cause a space battle just to land an Argan fighter on Prssk.

A corsair is a small space ship with room for a crew of ten, and enough cargo space for a profitable load of contraband, if you don't carry the crew of ten. Corsairs are tough little ships, well armed and well suited for small operations, and they are rather easy to handle with a crew of two. There are plenty of them flying around. That type of spacecraft is often seen on Prssk. Jeonk and Shok were flying the corsair without a crew. It was rigged so two people could operate its armament system, but the two operating it didn't expect to get into a battle. They wanted anyone who became interested in them to think they were out of work smugglers or pirates.

Jeonk and Shok are well known by reputation on Prssk but no one would be able to recognize them on sight unless they wore their usual uniforms or business clothing--that's what they thought. They decided to disguise themselves just to be safe. They wore the expensive clothing styled to the taste of self-employed space jockeys who were not precisely legal at any time. Jeonk filled out his disguise with a pair of false teeth he wore over his regular teeth to change the shape of his face. He wore a black cap with a bill on it and he had fake tattoos drawn on his arms, guaranteed to stay on until he removed them with chemicals.

Shok wore the same kind of clothing, including the same kind of hat, something like a French seaman's cap. He didn't have the false teeth but he did put on an eye patch he could see through.

Jeonk had the better disguise. There were enough Argans going in and leaving Prssk to give his lumpy headed Argan look the cover he needed. There are no Earth people on the planet Prssk and everyone knows Shok is from Earth. But, there is a race of people who come to Prssk occasionally from a planet called Enzurr. The Enzurrites look like Earth Caucasians except they all have brown eyes and brown hair. Shok's baldness took care of the hair part, and he wore contact lenses to make his eyes look brown. If anyone wanted him to speak the Enzurr language the game was up. He didn't have a clue about how it sounded. Argan voice translators didn't include Enzurr.

Both of them knew the first person they encountered on Prssk would be a tax collector, with the usual hand stretched out for the entry tax. Prssk Command doesn't like cheep skates coming to call and they get rid of them in a hurry. Neither of them worried about being recognized by the tax collector. If they had a problem it would occur as they moved around the commercial sections of Prssk.

They landed the corsair at the Prssk planet's port of entry, waited for the inevitable tax collector and paid the entry tax. Shok handed the tax collector a little extra so he would let them put the corsair in an easy area to get back to and leave from in a hurry if the need arose.

The taxman was glad for the extra gold, and his gratitude turned him into a fountain of information. Jeonk told him they were businessmen looking for profitable situations and they were low on cash. The tax collector didn't ask what kind of business. He assumed they were regulars in the trades. He gave Jeonk the names of places where others going broke in the pirating business could be found. He mentioned a few places that catered more to the smuggling trade. Shok slipped him another gold coin for his help. They were doing pretty good so far. The tax collector didn't ask Shok where he was from. Shok was glad the 'get the money and shut up' policy was still working on Prssk.

Shok and Jeonk headed for one of the more expensive pirate places the taxman told them about. The place was called, Klumika. Klumika's turned out to be a plush bistro whose customers ate the best food and watched expensive entertainment. The place had a fair number of expensively dressed people enjoying themselves. The space jockeys were easy to spot by the type of clothing they wore. Most of them preferred expensive fabrics with that shined, plastics, polished skins or cloth, and they all enjoyed wearing expensive metals, sometimes imbedded into the clothing they wore and sometimes in various parts of their heads. Knowing they were space jockeys was easy, but knowing which of them were pirates was another problem.

Jeonk and Shok passed through the dinner area to a back bar where there was a card game going on. The game was called Leeshtik. The Leeshtik deck has forty-five cards in it, and three different suits. Each suit is numbered one through fifteen. There are two red suites and one black suit. The object of the game is to get two red cards from different suites and different numbers and one black card whose number is in between the two red numbers. The winner is the person holding the hand adding up to the highest number. The best possible hand is a red thirteen in the red circle suit, a black fourteen in the black suit and a red fifteen in the red square suit. In the frequent case where there is no winner for one hand, the money stays on the table and increases the pot for the next hand, and so on, until there is a winner. Each player may discard one card and draw one card for each hand played. The largest number of people allowed to play in any one game is eleven but the players usually favored no more than eight. The game is played with only one deck and the cards are shuffled after each hand.

Leeshtik is a big money game on Prssk and it can be pretty emotional too. Cheaters are usually shot on the spot. Jeonk and Shok joined a game in progress but they had to wait a few hands until someone won. Five prosperous looking space jockeys were already in the game so it looked like a good place to start. One of the players was from Krex, two were Mogs and the other two were Gamacs. It's impossible to find a better recipe for pirate stew than a mix like that.

The dealer dealt for the house and lived off of tips from winners. Each player put one gold coin of equal value on the table for the ante. Then each was dealt three cards one at a time in turn. Jeonk drew a red circle eight, a red square twelve and a black eleven in return for his discard. His cards were good and he won the hand.

As the dealer began shuffling for the next hand, Shok started a conversation with the Gamac next to him, "We've been working the old Veolsh planets. The Veolsh Empire used to be pretty good but since the end of the war they're getting downright dangerous. They're out to get everyone in the business and they've stopped buying guns. The last time we were on Paraca, they tried to sell us guns. Our business has sure gone to blazes."

The Gamac answered, "The Argan King and that damned Shok screwed up everything in the area pretty good. Gun running was big business in the old empire. We supplied the rebels with guns and made money hand over fist. Now, we can't put a spacecraft down anywhere on the old Veolsh planets. Like you said, even Paraca is closing up tight. Paraca had some of our best ports."

"We're shut down until we can open a new territory," Shok remarked. "We're looking for business opportunities--if there's enough money in them. We have enough stashed to start something new but we're out of our usual territory. We'll have to look around for a while to see what's shaking and whose shaking it."

The Gamac let Shok in on one of the worst kept secrets on Prssk, "There's a pretty credible rumor that Arga is starting up a cargo line going from Arga to Earth. Earth is a blue planet way out on the edge of the galaxy. The Earth people have a lot of money, products and water. More than half the planet is water. Too bad we can't figure out a way to sell water. There'll be plenty of business for everyone when the Argan cargo line starts up. The big money people on Prssk are keeping an eye on that one."

"That's too big for us," Jeonk stated. "We don't have the fire power to go after an Argan cargo ship. Those people arm everything that flies. I'm an Argan and I know what I'm talking about."

"A bunch of small operators like us will go belly up in a star spot if we try to take them on," Shok commiserated. "We don't want any part of a small operation that dangerous. The bunch that took on the Veolsh and beat them won't be bothered by a few of us."

The Leeshtik player from Krex joined in, "Maybe it won't be a small operation. There's supposed to be big money and big players involved in this. We're hanging around to see if we can get some of the business coming our way. If I were you, I'd stay loose until the money decides to talk itself into business. I think there's plenty for everyone in this deal. All of us small operators may need to stay friendly in case the money people aren't that friendly to us independents. They could try to take over our fleets and keep everything for themselves."

Jeonk and Shok played, drank and swapped stories for another hour and a half. The other players didn't know anything of value. They didn't know or wouldn't tell the names of the source of money for the pirate operation. They knew of no time or place for a meeting of the people with the big money. They learned a little more than they knew before but nothing they hadn't already guessed.

Shok and Jeonk left Klumika's to meet one of Arga's informers for the Prssk area. The informer's office was in the business district. He was a longtime Prsskian businessman who knew Prssk's business people and their usual habits. As a Prsskian businessman, it wouldn't compromise him to have a clandestine meeting with pirates. Most of Prssk's businesses would be clandestine if they were on a different planet.

The informer, Boshtok Val, ushered them into his inner office for the sake of privacy. He had known they were coming so there was no need for questions about what he knew. He took a folder from his safe and opened it, saying, "The information you want is still not clearly defined. There is a rumor that the Veolsh are in hiding on some unknown planet while they wait for your cargo line to begin operation.

"I don't think it would be in their interests to attack anything as unprofitable as a cargo line, even one as large as yours. The Veolsh might decide to help the pirates just for revenge against the two of you, but they should be looking for a new home as quietly as possible. They still have thirty of the Veolsh Empire's Imperial Cruisers in operation. That's a powerful enough force to keep them safe anywhere unless you Argan's find them.

"It's been rumored that the Veolsh have a large amount of cash hid in a secret place, some planet the old regime hid it on. They may provide financing and organization for the pirate operation but I can't believe that is their main interest."

"Where does Prssk Command stand in the cargo pirating business?" Jeonk Asked.

"There is talk of Prssk Command operating a pirate organization from another planet," Boshtok Val answered. "That rumor comes from various sources and up to now I haven't been able to find out if the information is credible or not. Prssk Command might try it if they think they can remain undetected while profiting from the operation. They don't want a tough old space warrior like Fleet Admiral Rakoup dropping his fleet of Argan cruisers on Prssk to see how many butts he can kick and how high they fly. If I get any more information on the rumor, I'll pass it along to Shok's home office."

"Do you have information on the pirates themselves?" asked Shok. "We want to know who the leaders are, how many there are and which planets their bases are on?"

Boshtok Val laughed before he said, "The pirates are every smuggler, gun runner, pirate and slaver you two put out of business when you kicked the Veolsh Empire out of existence. All of them are looking for new opportunities. Most of them believe Prssk is the place to find those opportunities. I've never seen so many different races from so many different planets on Prssk at any time in the past.

"The present horde of money hungry pirate chiefs' command more than the usual one ship operations. Most of them have small fleets hid in places only they know. They wouldn't tell their mothers where their fleets are hidden.

"The one's you see here are trying to make the contacts they need to put their fleets back on the money trail. I think your biggest problem will be when they get tired of waiting for the, rumored, big money and decide to take you on with all of their fleets joined as one fleet.

"Prssk Command knows better than anyone else how powerful and how many ships are in the total pirate inventory, but they won't talk about it. Prssk Command has been beefing up its own military forces for several months. Its anyone's guess, so far, whether Prssk is beefing up its own fleet to join the pirates, or getting ready to defend Prssk from the pirates. I think it could go either way. That's all I have. If I get any more, you can contact me here or I can use my usual lines of communication to get the information to you."

Jeonk and Shok left Boshtok Val's office with no new information and left him no instructions to take another tact. Jeonk remarked, "So far, it's a useless trip. Your office already has more information than we've found here. We need to shake the tree and see what falls out. I was hoping we could discover who the principle pirates are and be introduced to their leader, but there may not be a pirate gang with one leader."

Shok thought over the possibilities as they walked toward a vyto taxi, "We have enough power to shake any trees we feel like, but we have to shake the right trees. We don't want Prssk going into business for itself and we don't want the Veolsh fleet wandering around waiting for a chance to organize the pirate fleets, Boshtok Val mentioned, into one big fleet."

His thoughts turned to space power and the Arga fleets, "Arga has nineteen fleets of sixteen cruisers each. It's the most powerful military force in the galaxy. Rakoup is the oldest Fleet Admiral and the most experienced. He's been past the retirement age for so long everyone has given up on getting his job. He's as hale and hearty as any of the young one's in the fleet. He married a young Argan lady less than a year ago and she spends a lot of time smiling. Rakoup is as strong as he is youthful. No one in his right mind wants to meet Rakoup when he's pissed, especially in a space battle. Rakoup has kicked Prssk's butt twice.

"Fleet Admiral Doskel is the other side of the same coin. He's the most technically expert of all the fleet commanders. He and Rakoup are opposites by nature. Rakoup is a mean slugger. Doskel is a technical wizard. Doskel's fleet turned off the power, all of the power, on the planet Krex before he attacked it. Doskel's and his fleet of sixteen cruisers followed a Veolsh Empire fleet of over sixty Imperial cruisers all over the galaxy before he took their hidden treasure away from them. Neither is likely to lose a battle and their enemies fearfully respect both.

"Fleet Admiral Brak designed the armament systems on the Black Cruiser fleets, and is the Fleet Admiral in command of one of the nineteen fleets. He is another tough genius with an interplanetary reputation for kicking butt. He knows more about Argan cruisers than any other admiral because he headed the team that manufactured the latest models."

Shok finished his thoughts and made this suggestion to Jeonk, "We should have Rakoup make a training and inspection tour of Prssk. He won't need to shoot anything. He won't need to land. All he has to do is keep his fleet over Prssk for a few days. He should be visible to those on the ground some of the time and he should scan the planet to take an inventory of everything that can move on Prssk. Rakoup's inspection may help Prssk Command decide to defend themselves from the pirates instead of joining the pirates. For the safety of Arga and the rest of the neighborhood, we need to keep Prssk under the gun.

"We should have Brak and Doskel's fleets find the thirty Veolsh cruisers. I don't know what the Veolsh fleet is up to but it's, for sure, up to no good. It's time we found the Veolsh fleet and kept tabs on it. A fleet that size could easily take over some weak planet and begin using it as a base. Wherever they are and whatever they're doing, we need to be able to put our hands on them at all times."

Jeonk agreed but he had an objection, "I hope it doesn't appear to the business people on Arga that we're doing these things just to protect our own business interests. We can take care of our business interests, and ourselves but I think your right. There are too many out of work criminal chiefs coming into Prssk to just pass it off as business as usual."

As they approached the vyto plak taxi, a Gamac signaled to them from the entrance of a bar. They followed him into the bar and the Gamac offered them chairs at a nearby table. As they sat down at the table, the Gamac said, "I understand you're out of work and looking for something with a little money in it." He spoke the Argan language. Argan is the business language of the inner galaxy and practically everyone involved in interplanetary business of any kind speaks Argan.

Jeonk answered, "How little is the money and what's the work?

The Gamac looked around suspiciously, as if his business would be too shady for the criminals on Prssk. He said, "I have forty boxes of goods for the Castu planet and I need someone to take them there. The boxes are number six size Prsskian shipping cartons. I'll pay you five hundred Argan gold skirbs to take the load. Can you handle that much on your corsair?"

Number six shipping cartons are about eight cubic feet each. Forty of them would fit nicely into the storage compartment of the corsair. Castu was one of the planets the Argans freed from the Veolsh. Jeonk and Shok knew the planet and were friendly with its people. Shok asked, "What's in the boxes and who do they go to on Castu?"

"The contents don't matter," the Gamac replied. "I want you to deliver them to a man who has a small space port on Castu. If you take the job, I'll give you his name and location."

"Five hundred skirbs isn't enough for a trip that far away," Jeonk objected, "and Castu is unfriendly to smugglers. We'll need fifteen hundred skirbs to take the load."

The Gamac's fingers fidgeted on the tabletop and he twisted in his seat as he considered the price. Finally, he made his counter offer, "I'll give you one thousand when your ship is loaded. You'll get the other five hundred when you deliver."

"How will the buyer on Castu know he has to pay another five hundred for the load?" Shok asked.

"I'm on my way to Castu now," the Gamac replied. "Your corsair is pretty slow. I'll be there before you are. I'll meet you on Castu with the extra five hundred skirbs."

Jeonk looked at the Gamac with the distrust any pirate would have shown before he said, "We intend to be here for another few days. We're looking for something bigger than freight jobs. If you don't mind waiting, we'll see that your boxes, of whatever they are, get to Castu."

The Gamac was dissatisfied but he agreed. The arrangements were made for him to put his load on the corsair and pay the one thousand gold skirbs when he began loading his forty boxes. Jeonk and Shok left the bar wondering what was important enough for such a high price.

They entered a vyto taxi a few yards farther down the street. The taxi climbed to the usual travel altitude before the pilot spoke. Instead of asking the usual, where to, he said, "You look like a couple of people who could come up with some pretty good money if you needed to."

"What have you got to sell that takes pretty good money?" Shok asked, "Do you have something special for us or are you just fishing?"

The pilot replied, "I know where there's something so special you'll pay me a gold skirb just to see it. I don't have it to sell and I don't know who is selling it but I can take you where it is--if you are interested."

"What is it?" Jeonk asked.

"It'll cost you one gold skirb to find out," the pilot retorted. "You'll know what it is when you see it."

The unbreakable Prssk Command rule is business people don't get robbed on Prssk. Neither thought the taxi pilot would try to rob them but he might lead them into some kind of a trap. Prssk had a different rule on traps; if anyone lets himself get into one, he's on his own. Still, The vyto pilot had their curiosity level raised. Shok said, "All right, show us this special, one gold skirb, sight."

The vyto taxi flew to a warehouse on the edge of the city. It looked safe enough from the outside. There were a few people passing on the street in front of it. The warehouse was large and it looked like an ordinary warehouse. They landed in the rear of the large building. The pilot went ahead of his passengers, opened a door in the rear of the building and waited for them to enter. Shok motioned for the pilot to go first. The pilot entered first with Shok and Jeonk following close behind.

Sitting across the floor of the warehouse were four Argan two man fighters. Jeonk and Shok walked toward them a few paces for a better look at the surprising find. Argan fighters are pretty well protected. Discovering how someone managed to steal or recover and repair four of them would take a fine tuned investigation. They stopped a few paces inside the door, giving the vyto pilots special one skirb sight a serious view. Suddenly, the vyto pilot turned and bolted for the door they had just entered.

They both knew it was a trap as soon as the vyto pilot moved toward the door. Shok grabbed him and punched him in the jaw. The punch was well placed, the pilot collapsed on the floor. Jeonk and Shok drew their pistols as he fell.   Several men of mixed races stepped out from behind packing crates that were spread around the warehouse. Jeonk and Shok began firing and backing toward the door. Jeonk took care of the attackers on the right. Shok shot the one's on the left. The surviving attackers were forced to escape the fire from four laser pistols fired by two gunfighters who rarely missed. The attackers retreated behind the packing crates they had just left, firing blindly behind them as they retreated. Shok and Jeonk managed to shoot down the assassins, who weren't quick enough to get behind the packing crates, as they made it out the door. They didn't wait to see if there was more assassins waiting around the outside of the building. Both of them quickly reentered the vyto plak and flew it out of there.

"I think we can forget those fifteen hundred skirbs and the trip to Castu," Shok remarked. "We were delayed by the Gamac to give somebody enough time to get the right vyto taxi to the right taxi stand. Someone knows who we are, or someone just doesn't like tall and short smugglers about to horn in on their business. I think we had better fly this plak to the corsair and get away from Prssk. It will take them at least a few minutes to organize another hit. Our corsair should be safe for that long."

"I'm sure as hell glad you and I work together so well in these situations," Jeonk said. "Someday, someone might get enough assassins together to make it really difficult for us. They'll have to do better than that bunch did."

They approached the corsair cautiously, making a swift overhead circle around it to check for an ambush. They saw no dangerous activity around the corsair. Shok slid the vyto plak to a landing very close to the corsair. Neither of them wanted to lose precious time going between the two crafts. They exited the plak with their pistols in their hands--just in case. Jeonk pressed the entry hatch control; both of them went in fast and were airborne a few seconds later.

Their quick climb to find some safe space wasn't quick enough. The corsair's rear scanner showed another corsair coming off of Prssk right behind them. Jeonk put the pedal to the metal on the souped up corsair to outdistance the bogey. The bogey on their tail was also souped up; they couldn't outdistance it. Shok flipped the gun switches and targeted it with the rear laser while Jeonk shifted to the right, trying to maneuver away from its forward pulse cannon.

The bogey fired and missed but Jeonk's quick turn took the bogey off of Shok's target scan. He fired a laser close to him anyway. Maybe the bogey's pilot was the worrying kind and a close shot might slow him down. The bogey pilot wasn't the worrying kind--he kept on coming. Jeonk slipped the corsair sharply to the left. The bogey countered with a left of his own which brought him into Shok's rear sight. Shok hit him with a laser that burned along the left side of his hull. The laser didn't hurt him enough to make him change course. The bogey fired his forward pulse cannon but he was out of position for a hit.

Shok said, "This guy sticks like glue. We better use our surprise on him." They had six very small missiles on board. Missile tubes aren't usually installed on corsairs but Jeonk and Shok like missiles so they had them installed. Shok fired a rear missile at the unfriendly son-of-a-gun. The unfriendly son-of-a-gun did some fancy maneuvers to escape the missile and he finally did escape it. Unfortunately for him, his maneuvering gave Jeonk a chance to come around for a forward pulse cannon shot at his amidships. With Jeonk coming in fast and aiming for the center of his ship, the bogey had only two choices, he could turn to face them or turn the other direction to get away. The bogey spun his corsair, choosing to get away. The bogey pilot thought his was the faster corsair, if push came to shove.

He quickly found out his wasn't the fastest corsair, but his retreat left him in a position to use his rear laser. He fired his rear laser at Jeonk and Shok as they pulled in behind him. The hit singed their hull on the starboard side but didn't cause any function problems. Shok had the bogey targeted on the forward scan. He hit the missile-firing button. This time the bogey didn't out maneuver the missile and his port thruster explode from the hit, causing the bogey corsair to yaw to the right as it lost forward motion. The exploding thruster put the corsair out of control, tumbling through space on its way back to the planet's surface.

Jeonk pointed their own corsair's nose toward deep space, climbed above the bogey and moved out of range of the active guns the pilot might still be able to use. He didn't want the bogey to win the battle with a dying shot.

"We got off of Prssk just in time," Jeonk assured Shok. "Another few minutes and we would have been up to our armpits in assassins.

"Let's not mention this little skirmish to our wives. They just don't seem to understand that these unimportant incidents are just a part of doing business."

Aslain is Jeonk's wife, and Alice is Shok's wife. They don't know much about their husbands businesses and the husbands don't bother the wives with the minor details. Their wives know they get into little scrapes now and then but they don't find it out from the husbands.

"We'd better take this Corsair into Meho for repairs," Shok suggested, "and get a pulse cannon installed in the rear in case we decide to use it again. The laser burn on the side will look terrible to anyone who isn't used to seeing them. Aslain and Alice never go to Meho and the security of the place will keep any of the Meho crew from talking about it."

"Good idea," Jeonk agreed. "We'll tell the wives that our business trip was just routine. They'll never know the difference."

The base at Meho was built and owned by Shok and Jeonk for the Black Ship. It's a special, hidden space base with an underground hanger built behind a cliff. The place looks like ordinary countryside until the camouflaged hanger doors are opened overhead. It's not far from the capital and their wives know about it but they have no reason to go there.

The Black Ship is a special cruiser Jeonk and Shok had built for commercial reasons. The same type of ship became the next generation Argan cruiser when the war with the Veolsh came on the horizon. Without the Black Cruiser class spacecraft, Arga would have lost the Veolsh war. Shok and Jeonk's original intention was to use the Black Ship to clear out the Prsskian pirates and make their cargo route safe. They used a variety of spacecraft for different travel needs but when business demands became dangerous, the Black Ship was the transportation of choice.

Neither Jeonk nor Shok wanted military involvement in their business but they sometimes ran into business situations where Arga's national interests were involved. This was one of those times. Jeonk said, "I'll have to call an Admiralty meeting to get Sitak Rakoup on board for the Prssk business. I think they'll all go for that all right. I'm not sure they'll be so happy about sending Brak and Doskel to find the Veolsh. Before I call the meeting, I want you to check with your sources on the old Veolsh planets to find out if there have been any of the Veolsh cruisers seen in their areas."

"I have continual coverage on those planets," Shok replied. "If there is a threat anywhere near them, I'll know about it as soon as I get to my office. I'll send a message to Chosteel on Paraca. He was in command of the rebel forces when we invaded the Veolsh planet. You remember him. He was that big tough looking guy who greeted us when we landed. He still watches the six planets like a mother hen. He set up a spy network with his old comrades in arms and the network covers all six planets. Chosteel thinks his spy network is a secret--don't say anything about it. If there's anything happening on any of the six planets, he'll probably be the one who knows what it is."

Jeonk was still concerned that the assassins had seen through their disguises so easily. Jeonk and Shok had been on Prssk many times before. They always went wherever they pleased and had no problems. He asked, "Who do you think tipped off the thugs who attacked us on Prssk?"

Shok didn't really have a clue so he gave him his best guess, "In a collection of professional scum that large it would be hard to tell. It may be that we have become so well known and hated that any two people who match the description of one big Argan and one standard Earth guy are considered to be us. They could be killed just because they're the wrong size and color. Every one of those bench-warming criminals blames us for putting them on the bench.

"I don't think we can travel around in the open like we did on Prssk any more any more. If we need proof, Prssk was the proof. From now on we better take some of our own military with us and no more disguises."

Jeonk was still thinking about it, "Do you think Boshtok Val may have helped set us up?"

"I don't think so," Shok answered. "He's been a good agent in the past but he does work for money, and there seems to be plenty of promises of big money on Prssk. I'll have him checked out through some of my other Prsskian sources just to make sure I'm right.

"I think Val was right about the Veolsh. They aren't pirates, they're conquerors. If they're the power behind the pirate activity, they aren't involved for what they can get in merchandise, and they don't need money. They'll want to destroy the cargo line for some other reason. We need to know that reason."

As they came into Argan atmosphere, Jeonk said, "Doskel and Brak may be able to get us the information we need about the Veolsh. Knowing the location of the Veolsh cruisers will tell us more about it. The old Veolsh Council only worked for itself. The survivors can't do whatever that is without their thirty cruisers and they can't do very much with only their cruisers. The Veolsh have a bigger plan, if they're at the bottom of this."

They landed the corsair at Meho, arranged for some new skin to replace the laser burned area on the corsair's outer hull, grabbed a command plak and headed for Poshalla. Plak is the Argan word for traveler. The most common vehicle is the vyto plak, the flying traveler. The command plaks are a larger and heavier version of the same type of traveler but filled with military communication gear and a few weapons.

Poshalla is the capital city of Arga. Jeonk, Shok, and their families live in separate buildings in the Royal Compound on the outskirts of Poshalla. From the street side of the compound, the buildings appear to be very expensive government buildings. Both buildings are ten floors high and have street accesses to their various business and military offices. On the opposite sides, away from the street, both look like beautiful palaces. They are very secure places to live, well guarded and very private.

Shok's palace belonged to Jeonk's brother, Tiskla, before Jeonk changed Arga from one to five kingdoms. Tiskla became king of the largest of the kingdoms and Jeonk remained the king over all other kings. Since Tiskla no longer needed the palace and Shok did, Jeonk asked Shok take it over. He's lived there ever since and it's been a good business, military and personal arrangement for Shok and Jeonk.

Shok landed the command plak on the rear pad of the Royal Compound. Jeonk went directly to Aslain and his two children in his palace. Shok went directly to Alice in his. Shok knew tomorrow would be a big day. The meeting might raise a few questions from the Admirals. There were twenty Fleet Admirals in Arga's Space Command. Jeonk remained in charge of the military as chief military officer for all of Arga. Shok was one of the twenty Fleet Admirals.

Alice was waiting for Shok when he entered. They kissed warmly and Shok enjoyed one of her tender welcoming hugs. She looked him over carefully, and asked, "No new laser burns and you aren't bleeding anywhere, I guess it was a routine business trip?"

He smiled at her concern and presented his story, "We were just checking some things out for our new cargo line, useless trip. We shouldn't have wasted our time."

Shok knew something was up when Alice said, "Is that what Jeonk is telling Aslain?"

He thought it best to wait it out and see what she knew. "Sure, why should he tell her anything else?" Shok replied.

Tears came to Alice's eyes as she answered, "Because Plask called here to see if you had gotten back yet. He said there was a gunfight in a warehouse on Prssk. You and Jeonk were seen leaving Prssk in that souped up corsair, you think we don't know you have, right after the gunfight. Another corsair followed the first one into space and one of them shot the other one down. Plask's friend on Prssk said he didn't know if yours was the one that kept going, or the one that was shot down. We've been worried about you ever since. Aslain has been crying, and I've been sick with worry. You two have got to quit playing this, this, wild-west days in the inner galaxy."

Plask is Jeonk's father. He abdicated and made Jeonk the King of Arga. He said he wanted to fish and live like an Argan again. Plask said he was tired of bureaucrats, paper work and diplomats. Plask's solution for his problem was simple. One day Plask walked up to Jeonk and told him it was time for him to be King. Plask has a castle in the Lersta Mountains and it's equipped to talk to anyone in Arga's area of the galaxy. He keeps in touch with his old friends and they keep in touch with him.

Plask's best and oldest friend is Sitak Rakoup and they have been in almost as much trouble as Jeonk and Shok but they won't admit it. Plask and Rakoup are generally on Jeonk and Shok's side in family discussions about the dangers of just being Jeonk and Shok, but not always.

Shok felt sorry for Jeonk. Aslain had been trying to get him to play king for a long time but Jeonk doesn't like the idea any more than his father did. Aslain was busily giving Jeonk hell about the gunfight and the 'little' corsair duel. Aslain is one of the finest and one of the strongest women anyone could want and she never tries to control Jeonk; she just wants him to be safe. Shok thought he had it much easier explaining to Alice.

Jeonk and Shok were in another of their unusual situations when Shok met Alice. They found Alice tied to a post, by the Mogs, outside of a mine operation on the Mog-5 planet. The Mog's tied her there to be eaten by an ugly little animal called Raka that ran in packs. The Raka are mostly teeth and three small legs. It uses its strongest leg, the one in the rear, to leap forward and snag its prey. If Jeonk and Shok hadn't been so active in personally solving their own and Arga's problems, the Raka would have made a meal of Alice. They were able to rescue her just after dark. The Raka are nocturnal feeders.

Shok knew Alice would understand, still, he chose his words carefully, "You and Aslain know Jeonk and I are very active. We're both hands on people. We get the best that can be done when we do it ourselves. We've done well for Arga and our families and we are what we are. We won't be going to Prssk anymore without an armed guard. In the old days we did and it wasn't dangerous. Now, we've become to well known.

"Jeonk and I were in a gunfight with Mog guards the day we met you, and I killed three of them that time. We're Argan warriors and we are sometimes in danger. We're both very good at getting out of danger alive. I'm sorry we upset you. We didn't think you would find out about the little gunfight in the warehouse. I'm sorry, OK?"

Then she began to cry in earnest. Shok's not very smart with women. He doesn't know what to do with them when they cry. She put her arms around him and rested her head on his shoulder. Shok just held her as she was and let her cry it out. After a while she said, "I know what you are and I wouldn't change you for anything. I love you. If you get yourself killed, I'll hate it. You do what you have to do but take more guns with you, and two of Sitak's cruisers when you and Jeonk go anywhere."

"I'll talk to Sitak about that," Shok answered. "Maybe I can add two cruisers from my own fleet, that will make four. Do you want us to take Plask and Rakoup with us? He and Rakoup haven't been in any trouble since the war ended. They'll both enjoy it."

The video telephone on the wall saved him from her retribution for his smart mouthed answer. The person who appeared on it was Jeonk. He said, "Will you come over for dinner, Bring Alice of course?"

The dinner was nice and Aslain wasn't as cool to Shok as he anticipated she would be. The dinner went smoothly and the ladies disappeared for after dinner women talk. Jeonk and Shok went into the library for a glass of wine and to discuss whatever Jeonk had invited Shok to dinner to talk about.

SPACE LINE BY MARIVIN E. FOX

Jeonk handed Shok a cigar and poured two glasses of wine. They lit their cigars and took a drink of the wine. "I think our gun fight on Prssk may have stirred things up a bit," Jeonk Remarked. "Not because of the fight, but because we didn't get killed. Plask has an old friend on Prssk, the one who called him about the corsair battle. His old friend told him something is going on with Prssk Command, but he wouldn't say what it was in an open conversation. He's sending Plask an information package by courier. I think we should wait until the package arrives before we have a meeting with the Admiralty. Plask is having Rakoup, Doskel and Brak for a visit to his castle tomorrow. You and I will be there with them."

Shok thought Plask might have a plan of his own. He didn't usually get involved with Jeonk and Shok's commercial business problems but he and many others, including Sitak Rakoup, had a financial interest in them. "Do you think Plask is just worried about your safety or do you think he's as worried about Arga as we are?" Shok asked.

"Maybe both," Jeonk replied, "he and Rakoup got into as much trouble as you and I get into. They were frequently off planet to check on things they considered important. He can't say too much about my safety. I think my Father feels some kind of trouble in the air and he wants to make sure it's taken care of. I have a feeling you and I are going for a small war council. My father, specifically, asked me to bring you with me. He probably knew I would anyway but he was specific about your being there."

They arrived at Plask's castle early in the afternoon. Alice and Aslain were, of course, with them. The four of them followed the Butler to Emira's kitchen where Emira and Iliaska, Jeonk's mother and Rakoup's wife, were waiting. Shok suffered through the usual greetings and small talk while he waited to get to the meat and potatoes of the visit. After a while, Emira said, "Jeonk, you and Shok go to Plask's library. He's waiting for you there. We ladies have things to talk about, and we don't need the two of you standing around while we're talking."

Plask's library was a big comfortable room filled with shelves full of books and there was a wealth of overstuffed furniture in the room. Plask and Sitak Rakoup were already there sitting comfortably at the large table in the center of the room. Plask said, "Sit down and have a Louisiana cigar while we wait for Doskel and Brak."

Rakoup opened up a little about the meeting. He said, "Plask thinks the cargo line has turned into a problem. It's a problem he thinks we need to take care of before you put it in operation."

Plask added, "I received a package from an old friend of mine on Prssk. It contains a number of documents outlining Prssk Command's plans for your cargo line."

The butler brought Doskel and Brak into the library as Plask finished speaking. Plask waved them to chairs at the table. They declined his offer of cigars.

Plask opened the folder he had previously laid on the table. He carefully looked at its contents for a few minutes before he spoke, "Prssk Command, helped by the Veolsh and their thirty cruisers, think they can knock your cargo line out of business. When they accomplish that, they intend to use their own cargo ships and take over the cargo business themselves. Prssk and the Veolsh are organizing the pirates and smugglers to hit your cargo ships so often and so hard you'll be driven out of business.

"We can't let that happen. If they succeed, we'll have contraband going to every friendly and unfriendly planet in our area of the galaxy. The Prsskians, the Veolsh and the Gamacs will get rich from the criminal trade and they will employ every out of work criminal in the galaxy. Your cargo line must succeed. We as a nation must not allow it to fail."

Doskel asked. "Why haven't the other Fleet Admirals been invited to this meeting? If it's a national matter, all of them will be involved."

"This isn't just a national matter," Plask answered, "it's also a family matter. According to the documents I have received from Prssk, the first priority of Prssk Command and the Veolsh is to kill Jeonk and Shok. They are sure they can make their plan work if Jeonk and Shok are dead. They don't believe their plan can be a success while Jeonk and Shok remain alive."

"What do you want us to do?" Brak asked. "I'm in from the beginning until the end but I think we need to bring the Admiralty into the picture."

Doskel added, "I agree with Brak. I think we need the other Admirals and their fleets in on this."

Jeonk agreed, "We'll bring the others into the picture but we need all of the intelligence we can get before we try to explain it to them. Father, do you have any information you haven't told us about? Who is this friend you have on Prssk?"

"Most of you know him," Plask replied. "He's the old Veolsh, Doctor Jssp, who escaped the Veolsh Empire long before it fell. He travels to several planets including this one. He owns a hospital on Prssk and he receives information only he can get because he treats most of the higher-ranking officials in Prssk Command. Not everyone in Prssk Command believes in the success of Prssk's venture into the pirate business. Some of them want out and they are afraid Prssk's involvement will only bring them more Argan grief than they already have. Those officials are the one's Jssp received the documents from. Doctor Jssp and his sources of information must be protected at all costs. That's one of the reasons this meeting is between the most trusted friends of the family. We aren't going to expose Jssp as our source, not even to the Admiralty."

Rakoup, by pre-arrangement with Plask, entered the discussion. "We are arranging special protection for Jeonk and Shok from this moment on. Plask has already ordered increased police protection for them and their families around the Royal Compound. I'm augmenting that protection with fighter protection over the Compound. There will be one of my cruisers in low orbit to back up the fighters if they need it."

Jeonk became angry as hell about the additional protection. He nearly exploded, "Who in the hell asked for more protection? We have enough protection without fighters hanging over the roof and a cruiser scanning every move we make. This isn't the first time Shok and I have been a target! We're almost always somebody's target."

Rakoup smiled; Doskel and Brak looked expectantly toward Plask to be the calming influence on the discussion. Shok was smart enough to keep his mouth shut as Plask's reply landed with both feet scuffing on Jeonk, "This is the first time you two have had somebody with thirty cruisers after you, and it's not the thirty cruisers worrying me. It's the six or seven hundred corsairs commanded by professional assassins--that worries me! Those pirates, and whatever else they are, are the best sneak attack force in the whole damn galaxy. They tried to kill you on Prssk and they will try to kill you wherever they can.

"The protection Sitak is giving you won't end with fighters over your roof! The fighters will follow wherever either of you go--until it's over! They'll go where Aslain and my grand children go. They'll go where Alice goes. I'm arranging the protection and I will not be put off in this matter. Arga is not losing its highest king and one of its most important admirals to a bunch of cutthroats. You and Shok will have to curb your activities until this is ended."

Jeonk still didn't like it but he knew his father was too serious to take no for an answer. He also knew the Admiralty would understand how serious the problem was as soon as Rakoup's cruisers and fighters began orbiting the Royal Compound. "All right," Jeonk agreed. "I'll call an Admiralty meeting immediately but I'll schedule it for two days from now. By that time we'll have some kind of a plan to present for the meeting.

"Shok's people are looking for the location of the pirate bases. Doskel and Brak can begin a search for the Veolsh fleet as soon as they can get their fleets in the sky. Only a few of the pirates will have their fleets with the Veolsh. The pirates don't trust the Veolsh any more than we do.

"None of the pirates brought their fleets to Prssk. They're afraid Prssk Command may want everything for themselves. The pirates don't want their fleets stolen by Prssk Command. Locating the Veolsh and the pirates should be our first priority. As soon as we know where they are, we'll put them out of business."

Brak added, "Doskel and I can split our fleets to cover a larger area. The Veolsh can't afford to lose any of their cruisers. They won't fight. We don't need two fleets flying together to find them. I'll get the archived fleet data on old pirate locations and make a tour of them with my fleet. I can check new locations as I go along. Shok can transfer any new information to Doskel and me while our fleets are in space. Anyone have any comments on that change?"

Shok decided it was time for him to get into the act. He suggested, "My fleet is on the ground at Perlta. I'll put six of my cruisers under Doskel's command and six under Brak's. It might be an unfortunate error for us to decide someone else won't fight. My cruisers added to Doskel and Brak's will bring their fleets up to the level of, they better not fight."

Plask voiced some worried thoughts on the subject, "Giving them your cruisers isn't going to be a way for you and Jeonk to join those fleets in space, is it?"

"No father," Jeonk growled, "we prefer a hot rod corsair and a couple of extra pistols. We'll have to find some other use for the four cruisers Shok is leaving on the ground."

Everyone in the room except Jeonk and Plask laughed at that. Rakoup said, "it seems to be settled. That's as far as we can go for now." All of them agreed with Rakoup.   Iliaska and Alice interrupted the end of the meeting with the announcement that dinner was being served.

Since the gathering of friends was formal, the dinner was held in the formal dinning room instead of Emira's kitchen. The small talk around the table was about families, fashions, jokes and old times. No one brought up the subjects of pirates and cargo lines. A formal dinner in the Lersta castle was for the enjoyment of the guests. Business of any kind was not a topic for discussion.

During the after dinner cigars and Louisiana beers, Plask announced, "I'm asking Dr. Jssp to stay here until this business with the cargo line is over. He's about the only honest person I know on Prssk and I think he may be in danger. I don't want to lose a friend because I didn't bother to invite him."

"Good idea," Jeonk remarked, "he can hold classes for the student doctors at Poshalla's Medical University. He hasn't been there for a long time and teaching at the Medical University will give him a cover story for leaving Prssk if he needs one."

"Who is Dr. Jssp?" asked Alice.

"Dr. Jssp is one of the most sought after doctors on several planets," Shok replied. "He almost always knows more about any particular race's medical problems than the resident doctors. His traveling office, laboratory and hospital are in a large spacecraft that actually looks like a flying saucer. His is the only spacecraft like it in our area of the galaxy and he won't say where he got it. When he visits Arga, everyone in the royal family circle gets a medical checkup. You have never met him and you are due for a medical checkup, ready or not.

Jssp can bring his ship into my base at Perlta. There will be plenty of room for it there and Perlta will put him close to Poshalla."

None of them stayed overnight at Lersta. Jeonk, Shok and the other Admirals, wanted to get started on the business at hand. Shok wanted to talk to Jeonk on the way to Poshalla but he couldn't while their wives were there. The subject was about tactics and he didn't think they would be interested. When the command plak landed at the Royal Compound, Shok said, "Jeonk, I need to talk to you. I'll see you in your library after I take Alice home."

As Alice and Shok entered their living quarters; Giama, Shok's personal secretary, said, "The men came to install the electronic thing you ordered. They went to put it in sub-level two."

" How long ago?" Shok asked, in a concerned voice.

"About two minutes," replied Giama.

Shok opened a panel near the communicator screen and pushed the silent Evacuate Building switch inside the panel. He took Alice and Giama by the arm and shoved them toward the door, saying "Go to Jeonk, tell him to evacuate his building and clear the area. Go with Jeonk when he leaves. I'll catch up with you when I'm done."

Before Alice and Giama were through the door, Shok grabbed two pistols from behind the panel he had just opened. He entered the small elevator nearby and went down to sub-level two. There was a large amount of electronic wiring in sub-level two and the only way to get to it was through Shok's living quarters. Shok knew Giama wouldn't have allowed workers in unless she was sure of them. Shok was sure of something else. He hadn't ordered any electronic 'thing' installed.

Shok stepped into the underground passageway from the elevator. He could hear two men discussing something but he couldn't hear well enough to understand what they were discussing. He turned quickly toward the voices. Two Argans were fifty feet farther down the passageway. They were standing still with a small package of about three cubic feet in volume held between them. Shok pointed a pistol at each of them and shouted, "Halt where you are! Don't turn around! Don't set that package down! If you move in any direction, I'll shoot!"

They both froze where they were and followed his order. Shok walked up behind them and said, "What are you doing here?"

The first one answered, "We were told to install this, whatever it is, according to the schematic it was delivered with. We checked the schematic before we left the shop and it seemed simple enough. We're here to do the installation."

The package was in a metal case with a lock on the case. Shok thought it was probably a bomb and it wouldn't go off until the lock was opened. He ordered them to remain where they were and not to move the case they were carrying. He removed his pocket radio and called the military police at the Poshalla Central Headquarters. Shok told them to send a bomb squad and some military police to handle the situation.

After twenty minutes the military and the bomb squad arrived. Shok explained to them. "I don't know what's in the package but it could be any kind of a bomb, including a small nuclear device."

The bomb squad's concern with the probability of an unknown type of bomb was immediate and serious. They took the metal case from the two workmen, and carefully slid it into a very sophisticated sealed transport case and removed it to a laboratory where it could be expertly examined. Shok would have to wait until they completed their examination to find out how the royal compound was supposed to be blown up.

Lower level passageways connect Shok and Jeonk's buildings. Sub-level one was used when it was inconvenient to walk from one building to the other on the surface. Sub-level two was full of electrical and electronic cabling to connect the various offices together. A powerful enough explosive device in either of the two passageways could destroy both buildings at the same time. A small nuclear device would make certain there were no survivors, and could destroy some of the closer buildings.

Shok ordered military guards for both passageways. The guards would remain on duty until Shok thought it was safe to relieve them. He also ordered ground troops to guard the compound and living quarters in the Royal Compound.

Having done everything he could to secure the compound, Shok left to find Jeonk and the rest of the family from the two evacuated buildings. Shok called as soon as he entered his command plak. He knew Jeonk would be waiting. Jeonk answered immediately. He had ordered the evacuating personnel from the two buildings to go home until they were notified to return. Jeonk took his family and Alice to the Krestam, a restaurant they all liked in Poshalla.

Jeonk said, "Alice has refused to order anything until you are at the table. You can explain what happened at the Royal Compound when you arrive. Aslain wont let us order anything until Alice does. I'm hungry and the kids are hungry, put the pedal to the metal. We'll talk about it when you arrive."

As Shok flew to the Krestam, it occurred to him that whoever was trying to blow them all to kingdom come would need to know when Jeonk and Shok would be in the building. It wouldn't have done them much good to blow the place up unless the assassins could get both of them.

Shok called Rakoup from his command plak, "Rakoup, have that hovering cruiser of yours look for a small spaceship, probably a corsair, with personnel scanning equipment on board. It will probably be hanging around in nearby space." Shok explained the situation about the bomb to him.

"I have more than one cruiser on duty in space," Rakoup replied, "Everything we have in space will be looking for your bogey. We'll board or force down anything big enough to carry a scanner."

He thanked Rakoup as he arrived at the Krestam. The family was waiting for him when he entered the dinning room. Alice ran to him from across the room. Shok thought she was going to give him a worried hug but instead, she took his arm and guided him to the table. As she pushed him down to be seated, she began a quiet but worried diatribe, "Kevin Kelly, do you have to do everything yourself? Why can't you let the police or the military take care of these problems? You didn't know what, or who, was in that basement. Why do you always have to be the first one in danger? Aren't you ever afraid?"

Jeonk stepped in to save Shok from Alice's fast paced misunderstanding of the situation. He remarked, "There were too many lives at stake for Shok to wait. He did the right thing. We might have lost some of the most important people in our organizations if he hadn't acted quickly."

Jeonk then turned to Shok and asked, "What's going on Shok?"

"You don't know what he was doing and you're on his side before you know?" Alice blurted.

Aslain quietly answered Alice, "When Kevin Kelly suddenly turns into Admiral Shok, It's best to stand back and let him do whatever he's doing. Tell us what went on in the compound Kevin. We're all curious."

Shok gave them the story, "Someone, through some ordinary work channel, was having what I think is a bomb planted in the sub-level two passageway between our buildings. I think the bomb is probably a small nuclear device large enough to blow up both buildings at the same time. Our return from Lersta was fortunately early. We arrived just as the workmen were about to install the bomb. I stopped them before they could begin the installation. The device is in military hands for evaluation and safe disposal. We'll know more about it when they finish with their evaluation. Rakoup has his cruisers checking nearby space for whoever was supposed to detonate it while we were in the building. That's all I know about it for the moment."

"Father was right," Jeonk said. "We'll have to beef up security around the compound until we can finish this business with the pirates."

Shok agreed, "I've already taken care of it. I ordered military ground troops to remain on the inside and outside of both buildings. The police have been relieved of the responsibility. They're not trained for this type of operation. Nothing, and no one, will get into, or go out of the compound, except through the military guards."

Alice apologized, "You did the right thing. I apologize for being concerned about your habit of jumping into everything first. You do what you have to do. I'll live with it, somehow!"

"Things should be closer to normal by the time we finish dinner," Jeonk advised. "You and I will have that talk when we return."

What was happening when the refugees from their own palaces finished dinner and returned to the compound wasn't precisely what anyone would call normal. The entire Royal Compound was flood lighted. Ground troops were busy setting up a military perimeter for five miles in all directions around the compound. General Sokeasel, the commanding general of The Argan National Army, the man in charge of the Argan ground forces on the planet Veolsh during the Veolsh war, was waiting for them.

General Sokeasel greeted them as they arrived and addressed Jeonk, "Your Majesty, King Plask has ordered maximum security for the Royal compound and asked me to personally supervise the security. I would have personally supervised the security anyway, but he did ask. King Plask didn't think Admiral Kelly put enough emphasis on the security problem. Your father is in route and will be here as soon as he can."

As the general finished speaking, one of Arga's finest fighter spacecraft came into the compound air space from the direction of the Lersta Mountains. It came in hot, did a quick aerial pirouette and slapped down on the landing pad in the rear of the compound. It wasn't difficult to figure out who would fly a fighter that way--Plask had arrived.

Jeonk and Shok sent their families inside. Alice chose to go with Aslain and the kids instead of to her own place. Jeonk and Shok left the general to greet Plask as he stepped out of his fighter. Plask was concerned, to say the least. He barked, "What's this business about a bomb being put inside the palace to blow both of you to hell? Rakoup tells me Shok found it and had it moved out. I want Aslain, the kids and Alice with me at Lersta. If you two get yourselves blown up, I'll have something to remember you by."

"What do you think Shok," Jeonk asked, "should we send them to Father's Lersta castle?"

"The pirates are probably willing to kill anyone to get the cargo line stopped," Shok replied. "Our families will need as much security at Lersta as they have here and so will your father."

Plask had never had a security problem like this. He balked for a moment before he said; "Sokeasel has more than five million men in his command. He can cover the entire Lersta mountain area if we need it. I'll speak to him immediately."

Plask waved General Sokeasel to where they were standing and explained the situation to him in his own short sentences, "General, I need the Lersta Mountains secured. Use as many troops as you need. Get them in there tonight."

He turned to Shok and continued, "Shok, you hang a couple of your cruisers over the place! Make sure they have Marines on board in case they need to do anything on the ground! Have them there as quick as you can!"

Shok and General Sokeasel picked up their radios at the same time. The General called for troops to move into the Lersta Mountains immediately.

Shok called his Vice Commander at his Perlta base and ordered four cruisers to patrol the Lersta Mountains immediately. Shok's cruisers would be over the mountains looking for bogeys, he hoped just bogeymen, in twenty minutes. He ordered the cruisers to land their Marines and form a line of protection around the castle until the ground troops arrived and relieved them.

"Plask, the castle is covered," Shok reported. "The cruisers will be over the castle in twenty minutes and my Marines will be protecting it in thirty minutes. General sokeasel's ground troops can relieve the Marines as soon as his troops get to the castle."

"I'll tell Aslain and the kids," remarked Jeonk. "You tell Alice. Aslain and the kids have plenty of clothing at the castle. Alice may want to pack a few things."

Plask interjected, "Alice has plenty of clothing at the castle. She won't need to pack anything. All of them spend a lot of time there while you two are gone. Alice and Aslain might as well be married to traveling salesmen."

That was Plask's last salvo before the families were ready to leave. Plask left his fighter sitting where he landed it. Jeonk put Plask and the families in a command plak as he and Shok said their short good-byes. The cruisers would be overhead and the Marines on the ground before their command plak reached Plask's castle.

Shok didn't think the Marines would flood light the whole area like Sokeasel's troops had done at the Royal Compound but he was sure there would be plenty of light around the castle after the ground troops took over.

Jeonk and Shok nearly made it to the library for their private meeting when Rakoup bellowed into their radios, "Shok, you were right. We found a corsair just sort of hanging around in space. We tractor beamed it into a cruiser and guess what they had on board." He didn't wait for Shok's guess, he continued, "It had a personnel scanner and a triggering device. A Gamac and a guy from Prssk manned the corsair. I'm having the cruiser bring them in at my base at Lipok. My interrogators are the best in the business. I'll tell my interrogators to wait until you arrive if you want to talk to them first."

"Tell your interrogators to wait," Shok replied. "I'll be at Lipok as soon as I can."

"I'll be there with Shok," Jeonk added into his radio. "This should be a very interesting question and answer session."

Rakoup wasn't one to be left out, "I'll meet both of you at Lipok. We'll get the truth out of those pirates. You have my word on it."

Jeonk and Shok had their private meeting in Plask's fighter on the flight to Lipok. Shok opened the conversation, "I don't think Doskel and Brak will find the Veolsh. They'll probably find a few of the pirate fleets but I think most of the fleets will be somewhere on the six planets we freed from the Veolsh. That's where most of the pirates and smugglers were working before the war. The pirates will know those planets haven't the equipment to find the pirates hiding places. They may not be able to do business on the planets but it's easy to hide a bunch of small fleets on any of them. Brak and Doskel will chase the ones who are hiding around here to the six planets and we need that done. When we get all of them in one area they'll be easier to deal with.

"We have another problem with the nations on the six planets. We can't take an unannounced fleet into their space without causing interplanetary problems. I think I had better go to the Veolsh planet and talk with the nations in the Galactic Forum. All of the Forum nations signed a treaty to ban piracy and I think I can get them to allow us to take a fleet in and wipe out the pirates because of the treaty.

"I'll talk with Chosteel; he's the one who will know more about pirate hideouts than anyone else. I don't think the Argan diplomats assigned to the Galactic Forum can handle this job. This will take someone who knows and has dealt with the freedom fighters personally. I'm the only one who can do it."

Jeonk asked, "How are you going to get there? What about the protection Plask insists we both have?"

"I kept four of my cruisers out of Doskel and Brak's commands to use but my four cruisers are now busy over the Lersta Mountains," Shok answered. "Rakoup isn't using all of his cruisers. I can ask him for four. Four cruisers should more than satisfy Plask's minimum protection standard and it's still a small enough force to keep the governments on the six planets from getting nervous."

Jeonk was in a joking mood. He said, "Wouldn't you rather sneak out and take that souped up corsair we hid at Tischel?"

Shok responded, "Have you noticed how many fighters have joined us on this flight to Lipok? There's a full load of them, and their mother ship is probably following them at low altitude. Our sneaking out days has ended for a while. Besides that, we may need a hideout corsair someday. We better keep it a secret."

Jeonk didn't say anymore about the plan. Shok knew he approved. If he hadn't, he would be asking questions and suggesting alternatives. Shok didn't know his silent approval included tthinking of a way to go along.

As they dropped down on Lipok, the fighter escort spread out and began orbiting the base. Rakoup was already at Lipok waiting for them. He escorted Jeonk and Shok into an interrogation room in his headquarters building. The two pirates sat nervously at a table with their backs to the door. One guard was in front of them and one behind. Jeonk and Shok walked around the table to face them before they began the questions.

Rakoup stayed outside the room and watched through a window but he could hear whatever went on in the room. Everything was being video recorded. Rakoup's interrogators were concealed in another room, and listening for any clues they might use in the later interrogations.

Shok was pleasantly surprised to see the Gamac who offered them the smuggling job on Prssk, and the vyto taxi pilot who had taken them to be killed at the warehouse on Prssk. Jeonk remarked, "I was afraid we had seen the last of you two when we left Prssk."

Shok gave them one of his friendliest smiles and said, "I'm really glad to see the two of you under such pleasant circumstances." He looked at the one from Prssk and added, "I hope the punch in the jaw I gave you hasn't been a problem."

Jeonk wasn't smiling when he said, "Do you know who Rakoup is?" They shook their heads yes. Jeonk continued, "Rakoup gave me his word that the two of you would tell us everything you know. I have only heard him give his word a few times in my life. He kept it each time. Rakoup is waiting just outside to see if you tell us everything you know. If you don't, Shok and I will leave and find out what you know from Rakoup."

The two pirates were about Shok's size. Rakoup is a little over eight feet tall, about the same as Jeonk. They both turned and looked at Rakoup through the window. Rakoup looked back at them with one of meanest expressions ever seen on his face. The two pirates looked sick after their quick look at Rakoup. Rakoup was well known on Prssk and Gamac, by reputation. Seeing him up close, and pissed off, wasn't a part of their plan.

Shok thought the pirates were about to become a fountain of information. He started by asking them questions he knew, or would know the answers to reasonably soon. "What kind of bomb did you put in the Royal compound?" Shok gave the Gamac a chance to answer first. He seemed the most frightened.

"Nuclear," the Gamac replied.

"What kind and how big?" Shok demanded.

"I don't know what kind, but I think it was a one kilo ton bomb," the Gamac answered.

Shok asked, "how were you going to set it off, and how would you know it would kill his Majesty and me?"

The Gamac squirmed before he answered, "We had a personnel scanner good enough to see the Royal compound and the people who were there. We would have set the bomb off with a remote trigger."

"Think very carefully before you answer my next question," Shok warned. "If you don't give me a straight answer, Rakoup won't need to come in here because you will be dead. You were waiting above Arga to kill the King, our families, and me. That wouldn't take a one-kilo ton bomb. Why did you use such a large explosive?"

The Gamac looked even sicker than he did before. He watched Jeonk as Jeonk drew his knife. The Gamac nervously responded, "We were paid to kill you, King Jeonk and all of the people you have in both of your offices in the Royal Compound. Our scanners aren't as good as the scanners you Argans use. We could make a mistake about your locations in the compound. We had to be sure we got everyone and everything with one blast."

Shok turned to the assassin from Prssk and said, "Your answers are under the same knife his answers are. Who paid you and how much?"

It was the Prsskians turn to squirm. His face gave them the impression that he might not answer or he might lie. Jeonk put his knife against the Prsskians throat and barked, "You have three seconds to start talking."

The Prsskian decided against losing his head. He stated, "We were paid one million gold skirbs but I don't know who hired us. The money came through middlemen who didn't identify the payer. The same people gave us the remote trigger and the scanner."

"Make a guess about who hired you," Shok demanded. "Who has a million gold skirbs to spend on one little job?"

The nervous Prsskian tried to squirm away from Jeonk's knife as he guessed, "I don't know; maybe a government, maybe a group of people got together to put up the money. You two aren't well liked in our crowd. I don't know who."

Shok pressed on for more information, "How did you know when the bomb would be active? You had to know when it was active to use the remote triggering device."

The Prsskian replied, "We were given a start time for the use of the remote trigger. After that time, we could detonate the bomb whenever our scanner showed both of you were anywhere in the compound."

"How did you get the bomb to Arga and how did you get it sent to the compound?" Shok asked.

"We don't know," he answered. "We didn't have anything to do with that end of the business. We were given a schedule and the stuff we had in the ship. We didn't have anything to do with anything else."

Shok thought he had exhausted the topic for the moment. He turned to the Gamac for his final questions, "Where are the people you ordinarily work with based? Where is your fleet?"

Shok saw the fear on his face. He could let them kill him now or let his pirate friends kill him later for talking. The time of death issue won the day. He answered, "We have a base on the planet Castu. I'll save you the next question; we have seventeen corsairs in the fleet."

Shok thought he had gotten everything he could from them for the moment. He turned to Jeonk and asked, "Do you have any more questions?" Jeonk shook his head no. He and Shok left to rejoined Rakoup outside the room.

Rakoup mulled it over for a while before he said, "The only thing you got from them that you didn't already know is how much they were paid and where their base is. I'll have my interrogators work with them, Maybe some long term questioning will turn up more information or something new. I have an old guy who can make them think he's their friend. It will take him a few days but he can get more from them than anyone else."

Jeonk turned to Rakoup; "We may need four of your cruisers and some Marines in the near future. Shok and I think we need to go to the Veolsh planet to talk with the freedom fighters there. The Gamac confirmed the location of at least one of the pirate fleets and we think most of them will be in the old Veolsh Empire area."

Shok noticed Jeonk's, "We need to go" in Jeonk's informational bulletin to Rakoup. Shok hadn't said anything about we. Shok had no idea how Jeonk expected to explain the new plan to his father. Shok hoped he wouldn't be there when Jeonk did but he knew Jeonk would have to make his explanation soon. If he didn't, Rakoup would have to inform Plask. Shok thought it would be a really bad idea for Jeonk to be the second one to tell Plask. Jeonk could tell his father that his father wasn't king any more and he, Jeonk, would do as he felt best, but Jeonk would never make a move like that. It just wasn't his style and he loved his parents too much to think of doing it.

Jeonk and Shok lifted Plask's fighter off of Rakoup's base and headed for Plask's castle with the fighter escort and probably one of Rakoup's cruisers following them. They were both anxious to see how the families were doing under the most extensive security umbrella Arga had ever seen. Neither of them said anything on the flight.

Shok flew the fighter and Jeonk sat thinking his own thoughts. Shok guessed he was considering how to tell Plask he was going to the Veolsh planet with Shok, without causing a family crisis. Both would be almost as safe on Veolsh as they were on Arga. After all, they were taking their military protection with them.

SPACE LINE BY MARIVIN E. FOX

The castle wasn't difficult to see. General Sokeasel had enough light around it to make it visible from anywhere in nearby space. Shok was glad he put four cruisers overhead instead of two. Shok considered, "With all the lights, I think I could eyeball a missile into the castle from a long way out in space." He lowered Plask's fighter to its usual pad. Jeonk and Shok entered the castle after being recognized by the security guards.

The family was gathered in Emira's kitchen, waiting anxiously for them to explain how they would have been blown up. Emira walked across the kitchen, leaned over, gave Shok a hug and a kiss on the cheek before she said, "Kevin, I pray for you every night when I pray for the rest of the family. You're one of the best men I've ever known and one of the dearest. I love you very much. If Plask ever gets mad at you, I'll kick him in the shins."

Emira didn't say very much as a rule. Shok knew she thought he had saved the family but he didn't know what he was supposed to say about it. He just gave her a hug and kissed her cheek in return. Shok finally said, "I just did the work I had to do. We were lucky to get home at just the right time."

Jeonk turned to where his father was sitting and said, "Shok and I have something to talk about, father. Let's go to the library."

Jeonk seemed unusually forceful with his father in the library, "Shok and I think we know where we'll find most of the pirate fleets and maybe the Veolsh cruisers. We're going to the Veolsh planet and talk to the freedom fighters that helped set up the Galactic Forum. The freedom fighters bought guns and ammunition from the pirates and smugglers during their decades of rebellion against the Veolsh Empire. If anyone knows where the pirates are hiding, it will be the freedom fighters.

"Shok thinks Chosteel, from Paraca, is the most likely one to begin with. It's best not to take a fleet into that area without doing some groundwork first. Shok knows them well and I've met many of them. There isn't anyone else who can get the job done. We'll take four of Rakoup's cruisers and their Marines. That should take care of our personal security problem."

Plask thought for a while before he said, "I know you're going whether I like it or not but I agree with you. You must go where the battle is. You two do what you have to do." He turned to Shok and asked, "Do you know how that bomb was delivered to Arga?

Shok shook his head no before he said, "Jeonk and I do a large amount of interplanetary business. My best guess is, that it came through some normal business channel from off planet. The instructions for delivery and installation were with it when it arrived. The police will investigate. I think they'll come to a dead end on whatever planet it was shipped from. It was a very slick operation. We were lucky it didn't work."

Plask barked, "Luck hell, you had the same kind of luck in the gun fight on Prssk. I don't know how you do it. The two of you are always the ones still standing when it's over. How did you win that fight on Prssk?"

Jeonk answered, "Shok shot three on the left; I shot three on the right, the rest of them dived for cover. We hit a couple of them as they went for cover, but I don't know how badly they were injured. We always know what the other will do in a fight. We don't have to plan it, think about it, or talk about it. We just do it."

Plask shook his head back and forth, then he chuckled, "The pirates don't have a chance. You two have a fun trip to Veolsh. Rakoup and I will keep the lid on things here. When are you leaving?"

Jeonk answered, "I've called an Admiralty meeting for tomorrow. We'll leave as soon as the meeting is over. I want this pirate business over with as quickly as possible.

"Enjoy your families as much as you can until then," Plask reminded.

Active men don't usually think about how important families are but when their families are in danger and need protection, family importance is brought into full focus. Shok and Jeonk had just left their families under massive ground and air protection. Both of them were sharply focused on their families' importance as their fighter settled to its landing at the Admiralty.

They expected the Admiralty meeting to be routine. Shok was sure the Admirals would be wondering how they could get their fleets into the action. Jeonk opened the meeting with the details of the pirate attempt to nuke the Royal Compound. Then he made his report on the security measures used for protection. Jeonk gave them his reasons for the meeting on the Veolsh planet with the members of the Galactic Forum.

Jeonk found it easy to convince the Admirals of the serious nature of the pirate threat the Argan fleets might be used to eliminate. "Your fleets will be involved in stopping the pirate threat to Arga and our neighboring nations, Jeonk explained. "Shok and I hope to locate the pirate bases in our meeting on the Veolsh planet.

"When the bases are located, I'll call for the fleet support needed to destroy them. We expect to have the full cooperation of any governments where the bases are located. Our main worry with the Forum nations is their fear of the loss of their sovereignty.

"Your fleets must be careful when they enter their airspace. We will not use air attacks on bases near towns or cities. We expect most of the bases to be in remote areas so that shouldn't be a problem. We'll us marine attacks covered by air support on any of the bases we find are not remote.

"If the pirates run, don't fire on them near a planets surface. Wait until they reach deep space, then fry them. If any of the pirates want to surrender, allow them to surrender. Put pilots aboard their ships and fly the ships to Tischel. Most of their spaceships are corsairs. They're tough ships, but no match for Argan fighters or cruisers. Are there any questions or comments?"

Fleet Admiral Skoltas' asked the question on everyone's mind, "How many cruisers are you going to need, and which fleets?"

"We don't know yet," Jeonk responded. "We won't know until we know where the bases are on the six planets and the total number of ships they have. We expect to learn that on Veolsh. We, and four of Rakoup's cruisers, are leaving for Veolsh as soon as this meeting is over."

The discussion, after Skoltas' question, was about the mundane details of fleet management for any operation. The meeting lasted another hour before Jeonk and Shok could leave for Lipok and put Rakoup's four cruisers in the sky.

2

THE GALACTIC FORUM MEETING

Shok was never comfortable on the sunburned sands of the Veolsh planet. He had spent eight months on it while helping the nations of Veolsh, and the nations of the other six planets establish the Galactic Forum. The Veolsh planet is a dry planet of shifting sands and high mountain ranges. It has little water. The Veolsh people didn't needed or use much water. They clean everything that can be cleaned in there homes with purified sand. Homes and their appliances are made of a common metal found on the Veolsh planet, and everything clean shines like newly minted silver. The metallic outside walls of their homes are polished by the wind and blowing sand. The inside of their homes is cleaned by whoever does that sort of thing. All of it has a mirror-like shine.

Veolsh storms were dangerous, wild, and beautiful to see. Piled up sand, blown by the wind, pours down the Veolsh cliffs like waterfalls. The canyons at the bottom of the cliffs never fill up with the sand. When the wind shifts to another direction it blows the sand around the cliffs and back where it came from. The shifted sand sits still, waiting for the next storm.

The exception to the Spartan like Veolsh home life was the mansions of the departed Veolsh Council members. Shok stayed in the Veolsh Council's Great Maxim's mansions while he worked to establish the Galactic Forum. It was very plush, had plenty of the scarce water, furniture covered with cloth, and all of the amenities any tyrannical potentate could want. Jeonk and Shok would be staying in the same mansion on this trip.

The Veolsh people and members of the Galactic Forum decided to keep the mansion in a pristine condition. They wanted an example of the Veolsh Council's imperial self-indulgence. They also considered it to be the birthplace of the Galactic Forum, so they thought of it as a historic sight on two levels.

Veolsh words are generally unpronounceable to anyone who isn't Veolsh but the name of their capital was an acronym. Magnificent Citadel of the Veolsh People was easier to say when grammatically shortened--pronounced, Pumg. The four Argan cruisers lowered into position one thousand feet above Pumg.

Shok and Jeonk used command plaks as landing vehicles for themselves and their Marine bodyguards. The Veolsh greeter from the Galactic Forum escorted them immediately to the mansion Shok thought they would be invited to use. It was near the Galactic Forum and had another advantage. The Veolsh tyrants were very fussy about self-protection. This mansion and all of their mansions were easy to defend. It would take a large force to successfully attack it.

Their first order of business was to meet with Chosteel. Shok had gotten to know him well enough to make friends with him and would be glad to see him again. Chosteel was a large man, about seven feet tall. He had the look of a man who had accepted many challenges, defeats, and victories with the fortitude to keep going in either case. He was a man to be reckoned with in a battle. Fortunately, he was on Arga's side.

Chosteel entered the mansion alone and was shown directly to the large office Jeonk and Shok were using. After the abrupt greetings were over, he said, "Your delegation to the Galactic Forum tells me you're having a pirate problem. We haven't seen many from that crowd since the fall of the Veolsh Empire. How can I help you?"

Chosteel was an old warrior, not a diplomat. Shok answered his question as directly as he had asked it, "The Pirates are threatening a cargo line Jeonk and I are starting. They want to destroy it and we want to destroy them. Our problem is, we don't know where their bases are. We know of one base on Castu and we think most of their other bases are on the planets of the old empire. We need information about their locations. We are hoping that information is available from you or some of the others in the Forum. If we can't find their bases with the information you or the Galactic Forum can supply us, we'll have to find them using our own resources. We'll need the permission of the nations in the Forum to allow our cruisers access to scan the six planets."

Chosteel thought for a moment before he answered, "Let me send a message to all of the nations in the forum. Your pirates could be spread out more than you think. They could be based on planets other than these six. It will take some time for all of them to check it out and return the information. I think that's the best way. I personally have no knowledge of any pirate activity in our area. I don't think the pirates are on the six planets in large numbers. If they were, I would probably know about it. I'll check to make sure."

He thought for another moment, and continued, "Most of the nations in the forum are very touchy about large space fleets entering their air spaces. Shok, most of them know you and his Majesty. They trust you because of your work on the Forum. I think I can convince them to allow your scans of their nations, if you or his Majesty commands the cruisers doing the scanning. Will you or his Majesty be in command of the cruisers?"

Jeonk answered, "Shok will be in command. I'll be with him but he will be in command of the cruisers."

Jeonk's curiosity had been aroused by Chosteel's assumption that we wouldn't find the main force of the pirates on the six planets. He asked, no one in particular, "If the pirates aren't in this area, and they aren't in our area, where can they be?"

Chosteel answered, "There are two planets farther out, more toward the edge of the Galaxy that the Veolsh didn't conquer. Shok met some of their representatives during the formation of the Galactic Forum. They were the ones asking him questions about Arga and the other members. Iklug is one of the planets. It had representatives at the conference but their representatives didn't ask for membership. Iklug was very friendly to the Veolsh Council and the Veolsh Council members frequently visited them, but I don't know who the Iklug leaders are. The Veolsh Council members either took vacations there or went there to confer with people as nasty as themselves.

"That's why I'm sending messages to all of the Forum members. Some of the others might have pirate problems or they may know where the pirates are based. I think the remains of the Veolsh fleet and the pirate fleets may be on Iklug. If the Veolsh fleet connects with the Iklugs and the pirates, they could be a danger to all of us. I think we'll all be ready to help you end your problem with pirates if you're ready to help us end our future problems with the Veolsh fleet."

Shok hadn't mentioned the Veolsh fleet to Chosteel. It's strange how a bad wind seems to circle around to spread it's bad smell. Shok added to Chosteel's worries, "We're pretty sure money from the Veolsh fleet is financing the pirates. If we find the Veolsh fleet and the pirate bases on Iklug, it means the three are working together. We come up with a very serious problem. We have to add what we know about the involvement of Prssk and Gamac to the pirate mix.

"We don't know what their ultimate agenda is. If it's good for them, it's bad for us. We know they intend to destroy the cargo line. We know that murder is their first order of business. They've tried to murder his Majesty and me twice, once on Prssk and once on Arga. They may think they can put together a power base strong enough to build a new empire."

Before Chosteel left the mansion, he stated, "I'll get all of the information I can for you-- and for us. I'm getting the commanders of the old rebel forces working on this. Everyone who was in the rebellion against the Veolsh Empire will want to help. We'll track the pirates down for you if they're in this part of the galaxy. We'll tighten security wherever we can.

"I think we need a general meeting of the Galactic Forum, but I would rather Arga didn't call for the meeting. I want to call for it in our interests instead of yours. Even the small chance of a new Veolsh Empire won't be ignored by any of us in the Forum."

Chosteel had given them a lot to think about. The general meeting would take a few days to organize and it would take time to get the national leaders to the Forum. The Forum's national leaders wouldn't be likely to allow their usual delegations to handle so serious a problem.

Waiting was always the worst part of any problem for Shok, and he could see Jeonk pacing around the mansion with the same impatience he felt. Shok suggested, "We might be more productive on a cruiser. We should call home to see how our families are doing, without using the Forum communications system. The Admiralty might have heard something from Doskel or Brak. Anything beats staying here and looking at the walls."

They were receiving a message coming from Arga As they entered the cruiser's command deck. Shok caught something about missiles. Jeonk said, "Wait until the message is finished. We'll listen to it on the recorder."

The recorded message was brief, "Three incoming missiles were aimed at Arga. One was launched to hit the Royal Compound; one was aimed at King Plask's Lersta Castle, and the third at the Admiralty. The missiles were intercepted and destroyed. They were launched from deep space. We could find no evidence of the launching spacecraft. Missiles fragments recovered from space indicate they were the type used by the Veolsh Council forces in the recent war. I strongly suggest his Majesty and Fleet Admiral Shok return to Arga immediately." It was signed, Plask Shap.

"We can't both leave Shok," Jeonk stated. "What do you think?"

"You're right but you must be the one to go home," Shok replied. "I'm needed here to keep things going on this end. I think we're about to go to war again. Our Admirals need to know what we know. Lets organize what we know before you go. We need a plan that includes the elements the Admirals don't know about."

Jeonk began the plan, "We need to put one fleet around Prssk and Gamac to stop the pirate traffic coming into or leaving either of those two planets. I'll have probes put in space to monitor planet Iklug for Veolsh Imperial or pirate activity. I'm not waiting for the Forum. I'll order one fleet to bypass the six planets to check Iklug. I'll protect Arga by locking it down tight, with three fleets overhead to prevent any further missile attacks. Is there anything you want to add?"

Shok added, "I think we need to beef up our ground forces on Krex and Mog. There are unfriendly elements on Krex and Mog that are certain to be in touch with the Veolsh Imperials. Krex and Mog were pirates themselves, and friends of the Veolsh Empire. They'll try to regain their former position with the Veolsh if they can. Krex and Mog would still be slave-driving tyrants if they dared. It might be a good idea to review our cruiser coverage of them. We need to lock everything out of Arga and we need to lock everything in on Krex and Mog. They'll join the pirates if we give them a chance.

"I think we need a full fleet here to protect the Galactic Forum. If we're threatened with a new effort to form the old Veolsh Empire, the new tyrants may decide to kill off the leaders of their former subjects in one quick action. I'll get to Chosteel and arrange whatever protection he can muster while I wait for the fleet to come in. I'll have him delay the meeting until the fleet gets here and provide its protection. I think he has that much clout with the members."

"Sounds good," Jeonk replied, "I'll call for a fleet immediately; it should arrive within the next few days. Sorry you can't have your own fleet. They're all busy. When your fleet is available I'll have it replace the fleet that's here.

"I'll return to Arga in two of the cruisers we have here. You keep the other two. My fathers four cruiser protection policy has just dropped off the scan but Alice's two cruiser policy is still in place, if you have a few extra guns on you."

Shok laughed and told him he would take a fighter back to the surface of the Veolsh planet. Jeonk and his two cruisers were on their way as Shok landed the fighter near the mansion.

The missile attack on Arga worried Chosteel. The Forum Charter said that any kind of attack on one nation was an attack on every nation in the forum. He reminded Shok, as if he needed it, "The Galactic Forum treaty says, if one of us is attacked, all of us go to war against the attacker. Whoever is attacking already knows that. They're using your cargo line to make the attack appear less than war. They evidently don't know that economic war against a Forum nation is the same as any other type of war. Every nation in the Forum will be with Arga in this war.

"I'll slow the meeting down long enough for the fleet of Argan cruisers to arrive. Get in touch with his majesty and tell him the Forum nations just gave him a shortcut to Iklug. The others will agree when I tell them the reasons. You have my word on it. I'll tell the national leaders to put as much protection around the Forum nations as they need.

"We're not the out of pocket rebels we were when we first met you and his Majesty after the war. We are the protectors of our own societies. We intend to fight and we intend to do some ass kicking in the process. We won't be behind you Shok. We'll be with you and sometimes in front of you. No one will ever try to take on the Galactic forum nations again. You be at that meeting. You have more respect from the Forum nations than you realize. Some of them are making statues of you. They think you're the one who really freed them."

Shok was touched by the words of the tough old warrior but he and those who thought Shok had won the war were wrong. Shok said, "Chosteel, the entire nation of Arga fought the war against the Veolsh Empire. If Jeonk Shap had been less of a king, we might have lost it. If our Admirals had been less prepared or less willing to fight and die, we might have lost it. If our lower ranking warriors had been less willing or less prepared to fight and die, we might have lost it. If you and the other freedom fighters hadn't been fighting the Veolsh Empire for so many years or hadn't been willing to die for your freedom, we might have lost it. We lost many of our warriors in the war. Your nations lost many more in the same war. We all won the war, those who died and those who survived. All of us deserve the credit for winning the war.

"You tell those people to lay off the statues. I don't need a statue of me standing in some park with birds crapping on my bald head."

Chosteel laughed and said, "I'll tell them, no statues without a crap deflector." As he left, he turned and repeated, "You be at that meeting."

The Argan fleet's arrival was overdue but the leaders of the Forum nations didn't wait for it. Each of them brought his own smaller fleet for protection. Shok was surprised by the number of spacecraft they had.

Their arrival gave Shok a chance to renew acquaintances with his friends among the members of the Forum. After speaking with many of them, he thought they were all willing to join Arga in protecting each other from the pirate threat and the threat of a new imperial takeover of the area. As it turned out, the meeting of the Galactic Forum would be more of a planning session about, how to do it, than a meeting to determine if it should be done.

SPACE LINE BY MARIVIN E. FOX

The time it took the fleet to arrive gave Shok some reason for worry. The Forum fleets protected the Veolsh planet very well near the surface, but it wasn't as well protected from a deep space attack. There was a great deal of traffic coming into Veolsh, with the arrival of spacecraft from six planets.

Most of the off planet nations used small military spaceships or passenger craft for diplomatic travel. Some of their spaceships were larger, and some smaller than the corsairs the pirates used. Shok thought it would be rather easy for the pirates to conceal their corsairs loaded with men and weapons in the incoming traffic, and set up an attack on the Galactic Forum.

The Oglaks sent two hundred night fighters to protect Shok in the Veolsh mansion. The Oglaks had a deep respect for Shok and believed him to be a very important person in a dangerous position. They took special pains to keep him alive. They weren't the kind to wait until they were asked if their protection was needed. They arrived unannounced at the mansion and they moved in to help his Argan night duty Marines.

Shok and the Marines were glad to have the Oglaks. They could see better at night than people using night vision glasses, and the Oglaks were tough fighters. Chosteel told Shok, "The Oglaks are an excellent night attack force. I've been with them on many night raids. The best way I found to work with them is this, don't try to keep track of them and don't expect them to be where you can see them. Trust them, if you need to know anything about the battle, an Oglak will find you and tell you."

The Oglaks were the strangest looking people of all the Forum members. Their most compelling feature was their eyes. Oglak eyes were big, flat surfaced and round looking but they weren't quit flat. The Oglak eye has a slight convex curve with eight segments. The segments probably have something to do with their ability to see at night. The Oglaks are about as tall as the average person from Earth. They have dark, almost black, rubbery looking skin and they are a thin people. Their heads are egg shaped with large ears and a rather small mouth. They have a three-inch bony growth on each side of their head above the ears. The bony growth points backward parallel to the ground, and the bony structures move around frequently. The bony growths are heat sensors used when it's so dark even an Oglak can't see.

The Oglak warriors protected Shok as if he was one of their own leaders who came to the Veolsh planet for the meeting. The other Forum members familiar with the Oglaks' abilities as night fighters wanted protection of the same quality. They asked the Oglaks to bring in more troops. There would be a large number of Oglaks around Pumg before the meeting was finished.

The cruisers from Arga arrived over the Forum complex a week late. When Shok was informed of the arrival he understood their reason for being late. Jeonk had brought two fleets and the Royal Cruiser. Twenty-six cruisers from the two fleets were spread out to cover the surface of the planet, which ended Shok's worries about pirate spacecraft getting on the planet. If pirates became a problem, it would be because they arrived before the Argan fleets. The Royal Cruiser was positioned in a low orbit over Pumg with six cruisers guarding it. Shok knew that meant the Royal Family was on board.

Shok immediately flew his fighter to the Royal Cruiser to meet with Jeonk and to find out what was going on. He wanted to know what Jeonk and the Admirals had decided and how many of the Royal Family were on board. He knew Alice would be there if Aslain was on board.

Jeonk met him in the cruiser's landing bay and answered Shok's first question before it was asked, "They're both here all right. I couldn't keep them home. My father is with Rakoup in a high orbit to direct the fleet. Our wives are inside waiting to see if you have any new scars or holes in your chest. We should go in immediately and let them see that you're still ambulatory."

"Where are Brak and Doskel?" Shok asked. "Have they found the pirate bases?"

"Doskel hasn't found the Veolsh fleet in our area," Jeonk replied. "Brak hit some small pirate bases in the area he was searching but most of them had left their hideouts before he could get to them. The ones he chased are headed in this direction. I've ordered Doskel and Brak to bring their fleets to this area as soon as they finish cleaning the home area of pirates. We don't want to leave any small pirate fleets behind us."

They entered the royal compartments to meet with the family. Alice rushed to Shok's side, gave him a hug and surreptitiously inspected him for damage. Aslain asked, "Did you have any gun fights?"

"I haven't even been in a good argument," Shok answered. "The Argan Marines and the Oglaks are guarding me. They throw anyone with a bad attitude out before I can get a chance to talk to him." Shok talked with the family for a while before Jeonk excused him. Both of them went to one of the conference compartments to discuss the pirate business privately.

Jeonk opened the discussion, "We have Gamac and the Prssk planet locked in. They can't make a move without our knowledge. We are stopping suspicious looking traffic from entering or leaving either of them. I took your advice about Krex and Mog. General Sokeasel has assigned another hundred thousand ground troops to each of them and we have tightened the cruiser umbrella over both. I don't think they'll be able to join up with the Veolsh and the Iklugs to establish a new empire. How have you been getting along on this end?"

Shok replied, "The Forum meeting will be a matter of how we can all work together to end this business. The meeting will probably begin tomorrow. Chosteel insists that I be there with the Argans assigned to the Forum. You should be there with me. They don't know you as well as they know me, but they have met you and they know you backed me when we established the Forum. The trillion gold skirbs you loaned them helped them big time. They will trust whatever Arga does as long as you and I are initiating the action.

"I haven't received any positive information about pirate bases yet. I think Chosteel's assumption that they are based on Iklug with the Veolsh Fleet is probably accurate. None of the Galactic Forum members have found pirate bases in their nations and that covers the surface of all six planets. The base we knew about on Castu cleared out before we arrived. Some scurrilous rat probably told them we had their leader in jail with a knife at his throat. I guess they knew him well enough to know he would sell them out.

"Our fleets are now welcome anywhere in the skies of the six planets. They can come and go as they please. I think we should send Doskel and his fleet on an inspection scan of Iklug. I think it would be a good idea if he takes my flagship with him. It has the most equipment on board, even more than Doskel's flagship. The quickest route to Iklug is by going between Paraca and the Castu solar systems.

"Scanning Iklug will take time. We need to scan everything Iklug has to fight with. If we are lucky, Iklug will be weak and willing to listen to reason or, maybe, won't be involved with the Veolsh and the pirates.

"We seem to be getting farther and farther from Arga to protect ourselves. We have had to spread ourselves over a third of the Galaxy in a very short time. Unfortunately, we have powerful, devious enemies but weak and honest friends. Thank God for our ability to maintain our strength and our sense of duty to Arga. Without that, we would already be lost."

"I'll go to the meeting with you," Jeonk stated. "We'll enter together. Where will you stay until then? Alice and the family want you to stay here with them."

"I'll have to stay in the mansion until this Forum conference is over," Shok answered, "and I don't know how long that will take. I must be available to the members of the Forum. They'll think I've become chicken hearted if I stay here and communicate with them by radio or fly to and from the meetings with an armed escort. The Freedom Fighters are still in control of their nations and they are the same tough people we first met here. They want someone to look at when they have something to say. A response from someone who has become chicken hearted won't do."

Jeonk looked happy about Shok's logic and decision. He stood up, put his hand on Shok's shoulder and said, "Good! We'll stay in the mansion. I'm not going to look chicken hearted either. You visit with Alice and the family the rest of the day. After dinner you can explain to our wives why we can't stay on board the Royal Cruiser. They'll understand, if you are the one who tells them."

Shok wasn't happy about being the bad guy. He said abruptly "You tell them! You're the king; that's your job!"

Jeonk smiled as though he knew he had Shok outmaneuvered, " I'm also Aslain's husband. You'll have to be the one who tells them; Aslain can't argue with you. Alice is easy for you to explain things to. She'll understand why you have to stay in the mansion. She won't get on your case about it. Aslain and Alice think you'll be staying here, safe on the cruiser. Don't tell them you won't be until after dinner."

As they left the compartment to join the family, Shok agreed to Jeonk's plan for making him the bad guy, but he didn't like it, and he didn't have much confidence in how easy it would be.

Jeonk and Shok spent the afternoon telling their wives how they thought the situation was developing and what both thought the best course of action was to cure it. During the conversations, Shok discovered why the Royal Cruiser was part of the fleet brought in by Jeonk.

Alice made it sound almost normal to bring the Royal Family on an outing to a war. She began, "Plask told us he and Rakoup needed to be here to protect you and Jeonk. They said the two of you had to be here and you would need their expert help to survive.

"They said both of you are too confident of yourselves, and you would fight all by yourselves if Plask and Rakoup didn't keep you covered. Aslain said she and I weren't going to wait around to see if the two of you were killed. If Plask and Rakoup were going to Veolsh, we were going to Veolsh.

"Plask didn't like that idea. He tried to get us to stay with Tiskla, in his kingdom. Aslain and I refused. We said, we are going to Veolsh! Jeonk can bring us in the Royal Cruiser he turned into a super cruiser that is, exceedingly, safe. Nothing in the sky or on the ground can touch it. Plask and Jeonk had a really long talk about it, but they couldn't think of any way to make us stay home.

"I told Aslain, I know how to pilot the corsair you and Jeonk think we don't know about at Tischel. If they leave us behind, we'll use it. Jeonk and Plask decided to load us into this Royal, super, Cruiser and here we are. We sent Emira and the kids to Tiskla. They have four cruisers, sixty fighters and a whole division of General Sokeasel's troops to guard them."

Shok was dumbfounded, thinking, "No wonder Jeonk wanted me to be the bad guy. He already failed to keep them from coming. After his failure, he wants me to find a way to get them away from the Veolsh planet and back to the safety of Arga--fat chance, they wont go back."

Alice and Aslain found out about the corsair at Tischel from one of their women friends in the space fleet. Shok knew their wives had many friends in the Argan Space Corps, but Tischel is four thousand miles from Poshalla. He and Jeonk thought the hideout corsair would be safe form prying wives eyes that far away.

"I know Plask and Rakoup would never miss a good fight," Shok thought. "As soon as Jeonk told them how big it was getting they wanted in on it. Plask must have felt very safe about the family's protection in his castle. He was right; nothing could get to them there. Plask misjudged when he decided to leave them alone at the castle so he and Rakoup could get into the battle together. The two wives refused to accept being alone at the castle no matter how safe it was.

Aslain and Alice are very strong-minded women. Once they decide to do something, the only stopping point is where it is no longer possible for them to do it. The best thing to do is to let them stay near the Forum on Jeonk's super cruiser. With two fleets hanging in soft orbits, they will be just as safe as if they were with Tiskla,"

Alice was sitting in a chair Jeonk usually sat in. The chair was much too big for her and she would have looked comical in it if she weren't so seriously sitting straight up with her hands in her lap. Alice waited for Shok to say something angry to her for going from the safety of the castle to the dangers of the Veolsh planet. Shok decided to let the situation perk until after dinner. He said, "Isn't dinner about ready? I'm really hungry."

The dinner was nice and afterward things were more relaxed. The two men enjoyed the quiet hours with their wives but it was getting time for Shok and Jeonk to leave for the mansion. Shok said, "It's getting late and Jeonk and I are going to have a busy day tomorrow. There are probably people waiting to see us in the mansion this evening. We must leave you lovely ladies and get back to work."

Aslain looked shocked and Alice said, "We thought you would be staying here. You can see those people tomorrow."

"No, we can't see them tomorrow," Shock insisted. "There are a whole bunch of nations represented in the Forum and most of their leaders are here now. They won't understand why two men, whom they consider to be great warriors, must hide out in a flying fortified palace. We must be on the surface and ready to work with them when they're ready to work with us. We don't have two choices; the one choice we do have is to stand with them and share the same dangers they face."

"You'll be in danger every minute you're there," Aslain declared. "The Veolsh planet is crawling with people who don't like you, and are willing to kill you."

Shok thought it was a good time to tell her about the mansions superb security, "We have one hundred Marines around the mansion and there are two hundred Oglaks helping them, especially at night. We have cruisers scanning the planet. There are fighter patrols overhead. I was safe here before you arrived. That safety has quadrupled since your arrival. Jeonk and I will be safe. We have to do what we have to do and we can't speak with people we need to speak with from up here. We, and they, need eyeball to eyeball contact to handle a problem like this."

Aslain and Alice exclaimed, at the same time, "We're going too!"

Shok wondered how one big beautiful Argan queen and one beautiful small town Earth girl could become two hard-nosed peas from the same pod. He hoped Jeonk would jump in with some help but Jeonk was watching Shok to see how Shok was going to handle the situation. Shok gave it a last ditch effort, "Neither of you can shoot very well, and neither of you have any battle experience. If we, through some unpredictable mishap, get into a bad situation, you won't be able to take care of yourselves. You might be hurt or killed. Jeonk and I would feel terrible, and we would blame ourselves. We need you to be where we know you're safe."

Aslain said, "We can shoot really good. Rakoup and Jeonk's father have been teaching us every time you two are gone. We've been practicing for months."

"Rakoup said we're both good enough to be military marksmen." Alice remarked. "He taught us to use the same pistols and knives you and Jeonk carry. If you don't take us when you go, we'll take one of the fighters from this cruiser and follow you down to the mansion. It won't be the first time I piloted a fighter from a cruiser to that mansion."

Aslain Added, "No one would dare to stop the Queen of Arga and her military aide, Major Alice Kelly, the wife of the great Admiral Shok, from taking one of the fighters. Alice, we had better get dressed; our husbands are in a hurry. I'll leave orders for someone to bring more of our clothing later."

After the wifely hard-nosed peas left, Shok asked Jeonk, "What's this stuff about Alice being Aslain's military aid and a Major? The last time I talked to her about being an officer in the fleet, she said she intended to give it up and she wasn't anyone's aid. Between then and know she's become a major and the military aid to the queen."

"Aslain has met many of the women officers from the fleets since Alice arrived," Jeonk informed him. "Aslain thought she needed a military aid to keep in contact with the military women because there are so many of them she and Alice know. Some of the lady officers recommended Alice. Everyone likes Alice and our wives lives next door to each other. Aslain thought the rank of captain was too low for a Queen's Aide. Rakoup promoted Alice to major for the new position. Aslain thinks her aide should be even higher in rank. Alice will undoubtedly be promoted again, by Rakoup, very soon."

Shok gave up on the rank bit and said, "I wish they would stop worrying about us getting killed. The worry makes them do strange things-like right now."

The two women appeared in the dinning room dressed for the planet surface. Alice and Aslain both wore military uniforms. They both had on combat belts with three pistols and a knife hanging from them. The knives were the same kind Jeonk and Shok carry when things get serious.

The four new battle buddies, two male and two female, left the Royal Cruiser in one of its shuttles. As they descended to the planet and the mansion, Shok worried silently about some unforeseen kind of action they might be forced into on the surface, "The most important thing in a battle isn't how well someone can shoot targets, it's how well someone can shoot someone who is shooting at him or, in this case, her."

There were too many things Shok was afraid they didn't know. He wasn't easy in his mind about the wives being in situations that began warm and fuzzy, but could turn deadly in an instant. The whole situation made him glad the Oglaks had insisted on guarding the Veolsh mansion. The Oglaks already knew Alice and they would get to know Aslain.

Shok felt Alice and Aslain knew Jeonk and Shok would be staying in the mansion before they left Arga. The two women had planned on staying with Jeonk and Shok in the old imperial mansion from the beginning. They had the uniforms and weapons already prepared for the surface. They also had all of their arguments prepared. Shok didn't believe their threat to take a fighter from the Royal Cruiser was a last minute inspiration. He had to admire their planning and admit they had outmaneuvered Jeonk and him, even if the results did worry him.

Shortly after they arrived at the mansion, the Oglaks informed Shok that they had reduced the amount of guards around the mansion to one hundred night fighters. So many of the Forum members had requested night guards that it made them short handed, and the Oglaks couldn't refuse them. The Oglak Commander told Shok that more Oglak troops would be arriving but it would take a few days.

Shok didn't think it was much of a problem. He could assign more Marines from the fleet if he felt the mansion needed more guards. If Plask knew about the change he would insist on having every Marine in the fleet guarding the four of them but Plask was floating high over the planet with Rakoup. Shok knew both of them would be keeping an eye on the place.

The meeting of the Galactic Forum began the following morning. Of course, Alice and Aslain insisted on going. While Jeonk and Shok were busy with the national leaders. Alice introduced Aslain to many of the friends she had made when she was in Pumg with Shok after the Veolsh war. The two wives were a big hit with all of the freedom fighters.

The general meeting began quickly. Chosteel introduced Shok at the meeting. Shok made a report to the forum on the seriousness of the situation. Chosteel had already told most of them what was going on during the unofficial meetings that were held while waiting for the official one.

The Forum nations agreed that Arga was in a war condition. The Galactic Forum Charter required them to enter the war on the side of the threatened member. They were doubly eager to defend Arga because they were certain to be the next target if the Pirate War against Arga succeeded. This would be the first real test of the Galactic Forum nations and their ability to protect each other. All of the nations in the Galactic Forum were eager to pass the test.

The fifty-three nations on the Veolsh planet were deeply interested. The major power behind the enemies aligned against Arga was also the surviving power of the defeated Veolsh Council. That power would certainly be trying to regain its power over the Veolsh people. The Forum nations had already outlawed the last remnants of the old Veolsh Empire. The Veolsh nations became adamant in their support for Arga against the Pirates, as they considered the implications. They felt a new Veolsh empire would not only destroy their newly formed republics, but kill the leaders and most prominent supporters of those republics.

The meeting boiled down to a planning session on the conduct of the war. Arga had enough power to take over the war preparations and end the war alone. Arga fought alone in the war against the Veolsh Empire until the last battle. This time, Arga couldn't say they wanted to take over the planning and they couldn't lock the other Forum nations out of the war. Arga was just another member of the Forum and they had to respect Forum treaty obligations they had with other nations. Those 'other' nations were more vulnerable than Arga, and they were getting ready for battle.

Doskel arrived and spread his fleet out in space, with Shok's six loaned cruisers, while waiting for the Forum's go ahead to scan the Iklug planet. Shok was glad to have his six cruisers back under his command, especially since his flagship had been with Doskel's fleet.

The Forum decided on a maximum of three people from each nation to be on the War Planning Board, which brought the number to more than four hundred That was a low number because most of the nations were represented by one person and many nations decided to accept whatever the planners decided without having a member present on the Board. The Argans were glad the situation was cut and dried and didn't need to be discussed by a large committee. The Forum committee quickly agreed that Doskel's fleet should immediately proceed to Iklug and make its scans without waiting for the conclusion of whatever plan the Forum decided on.

Chosteel wanted a consolidated fleet made up of spaceships from the Forum nations. Everyone agreed to the fleet. The nations of the six planets fielded a fleet of four thousand spacecraft of various sizes. It was decided to leave them based in their home nations for the time being. The Forum fleets would be used for home planet protection while the Argans were locating the Veolsh cruisers and the pirates.

The plan boiled down to a simple procedure. If the war were conducted against one planet, Iklug, Arga would take care of the Veolsh Imperial Cruisers and anything heavy the Iklugs could throw at them. The Forum spacecraft, assisted by Argan fighters, would destroy the smaller enemy spacecraft and whatever surface targets intelligence said they could handle. If there were surface targets to difficult for the Argan fighters or the Forum spacecraft, consisting mostly of corsairs, Arga's cruisers or missiles would blast the difficult targets.

Arga would place four of its fleets in space between Iklug planet and the pirates' bases on Gamac and Prssk just in case the pirates decided to run instead of fight. If the pirates tried to return to the six planets, the home guard fleets would destroy them or ask for cruiser assistance to destroy them.

The plans and variations on the plans were made for different situations. All of the planning would be for nothing if Doskel returned saying nobody's home. No one wanted to plan on that part of the war scenario. They were all sure Doskel would find thirty Veolsh Imperial Cruisers and several hundred pirate corsairs on Iklug. It was the only planet any one knew of where the Veolsh Imperial Cruisers and pirate fleets could be. The Forum had no idea what kind of power Iklug itself would bring to the battle. Doskel's scans of the planet would have to tell them about Iklug's defensive and offensive power.

For the next few days the Forum was in a waiting mode. Aslain and Alice kept busy filling notebooks full of information about old and new friends. They wouldn't have been busier if they had been working for votes to win a political office.

Jeonk and Shok kept busy by trying to lose their reputations, with their wives, for being brash, unruly gunfighters with a penchant for acquiring new scars and laser burns. They had dignified meetings with friends and Forum members. They quietly reviewed fleet activities. They had quiet dinners under the watchful eyes of the Marine and Oglak bodyguards. They watched the sandy looking sunsets on the mountains outside of Pumg. They had long talks with their wives and did their best to be real homebodies.

Rakoup interrupted one of their homebody evenings. He said his scanners were tracking a very large storm heading in the direction of Pumg. A weather front traveling over a hundred miles an hour was pushing sand clouds ahead of it. The sand clouds reached from ground level to more than a mile above the surface of the planet and the sand clouds would reach Pumg in about an hour.

Sand storms were nothing new to The Veolsh planet. They occurred at regular intervals and they could be very severe. The capital, Pumg, was built below the protection of high cliffs that put it in a good position during severe storm conditions. Most of the high wind and sand clouds would go over the top of Pumg. The sand dunes being pushed over the cliffs edges by the wind was the reason for the sand waterfall affect seen from below. Shok had shown Alice the natural wonder of the sand waterfall display when they were in Pumg before. Alice was anxious for Jeonk and Aslain to see the same spectacle. She had been amazed by it and wanted to share her amazement with them.

The four of them dressed to keep from being sand blasted instead of amazed. The standard fighter pilots gear was best for the purpose. The helmets' visors would protect their faces from the sand and they could talk to each other using the helmets' radios. The outer suit was tough enough to give some protection from laser hits and tough enough to withstand the wind blown sand. Each fighter suit had two side holsters for pistols, and none of them wanted to go unarmed. Jeonk and Shok always added an extra pistol and their personal knives for a little extra protection.

When the four finished dressing for their first Veolsh outing, they looked like people headed for a battlefield instead of a natural spectacle. The women's nice curves in their tailored uniforms kept them from looking as mean and ugly as Jeonk and Shok.

Fifty Marines and one hundred Oglaks traveled with them to the viewpoint. The Argan Marines dressed in the same type of protective clothing Jeonk and Shok wore, but their outer clothing was designed for ground battle conditions. They were the best protected in the party. The Marines carried a variety of weapons. All of them carried pistols. Some had laser rifles, others carried machine-guns that fired rocket propelled ammunition.

The Oglaks carried only two weapons. They carried a pistol Shok thought was heavier than a forty-four magnum. Their machine guns were even more dangerous. They fired a thin, brittle metal projectile covered with a soft metal jacket. The softer metal penetrated whatever was hit. The brittle interior metal exploded with the entry pressure, spreading its shards over a wide area like a small hand grenade.

The Oglaks wore protective clothing and helmets serving the same purpose the Marines clothing did. Their uniform was a dusty looking, non-reflecting black. The upper body of their uniform was crisscrossed with bandoleers for their machine-gun ammunition. The backs of their gloves were laced with sharp metal cutting edges for hand-to-hand combat. The Oglak helmets were large with protective covers on each side that allowed free movement for the rod-like heat sensors on their heads.

The knife the Oglaks carried was a vicious looking piece of cutlery. The blade was double-edged and eighteen inches long. The upper edge wasn't smooth; it had sharp pyramid shaped protrusions. The protrusions were very small and sharp on the forward edge but became larger and spread out on each side of the knife as they progressed to the rear. The lower edge of the knife was a series of small sharp wheels. The small wheels were sharp enough to cut bone or ride over it. Only some kind of nut would start a hand-to-hand fight with people armed like that. Maybe that's why there were so many of Oglaks left alive after the Veolsh war.

The party arrived below the cliffs on the edge of Pumg just before dark. The best view of sand pouring over the cliffs was from behind the same low building Alice and Shok had used when they viewed the strange sight alone. Shok pulled their command plak close to the building and waited for the Marine guards and the Oglaks to go through the building and surrounding area to make certain everything was safe. When they were given the all clear, they left the command plak and went through the building to a rear platform to watch the strange sand-fall phenomenon.

The Marines and the Oglaks quickly established a guard perimeter around the party. The Marines were closest with their Marine Assault Plaks spread in a semicircle fifty yards distance from the small building. The Oglaks circled fifty yards farther out in the same formation. Six Marines took close in positions around each of the four in the main party.

It was dusk when the sand began drifting over the cliff edges, falling like water to the canyon below. The fading sunlight filtering through the passing sand cloud gave an eerie light to the falling sand. The constantly shifting patterns of dark and muted light on the surface of the falling sand was the most beautiful thing any of them had seen on the Veolsh planet. The four of them watched in quiet appreciation of the beautiful sight until the sand blowing around the bottom of the cliff became so thick they could no longer enjoy the spectacle.

The four battle buddies were returning through the building to the command plak when shots sounded outside. Apparently, not every arrival to the area had come to see the sand-fall. Jeonk and Shok pushed their wives to the sides of the entrance to keep them out of the line of fire. They both stepped outside to confront whoever was doing the shooting.

SPACE LINE BY MARIVIN E. FOX

One of the Argan Marines pulled an assault plak a few feet in front of the entrance of the building to get them out. The plak settled to the ground and the Marine opened the door just as it exploded, hit by a hand launched missile, or explosive projectile. Jeonk and Shok rushed to the plak to see if they could get the pilot out but it was no use. The destroyed plak did give them some momentary cover.

The Marines and the Oglaks took positions around them and signaled for them to get back inside the building. Shok didn't like that idea, and Jeonk wasn't going that way either. A missile hitting the building would do the same thing to the building it had done to the assault plak. An individual in the open is much easier to miss with a missile than one in a building or a plak.

Shok took a quick look behind and saw Alice and Aslain running to join him and Jeonk. Both women had their two pistols drawn. The two men had to get the women away from the burning assault plak but not back in the building. Their helmet radios began filling with the battle commands of Marines and Oglaks as they pulled Alice and Aslain into a depression in the sand just a few yards to the right of the building.

Shok couldn't see the enemy but he didn't have to guess who sent them. He expected them to be pirates and he expected there would be many of them. They must have found their way to the Veolsh planet before the fleet arrived. What he did have to guess about was what kind of firepower they had.

The blowing sand made it difficult to see but there was laser fire coming from some low buildings on the other side of the sandy area. Shok told Alice to lie down at the same time Jeonk was telling Aslain the same thing. Shok called for the Marines and the Oglaks to put some heavy fire into the buildings being used by the pirates.

Shok's command plak carried some pretty heavy weapons. While the marines and the Oglaks kept the pirates diving for cover, Shok made his way to the command plak to get two of its heavy laser rifles.

As he was doing that, he heard Plask yelling at them on the command plak radio, "We can see your taking fire. Our scanners indicate four corsairs moving in on you from two directions. The sand is scattering our scans so their positions aren't certain. I'm sending fighters to cover you. We'll blast them from the cruisers if we can."

He didn't have time to answer Plask. He grabbed the laser rifles and ran back to the other three. Shok yelled at Jeonk on his helmet radio and threw him one of the lasers. He shouted, "four corsairs!" and pointed to the left and right. The corsairs couldn't see them yet but it was clear they had to move to a new position or be caught in the open. The Marines and the Oglaks picked up what Shok shouted on his helmet radio. They split to cover the direction of the incoming corsairs. The small defense force had to move forward or none of them would survive the corsair attack.

The cruisers couldn't blast the corsairs through a mile of blowing sand. By the time the cruiser's laser or pulse cannon shots hit the corsairs through the thick cloud of sand, they wouldn't have enough power left to toast a marshmallow.

Alice was stretched out on the ground with her pistols out in front to her. Her head was up so she could see what was going on. Shok told her, "Get lower!"

"I can't, my breasts are in the way!" Alice retorted.

"Keep your head down and stay where you are," Shok ordered.

She gave him a dirty look but she put her head a little lower.

Jeonk finished making Aslain as small a target as he could. They both expected to hear about it later. Jeonk signaled Shok and some nearby Argan troops to move forward. The Argans began pouring laser fire into some low buildings the pirates were using for cover.

The pirates kept firing from the buildings to keep the Argans in the open until the corsairs arrived. Jeonk and Shok began firing their heavier laser rifles into the buildings. That kept the pirates off balance well enough to prevent them from firing any deadly shots, but they were still too far from the pirates' buildings to stop the attack.

The Oglaks, more used to guerrilla tactics, had a better idea. They began positioning their plaks and troops to flank the buildings. As Jeonk and Shok fired their lasers to keep the pirates busy, the Oglaks moved in and began blasting the buildings at close range with their machine guns. The howls of the wounded pirates could be heard over the howling of the wind and sand. Within a short time, the howling and firing from the pirates' buildings stopped.

As Jeonk ordered the Argan Marines to advance, Shok signaled the Oglaks to stop firing and check the building for survivors. There were no survivors.

Shok turned to make sure Alice and Aslain would advance with the Marines. That was no problem, Alice was looking him in the eye as he turned and Aslain was close behind Jeonk. Both had followed as close as they could get, with their six guards trailing them.

Jeonk yelled, "The corsairs should be here by now." The corsairs were having visibility problems in the blowing sand and it caused them to move more slowly than Jeonk thought they should.

Plask had gotten on their helmet frequency. He instructed, "Hold your positions, fighters are one minute away."

One minute can be a long time in a battle and there was no certainty they had one minute left. The Marines on the outer perimeter, about twenty yards away, were on the same helmet ratios telling them the corsairs were coming into view on their left and right flanks. The corsairs couldn't see them through the sand yet, but it would only be seconds before they would. Shok ordered everyone to retreat to positions behind the buildings the Oglaks had just canceled the pirates' rental agreement on.

Alice was sticking to Shok like glue as they moved past the buildings looking for cover. They found a low sand dune with three of the small buildings behind it that would keep them from being seen by the advancing corsairs. The sand blinded corsairs would have to seek them out to make targets of them. The time the corsairs took to find them might give the fighters time to find the corsairs.

Shok signaled for the Marines and Oglaks to get behind the dune. Jeonk brought Aslain, the Marines, and Oglaks with him to the position behind the same dune.

The Oglaks didn't like the arrangement and Shok didn't blame them. There were too many Oglaks in the same position. Their firepower would be too concentrated in one area and the position was too small to face four corsairs coming from different directions--but there was no place else to go.

Jeonk and Shok's group waited for the fighters to catch up, hoping the corsairs' search for them would eat up the time until the fighters arrived. The Oglaks didn't wait for anything; they began spreading out in battle formation. They evaporated like ghosts in the night. It would be impossible for the corsairs to see them, especially in the darkness with poor scanner visibility in the blowing sand.

Shok pushed Alice down to the ground but she was still keeping her head up so she could see over the top of dune. He told her, "Get lower, damn it!"

She gave him another dirty look and said; "You think my breasts have gotten any smaller? You're higher than I am."

SPACE LINE BY MARIVIN E. FOX

"I'm not talking about your breasts," Shok yelled. "Keep your head down. My head has to be where I can see to shoot and see the battle area. That's just my tough break, not yours!"

The pirate corsairs hovered low, searching for them, then slid slowly into the battle area. Two came from the left and two came from the right. They moved quietly, just a few feet above the sand. The corsairs advanced on the building the party had been in when they were first fired on. The corsairs had lost their guide dogs, the pirates in the buildings, and they didn't know where the Argans were hiding. They could see the plaks the Oglaks and Marines were using spread around the area. The corsairs opened fire on the empty plaks at the same time the Oglaks opened fire on the corsairs.

All hell broke loose. The corsairs couldn't tell where the Oglaks were. The corsairs gunners began catching the Oglak machine gun fire coming at them from so many different directions they couldn't tell where to shoot first.

Shok grabbed Alice by the top of her helmet and shoved, pushing her to the bottom of the sand dune. Jeonk, Shok and the Marines opened up on the corsairs at the same time. The Argan lasers cooked a lot of pirates before they discovered the Argan position.

Alice squirmed back to the top of the dune and fired her pistols at the same corsair Shok's was blasting. Shok glanced to where Jeonk was firing his laser. Aslain had her pistols homed in on the corsair Jeonk was shooting. If laser pistols could bring down a corsair, the first two corsairs were toast. The laser pistol clip was a thirty-five round power pack and there were empty clips at Alice's feet.

The pirate corsairs had found the main party but they were slow in responding because of the intense fire the Argans and the Oglaks were pouring into them from different positions. The lead corsair on the left was burning and beginning to lose what little altitude it had.

The Oglak machine guns were doing so much damage to the lead corsair on the right that it was trying to turn and leave the area. The Oglaks didn't give it that much room to maneuver. The corsair suddenly shifted sideways, and hit the building near the plak the dead pirates in the small buildings had destroyed with their first rounds.

The lead corsairs coming from both directions were out of the fight. The Argans and the Oglaks shifted their fire to the second line corsairs as the Argan fighters dived into the action. Rakoup's fighters blew the two remaining corsairs to their natural end as junk metal. The fight was over. The Marines and the Oglaks quickly surrounded the downed corsairs to make prisoners of the pirate battle survivors.

Rakoup's fighters spread out to control the area, and make sure there was no threat from incoming pirates. That is, all of the fighters except one. It did an aerial pirouette, lowered its landing pods and slapped down in front of Jeonk. Plask had arrived again.

Plask and Rakoup exited the fighter and walked the few feet to where the four of them were standing. Plask said, "Damn, you would have taken those corsairs out without our help."

Shok replied, "Maybe, but not without the Oglaks. Their machine guns and their guerrilla tactics did more to bring down the corsairs than our weapons did."

"I'm giving the Arga Medal of Valor to every Oglak in this battle," Jeonk promised. "Shok is right about them. I want to get some of their machine guns for our ground troops. Those machine guns will shoot through almost anything and the Oglaks use them like artists."

Plask asked, "Why do you think the pirates came into the battle area low and slow instead of higher and faster?"

Jeonk answered, "They used the corsairs like ground attack vehicles because of visibility problems. They didn't expect much resistance. Don't you agree Shok?"

"That's right," Shok agreed. "We were supposed to be under fire from the pirates in the buildings and forced to remain in a convenient location to be killed by the corsairs. The attackers in the corsairs thought most of us would be dead and the rest of us would be pinned down inside the Sand Fall's View Point building. It's on the other side of the burned out assault plak you can see over there.

"We killed the pirates who were supposed to keep us pinned down and took their positions. Your warning about the corsairs gave the Oglaks and our Marines a chance to spread out and attack the corsairs coming at us. The corsair commanders thought we were easy targets. They couldn't handle the situation when we weren't."

Rakoup asked, "How did my two favorite students do in the battle?"

Aslain answered, "We would have done better if our husbands weren't so busy making us lay down with our heads in the sand. We shot hell out of the pirates after our husbands were too busy to keep us there."

Alice voiced her complaint; "Shok pushed me to the bottom of the sand dune when the corsairs began shooting. I had to climb back to the top just to get a few shots off. Aslain and I need guns that fire farther, faster and do more damage. Pushy husbands didn't help our aim either."

Rakoup sympathized, "I'll see if I can get Brak to make a couple of ladies pulse cannons for you. He can't do much about pushy husbands but he's a genius with weapons, he'll make something for you."

Jeonk asked, "Are you ladies ready to return to the mansion or would you rather we find some more pirates for you to shoot at?"

Shok thought Aslain would get mad at Jeonk for his remarks but she didn't. She took Jeonk's arm and replied, "I think we've had enough shooting for one evening. Maybe tomorrow we can look for more pirates someplace else. If you and Shok keep spending your nights like tonight, there wont be any bad guys left in the galaxy."

Alice didn't seem upset either, she put her arm around Shok before she said, "I have sand in my guns. I have sand in my shoes. I have sand in my eyes and I have sand in my brassiere. I expect you to clean it out."

"So, all right," Shok kidded, "I'll clean your guns."

"If you keep talking like that," she replied, "I'll clean your clock."

Jeonk and Shok both laughed at Alice's remark but Aslain didn't know what it meant. Alice could be counted on to explain it to her later.

Alice and Aslain stayed with their husbands in the mansion the night of the battle. The next day they said they would be returning to the Royal cruiser at night. Both had decided to join Shok and Jeonk at the Forum during the daytime but they weren't going on any more excursions. They decided their two gun fighting husbands had taken care of their wives safety before they took care of themselves and the pirates. The two ladies decided their men had a better chance of staying alive if they didn't have wives to take care of during a battle.

Aslain and Alice may not have thought much of themselves in the battle, but they had done really good for a first battle. Both certainly proved to be an asset in dealing with the Forum nations. They talked to the delegates for hours about things Jeonk and Shok had little interest in. They built important personal and political associations based on things having nothing to do with national security or danger. They formed lasting friendships with people Jeonk and Shok met only briefly and in an official capacity.

Shok watched the two women from a second floor balcony, looking down on them as they worked on the floor below. They talked with the leaders of nations or sat among them with their notebooks opened on their laps. They would ask questions and then write something in their notebooks. Men and women would approach them, take a seat nearby, and have long talks about whatever was of mutual interest. It wasn't long before Shok noticed more notebooks and more people writing information about other people. Shok didn't know what they were writing but he knew a galaxy of information was being poured into their notebooks. He wondered why they didn't use recorders like bureaucrats do and why he kept seeing more notebooks appearing on the floor of the Forum.

Alice looked up and saw him watching her from the balcony during one of the few times she wasn't busy with her question and answer sessions. She joined him on the second floor and said, "Aren't you busy? I hardly have a minute when I'm not busy with someone. Aslain is the same way."

"I'm not busy right now, Shok replied. "We're kind of stuck in limbo until we know what Doskel finds on Iklug. Our planning sessions are finished until we have more information. I'm sure we'll get busy as soon as Doskel gives us his report.

Do you mind telling me why you're using notebooks instead of recorders. I know you've filled several of your notebooks with whatever people are telling you. A recorder is easier to carry around and it's more efficient than a notebook. You and Aslain are both using notebooks."

"We don't like recorders," Alice replied. "When we ask people to talk into a recorder, they know every word they speak will be in it forever. Recorders make people feel spied on. People won't say the same things into a recorder they say if we are just having a conversation with them. Aslain and I write things we want to remember about people and the things they tell us.

We aren't asking them important things. We ask them how we can find them if we visit, how many children they have, what their children's names are, what kind of schools they have, things like that. We ask what kind of food they like and we ask a lot of questions about how they lived their lives when the Veolsh Council was in control. We ask how difficult it was to break away. Do you think we're talking too much?"

"No, I think you're doing fine," Shok answered. "I wish I could make friends the way you and Aslain do. Your notebook idea is infectious too. A lot of the people here are now using your notebook idea instead of recorders. They're apparently making friends with each other the same way you and Aslain are making friends with them. Keep it up. I'm proud of you. You and Aslain may be writing a new chapter in diplomatic relations." She gave him a kiss before she returned to her notebook diplomacy.

The days passed slowly for Shok. Doskel sent one of his cruisers back with a message and the scans he made of the planet Iklug. The message was, "Iklug has only half of the Veolsh Imperial fleet. The surface scans of Iklug show their defenses are insufficient to repel our cruiser attacks. They have only a few spacecraft large enough to be called cruisers. The Iklugs have approximately three thousand smaller military spacecraft of various sizes. All of the information I have is on the scan maps of the planet."

The scan maps, Doskel sent, showed the Iklug military to be too weak to rebuild the Veolsh Empire, even with all of the Veolsh space fleet and the help of the pirates.

Jeonk and Shok thought the Veolsh knew they would receive no help from the Gamac and Prssk planets. The Veolsh weren't fools; they knew Arga would nullify those two first.

Fleet Admiral Doskel noted, on his scan maps. "The Veolsh must have the remainder of their military strength hidden in other places to succeed. We picked up some intelligence coming to a Veolsh Cruiser on Iklug. The intelligence may have originated on the planet Egrin. I'm proceeding to the planet Egrin, three and one half light years beyond Iklug, to see if the missing Veolsh cruisers are there. If the Veolsh cruisers are there, we must assume the military capabilities of Egrin are also included in their war plan. I'll make scan maps of Egrin and return to the Veolsh planet when the mission is completed. I want to leave eleven cruiser guarding Iklug, and take eleven cruisers to Egrin."

Shok thought Doskel was right in his assumptions, but he thought Doskel was overextended. His fleet was covering Egrin with its back to Iklug. Doskel's sixteen cruisers and the six Shok had loaned him might not be enough to handle two planets. Shok liked better odds than that. Doskel had left fifteen Veolsh Imperial Cruisers behind him on Iklug and perhaps a more powerful fleet in front of him. Shok wanted to send him enough help to cover him in case the two planets decided to gang up on him and attack.

During the days of waiting, and before Doskel's message had been delivered, Fleet Admiral Brak had arrived on Veolsh. Brak's fleet consisted of his sixteen cruisers and the six he borrowed from Shok's fleet. The four cruisers Shok assigned to cover Plask's Lersta castle had been relieved and returned to Shok's command on the Veolsh planet. Shok now had ten of his cruisers back under his command and available for action.

Shok suggested to Jeonk, who was as bored with the inaction as Shok was, "We need to backup Doskel. He's too far out and he is exposed from the front and the rear. We need to keep the Veolsh cruisers on Iklug constantly covered. The Veolsh on Iklug might come in behind him if we don't. There is a good chance he's right about the Veolsh being on Egrin. It's very possible that he could be attacked from both directions at the same time. We should send Brak's fleet to cover Iklug before Doskel's fleet leaves. That will keep the Veolsh on Iklug and out of the Egrin situation, however that comes out.

"We should send another of the fleets we're holding here to patrol between the Veolsh and Iklug planets. The fleet we put between here and Iklug should be close enough to Iklug to be noticed by them. It seems our problem is centered there. With one fleet on this side of Iklug and Brak's over Iklug, the Veolsh cruisers and the Iklugs wont be able to arrange any surprises for us or Doskel."

"I like the plan," Jeonk agreed; "but I want another fleet guarding the Galactic Forum. I'll bring one more fleet to Veolsh to guard the Forum. Meanwhile, I think it would be wise if each of the member nations supplied some of their smaller spacecraft to make regular patrols of this planet and their own nations.

"You arrange a meeting with Chosteel and the other members, find out what they already have in the air. If it doesn't appear to be enough, get them to put more of their ships in the air. Shok, this business seems to be spreading. The farther we look, the more we find, and the uglier it gets."

Shok did as Jeonk suggested. Chosteel's original statement about the forum nations being sometimes ahead of the Argans was correct. They were patrolling their nations on a regular basis and they were in control of their planets airspace. The nations of the Veolsh planet were engaged in the same type of patrol activities as the other planets. The Veolsh civil police were looking for pirate terrorist groups in all of the Veolsh nations. The Forum nations were using the Galactic forum communications center as their central command center and their operation looked good to Shok. He couldn't find a way to improve on what was already being done.

Shok didn't enjoy being stuck in a diplomatic office. Part of his fleet was on loan, busy under someone else's command, while he waited impatiently to learn what they were learning first hand. If Egrin was working with the pirates, and Egrin was strong, it might start a battle with Doskel's fleet. It would take very little time for Egrin to prepare before they could mount an attack. Shok thought, "When there is a possibility for action, it's a Fleet Commanders duty to be with his fleet, not in some stuffy office doing paperwork."

Jeonk was sitting behind his desk as Shok entered his Forum office. He had an extra chair pulled nearby to put his feet on. Shok said, "Don't move, I like to talk to man who is comfortable. Everything is done here for a while. We have half of our ersatz empire builders in a position to get wiped out whenever they start something. The only wild card is Egrin. I think it would be a good idea if I rejoined my fleet to monitor firsthand what we're up against with the Egrin planet. Doskel and Brak left my flagship and most of my cruisers here. If I hurry, I can catch up with Doskel before he gets into trouble. My flagship is in orbit. I can grab the flag and be out of here real quick."

Jeonk wasn't very complimentary about Shok's plan. Shok knew Jeonk couldn't leave and he wanted to go as bad as Shok did. Jeonk said, "Bad idea Shok. If we leave, who do you think can take over what we're doing here? Who can coordinate Arga's activities with the Forum nations? You and I can't escape."

Shok gave him one of his best, thinking on his feet, answers, "I didn't say anything about 'we' but if 'we' go together, you can get your father and Rakoup to take over here. Your father doesn't have any friends in this area but he's well known and so is Rakoup. If you can get them to take over here, the 'we' can leave and do what we should be doing anyway. I should be with my fleet. Both of us should be doing our battle coordinating from a command deck--where we belong."

Plask and Rakoup arrived as quickly as Jeonk could get them to the surface. Plask said, "Rakoup and I will take care of things on Veolsh for you. You two haven't been in a good gunfight in the last few days; you must be getting pretty edgy."

Rakoup had to put his two skirbs worth in, "How are you two getting to Egrin? Have you found a souped up Veolsh corsair you can use?"

"We're taking my souped up flagship," Shok retorted. "It's in orbit overhead and waiting for us."

Plask added, "don't forget about the four cruiser policy for your protection."

"To hell with the four cruiser policy." Jeonk replied.

Rakoup found another two skirbs to spend, "What about Alice's two cruiser policy for Shok?"

Jeonk relented, "All right, I don't want to hurt Alice's feelings. We'll take two of Shok's cruisers."

Plask wasn't quit finished, "Don't forget to take some extra guns. Alice wanted extra guns."

When they left, Plask and Rakoup were still making jokes about things getting too tame for them. As their space fighter headed for the orbiting flagship, Jeonk said, "Don't pay any attention to their jokes. They wish they were coming with us. It will do my father good to deal with diplomats again, especially diplomats with as few diplomatic skills as Chosteel and the freedom fighters. He'll feel right at home with them in an hour."

They left the Veolsh planet at flank speed, regretting the time it would take them to rendezvous with Doskel's fleet and the six ships from Shok's fleet. They both enjoyed the feel of being back on a command deck. Ordinary problems seem to fade as the demands of flying a cruiser through space take over. Shok was on the command pedestal. Jeonk studied the course to Egrin with the navigator. They intended to bypass the two fleets monitoring the Iklug planet and go directly to Egrin. If there were any surprises, Egrin would supply the surprises.

As they approached the rendezvous, their scanners showed Doskel's twenty-two cruisers spread out in battle formation but there was nothing coming toward the fleet from the surface of Egrin. They couldn't tell from the scans if Doskel's fleet was in synchronous orbit in battle formation as a precaution or because Doskel thought an attack was eminent. Shok brought his flag cruiser as close to Doskel's flagship as he could. Jeonk and Shok took one of Shok's fighters to join Doskel on his command deck.

Jeonk raised the question, "Are you expecting an attack or are you being safe?"

Doskel replied, "We're being safe. They haven't taken any action against us but there is something going on in their capital. We're monitoring their transmissions, and their communications have become very busy since our arrival. I wish we had one of the Veolsh voice translators with us but we didn't expect to talk to anyone. We aren't leaving until we find out what they're doing."

"You can use mine," Shok offered. "The Veolsh council had the Egrin languages programmed. Is there any sign of fighting? Are the Veolsh cruisers on the planet? Are the pirate bases here?"

Doskel answered, "We haven't detected any war activities. The Veolsh cruisers are on the planet but the Veolsh cruisers can't go anywhere. If they launch, we'll nail them before they can clear Egrin's atmosphere. We haven't found any pirate bases on the planet."

"What kind of defense does Egrin have?" Jeonk asked. "How many and what kind of spacecraft do they have?"

"We've detected eight cruiser size spacecraft and about four thousand combat spacecraft of various sizes," Doskel replied. "They have a very good defense grid to protect the surface. We think some of their defensive weapons can destroy an airborne cruiser if it gets close enough to the planet's surface. If the Veolsh cruiser fleet, Iklug, Egrin and the pirates get together, they can beat the planet Veolsh and the other planets in the Galactic Forum. I don't think they would be a lethal threat to Arga but eventually they would have to try."

"If they were able to make a quick victory on the Galactic Forum," Shok stated, "Arga would have to fight because of our treaties with the Forum. That would force us to use our fleet patrolling the Krex and Mog systems. We would also have to remove or thin out our space patrols around Prssk and Gamac. Those four planets would be glad to fight against Arga if they could. Do you think the help they would have gotten from those four planets might have tilted the scale in favor of the newly forming empire?"

"It's a hell of a scenario," Jeonk answered. "If that's what they had in mind, they blew it by attacking the cargo line. Planning that bad in the face of planning that good doesn't match. The Gamacs and the Prsskians expect some kind of instant reward. Neither of them has been found guilty of long range planning."

"It does make sense," Doskel agreed, "if the planners intended for the Gamacs and the Prsskians to get on board long enough to insure the success of the plan and then cut them out of the rewards afterwards. Their reward was the cargo line and no fear of reprisals for their criminal activities. Prssk Command and the Gamacs were supposed to kill you and Shok, then keep Arga busy and out of this neighborhood long enough for the new empire to take over. The planners probably hoped that Arga, with a few new kings, would be weak enough for them to deal with successfully at a more leisurely pace."

"The Veolsh planners must have had Iklug and Egrin set up as new partners," Shok added. "With their other partners doing their dirty work close to Arga, it might have worked."

Shok turned toward the Communications Officer and said, "We should be getting some translations of the Egrin's chatter by now. Maybe we'll get enough information to put the whole puzzle together."

Doskel's fleet orbit was four hundred miles above the planet and the Egrins knew the fleet was there. Their radio transmissions were couched in language obviously designed to confuse unwanted visitors to the planet. There was some heavy back and forth discussions about pressing military matters and there seemed to be some disagreement about what actions should be taken. The Egrins had not expected an Argan fleet to show up on their doorstep.

Jeonk wanted to talk to someone in authority on the planet just to start things moving. He said, "Doskel, open a channel to the whoever is receiving the most traffic. I don't want to talk to them personally unless I must. Shok, you talk to them and try to find out what's going on."

Doskel opened a channel with enough power to override all other inputs to the location. Shok began, "This is Fleet Admiral Kelly of the Argan Admiralty. I want to speak with the highest ranking person available on this frequency."

They waited for about a minute before they received a response, "I am Marshall Treast, Commander of the Egrin Space Command. I will speak with Admiral Kelly of the Argan Admiralty."

Shok gave him the full treatment, "This is admiral Kelly speaking. I'm glad to have this opportunity to speak with you Marshall Treast. You have fifteen Veolsh Imperial Cruisers on the surface of Egrin and in your planetary control. The criminal Veolsh crews flying the cruisers were instrumental in perpetrating deadly attacks on the Argan Royal family, the Argan Admiralty, and the private businesses of Argan citizens. We further believe they intend to make war on the member nations of the Galactic Forum. Arga is one of those member nations. We want them for their crimes and we want you to release the Veolsh criminals into our custody. How do you respond?"

There was a pregnant silence before Shok received a reply; "We wish to speak with your king on this matter. Matters as important as the accusations you have made are only settled at the royal level."

Shok responded, "I have the authority of the king in these matters. Speaking with me is the same as speaking with the king. I strongly suggest you answer the questions I have already asked."

Shok turned to Doskel, "If they, or we, start shooting, kill the fifteen Veolsh cruisers on the ground then get high enough to beat hell out of Egrin Space Command without taking fire from their ground defense units."

Doskel said, "If it's going to turn hot it will be turning soon."

Marshall Treast came back to them, "Admiral Kelly, His Majesty, King Verstra, King of all of the planet Egrin, has authorized me to say, 'This matter is a simple one and easily settled between his Majesty, the King of Arga and his Majesty, King Verstra.'"

Jeonk started to answer but Shok warned him, "They're playing a political game to gain time and figure out what to do. They know it's too late to hide their connection with the Veolsh. If they find out you are here, they'll think it is win or lose right now. The Veolsh cruisers will launch; Egrin space Command will launch, and we may not be strong enough to beat them. Some of our cruisers could be lost. We've got them boxed. They are vacillating; let them squirm for a while. Let's call in another fleet and cinch their undying cooperation."

Doskel said, "We can take them right now."

As Jeonk opened his microphone, Shok wondered when Doskel began taking Rakoup lessons. Jeonk barked into the microphone,' "This is Jeonk Shap, King of Arga, I will speak with King Verstra of Egrin. When will he be available?"

Marshall Treast answered, "He will be available in twenty minutes."

"Jeonk," Shok remarked, "Doskel can transfer the conversation to my flagship. If we hurry, we can get to it before they launch everything they've got."

"All right but I think you're being pessimistic," Jeonk replied. "We may be able to work this out without going to war. The Egrin king might consider it safer to give the Veolsh to us than go to war with us. If he doesn't, fighting Egrin now will save us the trouble of fighting them later. Why do you think he wont talk?"

Shok gave him one of his best guesses as they walked to the launch bay and the fighter. "The King of Egrin wanted to be one of the bosses of a new empire. Arga was to be a part of the new empire. Verstra knows we know that. He was willing to kill or allow someone else to kill us to be the new boss. He won't believe we will allow him to live. Egrin Space Command is set up to launch and it will in less than twenty minutes. King Verstra doesn't want to talk; he wants to kill us. I think they still have some hope for the new empire if you and I are dead. Now, they know where we are and they have a chance to kill us."

As they entered the command deck of Shok's flagship, the gunnery officer said, "We have incoming from the surface of Egrin--all kinds. The Veolsh cruisers are launching and so is everything else."

Jeonk laughed and said, "You were right Shok, I think they want to fight. You better get this fleet moving. You bring any extra guns?"

Doskel fired at his fleets initial targets as his fleet gained altitude fast to avoid Egrin's ground batteries. There was no time to see what Doskel's gunners had hit. Shok had to get his cruisers higher to keep from becoming a target for the same ground batteries. Shok gave the marching orders to his fleet of eight cruisers, "Launch fighters. Navigator, take us one thousand miles high and put is on grid one, seven, seven, six. Attention all cruisers and all fighters. We are moving our cruisers away from Fleet One. I intend to put the incoming spacecraft in our crossfire as they approach Fleet One. Be ready to go in hot and hard on my signal. Disperse in battle formation four. Fire on any targets you can hit as we position for battle."

In seconds they were in position and as Shok expected, the incoming was concentrating on Doskel's fleet. The Egrins' intense focus on Doskel's fleet gave Shock's cruisers a nice flank to attack. First, Shok's fleet had to fight its own incoming enemy. There was one Egrin cruiser, about forty fighters, a half dozen corsairs, and whatever the other thirty was; he didn't have a name for them, coming directly at Shok's fleet to keep his cruisers and fighters from protecting Doskel's fleet.

Shok blasted the Egrin cruiser with a forward pulse cannon and told Jeonk, "If I knew Egrin cruisers were such cracker boxes I would have let the fighters take care of that one. Fighter pilots like it when they can take out a cruiser."

Shok's fighters punched their thrusters as they lunged into dogfights with the Egrin fighters. The ferocity of the Argan fighters shook the Egrin pilots. They broke formation to sweep around the Argan fighters. Half of them broke to the left side and half to the right. The dodging Egrin fighters were trying to continue their original assault on Shok's cruisers.

That was a bad move for the Egrin fighters to make against the more experienced Argan pilots. The Argan pilots split their formation, slipped sideways, and punched their thrusters one more time to use their forward lasers and pulse cannons on the broadside of the Egrins' split formation. One big mistake is usually the only one you get in a space battle. The Egrin fighters were so thoroughly pummeled by the Argan pilots that none in that formation survived.

The Egrin corsairs and the spacecraft Shok had no name for, something in between the size of the fighters and corsairs, attacked Shok's small cruiser fleet while his fighter protection was taking care of the Egrin fighters. The Egrin pilots obviously had no knowledge of Argan Cruisers. The Egrin fleet tried to attack the belly of the Argan cruisers. That move avoided the very powerful Argan forward pulse cannons but those pulse cannons wouldn't have been used on such small spacecraft anyway.

It was almost a shame to send a fleet like the Egrin fleet against such powerful spacecraft as the Argan Cruisers. The Egrin fleet could only kill a cruiser if enough of them hit the cruiser often enough.

Shok's belly gunners opened up on the Egrins, blasting them with a mind-numbing array of firepower. Eight Argan cruisers spread arrows of laser fire and hot balls of pulse cannon lightning into the hulls of the Egrin fleet. Some of Shok's cruisers rolled over so their port or starboard gunners could get in a few shots.

The Egrin pilots weren't on a suicide mission. Their Pilots on the lower end of the attack spun and dived to get away from the withering fire. Shok ordered his fleet's gunners to ceasefire and let them make it back home.

As Shok's fleet wheeled into the flank of the Egrin attack on Doskel's fleet, his holoscan showed two Argan cruisers attacking Egrin close to the ground, about building top level. He didn't know what Doskel had in mind. Doskel had told his crews to stay away from the ground defenses.

The two lone cruisers lasers and pulse cannons fired at every target in their area but they were concentrating on the position Marshall Treast had been transmitting from. Shok thought Doskel must have decided to blast the Egrin Space Command out of business. The two cruisers' fighters were battling with Egrin corsairs attacking them.

Shok didn't have time to keep a running check on the two cruisers. Jeonk noticed them the same time Shok did. He asked, "Did you see where those two cruisers come from?" Shok answered quickly from the fury of the battle, "I don't know, and I have to make a flank attack." He gave the order for the flank attack.

Doskel's fleet was now being fired at from all directions by the Egrin spacecraft coming from the surface and those that had survived and gotten above the fleet. The surviving Egrins cruisers and the ten Veolsh cruisers, Doskel's gunners missed on the ground, were in the sky and firing at Doskel's fleet. There were five hundred other ships of various descriptions attacking Doskel's fleet with the Egrin and Veolsh cruisers.

Three hundred and fifty Argan fighters defended Doskel's cruisers. The firing had become so intense that it was almost impossible to keep track of individual Argan fighters. Fortunately, the Argan computers recognized every one of them and prevented friendly fire by the home team.

Shok ordered, "Fighters, fire one, number four" Meaning, fire at any target any time you can and spread out to cover the entire battle area. Shok's fleet fighters were no longer to remain in position to protect their cruisers. Shok gave the same general order to the cruiser commanders. Shok spread his fleet of cruisers to hammer the flank of the enemy ships. Doskel's cruisers fired below his own fleet with a constant barrage of lasers and pulse cannons. The enemy spacecraft lucky enough to work its way above him through his massive defense would be taken care of by his fighters or his upper deck gunners.

The real worry was the Veolsh Imperial Cruisers. They weren't in their usual diamond formations. The Veolsh cruisers remained below the attacking Egrin ships, advancing behind them and using the Egrin ships for cover so the Imperial Cruisers could get close enough to kill Doskel's cruisers without themselves being killed.

Shok's flank attack had brought his cruisers in below the attacking Egrins protective umbrella and made the Veolsh cruisers prime targets for his fleet's forward pulse cannons. Ten Veolsh Imperial Cruisers were in the attack formation. Doskel's initial firing pattern hadn't been as deadly as he predicted. Doskel had predicted he would destroy all fifteen Veolsh cruisers while they were on the ground. He destroyed only five.

Shok felt a shred of sorrow for the Egrin crews. They were fighting bravely but futilely to kill Jeonk and Shok. The Egrins no longer knew where to find Jeonk and Shok, and were being out flanked by the two they intended to kill. Too Bad!

Shok ordered his fleet cruisers to ignore the Egrin cruisers. They fighters could destroy the cruisers. He had little respect for Egrin cruisers and wanted his maximum firepower concentrated on the Veolsh cruisers. He had a grudging respect for the Veolsh cruisers, and he knew they could destroy Doskel's cruisers if they got as close as they intended.

The Veolsh cruisers commanders were fixated on destroying Doskel's flagship. They thought Jeonk and Shok were with Doskel. In their zeal to kill Jeonk and Shok, they neglected their flank. It was an old Veolsh failing and one the Argans had taken advantage of before. The Veolsh commanded powerful ships, but used weak tactics. Shok's eight cruisers blasted through the Veolsh fighter protection, destroying their two hundred fighters as fast as they could target them.

Shok's fleet fired its forward pulse cannons that lashed the Veolsh cruisers with devastating affect. The Veolsh commanders quickly discovered their mistake in pitting all of their fire against Doskel's fleet. They tried to correct that mistake with another mistake. They tried to wheel into their diamond formations to repel Shok's flank attack.

Shok's fleet's guns lit up the exposed sides of the Veolsh cruisers as they wheeled. The sides of Shok's eight cruisers began lighting up as they took hits from the Veolsh lasers and pulse cannons, but the Argan cruisers could take more hits than the Veolsh. The out positioned Veolsh cruisers were taking most of the hits. The Argan pulse cannons began punching holes in the tough outer skin of the Veolsh cruisers. Argan lasers burned holes in the Veolsh hulls as they closed on them.

Doskel finally realized the fire from the decreased number of Egrin spacecraft was too little to do his fleet any serious damage. He ordered his cruiser gunners to ignore what was left of the Egrin swarm. His fighters could take care of them.

Doskel began concentrating his fleet's major firepower on the Veolsh Imperial Cruisers. His fleet's firepower and Shok's fleet's firepower finished the battle with the Veolsh. They were beaten seconds after both fleets began hitting them at the same time.

SPACE LINE BY MARIVIN E. FOX

When the Veolsh cruisers died, the Egrins got the message. They wheeled their ships and left the battle at flank speed, diving for the Egrin surface to find safety from certain death.

Shok opened his cruiser's blast shields to take an eyeball view of what they had done. The burning Veolsh cruisers he watched disintegrate were the fruit of an evil empire's first effort to rebuild itself and, he hoped, its last effort. There were no Veolsh fighters seen leaving the battle area with the Egrins. All two hundred of them were destroyed. There were so many lifeless Veolsh fighters and Egrin ships floating silently into oblivion that it wasn't worth the bother to count them. The burned out spaceships would be drifting away from Egrin for a long time before they found their final graves on strange, distant, lifeless, floating islands of dirt and rock.

Doskel's cruisers took many hits in the battle. The concentrated fire from the Egrin fleet had hurt his fleet but he had lost no cruisers. Seven of Shok's cruisers suffered damage but all of his ships could still fight after the battle ended. Many Argan fighters were damaged and a few were lost but most of the pilots were recovered from the damaged fighters. The Egrin's spacecraft didn't have enough punch to kill them and the Veolsh cruisers didn't have enough time to kill them. Shok had the last word on the Battle, "It was a good battle. We lived, they didn't."

Shok's flagship picked up the communications between the two Argan cruisers fighting on Egrin's surface as the Egrins retreated from the battle. One voice said, "Rakoup, we've got more than one hundred fifty ships coming at us. You better recall your fighters to take care of them."

The other voice replied, "I've got them Plask. They seem to be peeling off to avoid us. Do you think we should go after them?"

Plask answered, "No, let them go. They're running for their lives. They can go anywhere they like. They will sure as hell get no instructions from this command center and knocking out those ground pulse batteries was sure lucky for Doskel and his fleet fighting overhead."

Rakoup added, "that's right Plask, the fleet might have gotten low enough to get hit."

Jeonk looked at Shok and said, "That's the way they're in charge. We might as well have left our wives in charge. I'm going to ask them to come up here for a meeting."

As the two cruisers pulled close to Shok's flagship, he could see the damage they took while they were destroying one command center, a bunch of fighters, and a few of the pulse batteries the fleet had avoided by moving out of range. Both ships had numerous holes in their outer skin heat shields and several holes in their secondary heat shields. The white of the ships' hull insulation could be seen down the entire length of both ships. The damage was an expected result of being the target for every gun on the planet firing at them at the same time. Getting hit that often and that hard does it.

Plask and Rakoup took fighters from their separate cruisers and landed in the landing bay at the same time. They came forward to the command deck together. Jeonk didn't waste any time with preliminaries; he was mad at them. Since they had survived the battle, the near fatal damage to their cruisers didn't even enter his mind. He demanded, "Who is in charge on the Veolsh planet. Who did you leave to do the job you said you were going to take care of for me?"

"Don't get overheated son," Plask answered, "everything is being taken care of just like I said it would. We knew you and Shok would start some kind of fight. We had to be here to make sure it didn't get too dangerous for you. We promised Aslain and Alice we would take care of you and Shok."

Jeonk interrupted, "But who did you put in charge? The Galactic Forum members need someone who can speak for Arga, someone who can speak with authority."

"We left Aslain and Alice in charge," Plask replied. "They know more about the Galactic Forum business than anyone else. They know most of the members by their first names. Alice said Shok was proud of her and Aslain's diplomatic skills. She said Shok told her the two of them were writing a new chapter in diplomacy."

Jeonk wasn't satisfied with what he considered to be skimpy logic, "And what do Aslain and Alice do if the fleet has to move? What will they do if there's a fleet emergency?"

Plask hesitated, so Rakoup added, "Plask and I have been teaching them fleet maneuvers and fleet tactics for a long time. I'm surprised they haven't told you about it. They're really quick learners. Besides that, the Fleet Admiral guarding the Veolsh planet may know something about fleet movements and emergencies. If he had to ask for instructions to take care of an emergency, he wouldn't be a Fleet Admiral."

Shok didn't want to get between the heated remarks, but he couldn't resist one question, "What military rank do our wives hold?"

Plask answered, "Aslain can hold any rank she wants; she's the Queen. Alice has been promoted, at my insistence, to Vice Commander. If she does well in this job, and I know she will, I'm having her promoted to Commander. People with a special talent deserve the rank their talent qualifies them to hold."

Arga had women of higher rank but Shok wasn't married to them; none of them were being taught cruiser battle tactics!"

"All right,' Jeonk said; "you and Rakoup take over here. I'll call in another fleet and some ground troops to keep control here until we can get this mess stabilized well enough to prevent the Egrins from causing further trouble. The King's name is Verstra. Force him to come to you for a meeting. Scare hell out of him so our ground troops won't have to fight a war to gain control of the planet.

"If Verstra causes you any trouble, tell him Arga will appoint a new king over his dead body. You better keep him on board until it's over. We don't want him escaping to a planet we've never heard of and talking them into helping him.

Shok and I are going back to the Galactic Forum to see how things are going there. I'll leave Doskel's fleet and six of Shok's cruisers to keep a lid on things here."

Shok added, "It might be a good idea to prevent anyone from leaving the planet. The first one to leave will be King Verstra."

"Well Jeonk," Plask remarked, "you have finally found something decent for two old warriors to do. With good luck, maybe Verstra will try to fight his way off the planet."

Jeonk and Shok took his flagship and one other cruiser to the Veolsh planet to find out what their wives were doing to keep the Galactic Forum nations lined up. It appeared the Egrin battle had sharply reduced the threat of war. Each of them hoped, with less of a threat of war on the horizon and no immanent threat to his personal safety, his wife would quietly slip back into her wifely duties without carrying three pistols and a knife when she left the house. Shok thought, "One thing is sure, I don't want my wife with me on the command deck during my next cruiser battle."

Shok's flag cruiser and his escort cruiser had exterior battle damage. The two cruisers hadn't taken as many hits as Plask and Rakoup's but both were hit hard and often enough to become a tourist attraction. Many of the Forum members flying their corsairs and fighters came to meet the damaged cruisers on the way in. They had a large escort to their airborne anchorage over the Galactic Forum. Everyone who could find something that flies circled the two battle damaged spacecraft a few times.

The Galactic forum was still running smoothly in spite of Jeonk's fears. Aslain and Alice had done well as Plask had predicted. Chosteel and his Paracans had insisted on helping the Argan Marines and the Oglaks to guard them. The ladies had moved back into the Veolsh Council mansion while their husbands were gone. The new Oglak troops arrived and were guarding the mansion and the ladies at night. With all of the guards they had, a sand flea couldn't have gotten to them.

Aslain and Alice had explained to those who were afraid they might not have the necessary military skills, that they were standing in for their husbands and their husbands were still in charge of the Argan effort. The members were satisfied with their explanation and most of them paid compliments to the ladies for their expert handling of the diplomatic chores.

Jeonk called a meeting of the Forum to give his report about the activities in space over Egrin. He explained the present military position on Egrin and that Arga was bringing ground troops to control its capitol and military bases. He asked for the help of the Forum members, "Arga doesn't have enough troops to control the Egrin planet alone. We'll need your troops and their commanders for effective control of the planet on the ground and in Egrins surrounding space. We can decide how it is to be done in strategy meetings among the members.

"I think we may have a similar situation with the Iklug planet. There are presently fifteen Veolsh Imperial cruisers on Iklug and we must deal with those fifteen cruisers. The Iklugs themselves are militarily weak. Arga currently has one fleet over Iklug and one fleet between Iklug and the Veolsh planet at this time. We haven't attacked and they can't escape.

"Fleet Admiral Shok and I will go to Iklug and ask for their surrender. If they don't surrender, they wont have a military to fight with anyway. We'll blast it out of existence. We want to speak with those members who are familiar with the Iklugs before we do anything in their area. We have no interest in fighting them if we can get them to become peaceful and remain peaceful. If there is someone on friendly terms with them in the Forum, we would like him to come forward for consultation. A friendly member may be the best person to approach the Iklug leadership.

"We haven't yet located the pirate fleet. We think it may be as large as seven hundred spaceships. We expect most of those spaceships to be of the corsair class. We believe the pirates have joined into one cooperating fleet. That's far too many pirates, and too much criminal fire power for us to leave wandering around loose.

"The pirates are apparently familiar with parts of the galaxy the rest of us are unfamiliar with. Their hiding place is somewhere none of us have been. We are fortunate to have one of the best interplanetary hunters in this galaxy with us. That hunter is fleet Admiral Doskel. So far, we have had him searching in specified areas. His fleet found the Veolsh cruisers on Iklug and Egrin. When his fleet is free, he will be turned loose to hunt anyplace in the galaxy he wishes to look. We must find the pirates. Sooner or later they will cause trouble for all of us, and they were our original targets. They will remain our targets until we deal with them conclusively.

"There will be a meeting of primary national delegates in two hours according to the schedule Admiral Chosteel has given me. If any of you have questions about planning, please give them to your primary delegates. Your answers will have to come from the meeting, depending on the decisions of the Forum. Admiral Shok and I will be available to answer any questions we can answer individually until then."

The planning of what to do about Egrin was comparatively simple. It had one government, one currency and one social structure. The major problem was getting enough troops to keep it's military under control. The Forum thought a land war waged against ground troops whose leaders had squandered their air support wouldn't be a long war.

The Forum nations decided to occupy Egrin's major cities and its military bases. Egrin's military bases were widespread but there weren't very many of them. The nations of the Forum had enough military personnel of their own to maintain control of the Egrin military and the cities. Arga would only supply ground forces if Egrin's military decided to put up a strong fight. The troops of the Forum nations would then back up the Argans as needed.

The Forum nations didn't expect the social life on Egrin to be greatly affected by their takeover. No plan was made to restrict the activities of the average person or business. They wanted normal personal and business relations to continue as undisturbed as possible. They had no idea what normal was on Egrin. The Forum nations made no plan to confiscate personal property or money. When the Forum troops got on the ground, they didn't want a door-to-door war with an irate population trying to protect itself from a greedy conqueror.

Iklug was different. It was a wild card. The Argans had it nailed down but they couldn't hold it that way forever. Jeonk didn't want to tie up a fleet orbiting Iklug for a long period of time. The Forum nations didn't have enough firepower to substitute for the Argan cruisers orbiting Iklug. The Iklug problem had to be solved as quickly as possible.

Jeonk had already decided he and Shok would take on the Iklugs. He had gained a new confidence in Aslain and Alice; he would leave Arga's Forum interests in their capable hands. Besides, Jeonk couldn't hope to keep Plask and Rakoup on the ground for more than a few minutes at a time, so he had no choice. He had to have someone who was knowledgeable about the immediate problems and who was known and trusted by the Forum members. Jeonk may have regretted leaving Arga's regular Forum diplomats out of the situation in the beginning. Shok knew him to well to ask him about it when he wasn't in a good mood.

The two women had done better than good so far. They had the Forum looking like a family reunion. People were showing each other pictures of their kids, table hopping, waving across the room at each other and there were more people with notebooks at work on the floor than Shok had seen anywhere. Formal diplomacy would be a thing of the past in the inner galaxy if the two women kept up their assault on it.

Jeonk and Shok took two undamaged cruisers from the orbiting fleet for the trip to Iklug. Both had time to say good-bye to their wives. Aslain gave Jeonk a hug and a kiss and told him she and Alice would take care of everything while he was gone. She slipped an extra pistol into his pocket as she kissed him. Alice gave Shok a kiss and, as she hugged him, she slipped an extra pistol into his pocket, as though there aren't enough pistols on cruisers. Shok thanked her for her good thought and didn't bother to mention the large number of extra pistols in cruiser armories.

On the flight to Iklug, Jeonk asked, "What do you think we should do about the Veolsh cruisers?"

"Blast them," Shok answered, "do it before we talk to anyone."

"Good idea," Jeonk agreed, "they're easier to hit on the ground than in the sky. Their pulse cannons don't work worth a damn on the ground."

"Too bad we couldn't find someone who knows the Iklugs well enough to talk to them," Shok mentioned. "The Iklugs may have something to say about the splattered Veolsh cruisers. I guess we can use a voice translator to ask if they would prefer to surrender or get splattered like the cruisers."

Jeonk didn't agree, "I'm getting damned tired of these galaxy conquerors. Every time we get rid of one of them there's another waiting to take his place. It's better not to talk to them. It's better to kick the crap out of them and get it over with. I don't intend to listen to any more longwinded speeches about how misunderstood they are. I don't mind asking them to surrender, that's all right. If they don't surrender, kick the crap out of them."

Jeonk's last remark exhausted the very short planning phase of their upcoming association with the Iklugs. Jeonk turned to their most complicated and mystifying subject, their wives. Jeonk reached over and tapped the pocket Alice had put Shok's extra pistol in. "Aslain put an extra pistol in my pocket as we left," he remarked. "I can't tell if Aslain is getting to be more like Alice or Alice is getting to be more like Aslain. Maybe they just met in the middle somewhere. Maybe they were always the way they are now and by strange circumstances happen to know each other. I don't understand how two women who were born so far apart, on different planets, can be so alike."

Shok would have liked to clear the matter up for him but he didn't have any more clues on the subject than Jeonk. They cruised into Brak's fleet as Shok spoke, "I don't know any more about it than you do. The deepening mysteries of Aslain and Alice make them all the more interesting. We've both got the wives we want and need. Let's just count our blessings and keep right on loving them."

Jeonk made the final assessment on the subject of wives, "Let's take a fighter ride to Brak's cruiser and let's not forget our extra pistol. Brak may want to shoot one of us."

Brak reported his and the Veolsh conditions, "I have the Veolsh cruisers targeted. If they make a move to leave the surface of the planet, I'll destroy them on the ground. I'm sure they know we have them on our target scans. If I were the Veolsh, I would have tried something by now. I don't understand why they've done nothing."

Shok thought he could bring some clarity to the matter, "When we were on Egrin, we called for negotiations in an attempt to avoid war. The time it took for the negotiations to begin was the time they used to launch into battle. They are probably waiting for us to do the same thing here. Where are the Veolsh cruisers on the planet?"

Brak answered, "The Veolsh spread them pretty evenly around Iklug. That isn't a problem. What do you want me to do?"

"Hit all of them at the same time, right now!" Jeonk ordered.

Brak had positioned one of his Argan cruisers to cover each of the Veolsh cruisers. He put his finger on the simultaneous fire button on his command pedestal and pressed it once.

All of the Argan cruisers began their fire patterns at the same time and the Veolsh cruisers on the ground began exploding. Some of the Veolsh missiles, those already loaded into the cruiser missile tubes, were launched from the effects of the explosions. The missiles began hitting targets indiscriminately on the ground. Secondary explosions repeatedly occurred near the burning cruisers. Flames poured from everything combustible anywhere near the destroyed cruisers.

The Argan cruiser holoscanners displayed intense ground activity around the cruisers, but no spacecraft were launched. There was no answering fire from the Iklug ground batteries. The Iklugs had undoubtedly been informed of the battle on Egrin. They didn't want Plask and Rakoup blasting their command centers if they fired.

The Argan radio receivers burst into activity. A highly disturbed voice, obviously from a voice translator, said, "Why have you fired on the peaceful Veolsh warriors protecting the peaceful people of the planet Iklug? Is this one more instance of the Argan propensity for unwarranted sneak attacks on their neighbors? We would have surrendered any time you gave us safe passage to go peacefully on our way. You have destroyed the last hope for sanity in this galaxy.

We find it wise to bear you no ill will. We await your instructions, and hope to come to some agreement with the powerful king of Arga. If he is present, please have him communicate with us."

Jeonk was really pissed. He barked at Shok, "Didn't we take care of all of those Veolsh Council tyrants? That sounded like one of the fat cats on the Veolsh Council."

"I thought we did," Shok replied, "but I'll bet my bottom gold skirb we just heard from one we missed. I think we should bypass the little rat and contact the Iklugs. Brak, You've been here the longest, do you know who the leader of this messy planet is?"

Brak was mystified, "We weren't interested in who the Iklug leader is. We are here to keep any spacecraft of any kind from leaving the planet. You two have been with the Galactic Forum people, didn't any of them know about the Iklugs?"

"The Iklugs are long time friends and associates with the Veolsh Council," Jeonk informed him. "The Veolsh Council and high ranking Veolsh government people came here for vacations or whatever the Veolsh did with their friends. No one in the Forum knows the Iklugs well enough to give us any more information than that.

"I think Shok is right. We need to bypass the Veolsh Council member--who seems to think he can speak for the planet Iklug, and go directly to whatever leadership the Iklugs have. We may be able to prevent any further destruction on the planet."

Brak was hell on wheels when it came to shooting anything that needed a little firepower laid on it, but he was no Doskel with communications. Shok had to use Brak's communications gear to raise someone of importance, who was also an Iklug. He transmitted on the entire frequency spectrum Brak had received since his arrival. Shok's message was simple, "This is Fleet Admiral Shok of the Argan Admiralty. I wish to speak with the highest authority of the planet Iklug. Veolsh council members, their subordinates or citizens of the Veolsh planet shall not comply with this request."

After what Shok thought was a decent interval, his call was answered, "I am Fogeek Lastri, king of the planet Iklug. I am waiting for your communication, please proceed."

Shok turned to Jeonk and asked, "Do you want to talk to him?"

Jeonk answered, "No, I talked to the last king and it started the war on Egrin. It's your turn, you start this war."

Shok began with what he hoped wouldn't be a war starter, "We regret the inconvenience of the few explosions and fires that occurred when we destroyed the war cruisers belonging to the Veolsh Imperial Council. We hope none of your people were injured, and collateral damage to Iklug property was kept at a minimum. We applaud the efforts of your ground crews to limit the unintentional damage to your property."

"Damn it Shok," Jeonk interrupted, "just get to it. We're not trying to make friends with the guy."

Shok retorted, "Don't bang my ear about my best effort at diplomacy. I'm trying to keep from starting a war here and I would have already been to it if you hadn't interrupted."

SPACE LINE BY MARIVIN E. FOX

He continued his conversation with the king in his usual way, minus the diplomatic effort, "We have enough fire power over your head to blast all of you into political oblivion for years to come. If we are fired on, or you launch your spacecraft against us, we will blast you into oblivion. But, that isn't our first choice. Our first choice is this. We want you to hand over the remnants of the Veolsh Council and the Veolsh citizens who are with them. Those you hand over to us will be treated fairly, but they will go on trail on their home planet and possibly on other planets where they have taken many lives. The planet Iklug will be occupied by Argan military personnel, and reinforced by the Galactic forum nations. As long as you are peaceful, you and your people will be treated with respect by the occupying forces.

"Arga and the Forum nations need nothing of yours. Your money, national treasures, personal possessions, private money accounts and your persons will not be endangered. If our first choice is your first choice, you and yours will be spared further damage. What is your reply?"

King Fogeek Lastri answered cautiously, "We are longtime friends of those you wish us to help you capture. We are not in a position to refuse your request, but it will take us some time to capture them ourselves and transfer them to your custody. Perhaps, knowing our desperate situation, they will volunteer to go with you and spare us the national regret of taking them by force. Will you allow us the time we need to ascertain their wishes in this matter? We will allow them to surrender or we will take them by force if they do not."

Brak said, "He's trying to buy time to get the Veolsh and himself off the planet."

Jeonk said, "You tell King Lastri, his last try wont work. He either gives the remaining Veolsh to us or we're coming to get them, now."

Before Shok returned to Lastri's last try, he said, "Quick Brak, make sure every scanner in the fleet is looking for some kind of an escape craft. It will be fast and probably small."

Brak got busy with the fleet and Shok returned to Lastri, "Your Majesty, we will not wait. We are beginning our scans of the planet for military facilities and power sources. We will begin destroying whatever is necessary to neutralize the political, military and civilian infrastructure of your planet in preparation for our invasion of it. What is your answer?"

Shok waited; there was no answer. Brak reported sharply, "A small craft is leaving the planet from the other side. I've never seen anything move that fast."

Jeonk slapped his hand on the command pedestal and said, "Get two cruisers after it now! Shoot the damn thing down!

Shok watched the holoscan on the command pedestal as the escape craft disappeared. Brak managed to make a scanner readout of its speed and dimensions. Unless it cloaked as it went out of range, it was the fastest any of them had encountered. Everyone on the command deck realized they were witnessing a new technology in the speed of the small spacecraft, a technology the Argans didn't have. Speeds in multiples of light speed were common but the speed of the escaped spacecraft was a quantum leap above the speeds they were familiar with.

Shok suggested to Brak, "Keep the two cruisers after it as long as their commanders can find some trace elements in its trail to follow. When they lose any method of following it except its last position, and supposed course, bring them back. It will change course as soon as the pilot feels safe to do so. Attempting to follow it will do no good. We'll have to use some other method to find out where they're going."

Admiral Brak computed the data trail of the escape spacecraft and put an animated model on the command pedestal holograph. The ship was unusual, twice the size of a corsair with four huge external thrusters. The external thrusters gave them the answer for its surface atmosphere speed but not the answer for its speed in space. Brak turned the computer model to view the ship from every angle. They found no answer for its speed in space from what they saw on the model.

Brak programmed the display to reproduce the escaping ships course to the place where they lost it. The model was normal until it disappeared. Just before it disappeared, it lit up like a pulse from a pulse cannon, and then just vanished. None of them knew what technology it used but they all knew they couldn't afford to be without it. The technology wasn't Veolsh and no one they knew had anything similar. Whoever gave the technology to the Veolsh was friendly enough to share the technology with them. The sharing of technology, with a dangerous enemy of Arga, made it dangerous for Arga.

Jeonk voiced his disappointment, "I hate to lose Lastri. We might have been able to finish this business here. Shok, get back on the radio and find out who's in charge. I still don't want to start blasting things if we don't need to blast them."

The channel Shok was on opened as Jeonk finished speaking, "This is General Vrastklo of the Revolutionary Army of Iklug. I wish to speak with Admiral Shok, sometimes called Kelly; is Admiral Shok available?"

Shok answered, "General Vrastklo, this is Admiral Shok, what do you wish to say?"

The General returned, "There has been a change of government on Iklug. We ask you not to fire on us. All of the Veolsh personnel on this planet are now under arrest and in the custody of the Revolutionary Army. We offer them to you now, as you demanded from the previous government. We will accept your occupation of Iklug for your determination of our peaceful intentions.

I am familiar with Arga's occupation policies from my observations of them on the planet Veolsh during your occupation of that planet. I can assure you of the support of the revolutionary Army and the people of Iklug while you are here. You may stay as long as you like and leave when it pleases you."

Shok asked, "What happened to the former government and why have we detected no conflict on the planets surface during your revolution?"

The General replied, "I was formerly a high ranking general in the Iklug Army. I was also one of the observers on the planet Veolsh during the formation of the Galactic Forum. I have known for a long time that we on Iklug were under the same type of tyranny the Veolsh people suffered with the Veolsh Council.

When you defeated the Veolsh Council and gave the people of Veolsh and the other planets freedom, I believed we could also be free. I decided to use my military connections to overthrow the former government. I have been working to bring the Iklug people, who believe as I do, into the revolution since I was an observer at the Forum.

King Lastri became aware of the revolution but he made the mistake of putting me in command of putting it down. King Lastri never discovered his mistake. I managed to put together a revolution based on a large number of dissatisfied high-ranking military people who were also patriots of Iklug. We were about to remove the king from power when the Veolsh descended on our planet with their cruisers.

With the certainty of Veolsh help, the king could have defeated us. I halted our revolutionary efforts until after the Veolsh cruisers were destroyed. Our delay of the revolution avoided our defeat by king Lastri. The Veolsh and their cruisers had been here for a long time before your cruisers entered our airspace. With your cruisers overhead, I knew the Veolsh Council influence on our planet would be ended rather soon. I put my revolutionary army back into position and waited for that moment to begin our revolution.

When you destroyed the Veolsh cruisers you destroyed any possibility for the king to remain in power. The king realized this and so did his Veolsh friends who survived your attack. The king, his mistress and the highest-ranking members of the Veolsh survivors left in the spacecraft you most certainly observed as it left this planet.

I don't know their destination and I have no information on the type of spacecraft they used to leave the planet. I realize you must be intensely interested in the design of the spacecraft they escaped in. I will share that information with you if it is in the imperial records.

You are welcome here. The area is secured and we are waiting for your arrival. I would like to speak personally with Admiral Shok on matters concerning the structure of our new governments. I have set a landing beacon for you on a frequency of ten gigahertz. You may follow the beacon to the landing sight. There is sufficient room at the landing sight for several of your cruisers if you decide to land."

The beacon came on as the General indicated. Shok looked at Jeonk and said, "That was what we Americans call, saying a mouthful. Sounds great, and no war, if it isn't some kind of a Veolsh trap."

Jeonk was as trap jumpy as Shok. He turned to Brak and ordered, "Send three of your cruisers to the beacon sight. Have one of them land. Have its Marines debark and check the security in the area. Keep the remaining two cruisers off the ground with their fighters launched. Hold that position until the Marines on the ground make sure we aren't walking into a trap. If it looks like there is no trap, land the other two cruisers and have the Marines from those two join the Marines already on the ground. Put the two cruisers back in the sky while the Marines make a more extensive inspection of the area. If they find nothing, Shok and I will land in the cruiser we came in.

"Put extra fighters from your fleet overhead to cover the Marines and do the close work just in case the Iklugs spring a trap. You remain here with your two fleets on constant alert. If it looks like we have walked into a well designed trap, don't wait for my instructions to start shooting."

Jeonk and Shok returned to their cruiser to wait for developments. It was several hours before the Marines were satisfied with the security of the area. The two finally received Brak's, "all clear" and started their descent. During the descent, Jeonk asked, "Shok, do you want to stay here and help these Iklugs the same way you did the Forum people on the Veolsh Planet?"

"No, we have other things to do," Shok answered. "I can talk to General Vrastklo and get him started in the right direction. I'll call on the member nations of the Galactic Forum to give him as much help as I can. The forum people will be able to give him as much help as I can and maybe more."

Jeonk voiced his satisfaction, "Good choice, we have some detective work to do. We haven't found the pirates yet and we must find out where the high ranking Veolsh and King Last Try are bound for."

The descent and landing was uneventful. Argan Marine guards waited for them at the landing sight and stayed with them constantly. General Vrastklo and several of his aides were waiting to greet them. The General made the welcoming speech. Jeonk and Shok were welcomed as friends and benefactors of the Iklug people. The General introduced them to the other revolutionaries in his group. The revolutionaries greeted them with great thanks and their gratitude because Admiral Brak hadn't shot hell out of the place.

The General finally got to the meat and potatoes of the meeting and he seemed to have plenty of both in his larder. General Vrastklo stated, "We need no financial help. We managed to keep the national treasury intact. We thank you again for attacking the Veolsh in such a timely manner. We would have lost nearly one third of the treasury if the Veolsh had been able to leave the Planet. But, we are still removing our gold and jewels from their destroyed cruisers.

"Our communications network is in operation, and our Army is under the control of revolutionary generals. Most of our military people were not loyal to the king. His Majesty depended on an inner circle of bureaucrats and generals to maintain his power. Some of the inner circle, as myself, didn't like him. As soon as he lost the protection of the Veolsh Council, thanks to you, we decided to depose him. We have accomplished that.

"I am calling a council of leaders, those not friendly to the king, for an alliance of freedom and a realignment of the government on the planet. It seems to us that many separate nations with unbreakable sovereignty will offer more security for our people than one government with unbreakable control. The council I am calling will consider our options for that purpose. I remember Admiral Shok, as the organizer of the Galactic Forum. We want to start a Planetary Forum on that same plan and have each of our nations seek admission into the Galactic Forum.

Admiral Kelly, is it possible for us to have a Planetary Forum and have each nation in it be eligible for membership in the Galactic Forum?"

Shok gave his question some thought, and answered, "Yes it is possible and it's a good idea. You would have a problem if you consolidated the nations into one planetary government again. If that happens, the consolidated nations belonging to the Galactic Forum will no longer be eligible for membership. The major government would be eligible for membership. The consolidated nations would become subdivisions of the major government and subdivisions of governments aren't eligible to be members in the Galactic Forum."

General Vrastklo had another question; he looked at Shok with great intensity, and said, "Admiral Shok, will you help the people of Iklug as you did the present members of the Galactic Forum after your war with the Veolsh Council?"

Shok understood how important the question was to the General and he hated the answer he had to give, "General, I would like to give my personal help but I cannot. However, there are many willing hands among the nations of the Galactic Forum. I know Iklug can get all of the help it needs from people who have already completed what you are beginning.

"You may be assured, there will be an Argan diplomat among them, one who can seek my assistance, the assistance of King Jeonk, and the assistance of the Argan government to resolve any problems you may encounter. I'm sorry but my services are needed to resolve our present problems.

"His Majesty and I will be leaving soon to confer with the Forum member nations on the planet Veolsh. You may send those of your choice with us to supervise the selection of those who will be willing to help you, or you may allow me to put together a team to assist you. However you wish to proceed is acceptable."

General Vrastklo had one more request; "I talked with the lady, who I assume is now your wife, when I was an observer at the formation of the Galactic Forum. We spoke at some length. I admired her greatly for her grasp of the situation and her hopes for its success. Admiral Shok, we need your prestige at this conference. If you cannot be there yourself, may we ask for her services in your place? She will bring your prestige with her, and that may supply the help we need. I will personally guard her life with my life.

"Most of the people on Iklug know of the fear and hatred you and His Majesty caused in the Veolsh, and our quickly departed king. Neither of you are available because of the importance of what you are doing. The prestige of Arga, and you, will be present in that one young lady. I think her help may insure our success."

Jeonk took the question out of Shok's hands, "Of course she can help. I'll make sure she has enough advisors from the Forum nations to take care of any technical or legal problems that may arise. I am reassured by your offer to protect her and I thank you for it but I must insist on having Argan Marines in charge of her safety. Alice, and all of us, will be glad for any added protection you provide. One of our cruisers will leave within the hour to bring her and the necessary advisors to Iklug and your Planetary Forum meeting."

General Vrastklo was very happy with Jeonk's endorsement of his request. He stated, "Admiral Shok's wife and her party will be staying in the royal palace of King Lastri. I will have it prepared for her immediately. If she wants for anything, anything at all, it will be given to her if it is possible for Iklug to provide it."

Jeonk used a voice recorder message to Alice, mentioning how important Alice and the prestige of Arga was to the success of the formation of the Iklugs' Planetary Forum. He laid it on pretty heavily about the importance of Arga's prestige and the difficulty of the job.

Shok knew they wouldn't be able to leave until after Alice's arrival. Anyway, they couldn't go until the two cruisers chasing The Veolsh and Lastri's double cross corsair returned and none of them knew when that would be.

General Vrastklo became very busy with the affairs of his newly forming nations. Two of his aids accepted the task of showing Jeonk and Shok around the planet. In the larger cities the planet looked reasonably good. The farther they went from the capital, the worse it looked. There were large areas where people lived in poverty. The best looking buildings in those areas were always the government buildings. Population support systems were in poor condition. Shok could see why General Vrastklo decided the planet needed some kind of new government arrangement. The General did well in considering a Planetary Forum of cooperating but separate sovereign nations and their inclusion into the Galactic Forum.

The two cruisers returned from their fruitless effort to catch the escaping spacecraft. They never caught sight of it but they were able to follow a photon trail it left behind. The photon trail petered out and with no other way to follow the ship, they returned as instructed.

To say the return of the two cruisers brought disappointment with them would be an understatement. The two cruisers brought worry with them, that's an accurate statement. The photon trail they followed confirmed the new technology. The Argans now knew there was a technology they didn't have. They also knew it wasn't Veolsh technology, and whoever gave it to the Veolsh hadn't given them enough of it to use in a war; that was the good news.

The bad news was, whoever invented the technology obviously knew about the Argans but the Argans didn't know about them. If the owners of the new technology were friendly, the bad news wasn't very important. If they were unfriendly, the bad news was of Galactic importance. None of the Argans believed anyone who was willing to give the Veolsh Council a superior technology could fall on the good news side of the importance equation.

Shok spent the next few days with more than his usual amount of impatience. Jeonk and Shok had full schedules for the future but they couldn't leave before the cruiser from the Forum arrived. If they left, they would be leaving the Iklugs seeking nationhood in the lurch. Their leaving might tip the scales against the revolution and the two of them would be responsible for its fall.

The cruiser bringing Alice and her advisors to Iklug finally arrived. Jeonk and Shok were on hand as the cruiser made its descent. The first two people out of the cruiser were Alice and Aslain. Both carried notebooks. Shok was sure Jeonk hadn't expected Aslain to sign on with Alice to help the Iklugs. Jeonk had made the mistake of mentioning the prestige of Arga in his voice message. Shok didn't say anything to Jeonk in his moment of shock, but he was sure the subject would come up later, on the next space flight.

Immediately behind Alice and Aslain were Plask and Rakoup. They said they came along to make sure the security for Aslain and Alice was broad based enough to keep them safe. Shok thought that sounded like a reasonable excuse to find out what Jeonk and he were up to--and get in on the action. They had, fortuitously, brought with them the locations of all of the planets the Veolsh Council had shown any interest in, to aid in the search for the pirates. Rakoup had his fleet standing off in space just in case Jeonk and Shok needed transportation and, perhaps, as a backup for a future, undetermined emergency.

Shok could see Plask's diplomatic skills at work here. He and Rakoup didn't know what the plan was but they didn't want to be left out. They used the defeated Veolsh Council's archives to do the detective work they knew the plan would require and presented the results. Neither of them was needed on Iklug and the Forum was getting too quiet for two old warriors to be bothered with. The only reasonable thing left to do was for them to join Jeonk and Shock in their quest against the pirates.

Following the royal party from the cruiser was the advisors from the Galactic Forum, about thirty of them. It must have been quit a sight for those leaving the cruiser. The Argan Marines and the Iklug guards were waiting in formation to protect them. More Argan Marines left the cruiser's exit hatches and took their positions with the other guards. The Commander of the Iklug planet's freedom fighters waited to greet them and escort them to the former king's royal palace.

Alice was farther than she had ever been from Decatur, Illinois in distance and situation. She was now a well-known and highly respected person on several planets and she was about to become the chief planetary advisor who would aid in the formation of every one of the new governments on the planet Iklug. Even Shok was impressed with his wife's accomplishments.

Jeonk and Shok stayed in the background as General Vrastklo and the Iklug freedom fighters took Alice, Aslain and the Forum's advisors to their quarters in the royal palace. They did have an opportunity that evening to see their wives privately and they stayed overnight with them in the palace. Alice was as loving and warm as always.

Shok felt reassured that her growing fame wouldn't cause them family problems. He explained to her what Jeonk and he had to do and apologized for not being able to help her with the job ahead of her. He told her of his confidence in her ability to get the job done right. She cried in his arms as he told her he had to leave in the morning and didn't know when he would return.

SPACE LINE BY MARIVIN E. FOX

3

THE LAST TRY QUEST

Plask and Rakoup joined Jeonk and Shok in the search for the pirates, King Last Try, and the Veolsh escapees. Jeonk and Shok flew into the unknown in one of the two cruisers they had flown to Iklug from the Veolsh planet. Plask and Rakoup flew beside them in Rakoup's flagship. Rakoup's fleet followed close behind as they headed for the last known position of the double corsair. They believed the corsair and the pirates would be found in the same place. The escapees in the corsair needed allies and the pirates were the only allies they had left.

The Argans needed someplace to begin to look. With an entire galaxy to consider, they weren't too sure where that was. Plask and Rakoup joined Jeonk and Shok in Shok's cruiser to give as much help as they could. They were the ones who had done the research on planets the old Veolsh Council had shown an interest in. Their experienced research made them the galactic experts on hiding places for pirates and fleeing tyrants.

The command pedestal global display was programmed to show as much of the galaxy as they knew about. When Plask and Rakoup came on board, the first thing Plask said was, "I had Alice promoted to Fleet Commander before we arrived on Iklug. When she's finished with Iklug, I'm having her promoted to Vice Admiral. She'll deserve it if she keeps the Iklug situation stabilized."

"Congratulations Shok," Jeonk offered. "If we go to war one more time, you'll be sleeping with a Fleet Admiral. Even her promotion to Vice Admiral will make the two of you a first for Arga, you'll be the first Admiral in Arga to go to bed with another Admiral."

Shok thought he could do without the usual round of jokes. He wanted to finish this job and get back to sleeping with his beautiful Admiral. Shok introduced a serious note into their levity, "This job is like looking for a needle in every haystack in the galaxy. We'd better begin updating this display with every new planet we can find in the Veolsh records. They did more traveling than we do, and it may take a while to put their information into some form we can use."

They spent hours updating the galactic display. Fortunately, Plask and Rakoup were old experienced space travelers themselves. They had researched the Galactic coordinates of every piece of floating real estate the Veolsh council had recorded visiting. When the display included all of the information Plask and Rakoup found, it contained nearly one hundred new locations. A few of the locations were referenced as inhabited planets, but most of them were raw coordinates with no information on the conditions of the planets in question. All of them were a long way from the present position of the Argan searchers.

The four of them stared at the completed display for several minutes trying to find a key that might lead them to a quick discovery of the pirates. They reprogrammed the display to show the new locations in red. The little red orbs blinking at them from the display looked like a shotgun blast toward the center of the Galaxy. It wasn't a very even shot pattern and there was no key to a quick success.

"Are there any suggestions?" Jeonk asked.

Rakoup answered as he pointed to a location on the display, "I think we should have a fleet supply ship meet us right here. This search will take a long time to finish."

Plask suggested, "We can send each of the cruiser to different targets. That will give us a broader search area and shorten the time for the entire search."

Jeonk didn't like that idea and he objected, "The cruiser that succeeds in finding them will be faced with seven hundred standard corsairs plus the big one that got away. We don't know what else they have in their hideout. Some of the pirates' cargo ships are big and they are fitted with cruiser armament like the cargo ships we destroyed on Prssk. We need to keep the fleet together. We have no idea how much power we may have against us when we find them."

Shok's suggestion would take more time initially but it would be shorter in the long run, "They are in hiding. We could look for them forever and not find them. We need Doskel in this search. We can place his cruisers in a pattern to cover the entire area. Each of his cruisers can remain in deep space and monitor the communications traffic in each cruiser's selected target area. When something breaks for one of them, our fleet will be in a central location to respond as quickly as possible."

Jeonk thought there was a problem with Shok's suggestion, "Doskel's fleet is covering Egrin and Egrin could get hot any time. It will take too much time to replace him and get him here."

Rakoup liked Shok's plan. He offered, "We have one fleet over Iklug and one fleet between Veolsh and Iklug. The Iklugs have become friendly, so far. We can shift Brak's fleet to Egrin and put the other one on Iklug. If the Iklugs decide they want to become unfriendly, one of the fleets hanging over the Veolsh planet can back them up. Brak is the best gunner in the fleet. He should be taking care of the Egrin situation anyway."

Plask added, "It will take less time to get Doskel's fleet here and follow Shok's plan than it will for us to hunt these rascals down one planet at a time. We don't know if the pirates are actually on one of our target planets. Doskel and his fleet have more expertise in high tech hunting than any fleet in the galaxy. We need that expertise.

"You and Shok head for Egrin and get Doskel ready to join us. Rakoup and I will take care of transferring Brak's fleet from Iklug to Egrin. When we get back here, Rakoup and I will spread this fleet to cover what we can until you return."

Jeonk gave the problem more thought but finally gave his OK. Plask and Rakoup returned to their fleet. Jeonk and Shok set their cruiser on a course for Egrin and Doskel's fleet. Jeonk still had some misgivings about using Doskel's fleet, "Most of Doskel's fleet was damaged in the battle with the Egrins. I know they are still space worthy but I don't know how many more times they can be hit without losing some of his cruisers. If he still has Marines on board, I'll transfer them to Brak's fleet. We wont get Doskel's Marines killed if anything goes wrong."

Shok knew Jeonk was right about Doskel's cruisers. He had seen the damage from the same command deck Jeonk had. Shok didn't expect Doskel's fleet to go into battle. He only wanted their communications expertise. Shok tried to put Jeonk's mind at ease, "Doskel's fleet won't be put in a position to go into battle. That's our job. Our fleet is fresh and we'll have to handle the pirates no matter how many of them there are or what they have with them. Doskel will put his probes near every planet we have targeted and everywhere else that squeaks in this part of the galaxy. He's our best, maybe our only hope of finding the hideout."

Jeonk and Shok arrived over Egrin before Brak's fleet could relieve Doskel. Coming in over Doskel's fleet was an experience. Most of his cruisers clearly showed the damages they received from the Egrin laser and pulse cannon fire. If Jeonk wasn't so familiar with the capabilities of the cruisers, he would have sent them immediately back to Arga for repairs.

Jeonk and Shok, once again, flew to Doskel's flagship in one of their fighters. As they stepped onto his command deck, Jeonk asked, "Is your fleet capable of doing a mission in deep space or will your external damages be too much of a problem?"

SPACE LINE BY MARIVIN E. FOX

"We have some skin abrasions and a few dents but we can go anywhere and fight anyone," Doskel replied.

"That's good," Jeonk, remarked, "Shok thinks you are the only one in the fleet who can do what we need. My father and Rakoup agree with him, and so do I. You'll be relieved by Brak as soon as he can get his fleet here from Iklug and he is on the way.

"Our communications man is transferring the data for your mission to your computers now. We'll talk about the problem after that's done. Meanwhile, how are things going on Egrin, any problems?"

Doskel was optimistic about the Egrin situation; "We haven't had to fire a shot since you left. The Argan ground troops have had frequent firefights with the Egrin military but they haven't asked for any coordinating fire. I keep a few fighters in their area in case they need support but they don't ask.

"General Sokeasel is in charge of the ground troops. He apparently knows where the opposition is going to be before the opposition knows where it is. He doesn't seem to require any assistance. He has everything screwed down tight. Sokeasel believes the situation is firmly under his troops control. He has had no problem from guerrilla activity. I don't know if that's because no one wants to help the military or because they don't have any guns. One way or another, things are getting pretty calm.

"Sokeasel has secured the capital and most of the larger cities. The merchants are doing a good business, the transportation system is functioning, and the planets communications system is working very well. I think it's about time we sent in some kind of diplomats to start leveling things out politically."

Jeonk said, "There's a team of people on Iklug now. Maybe we can get them here when they're finished with the work on Iklug."

Shok took the bait, "Why not get a new group from the Galactic Forum? The Argans who are still there can put a group together and be here much quicker. The team on Iklug will probably be busy for months."

Doskel, as one would expect, kept himself informed about conditions on Iklug. He rubbed his chin and said, "I don't know, there's some woman in charge on Iklug and I hear she's an amazing diplomat for a fleet officer. I heard she was going to be promoted to Fleet Vice Admiral if everything went well on Iklug. It would be a shame not to give her a chance at making Fleet Admiral for the work she could do here."

"She can probably handle two planets at one time," Jeonk kidded. "After all, she's another Shok."

Plask and Rakoup had apparently told every admiral in the Argan Space Command about the planed promotions for Alice. Brak's arrival saved Shok from further embarrassment. Brak put his cruisers in orbit to replace Doskel's. Doskel's fleet, with Jeonk and Shok's cruiser, headed for deep space where things were serious enough to cancel the jokes about Alice and Shok.

Doskel made his plans as he was briefed on the way to the galactic search area. His fleet was spread to monitor communications in the largest area he had ever monitored. His fleet, although burned and dented, was still capable of finding the hiding pirates. If the last member of the Veolsh Council knew it was Doskel hunting him and his pirates down, he would be sweating buckets of water and Veolsh don't sweat.

They hoped to find their den of thieves on the planet the Veolsh corsair technology came from. After months of searching, they found no evidence of a planet with that technology in the search area. They were able to eliminate many of the planets with the help of Doskel's technical experts. Those planets were uninhabited and uninhabitable. The thieves needed an inhabitable den to bury themselves in while they decided on a safe method to resume their pirate businesses.

They discovered sixteen planets among their blinking red lights to be inhabited. Doskel put probes around all of them and monitored their communications traffic. They thought the pirates would be on one of them but they didn't know which one. The searchers would have to wait until there was a recognizable transmission from the guilty party to know which.

The remainder of their blinking red lights fell into the uninhabited and uninhabitable class. They decided to wait for a more convenient time to find out why the Veolsh had bothered to list so many dead planets in their galactic digest of places to visit. Plask speculated that the Veolsh were cataloging locations of natural resources they might need in the future or places to hide some of their ill-gotten treasures. In either case, later was a better time to explore the possibilities than now.

Time was dragging for the searchers. They had discovered nothing about the pirates. The fleet supply ship was the busiest ship in the fleet. Doskel's fleet was constantly on the go but Rakoup's cruisers sat in deep space like greyhounds waiting to see the rabbit.

The inhabited planets in the search area had some communications traffic but it was always the wrong kind of traffic for the search. The didn't seem any closer to success than they were on the first day, but no one wanted to give up. All of them believed they were searching in the right area and would eventually find the pirates' den.

The big break came right after their boredom changed to frustration. One of Doskel's cruisers intercepted a message intended for someone on the planet Prssk. The message didn't come from one of the blinking red light planets, as they expected, but it did come from a location on the outskirts of the immediate search area. The closest inhabited planet to the source of the message was Prssk. The message requested clearance information for a spaceship bound for Prssk.

The return message from Prssk convinced the search team that the message was from the pirates. The return message said, "Clearance denied. An Argan fleet is patrolling Prssk for pirate activity." No one needed a clearance to land on Prssk. It was open to anyone who was careless enough to go there. The only space travelers who would be asking about clearance were the pirates the Argans were searching for. The message from Prssk gave Rakoup's greyhound fleet its first scent of the rabbit.

As they set the headings for the source of the first message, Jeonk Said, "The pirates have a good hideout. We would never have found it without Doskel's expertise in tracking down anyone in the whole damn galaxy. I know of no inhabited planet in the area the message came from. It doesn't show on any charts we have and it isn't located in any of the Veolsh's documents. What do you think Shok?"

"I'll bet big money the Veolsh Council was using the planet for some reason," Shok replied. "I believe our last Veolsh Council member knew about the planet and he knew it was uncharted. He will be there and is using the planet to hide his most useful friends. I think we'll find the new Veolsh Maxim, the pirates and king Last Try are hiding there waiting until the heat is off.

"The message to Prssk may have been from one of the pirate chiefs who is ready to jump the Veolsh ship and get back to work. Pirates are hard working crooks and they don't like being idle for long periods of time. The pirates in this part of the galaxy have been out of work, on the run, or hiding for a very long time. We may have quit a battle when we find them."

Plask and Rakoup flew a fighter over to discuss the battle plan with Jeonk and Shok. Neither Jeonk nor shock knew what the battle plan would look like. They didn't know what the battle area looked like. Doskel's cruiser, the one receiving the messages, and the nearest to its source, was still making some discreet scans of the area. The plan would be formed from the scan data.

Plask and Rakoup ordinarily wanted to go in with their guns blazing but in this case they had some misgivings. Plask raised their concern, "We don't know anything about the people on this planet. We aren't sure there are people other than the pirates on the planet. Rakoup and I think we should take a cautious approach to avoid any collateral casualties in case there is a population of innocent people on the planet."

Jeonk allayed their concerns, "Father, when we receive the scan data from Doskel's cruiser, you, Rakoup, Shok, and I will make our battle plan together. We won't attack anything we don't need to attack. Any innocent people on the planet will be protected as well as we can protect them.

This planet is closer to Arga than Arga is to Mog. Its difficult to understand how it has remained unnoticed. I know the pirates haven't used it before or we would have tracked them to it. Shok thinks it's a special purpose planet the Veolsh Council was using. I think the Veolsh kept it uncharted so they would have a hideout if thing got tough for them. If either of us is right, we'll know the purpose after we land on the planet.

"I hope you and Rakoup will stay on this cruiser with us until the scan data arrives. All we're doing now is eating up space and time until we can make a plan to get rid of the pirates. You can fly back to Rakoup's flagship after that."

Doskel transmitted the scan data for the planet while they were one day away from visual contact. The scans showed the planet to be very thinly populated and the populated areas were close together in the center of one continent. The population appeared to be farmers. There was one small area that looked something like a village. It had some small buildings in it, and it was a few miles from the farmland.

The scans showed the pirates to be bunched up in a small space on a large island about seven hundred miles long and nearly three hundred miles wide. The island was almost a thousand miles offshore from the farmers' continent. The only sophisticated technology on the planet was in the pirates' lair.

Plask and Rakoup were happy. They had a small area to attack and no possibility of any collateral casualties. Rakoup presented his plan of attack, "We should put one cruiser over the buildings trying to pass as a city and make sure nothing can escape from them. The fleet should come out of space on the dark side of the planet away from the pirates. We'll spread the fleet around the planet and come at them low and fast from all directions. We'll have them surrounded.

"If the pirates want to surrender, we'll give them a quick chance. They have no place to go if they escape. Most them are wanted on every planet in our part of galaxy except Prssk and Gamac. I don't think they will surrender. Spacecraft that well armed and manned by pirate crews should provide us with a serious battle."

Plask added, "The scans show over seven hundred spacecraft bunched on the Island and most of them are close together. There are five cargo ships. You can bet they're fitted with cruiser armament. The cargo ships will try to blast a hole in the fleet for the others to escape through. Rakoup's gunners will get them first. The others will know they have nowhere to go if they escape. We found them here and we'll find them everywhere else. The pirates will fight to their last corsair. What do you think Shok?"

"That sounds like the best plan for a worst case situation and it could be the way the battle goes," Shok responded. "I think I would launch all fighters in that fast approach just in case the pirates try an every man for himself battle and try to make their escapes in all directions."

"Good plan," Rakoup answered, "we intended to do that. Where will you and Jeonk be in the battle?"

"We'll be over that small city," Jeonk replied. "This is a Veolsh planet and the Veolsh we're searching for love their comfort. The little city looks like the only comfortable place on the planet."

Shok added, "Our gunners have already been briefed to instantly target and kill anything coming off the planet. We hope to find and capture that little fireball we lost when it made its quick exit from Iklug. You should brief your gunners to be watching for it just in case we're wrong about where it's hiding. I don't think we will be able to capture the fireball."

After Plask and Rakoup went back to the fleet, Jeonk asked, "Why do you think they believe the pirates will fight to the last corsair?"

"I don't know but this is my best guess." Shok responded. "Your father and Rakoup are both brave, honorable men. If their fleet were trapped, they would fly their cruisers into a head on fight and pull every trick they knew to save their fleet from destruction. Plask and Rakoup give the pirates more credit than the pirates deserve. I think half the pirates will fight and the other half will surrender. About half of them would rather go on trail than to their graves."

Jeonk didn't care for Shok's surrender prediction. He favored Rakoup's fight to the last pirate's death. Jeonk's hope for the battle was simpler, "I don't care if they fall down and break their damn necks, as long as we are finished with them."

The fleet approached the planet on its quiet side to avoid alerting the pirates in their island lair. The fleet dived low and split, half spreading its charge across one side of the planet and half making their run from the other direction. The pirates would know they were targets only seconds before Rakoup's cruisers converged and surrounded them.

Shok brought his cruiser in hot and fast, slamming it to a halt over the small city. If a cruiser could skid to halt, his would have skidded to a halt at two thousand feet above the city. The buildings trying to become a city weren't much, a few buildings and almost nothing else. Shok set his scanners for deep scans, attempting to locate the Veolsh corsair.

Everyone on Shok's command deck could hear Plask and Rakoup directing their fleet but they were too low for a visual sighting of the battle. It sounded like all hell had broken loose with pirate corsairs going in every direction. They heard Plask direct one of the cruisers to get after a pirate cargo ship that made it off the ground. Plask and Rakoup had flown into their best possible battle situation, a target rich environment with a vicious enemy who needed to be gotten rid of.

Shok's deep scans began showing signs of life in the slow lane. The Veolsh corsair was detected in a tunnel system below ground and it began its move. Shok kept his cruiser above the corsair, creeping along in pursuit of the slow moving spacecraft. He and the crew would have to be content with Plask and Rakoup's later description of the pirate battle.

Jeonk snapped his fingers and said, "We've got him. Where's he going to surface?"

Shok could give him no answer. The fireball ship was on the move down a long tunnel, a favorite Veolsh hiding place, and it had to move slowly until it cleared the exit. Shok kept the cruiser following above the fireball as it moved toward its exit. The gunners were waiting to blast the ship as soon as it was out of the tunnel and punched its thrusters. Shok thought he had the exit targeted but at the last moment the fireball changed directions and made its escape try from an alternate exit. Shok's port gunners opened up on it. It was difficult to tell if the little ship gained enough speed to make the gunners miss or if the fireball corsair was tough enough to take the hits. One way or the other, it was still going.

It was certain, if they didn't destroy the escaping ship within the next three second, they would lose it again. Shok quickly set the forward pulse cannons to continuous fire, set target acquisition to fire ahead of the Veolsh corsair with a spread pattern firing sequence, then hit the fire switch. The Veolsh corsair tried weaving and darting from side to side to avoid the pulse cannons. It hadn't yet reached the speed necessary to outrun the incoming pulses of super heated destruction, but it was flying to fast to keep from flying into them.

After the first hit, it was all over for the Veolsh, and the corsair. Several of the forward pulse cannon bursts found their target as the corsair lost speed. The fireball corsair exploded and became a real fireball in midair. By the time its debris hit the ground, Shok knew they wouldn't be getting any help with new technology from the wreckage. The last Veolsh Council member was dead and King Lastri's last try was a failure.

Jeonk tapped Shok's shoulder and exclaimed, "Nice shooting Shok! For a minute I thought we were going to lose it again. I wish you could have saved some of the pieces; we might have gotten some information on its propulsion system."

The cruiser returned to the city and landed its Marines to secure whatever information the city records might contain. Shok ordered two fighters to cover the Marines in case they encountered resistance in taking the city, but he didn't think they would be needed. The original scans hadn't shown any resistance capability.

Shok wheeled the cruiser and headed for the island battle area.

Two escaping pirate corsairs popped up on a collision course with Shok's cruiser. The surprised pirates tried to swing out of range but it was a futile attempt. Gunners brought them down with well-aimed laser fire.

More pirate corsairs, with fleet fighters in pursuit, appeared on both the right and the left sides of Shok's cruiser. The pirate corsairs were trying to gain altitude in some vague hope of escaping the following space fighters. The pirates' hopes were too vague. The fleet fighters downed four of them before the others wheeled for their return to the insecurity of a lower level escape.

Shok's command deck officers could hear Plask and Rakoup giving orders in the calm measured voices of experienced battle commanders. Their lack of excitement reminded Shok of someone reading the orders of the day to a troop of bored soldiers.

The main battle was in space with the pirates who hoped to escape with a quick climb into the vast no-man's-land of deep space. Half of Rakoup's fleet cruisers were in stationary positions over the battle zone. The other half was with their fighters in the pursuit of escaping pirates.

The pirates were fighting an every man for-himself battle, trying to stay as far from the cruisers as their speed and maneuverability allowed. The pirates who made it off planet, desperately searched for any kind of empty space to put between them and Rakoup's fleet of expert pirate terminators. The pirates near the ground hoped Rakoup's fleet's intense effort to control the planet's space would deflect its attention form themselves and allow them to escape using low altitude routes.

Shok's cruiser was too low to see the entire island on its command pedestal holoscan, but he noticed a small fleet of corsairs scooting away from the battle at less than fifty feet altitude. He thought the corsairs were probably on the outside edge of the main battle area before the first attack. The pirate fleet waited for the battle to get into full swing before making its move, hoping to go undiscovered in the battle confusion.

The eleven corsairs was probably the entire fleet of one of the more prosperous pirates. Shok guessed one man commanded them because they were flying in close formation instead of breaking and running individually.

Jeonk pointed to them on the holoscan as they disappeared behind some hills. Shok gained altitude to put them back on the display and his scanners painted a new picture as the cruiser flew above the corsairs. The pirate fleet found a deep canyon to follow and probably thought they were about to make their escape. Shok pulled the cruiser directly above them and rolled right a few degrees to give his starboard gunners a field of fire, while still allowing the belly gunners to target the pirates.

Shok gave the order to fire while the pirates were still in the canyon. They couldn't go left or right without hitting the canyon walls. They couldn't go up because the cruiser was flying above them. The cruiser's pulse cannons and lasers hit the pirates with devastating results. Three of the corsairs in the rear of the formation stopped their forward flight, pitched up and returned fire. Their pulse cannons heated the cruisers aft section when it was hit but the cruiser's gunners hit them quickly, crashing the corsairs to the floor of the canyon. The six in the middle were hit by pulse cannon and laser fire, bouncing them into the canyon walls before they joined the first three pirate corsairs at the bottom of the canyon.

The two corsairs at the front of the formation put their thrusters to max', trying to distance themselves from certain destruction. Shok's cruiser wasn't the only one who noticed the clever escape attempt. His cruiser's gunners had to hold their fire to keep from hitting Rakoup's fighters coming down the canyon toward the pirate corsairs. The two corsairs made a quick attempt to jump out of the canyon and find safety by putting some hills between them and the fighters. It wasn't a good day for pirates. The fighters sent them bouncing along the valley like losers in a demolition derby.

"This is the last stand for the pirates," Jeonk stated. "Most of them are wanted on so many charges on so many different planets that surrender is out of the question for them. If they fight they die. If they're captured they die. Most of them would rather die as they lived, low down and dirty."

Shok couldn't argue with him about it but he still thought enough of them would surrender to make processing them to the various planets waiting to hang them a real mess. He said, "Let's put this cruiser up a hundred miles and make some wider scans, maybe we can stop any more of them from trying to sneak away from Plask and Rakoup."

Jeonk wasn't very hopeful. He answered, "OK but those two don't miss very much. If any of the pirates escaped, they're already gone and you can bet there are fighters in hot pursuit."

SPACE LINE BY MARIVIN E. FOX

Jeonk was right; there were no unattended escapees in the sky. Plask and Rakoup's fleet fighters were scattered in nearby space, all of them busy in pursuit of pirates who weren't going to make it. Shok felt sure that some of the pirates had escaped in the first moments of battle, but not very many. His scanners showed downed pirate ships in every area of the large island and there were a few newly opened impact graves on the mainland. Plask and Rakoup had the pirates, who chose not to try an escape, surrounded with a tight network of cruisers and fighters overhead.

Eight of Rakoup's cruisers landed, and their Marines began surrounding the battle area on the ground. It was a very large battle area for the small number of Marines to surround but the pirates knew the battle was over. They were drifting toward the center of the area to keep from being shot for presumed belligerence. Shok had been right. It would be a mess to process that many pirates.

Jeonk didn't want to get involved in the cleanup. It was a complicated job and somebody had to do it. He decided Plask and Rakoup were the only one's available who could do it. Jeonk was curious about the same place Shok wanted to look into, the cheesy little Veolsh city on the mainland. Why it was so far from the main population was very curious. Why it was on this planet at all was even more intriguing.

Shok found an open cruiser parking space in the open country right near the down town area and dropped his cruiser into it. The nose of the cruiser extended well into the downtown district.

The Marines who had been left there earlier were sifting through paper work written in the Veolsh language. The paperwork wouldn't be difficult to translate but there was neither the time nor the equipment to do the translations here. Shok ordered the Marines to package every piece of paper with an appearance of information on it and store it on the cruiser.

Jeonk took a voice translator and headed for the three Veolsh guards who were being held prisoner in the main building. There were no other people in the city. Shok joined him to satisfy his curiosity about the strange place. The Veolsh guards knew very little. They had been stationed there to protect the place from the local population. They had a very easy job because the local population wouldn't have anything to do with the collection of small buildings. The guards said the place was used for scientific research of some kind but they didn't know what kind. There was no activity in the place when they arrived and none since they were stationed there.

The Guards began griping to Jeonk and Shok because they had been there so long without being relieved to go home. Evidently, GIs are the same on every planet. Jeonk asked them about the spaceship Shok shot down. The leader said he knew about it but it didn't need anything from the guards and the guards couldn't get anything from it. It had arrived, flew somewhere from time to time, and returned to its tunnel. The guards didn't know where it went. They didn't care if it came back.

The guards appeared to have been on the planet for a long time. Their uniforms were old and none of the three looked well fed. Shok asked the guards how they found food. The senior of the three guards told him one of them would go to the farmers and get food from them. Shok asked, "Who are the farmers? Are they Veolsh or some other race, and if they are another race, what other race?"

The Veolsh guard answered, "They are like you, men and women like you."

It took a while for his answer to sink in. Finally, Jeonk broke the silence, "Shok, we had better take a look at some of the farmers. It sounds to me like he's saying this planet is populated by Earth people."

Before they left the Veolsh guards in the custody of the Marines, they assured the guards they would be returned to their home planet. Jeonk and Shok entered the cruiser for the short hop to the farmlands and put the cruiser up high enough to get a good look at the farms beneath them.

There wasn't a large amount of land under cultivation and the farms were scattered. The farmers had built their houses in central locations where the most cultivated areas joined. There were many collections of houses in similar areas, like villages. They didn't make scans of the nearby mountains for inhabitants, but they could do that later if it became necessary.

Shok lowered the cruiser to a clear area near one of the collections of houses. He didn't want to frighten the inhabitants so he asked Jeonk, "Do you mind waiting in the cruiser until I make contact with them and assure them we are friendly. If they see you they might panic."

"I don't look any worse than the Veolsh," Jeonk answered, "but I'll wait for your signal."

No one was in sight as Shok exited the cruiser. The houses appeared deserted, and so did the fields, but the people had to be somewhere. He called out, "My name is Kevin Kelly and I'm from the planet Earth"

A head popped up above a windowsill in the nearest house. The head said, "Be you Devil or friend?"

Shok called back, "Friend, and I will speak with you if you are willing."

The head replied, "You've not the look of the Devils; speak as you will. I will answer. Are you of the flying ships darting here and yonder?"

Shok answered, "I'm one of those who made war on the flying ships that came here many months ago. We defeated them in battle. We will give you help if you need it. We are your friends, if you will allow us to be."

After a few seconds, a middle-aged man came out of the cottage. He extended his hand and said, "I'm called James Collier. My family lives here with other families near to us."

"How did you get here from Earth?" Shok asked, "and where did you live on Earth?"

He answered, "Many generations of us are here. The Devils brought our forefathers here. We don't know why. The Devils have done nothing for, or against us, for many years. Have you done battle with the Devils and won?"

Shok understood he was referring to the Veolsh as the Devils. Shok assured him, "We have beaten the Devils in battle in many places, in all of the places the Devils had power, and we have beaten the Devils in this place. You will be free of the Devils from this day forward. Where did your forefathers live on Earth?"

"Mine, England," he replied, "others, other places."

People from the other cottages became less afraid and were slowly coming toward Shok. He noticed there were only old people and guessed the young ones had been sent to the mountains sometime after the pirates arrived or at the first sign of the battle above their farms.

A few people had gathered and Shok thought it was a good time to introduce Jeonk to them. He said, "I have many friends with me. They will look very strange to you. My friends are very big and they are a blue color. They look fierce but they are friendly to all people of peace. I, and they, fought the devils. I will ask one of them to come from this flying ship and I will introduce him to you, if you will allow it."

James Collier consented, "I will shake the hand of any who fought the Devils. Only the fierce could have won."

Jeonk was waiting for Shok's invitation. He stepped from the cruiser and walked forward. There was a gasp from the small group as they sighted him but none of them ran away. Jeonk walked directly forward, stuck out his hand and said, "My name is Jeonk Shap, I'm glad to meet you Mr. Collier."

James Collier hesitated for only a couple of seconds before he reached out and grasped Jeonk's big hand, and said, "It's proud I am to shake the hand of a fierce man who fought and beat the Devils." Mr. Collier then turned to one of the nearby women, "Mrs. McGuire, sound the alarm for the young ones. They have friends to meet."

Mrs. McGuire's alarm, a large iron triangle struck by a short iron rod, started a flurry of alarms across the farmlands. Within a short time, the younger people in the community were coming toward them from the mountains, walking beside smaller children and some were carrying children in their arms.

It was nearing dusk and Shok didn't think anymore could be done with the farmers until the next day. He suggested to Mr. Collier, "After sunrise tomorrow we can meet with any of you who care to speak with us. It will be full dark before your young ones return home. Tomorrow, I would like very much to speak with those who will allow us to speak with them. Can you give them that message?"

Mr. Collier replied, "I can and you are welcome to sup with us. We have little but enough to share our table."

Shok accepted the invitation for Jeonk and himself. The supper was simple but delicious, baked meat, bread, a vegetable and a soup made of grain and broth. The farmers had adapted to the planet by using anything similar to what they had on Earth to sustain them. They spun their thread and weaved their own cloth for clothing, made their own simple farm implements, built their houses and lived close to the land they tilled. They seemed to be healthy and secure from everything but the Veolsh.

Jeonk and Shok returned to the cruiser after supper with the Colliers. Both were lounging around the command deck when Jeonk asked, "What do you intend to do with them Shok?"

Shok was surprised by his question and answered, "What do you mean, what am I going to do with them? I don't know what to do with them."

Jeonk wouldn't give it up, "They are your people and you always have a plan. What's your plan?"

"I don't know, "Shok replied. "They have been here for about two hundred years. If we take them back to Earth, even if they want to go, this population will be an oddity the Earth people will study, question, write reports about, control them in micro detail and make them feel like animals in a zoo.

"The present day Earth language is different, its customs are different, its technology is different; everything on Earth is different from what they knew on Earth and what they have here. I'm not sure it is possible to integrate them back into the societies that have grown on Earth since their forefathers were brought here.

"I think what we should do for them is set up a communications system between Arga and them, and between Earth and them. We can update their farm technology very easily. We can slowly introduce them to advances in Earth technology. We can put them in contact with people with the same names who live where they used to live. Other than that, I think we should ask them what they need or want. If we can provide it, we should. They seem to be very good people. Our help should be natural and friendly.

"We will need constant patrols over this planet to make sure they are kept safe. Prssk, Gamac and everyone else will know they are here after this battle. We found them and we do have some responsibility for them. We can't allow them to become a source for slavery."

"I knew you had a plan," Jeonk said. "It sounds pretty good. As soon as they find out there are people here, Aslain and Alice will be here with notebooks to document their lives."

Jeonk then changed the subject to something much more personal, "I'd like to have a vacation home in the mountains behind our cruiser. You want to go halves with me? The hunting and the fishing must be really great. We can get away from society and associate with real people. We can travel back and forth in one of the hot rod corsairs we hid out."

"Sure," Shok agreed, "I'll go halves--but let's use one of the corsairs Alice and Aslain already know about.

"I saw a nice place for a lodge on the scanner as we landed. It's on a river about halfway up the mountain. It has a waterfall nearby and good cover for hunting."

The next morning Shok felt good. Jeonk had jump-started his mind with questions and Shok knew what needed to be done for the people waiting for them. Some of the farmers were leaning on the landing pods while others intently inspected the exterior of the ship, pointing at everything that looked unusual to them on the outside skin of the spacecraft.

Jeonk and Shok talked to many of them. They discovered there were many different groups in the population of the planet. All of the groups were form northern Europe. There were one or more groups from England, Scotland, Ireland, Germany, Denmark, Norway and Sweden. The Veolsh had forced the groups to settle in different areas by nationality. The entire population of the planet was the offspring of people abducted from their homes on Earth and brought to the new planet nearly two hundred years ago.

The Veolsh kidnappers didn't pay much attention to them after putting them in separate areas. In the beginning, the only authority the Veolsh exercised was to force them to stay in their own national groups, and each group was frequently given medical examinations.

During the last fifty years, there had been no Veolsh presence on the planet except a slowly dwindling number of guards in the small Veolsh city the Argans had captured. The nationally different groups began drifting together as the Veolsh presence dwindled. The groups maintained their original settlements but their populations became mixed. None of the people knew what the Veolsh had in mind by kidnapping them and resettling them on this planet.

They had received no news about Earth in all of that time. They listened in amazement as Shok explained the changes the different nations on Earth went through while their families were on this planet. To help them get first hand knowledge of the present conditions on Earth, Shok taught some of the young men and women how to use the unfamiliar communications gear needed to talk to Earth. He promised to put them in contact with people on Earth as soon as he could arrange a point of contact on Earth for them.

The cruiser's scanners gave a population count of about eighty thousand. Two hundred years of having babies had increased their numbers but none of them knew how many were originally brought to the planet from Earth.

Shok thought some of them would want to return to Earth. He explained that they could return, but it would have to be at a later date when the arrangements could be made. He explained it would be better for them to make contact with people on Earth and become more informed about what a return would mean in their lives. He thought most of them would want to stay where they were, especially after their living conditions were improved. He explained to them that the Argans would bring in modern farm implements. The equipment would be supplied that was needed to improve their transportation and communications system.

The Argans stayed with the farmers for several days and familiarized them with the crew of the cruiser so they wouldn't be alarmed when other Argans arrived to help them. They took many of them on tours of the cruiser to let them get a feel for a new technology.

In those few days, the sons and daughters of planet Earth became more familiar with Shok and the Argans. They came from miles around to see and offer their greetings to the friendly strangers.

The people living in the farm area didn't have a name for their planet and Shok wanted a name he could use as a reference for it. He called the planet, Nordic, after the area on Earth the new owners of the planet had originally lived. By the time they said their good-byes, Plask and Rakoup had finished their pirate clean up duties and were gone. Shok lifted the cruiser off the surface and put it on a heading for Arga. He and Jeonk still had the matter of putting their cargo line into operation.

4

TRIUMPHANT RETURN TO ARGA

Shok informed the Argan Admiralty of the time his cruiser would land at his Perlta base and asked them to inform the families of the crew. The cruiser crew had been separated from their families for many months and deserved the landing reunion. Jeonk and Shok hoped to have a reunion with their own wives when the other crewmembers had their reunions. The Admiralty gave them good news. Their wives had returned from Iklug and Egrin.

Waiting for them as they disembarked from the cruiser was Plask, Aslain, and last but not least, Alice in her brand new Vice Admiral uniform. She had obviously done well on Iklug and just as obviously, had done well on the planet Egrin. Jeonk took his family to a waiting command plak, leaving Alice and Shok alone.

Shok was proud of Alice even though she had told him she would take off the uniform and never put it on again after they were married. Shok grabbed her by her shoulders and gave her a long kiss. As she hugged him, he said, "This is going to be the first time an Argan Admiral has ever slept with another Argan Admiral. Jeonk was right, Vice Admiral Kelly, they'll be calling us the Shok's of Arga."

Alice laughed and retorted, "Your still the only one who gets to fight the bad guys. All I heard on Iklug was what great warriors you and Jeonk are. On Egrin, they wouldn't make a move until I convinced them the Galactic Forum plan I used was the same plan you introduced on the Veolsh planet. I was so proud of you! It made me lonesome for you.

My new rank allows me to have one of those flying communications arsenals like yours. Let's take 'my' command plak home, I'll pilot."

"Did you get any Veolsh sand in your brassiere on your way home?" Shok asked.

Alice added a little sand of her own, "No but you didn't get it all out the last time. We wont have time to bother with it when I get you home. You'll just have to settle for sand scratches on your chest."

The pressure of war was off and the pressures of business could wait. Alice and Shok spent the evening alone at home. Shok put the, don't bother us, or else, sign up for incoming communications until further notice. He intended to take a long vacation with Alice.

He planned the vacation to last at least a month, and for as much of the month as he got, the vacation was wonderful. Alice was his warm, tender, loving woman. She made him glad for every moment they were together. They shared their lives and vacation with Jeonk, Aslain, the family, and many of their friends on Arga.

The guest rooms in Shock's Lersta Mountain cottage were kept busy with fun loving guests. Even Rakoup and his wife Iliaska stayed for a couple of weekends. Shok didn't see a uniform the entire time. He began to feel like a man with his feet planted on solid ground until some really bad news flew high enough to get over his, don't bother us, or else, sign.

The mile long cargo ship built to haul merchandise between Arga and Earth was being tested in space. The ship was built in ten sections that could be connected or disconnected in space. The large spacecraft could be used as one ship or ten ships according to cargo demands. The ship was on its first test flight in deep space. The long ship had been loaded with dummy weights to simulate cargo.

The individual cargo sections were not maneuverable after they were connected with the mother craft. The connected cargo spacecraft was less maneuverable than a smaller spacecraft would be. A space rock had hit the sixth section from the front of Shok and Jeonk's brand new cargo spaceship. The fear was that the asteroid hit had wrenched the ships interlocking frame, making the separate cargo sections unable to disconnect. The hit had caused a severe bend in the structure of the sixth section section where it hit.

The mile long cargo carrier was drifting in space, unable to power up because the leading edge was no longer pointing in the same direction as the lagging edge. It was drifting out of control and it was drifting at one hell of a speed. The ship's braking thrusters couldn't be used to slow it down and it couldn't change course. It would soon crash into the planet Gamac.

5

CARGO SHIP OR HOLE IN THE GROUND

Jeonk and Shok had six days, twenty-three hours and seven minutes before the unbelievably expensive flagship of the new cargo line crashed into the rocky surface of the planet Gamac. It would take two days to put a crew of space repair specialists together. Another four days were needed to get to the damaged cargo ship at a docking point near Gamac.

Jeonk and Shok had twenty three hours and seven minutes after they reached the damaged ship to either separate the ten sections or cut the meteor damaged cargo ship into two pieces so it could power up and maneuver. If both of those plans failed, all they could do was evacuate the crew and measure the depth of the hole the ship made when it slammed into Gamac. The Earth to Arga cargo line would be finished.

There were plenty of specialists among the civilian population who were familiar with spacecraft repair and recovery. The recent wars employed several who would be willing to take on the job. The equipment was available to do what needed to be done. Everything from one man space platforms using laser cutting equipment to large clamping ships capable of clamping and holding a space cruiser in its jaws was available.

Shok contacted an Argan man named Jarl Gast who had been in charge of cleaning up the hundreds of spacecraft destroyed in the Veolsh war. He was the best of those who would have the expertise to get the cargo ship moving under its own power. Shok gave him the blue prints for the ship and the information he had about the problem. He instructed him to leave sooner than possible with the crew to do the job.

Jarl looked at the blue prints and said, "I can't believe you actually built that thing and got it to fly. One section of it could hold several cruisers. If I had just one of those sections, I could salvage anything in space, make a fortune. How much do you want for one of them?"

"They aren't for sale," Shok replied, "but if you save the nine sections we can still use, I'll give you my okay to build one of your own. You can't save the ship by sitting here wondering about it. How about getting on the move?"

Jarl was unimpressed by Shok's urgency, "I'll take the job and I and my crew will be there before you will. I'll give you the bill after we're finished and know how much you have to pay. I can't give an estimate on a job like this."

Shok removed one of his standard cargo ships from service to rendezvous with the drifting cargo ship. In the hold was five of Jarl Gast's two man space repair modules fitted with laser cutters, magnetic clamps, powerful mechanical grapples and the smaller power equipment used in space recovery. The space repair modules would allow Shok and Jeonk to move around the damaged ship, evaluate the damage and help in the recovery.

Alice and Aslain insisted on coming along. Jeonk and Shok didn't have time for the protracted discussions needed to keep them home, even if their reasons for leaving them home worked. Alice could still fly a fighter. Plask and Rakoup were teaching Aslain to fly everything Alice could fly. The two women were, grudgingly, allowed to come along. Plask and Rakoup insisted on coming along to protect their financial interest in the cargo line. Since two of the wives were coming along, Rakoup couldn't refuse to leave his wife, Iliaska, at home alone; she signed on as a crewmember. Shok wondered if they were headed for a disaster area or a family reunion; maybe, they're the same thing sometimes.

The family reunion/disaster crew lifted off of Arga's surface one day after news of the asteroid hit was delivered. They were one day ahead of Jarl Gast and his crew but Jarl had more preparations to make than the disaster crew did. Jeonk and Shok would have an unexpected, additional twenty-four hours to sort things out for the impacted cargo ship. If things looked too bad, they could use the space repair modules to evacuate the crew of the damaged cargo ship to the cargo ship they were bringing alongside.

The cargo liner was a mile long, one thousand feet thick and one thousand feet wide. It was the first ship of its size ever built. Their first look at its damage was a shock. It looked like it had been t-boned from the top. The ship had a fifteen-degree bend in the sixth section that put the nose and tail sections at the top of the V formation. The other sections had no visual damage. Wrenching and twisting of metal throughout the structure wasn't apparent by looking at it.

The wreck looked like a simple problem in space mechanics. They would cut through the sixth section. That would divide the sixth section in half. Releasing the other nine sections from the damaged sixth section would allow the other sections to power up. The whole mess could then be flown back to Arga for whatever repairs were needed while the big ship was in a fixed orbit over Arga.

An Argan cruiser on patrol between the planets Prssk and Gamac had gotten to the stranded ship first. A few Gamac corsairs and some passing thieves from the planet Prssk were on hand to add anything they could to the problem.

The cruiser Commander had launched his fighters to guard against the unemployed pirates from Gamac, and the uninvited thieves from Prssk. The light-fingered tourist would be no problems as long as the cruiser was around.

Jeonk and Shok flew one of the space repair modules along the outside of the damaged ship to see if a closer inspection would highlight any unseen catastrophic damage.

They were especially concerned about the alignment of the ship's thrusters. Each section had separate thrusters and each thruster had to be properly aligned with the all of the others to keep the ship safe and on course. If the thrusters were out of alignment when they were fired, the ship could be torn apart by the force of the poorly aligned thrusters. The thruster alignment could be varied using the command deck controls but it was absolutely necessary to know that the alignment was correct. The thruster alignment was calibrated on the internal structure of the ship and the internal structure of the ship had been damaged enough to prevent separation of the different sections. The exterior inspection didn't tell them if the ship was damaged badly enough to cause a thruster alignment problem.

None of the crew had been hurt in the asteroid collision. In flight, all sections could be operated from all of the other sections. Only the first section and the last section had crews in them for the test flight, and the crews were still in their sections. Jeonk spoke to the two crews on the damaged ship and found they weren't unduly concerned for their safety.

The cargo crew had confidence in the disaster crew's ability to get them out. They had refused to allow the protecting cruiser to remove them until Jeonk and Shok arrived and determined that their removal was necessary. So far, their removal hadn't been determined as necessary.

While Jeonk and Shok slowly made their inspection, two more space repair modules left the family reunion cargo ship. The two repair modules were close together checking the bent sixth section to find a way inside to inspect its internal damage. Aslain and Alice were in one module; Rakoup and Iliaska were in the other. Plask was probably playing cards with the family cargo ship's crew.

Jeonk and Shok's inspection showed many small holes in the exterior skin of the sixth section but none of them was large enough for entry. They found a similar pattern of holes when they moved to the other side of the ship. Jeonk said, "We need to go inside and check the interior structure of the ship." They cut a large entry hole with the repair modules laser. When they removed the cut section with the mechanical grapples, they could look right through the ship. Rakoup had cut a similar hole in the opposite side and was about to lead the family in.

The inside of the section was big enough for Jeonk and Shok to maneuver around the family inspectors while making their assessment of the damage. The wandering space rock went through the top rear of the section and struck the metal of the dummy cargo just forward of center in the section. The speed of the spaceship and the speed of the rock, both traveling in the same direction, were close enough to prevent the full-scale explosion that would have destroyed the entire ship. The two speeds were different enough to throw exploded metal and rock throughout the section.

The exploding spray hadn't penetrated the rear bulkhead of the section it hit but it had penetrated the rear bulkhead and the forward bulkhead of the next section forward. The cargo hold of the forward section could be repaired with ease if the exploding metal shards hadn't penetrated its thruster pods. All things considered, the damage could have been worse. They knew they would lose one section, maybe two.

Jeonk and Shok received a call from Plask at the end of the damage inspection. Plask informed them, "Jarl Gast and his crew have arrived. He 'ordered' me to tell you to get the hell out of the way so he can go to work."

Jarl had brought a large array of equipment. An impressive sight for mortal eyes awaited them as they exited the damaged cargo section. First in view were two massive space tugs with heavily reinforced noses. Grappling clamps extended above and below the thick metal noses used to push or maneuver large objects in space. The tugs thrusters were arranged on massave pivots to give them control in any direction. Thick metal catwalks on the forward sections allowed the space suited work crew access to whatever the tug was pushing, pulling or destroying.

Jarl brought a recovery ship large enough to grab and move a space cruiser in the giant tongs extending from its belly. It wasn't big enough to grab one of the cargo sections but it was big enough to handle the wreckage they would cut away from it.

None of Argans liked the Gamacs, but they didn't want the wreckage to destroy anything not specifically targeted on the planet. Jarl had to clean up the wreckage. Some of it might miss a pirate target of opportunity on Gamac and hit something important, like an ordinary citizen.

Several smaller spacecraft used for a variety of jobs were in Jarl's fleet. That included space modules capable of cutting, burning, bending, exploding or otherwise demolishing some very expensive space hardware. It was the hope of all of family, with more than just a financial interest in the cargo shipping business, that the demolishing part of this operation would be held to a minimum.

Jarl's plan, with a little urging from Jeonk and Shok, was simple. He would remove part of the outer skin around the damaged section, expose its metal structure, set shaped charges to cut through the structure and free the two parts of the ship on each end.

While the clearing work was being done, he would make laser measurements of the thrusters on the other sections, and make sure they were still properly aligned. If the thrusters were properly aligned, they were in business. Each of the cargo sections had sixteen thrusters. The divided ship could still make it home if a few of its thrusters had to remain powered down during the voyage.

SPACE LINE BY MARIVIN E. FOX

There was nothing any of the early arrivals could do but wait out the hours while the planet Gamac came closer with each tick of the clock. Something very heavy and a mile long hitting a planet going in the opposite direction could do some serious damage.

The space, sidewalk, supervisors made some calculations during the waiting period. They calculated the possible impact to be very close to the city usually considered to be the capital of the Gamacs ruthless kingdom of unemployed pirates.

The possible impact on his palace might be the reason the CPIC (Chief Pirate In Charge) called to protest. Plask and Shok were both eager to answer the CPIC's call but Jeonk was in a foul mood and needed a particularly useless piece of trash to work it off on.

The caller identified himself, "I am Chokng Fould, Emperor of the Gamac Kingdom, which underling am I addressing?"

Jeonk smiled and sat back like a man whose prayer had just been answered, then he replied, "I am Jeonk Shap, King of Arga, recent destroyer of Gamac pirate fleets, demolisher of Gamac smugglers, bringer of justice to Gamac thieves, and a frequent ass kicker of Gamac slavers. What is it you wish of me, Choking?"

His Majesty, or Emperor Chokng was undeterred by Jeonk's list of accomplishments. He made his demands, "I demand you destroy that space monstrosity you are, fruitlessly, trying to save to increase your ill gotten gains from other planets. In sixteen hours, your broken leviathan will crash into my capital city. Thousands, no, tens of thousands may die in the spread of its debris throughout my capital. That floundering wreck of your ridiculous ambition might destroy my very own new royal palace.

"You have the equipment in your fleet of planet destroyers to easily push it off of its present disastrous path. I order you to spare the peaceful Gamac people the tragedy of having their homes and their persons obliterated. I demand you move it and destroy it elsewhere--using the means you have at hand."

Jeonk's rejection of Chokng's demands was a lesson in straight talk. "We are not moving it. If worse comes to worst, and we can't save it, the most useful purpose it can serve is to get rid of you and your foul crew of criminals who are responsible for at least fifty percent of all crimes committed in this part of the galaxy. If I knew for certain my 'monstrosity' would hit your palace and its den of murderers, I would stop the effort to save it and consider the loss as money well spent. I have wanted for a long time to get rid of you and the gang of filth now lording it over the unfortunate people of the planet Gamac. If you make one more demand, I'll have a fleet of cruisers obliterate you and your rotten palace--if our cargo ship does not. Choking, I hope you have a nice day, end of message."

Aslain was familiar with hard talk among enemies but I think Jeonk raised her awareness by a quantum leap. She said, "No wonder the Gamacs are always shooting at you and Shok. You didn't say one nice word to their King, or Emperor, whatever he is."

Jeonk growled, "I did too; I told him to have a nice day."

Iliaska was about to put in her two cents worth but Rakoup tapped her on the shoulder and signaled her to keep quiet. Plask, who disliked the pirate king as much as Jeonk, began laughing and he started Alice laughing. They were all in a good mood after that, even Jeonk lightened up. Chokng Fould, Emperor of the Gamac kingdom, didn't make any more demands.

Jarl Gast and his crew finished the removal of the skin on the damaged section. Setting the shaped charges to cut the damaged section's superstructure into two pieces was completed. All of the space sidewalk supervisors got into their space repair modules and went outside to watch the fun.

Jeonk was in one module. Shok was in another. Alice and Iliaska were in another, Plask and Rakoup were in a fourth and Aslain volunteered to remain on board the cargo ship to mind the store. Alice and Iliaska seemed to have trouble positioning their module to see the display. They kept jockeying the module back and forth for a better view. At least, Shok thought that was what they were doing.

The gravity from the Gamac planet had begun to pull on the huge cargo ship. The damaged ship was beginning its quick trip toward the Gamac surface with only thirty-one minutes left before it would be destroyed in the Gamac atmosphere. There would be little margin for error after Jarl Gast put the finishing touches on his explosive charges.

All of the charges did their cutting work, except one. The two ship's sections shifted after the explosion of the shaped charges and hung like a wounded bird with a broken wing on the last uncut metal beam holding it together. Gast, quickly, swung one of his space tugs to the other side of the cargo craft and turned a laser on the unexploded charge. The last charge exploded, cutting the last beam holding the two sections together.

The Gamac planet was in broad view as Jeonk ordered the separated cargo ship's crew to start their thrusters and head the two parts of the separated ship back toward Arga to put the finishing touches on the repair. The forward and the rear sections' thrusters put them on their way, barely brushing the Gamac atmosphere as they lifted into deep space. Old Chokng Fould would be delighted with the safety of his palace.

After the cutting of the superstructure, everyone but Jeonk and Shok returned to the family reunion cargo ship. Jeonk and Shok stayed to watch the damaged ships thrusters come on line and get the two sections on their way. If they didn't start, they could wring their hands and curse their luck in private. The two men had billions tied up in that ship and they both wanted to be outside and up close to view its recovery or the calamity.

They both returned to the family cargo ship and walked across the cargo bay at the same time. Jeonk was in a good mood as they passed the other repair modules. Shok noticed the repair module Alice and Iliaska used had a missing claw. The repair module had two four hundred pound claws in its forward section and two in the rear. The claws could be jettisoned to free the module if one the claws got the repair module stuck in some kind of space debris. Shok remarked, "The girls lost one of the forward claws on their repair module while they were outside."

"Forget it, where could it go?" Jeonk asked.

They both continued on to the command deck of the cargo ship. Everyone was happy about the good luck of recovering the expensive hardware. Neither Alice nor Iliaska said a word about the missing claw. Shok decided to let the subject drop. After all, as Jeonk had said, "where could it go?"

Plask was giving the order to get underway when Chokng Fould made his final hysterical accusations. Anger and frustration were apparent in his voice coming in short gasps through the voice translator, "Do you think I don't know who the murderers are on the crew of that ship? Do you think I don't know a missile when one hits my palace? You have ruined my palace in your attempt to murder me. Your missile did not explode until it went completely through my palace and landed in the dungeon. You killed no one, even my dungeon was empty."

"Who are you?" Jeonk interrupted. "Unidentified raving maniacs should stay away from transmitters. Identify yourself."

"You know who I am." Chokng screamed. "I am Choking Fould, Emperor of the Gamac Kingdom, the one you just tried to kill with your missile."

"We don't carry missiles on cargo ships." Jeonk replied. "If we did, I would be glad to hit your rotten palace with it. Go back to bed and sleep it off, you'll feel better in the morning."

"My bed is in the dungeon with the rest of my bedroom," Chokng shot back. "If I had been sleeping in it, I would be there too--dead. A day of revenge is coming--you blue Argan monster. I know you and that miserable Earthman, Shok, did this to me. A day of revenge is coming."

"That's a really pissed off Gamac," Plask remarked. "What did you and Shok do to him?"

Shok thought he had it figured out but he didn't know for sure. He thought he had better give some kind of an answer for Jeonk and himself, "We didn't do anything to him. He may just be in a cranky mood because we recovered our cargo ship instead of dumping it on Gamac like he thought we would."

Jeonk added, "maybe a piece of equipment got lost and hit his palace. There was a lot of stuff floating around after the ship was separated. Something may have gotten loose and tumbled into his palace."

Iliaska added some additional information with a possible reason for Chokng Fould's foul mood, "Alice and I lost one of the claw things on our repair module. All you have to do is push one little button and the thing shoots right off the end of its arm. Maybe it accidentally hit his filthy palace. I don't feel bad if it did. Chokng Fould and his Gamac slavers are the one's who kidnapped Alice and nearly got her killed in that Mog mine."

Rakoup was supportive, "Too bad you missed. The next time you dump a claw on his 'filthy palace', call ahead and make sure he's home."

Jeonk promoted Iliaska to Commander for her well-manicured button pushing. One more claw dumping and she'll be a Vice Admiral. Skish, one of Shok's fleet's best navigators, had previously told Shok, 'Iliaska is an excellent navigator.' Shok thought, "I don't think so, no matter how good a navigator, and how much she dislikes Gamacs, a shot like that is impossible--on purpose."

Alice, who was sitting next to Iliaska in the repair module as the errant claw made its departure toward the hysterical arms of Choking Fould, didn't say one word about the wandering claw. Shok thought, "I'll ask her about it sometime when we're alone, especially about all the maneuvering they were doing while they were waiting for the shaped charges to be set off."

6

THREE CARGO SHIPS

When the test crew for the huge ship was debriefed, it was discovered the crew had seen the space rock coming on the ships scanning equipment. The large ship was so complicated to maneuver that the crew couldn't move it out of the flight path of the wandering rock fast enough to avoid the damaging impact.

Jeonk and Shok decided to break the large ship into three smaller ships instead of one ship a mile long. They thought it was safer to use three ships, each three-tenths of a mile long. They could still connect the three together if they found a special purpose for a larger ship. The shorter ships would give more maneuverability for space travel. If they needed more cargo space, they could build more sections later.

The cargo ship was repaired in orbit and loaded for market. Shok did a little research the last time they were on Earth. He discovered there was a market for vyto plaks. They loaded two of the shortened cargo ships with thousands of vyto plaks bound for Earth markets in various countries.

The return loads would be crude oil. Jeonk and Shok thought it was a good trade. They would make a bundle of money on the plaks and make money on the oil at home. Vyto plaks used no gas or oil. They could sell their vyto plaks for slightly more than the cost of an Earth luxury car.

The sale of plaks would reduce the need for crude oil on Earth; that would create an excess supply of the Earth's crude oil, which could be used for some of the chemical needs of Arga. Arga produced very little crude oil. It would be cheaper to buy and transport it than to find it, if there was any of it to find.

There was no cargo available for the third ship, but Jeonk and Shok found a use for it. Neither wanted to go to Earth any time soon. Everywhere they went on Earth, someone took their picture and someone else began asking questions. They thought another visit to Earth would end up being more political than pleasure, and a very nosy place in the bargain. They had more interesting places to spend their time.

They loaded the third cargo ship with farm machinery, guns, books, technicians and household items for the planet Nordic. The hunting lodge they wanted to build didn't have anything to do with them going to Nordic; but they decided, while they were in the neighborhood would be a good time get the lodge project started. The real purpose of the trip was to help the Nordics bring themselves into the present century.

When the Nordic business was finished, they would set a course for the planet Egrin. The market possibilities on Egrin needed to be explored. Egrin would be building after the war. Shok remarked, "I don't think the Egrins are still mad at us for attacking their planet. It was a short war, as wars go, and we were about as nice to the Egrins as we could be."

They planned a stop on the planet Iklug after they were finished on Egrin. Jeonk remarked, "They seem friendly enough since we got rid of the last Veolsh tyrant for them. I think we can do business with them. We should go to the other planets we freed from Veolsh after we finish with Iklug. If things work out the way we want, we'll have markets on every friendly planet in the galaxy. We'll skip Prssk, Gamac, Krex and Mog. They don't manufacture very much, and they tend to steal instead of purchase. We should cross them off of our cargo list."

Jeonk and Shok had the trip set it up pretty well for themselves. They would buy products, show Argan manufactured goods, sell and buy options for products and meet old friends and new people all the way down the line. Arga was now safe, and its enemies were conquered, or made into friends. Jeonk and Shok thought it would be a nice, quite, few months, out in the galaxy, traveling light and moving fast--just the way they liked it.

There was one problem with traveling light and moving fast, and that problem had several heads. Jeonk and Shok thought they could handle all of the heads the same way. Alice and Aslain found out about their itinerary; a planet-hopping itinerary is hard to hide from observant wives.

Both wives insisted on going along so they could visit their friends on Iklug and Egrin, the friends they made while Jeonk and Shok were busy fighting the last of the Veolsh Council and the pirates.

After Alice was promoted to Vice Admiral, Iliaska was assigned as Aslain's new military liaison officer. She had to come along because of her new status, and Aslain wanted her along. Being Rakoup's wife didn't hurt her case either.

Plask and Rakoup thought there was nothing Jeonk and Shok could do that wouldn't stir up some kind of trouble, and they wanted to be on the ground floor of any new trouble. Plask and Rakoup were large investors in the space cargo business. They insisted on the complete exercise of an investor's responsibilities by going on the business trip.

Aslain wanted Jeonk to take the Royal Cruiser along. She didn't want to be embarrassed by looking like an impoverished queen. Plask insisted on at least four of Rakoup's cruisers accompanying them to guard the royal personages, and to help with the trouble Jeonk and Shok would undoubtedly stir up.

Jeonk and Shok had a beefed up hot rod corsair they stashed in the cargo ship's hold; that's all they wanted on the trip, not the whole family.

Shok realized all of the heads had been handled in the same way; that was an inescapable conclusion. He turned thoughtfully toward Jeonk and said, "I wish you and I had told Aslain and Alice about our plans for a hunting lodge on Nordic. Ah, well, maybe we can find a way to let them discover the place we picked to build it, and let them tell us what a great place it would be to build a lodge."

7

THE FRIENDLY SPACE LINE

The hot rod corsair was safely aboard the cargo ship in its special, newly constructed, takeoff and landing bay. Jeonk and Shok were safely on board the Royal Cruiser with their wives, along with forty under-worked servants and a few select friends. Jeonk thought of putting the hot rod corsair in the shuttle bay of the Royal Cruiser but it wouldn't fit. It was six inches too fat because they had added additional missile tubes and a couple of extra pulse cannons. Shok and Jeonk could probably kiss flying their hot rod corsair good-bye for this trip.

Plask and Rakoup stayed with the family in the Royal Cruiser. They knew about the fast corsair in the cargo ship and they wouldn't let Jeonk or Shok out of their sight for fear of missing whatever trouble they got into, and they wanted their share. Jeonk and Shok stayed busy trying to convince everyone they didn't expect trouble. The only people they were going to see would be friendly. Shok asked, "How can we get into trouble in a Royal Cruiser built like a palatial interplanetary tank?" The skeptics weren't impressed by his logic. The women had made sure their protective clothing still fit from the last time they traveled with their husbands. Their guns were cleaned and loaded.

The women were anxious to see Nordic, the planet of Earth people in the inner galaxy. They also wanted to see the island where the pirate fleets were finished off by Plask and Rakoup. Nothing but a first hand look at the battle zone would satisfy them.

The group came into Nordic slowly because the cargo ship wasn't as fast as a cruiser and they wanted to land on Nordic at the same time it, and the equipment it was carrying, landed.

Admiral Brak, he was usually in command of the Royal Cruiser when it was off planet, came into the community compartment. They were all gathered there for the approach. Brak announced, "We'll be landing in a few minutes, but we have some spacecraft activity on our scanners. I ordered one of the cruisers to check it out before we arrive, just a few small ships. We should have a report momentarily."

"Probably a bunch from Prssk," Jeonk guessed.

"What would Prssk's spacecraft be doing this far from Prssk?" Alice asked. "These people have nothing to steal."

"We left a few hundred damaged spacecraft on the surface of Nordic," Shok reminded her, "and they may be here to see if they can salvage parts from them."

Rakoup didn't think spare parts was the purpose, "I think they're here to kill Jeonk, Shok and maybe Plask and me. The four of us are responsible for ruining the Prssk market for hideouts. Most of Prssk's paying customers are dead or in prison on several different planets. Our little skirmish with them on Nordic was the final act in putting Prssk out of business. They may be taking it hard."

"They aren't going to ruin this trip," Aslain stated. "We have four cruisers with us and Jeonk told me he put a few extra guns on the Royal Cruiser."

Plask didn't think we would have a problem, "Only idiots would attack a party this size and no one on Prssk knew we were coming to Nordic. I think Shok is right."

Iliaska wasn't so sure, "The bomb attack on the Royal Compound had help from Prssk Command. Even if they are here for spare parts, I think we should attack Prssk and get rid that bunch of thieves. The whole galaxy will sleep better when they're gone--and we can throw the Gamacs in with them at the same time."

Brak's return with the report from the cruiser saved them from their own speculations, "It appears the spacecraft were Gamac. They were headed for the island the pirate fleets were using for a base before we cleaned the pirates out. They left as soon as the cruiser began scanning them at close range. None of them landed."

They finished the approach, landed the cargo ship and the Royal Cruiser in a large meadow between two of the Nordic settlements. The cargo crew was unloading the farm equipment before they were approached by any of the Nordics. The Argan farmers and technicians they had brought to show the Nordics how to use the equipment were moving the tractors, cultivators and harvesters into neat rows as the Nordics arrived.

Shok gave each of the Argan farmers and technicians a voice translator programmed with the Earth languages they would need. The translators' languages were modern while the Nordics spoke older versions of the same languages. Shok could help with the English and maybe a little with the German but he didn't intend to be around to do that. Shok knew the difference between the Nordic's old and the Earth's new languages would be a problem, but the Nordics and the Argans would have to adapt as best they could during the few months of the project.

The Nordics Jeonk and Shok had met on the previous trip were not among those who first approached the strange goings on this time. Before the landing, Shok had contacted the Nordics on the radio he left with them the first time he was on Nordic. The Nordics knew the party was coming but they certainly didn't expect them to arrive with something as big as the cargo ship. Still, they didn't seem to be afraid. Shok could see many of them in the distance walking toward the cargo-landing site. They let the crew of Argan teachers try to communicate with the Nordics who were shy and unable to understand the big blue strangers.

Jeonk and Shok would have to renew their Nordic contacts a little later. The ladies were anxious to see the island battleground and hear the explanations of how the pirates were brought to justice from those who performed that magnificent feat. Plask loaded everyone into one of the Royal Cruiser's shuttles and proceeded directly to the offshore island to regale them with the superhuman exploits of Rakoup and himself.

Plask and Rakoup had the honor of explaining the situation to the ladies. They took turns explaining how the fleet was positioned to control the battlefield, it seemed theirs were the only two cruisers in the battle. Iliaska gave Rakoup a wifely, doubting look. Aslain and Alice were transfixed by the explanation of courage and cunning in the face of danger from seven hundred ferocious pirate spacecraft and their murderous crews. Aslain gave Jeonk a doubting look in the middle of the explanation. Alice elbowed Shok in the side as Plask described beating off the attack of twenty-five corsairs trying to even up the battle by destroying the cruiser he commanded. Both women knew the pirates' corsairs didn't have a chance in a battle with an Argan Cruiser.

The hundreds of corsairs and the few larger spacecraft in the area looked more like a spacecraft junkyard than a battleground--if you didn't notice most of the junk had holes burned in the sides and tops. They went through some of the ships for evidence of parts removal and there were parts missing from most of the ships they went into. The missing parts were mostly black boxes someone could use on similar spacecraft. Judging from the number of removals in the few ships they looked at, the removal operation was pretty big.

Having gotten the last dregs of admiration from their ladies, they took the shuttle and returned to the main party. Mrs. McGuire, a lady Jeonk and Shok had met previously, was trying to tell one of the Argans something important, but the translators couldn't translate her message. Shok asked her to tell him about it. She said, "They be devil men in yon mountains. Fiercer ones ich ne'er saw, with skin on 'em like old iron. We cry beef, come they for thievin'."

SPACE LINE BY MARVIN E. FOX

"What did she say?" Iliaska asked.

Shok replied, "She said, there are Gamacs in the mountains and the people here raise an alarm when the Gamacs come to steal from them. The Nordics think the Gamacs are devils because they have skin the color of rusted iron."

Shok explained to Mrs. McGuire that the Argans would take care of the Gamacs and the Gamacs weren't devils, just thieves like any other thieves. Mrs. McGuire seemed relieved to find the Gamacs were just people and the Argans would take care of them.

Jeonk said, Shok, you and I can take one of Rakoup's fighters and locate them if they haven't gone into hiding."

Aslain wasn't happy with Jeonk's solution. "Let the Marines take care of it. They can find them with their scanners."

Rakoup corrected Aslain's wrong assumption, "The scanners can identify people but not nationalities and the Gamacs are the same size as the Nordics. Plask and I will be in another fighter with Jeonk and Shok. Right now, Shok is the only one of us who can speak with these people and we'll have to talk with the Nordics living in the mountains to find the Gamacs."

"We're going too!" Alice demanded. "We can use the shuttle. It flies slower than a fighter and we can help you look for them."

Aslain and Iliaska chimed in with their approval of Alice's plan. "We don't intend to fight the Gamacs after we located them,"

Jeonk said. "We'll call in the fleet Marines and go on our happy way while the Marines do the dirty work."

The women were adamant in their demand to go along. The men reluctantly agreed to let the women help with the search, and to search in the shuttle. The search would also give Jeonk and Shok a chance to let their wives discover the place Jeonk and Shok wanted to build the hunting lodge.

Plask and Rakoup were always well armed. The three ladies opted to carry three pistols each and the same combat knife Jeonk and Shok carried in the field. They wore the standard combat thermal uniform the Marines wore into battle. The women looked real cute in their Marine uniforms.

Rakoup told Plask. "We'll probably get into some kind of trouble for doing this the wrong way." He alerted one of his cruisers to keep tabs on them from a low stationary orbit. The cruiser was one hundred miles above them. Shok didn't think it could do much good, unless a large party of Gamacs attacked the party.

Jeonk took a quick look at the small hill with a waterfall on low side of it, the same hill he and Shok wanted their hunting lodge on. As they lifted above the meadow in the shuttle, Jeonk said, "We should check that hill to see if the Gamacs are using it for a lookout point. They know we're in the area and they will want to spy on us from somewhere. That looks like the best spot for them."

Jeonk is smart. He was taking them to the future lodge sight before they tired of looking at hills and forests. The ladies were thrilled with the place. The view of the valley was great. If they had brought fishing equipment, Plask and Rakoup would have forgone the pleasure of getting into trouble with Jeonk and Shok to go fishing in the river. Everyone thought some kind of nice place should be built there. Jeonk remarked, as though it was a new idea, "What do you think Shok, is this place good enough for a hunting lodge?"

"I haven't seen a better place in years," Shok agreed. "I'm glad you accidentally stumbled onto this place. We can thank the Gamacs for this before we get rid of them."

After a brief period of appreciation, they left the new lodge site to check out the areas closest to the settlements. Shok suggested, "If the Gamacs are stealing food, then they must be on foot." All of them suspected they were on foot because the Gamac's spacecraft had been destroyed in the island battle. That would force the Gamacs to remain close to the food source. They flew the shuttle back and forth through valleys and across mountains searching for campsites or any other sign of human life. They saw nothing.

It was about one and a half hours before dark when the women began to tire of the search. Plask suggested the search be abandoned to let Rakoup's cruisers and fighters take over the problem. Their scanners would log the inhabited places and life forms in the entire mountain range. The suspected life forms could be checked out individually the next day.

The shuttle was flying low through a valley on their return trip but still thirty miles from the farms they had launched from that morning. Jeonk suddenly jerked the shuttle to the right. Something had exploded on the lower left side damaging the shuttle's anti-gravity unit. The shuttle quickly began to lose altitude as Jeonk arched it into the bottom of a shallow river on the floor of the valley.

Shok made a quick check of the mixed crew and found they were still healthy. Rakoup exclaimed, "We've found the Gamacs. We had better get the hell out of this shuttle before they find out we're still alive."

They blew the emergency exits. The inside of the shuttle was knee deep in water before they could get out of it. Jeonk, Rakoup and Shok hesitated before leaving to make sure their wives got out all right. Plask, who was wife free on this mission, reported, "There's some cover on the river bank. We better get to it before the Gamacs start shooting. They can't be very far away."

Shok caught a glimpse of furtive movement on the crest of the hill above them as they waded toward the cover Plask had found. Shok quickly drew one of his pistols and fired two shots at whatever it was. The women saw where he fired, drew their pistols and fired at the same place. They fired about five times each and the shots were nicely spaced laser blasts. If it was a Gamac on the hill, he was either killed or someplace else before they fired.

All of them reached Plask's cover without being fired on. Plask got to the cover first and immediately began studying the hillside for a better site to fight from. He saw a wood covered knoll about eighty meters uphill that looked better to him. The three women and the three men followed him cautiously up the hill, with a wary eye for any movement in the surrounding area. They made the knoll without trouble and no shots were fired in their direction. Plainly, the Gamacs hadn't gotten into an attack position. Jeonk had been able to maneuver the shuttle after the hit and his maneuvering put them farther from the Gamacs than they would have been if he had landed quickly.

The knoll appeared defensible. There were several trees to stop laser rounds and plenty of bushes to obscure their positions from a distant observer. The downed searchers had managed to gain the high ground for small arms fire. The Gamacs would have to climb the knoll to attack, but they could win if there were enough of them in the attack.

Shok didn't like the situation. The cruiser above them probably thought they had landed to look at something. Until the cruiser crew became concerned, they wouldn't realize the party was down and damaged. Until then, the cruiser crew would take no action.

On the other hand, the Gamacs knew they had a limited time to fight and they might know that Jeonk, Plask, Rakoup and Shok were in the party. The four of them had destroyed the pirates' spacecraft and killed many of their pirate friends. The Gamacs wouldn't wait for an invitation to kill. The time the party had to prepare was the time it would take for the Gamacs to get to them and start shooting.

Shok suggested, "The Gamacs are still down river from us. They won't come at us from the riverbed because there is too little cover. I think they'll be coming over the large hill to our left. I'm going to work my way up the hill to a position where I can ambush them as they crest the hill."

"I can go with you and help." Alice offered.

"Thanks but you can't," Shok replied. "I have guerrilla fighting experience and you don't. This is pretty good guerrilla country. You don't know what to do in it."

Jeonk made his offer, which reassured Alice but worried Aslain; "I'll take care of Shok for you. We'll get them in our crossfire. If any of them get past us, you get to shoot them."

Aslain remarked, "If you get killed and I have to marry someone else, I'll marry someone who was born without a trigger finger." Plask and Rakoup thought the remark was funny but they had to stop laughing because the three women gave them dirty looks.

Jeonk instructed Rakoup, "When you get your radio dried out, call in some air support on that hill. Tell them not to shoot the two guys with the big trigger fingers."

Jeonk and Shok left the knoll to work their way up the hill in search of good place to ambush the Gamacs. Neither thought they had much time, but the Gamacs wouldn't be good woodsmen because the planet Gamac didn't have anything like good woods. Both men felt the Gamacs would probably be noisy as they advanced and it would be easy to hear them coming. The terrain Shok and Jeonk crossed was rough woodland and there was plenty of cover. They could hear the Gamacs coming up the other side as they worked their way toward the top of the hill.

Jeonk positioned himself in a spot with good cover behind trees and rocks. Shok found a position fifty or sixty meters away behind some fallen trees. They would wait until the pirates crossed the crest of the hill and were on the down slope. The pirates didn't seem to be concerned that they might be walking into an ambush, probably because there were so many of them.

The Gamacs walked three or four abreast in a loose formation, like a bunch of guys in a hunting party. Not all of them had reached the top of the hill when the first of them drifted into the position where Jeonk and Shok had to start firing.

Jeonk and Shok began laying a fast laser crossfire into them as the first of the pirates crossed the open space at the top of the hill and were about to enter the protection of trees and undergrowth. About forty pirates were in the crossfire. The pirates were stunned by the crossfire, and for three or four seconds Jeonk and Shok had a clear field of fire with no return fire from the pirates. Three or four seconds is a long time in a gunfight. They finished off about twenty of them while the pirates mulled over their options and made their move.

The Gamacs in the rear found their wits first and bolted back down the other side of the crest of the hill. The pirates who didn't think they could make the trip back across the hill, drew their pistols and began firing, but they couldn't locate Shok or Jeonk in the rocks and undergrowth. The two Argans finished that part of the gun battle with little danger to themselves. Shok saw a few laser blasts go into the bushes near him but none hit him. Seven more Gamacs fell before quiet returned to the forest.

SPACE LINE BY MARIVIN E. FOX

Shok checked to see if Jeonk was all right. Jeonk waved to him and signaled for them to go around opposite sides of the hill to take care of the pirates who escaped. They both took a high line, following the cover of the trees and brush as they worked their way toward the Gamacs. Both knew, without either of them saying it, the pirates weren't finished and they would try to flank their positions by coming around behind and below them. There was plenty of cover for the pirates and they would be using all of it they could.

As Shok worked his way carefully around the hill, he could see lasers firing from the knoll the rest of the party was using for cover. He guessed they were being attacked by a group of pirates who had come up the riverbank he hadn't thought they would use. Plask and Rakoup would have positioned themselves and the women for their best firing positions. Shok thought he and Jeonk were covering the main party of pirates, so he wasn't unduly worried about the party on the knoll. Everyone on the knoll was a good shot and none of them were shy about shooting.

Shok found a position where he thought he should be seeing some of the pirates moving through the trees but he wasn't. He decided to stay hunkered down where he was and make sure he hadn't missed them as he passed by. He remained behind some low bushes to wait them out. He listened but heard nothing coming from Jeonk's side of the hill.

Suddenly, He saw a flash and felt a burning in his right arm. A laser blast grazed the muscle of his upper arm. He wasn't badly burned but it hurt like hell. Then he saw the pirates. They hadn't traveled around the hill to flank him. They dug in behind the best cover they could find on short notice, and waited for Shok to come to them.

Shok quickly moved behind a stand of nearby trees to get a little of that short notice cover for himself. Shok was glad he had waited. The pirates were still ahead of him and he hadn't let them flank him. They would have killed him if he had kept going.

Pirates are a wary bunch, not given to taking personal risks. Shok watched the firing patterns of their lasers, and discovered they were in small groups behind any kind of cover they could find. They fired blindly from their safe positions, trying not to expose themselves to his fire. They weren't hitting him or anything else that would do them any good.

The pirates were hoping one of them would get lucky or someone in their group would stand up to take a well aimed shot at him. The first one who fired at him had made their best shot. Shok watched their sporadic fire for several minutes without firing, hoping some of them would stand and fire so he could get a clear enough shot at them to help them join their dead friends on the hilltop.

Dark was approaching and the dark would give the advantage to the pirates. The approaching darkness was forcing Shok to do something quick. Jeonk had seen the problem from where he was coming to help Shok. Jeonk flanked the Gamacs, putting the pirates between Shok and himself, before he began firing at them. His laser fire started a serious deterioration in the pirates' positions.

Jeonk's flank attack stopped Shok's worrisome thinking about the approaching dark. Shok realized Jeonk hadn't met any pirates as he worked his way around the mountain. The pirates stayed together as they found places to hid and wait. Shok kept a steady pace of laser fire as he worked his way toward them from below.

Shok's steady laser rounds forced them to bolt from their protected positions and begin firing at Jeonk to get him out of their way. The pirate's flight to better protection gave Shok the targets he had been waiting for. The pirates were, once again, between Jeonk and Shok and they were in the crossfire. The Pirates fell at a rapid rate; the crossfire took its toll. Pirate and Argan lasers punctured the spreading dusk.

The Gamac pirate's normal lack of courage and their inborn conviction to give up when they think it's too dangerous, gripped the pirate group just as one of Rakoup's fighters swooped down and zeroed in on their position on the hillside. The Gamacs dropped their weapons and kept their hands well over their heads.

Marines rapidly left the cruiser that hovered near Plask's knoll, where the rest of the Argan party was firing. Jeonk and Shok marched the defeated pirates to the waiting cruiser. The cruiser would take them to whichever planet had the most or the most serious warrants for them. Jeonk wanted to give the pirates to Iliaska and Alice in the hope the two of them would drop the pirates on Chokng Fould's castle but he didn't think Aslain would approve and he wanted to keep her happy. Letting the Marines put them on Rakoup's cruiser was the only alternative.

Jeonk had a laser burn on each arm and Shok had collected one on his right arm and another on his left leg. Both of them slept on their sides. They wouldn't be doing that for a few days. Alice and Aslain were worried about them. They could see the lasers firing in the dusk and they were sure their husbands would be killed or badly wounded. They were very relieved when their worst worries appeared behind the captured Gamacs.

The remainder of the time on Nordic was uneventful compared to the evening with the Gamacs. Jeonk and Shok were convinced there were more pirates hiding out in the Nordic bush and they refused to leave the Nordics unarmed to face armed pirates. They left the Nordics with enough laser pistols to take care of the pirates. They assigned one of Rakoup's cruisers and its Marines to teach the Nordics how to use them. The Argans also set up a power station to provide the Nordics with electricity. The Nordics could recharge the laser power packs and have no fear of being unarmed in case more pirates showed up.

The party stayed a month on Nordic. By the time they left, the Argan technicians and farmers were beginning to understand each other, and the Argans seemed to be getting along well with the Nordics.

It looked like a good trip to Shok. The Nordics were learning modern farm techniques and how to use mechanized farms equipment. Better farm methods insured the Nordics of an abundant supply of food, plus, Jeonk and Shok would have a source of farm products to buy for people on other planets who might, from time to time, have the need. Jeonk and Shok hired the Nordics to build the hunting lodge, which appeared to be everyone else's idea. Alice and Aslain filled several more notebooks for their galactic record on everyone alive in the galaxy.

Alice and Aslain were filled with sympathy for poor wounded Jeonk and Shok, wounded while facing death to defend their wives in the face of the unprovoked Gamac pirate attack. Sympathy like that might be worth one hot rod corsair trip without having wife trouble even if they happen to run into some insignificant danger on the trip.

8

EGRIN AND BUST

The ladies expressed their sorrow at having to leave Nordic so soon but they were secretly happy to be on their way. Plask and Rakoup's conviction that Jeonk and Shok would find some kind of trouble wherever they went was reinforced by the battle with the Gamacs. The interplanetary travelers lost two of their escort cruisers, one to the job of taking the Gamacs to jails on various planets. The other stayed to teach the Nordics to defend themselves with modern weapons. Plask insisted on replacing the two cruisers with three more from Rakoup's fleet. Shok's fleet of sixteen cruisers sat idle on his base at Perlta, but he didn't want to insult Plask and Rakoup by suggesting his would do as well as Rakoup's.

Jeonk thought they were beginning to look like a war fleet instead of commercial visitors to friendly planets. He suggested the slower pace they would have to maintain because of the large, slower moving, cargo ship would cause them to lose business time on the various planets they intended to visit. He insisted on leaving two cruisers to lumber along with the cargo ship.

The smaller number of three cruisers and the Royal Cruiser could make the trip to Egrin much faster. They intended to be on Egrin long enough for the cargo ship to catch up. The ladies were happy with the plan because they were anxious to see old friends on Egrin. Plask and Rakoup couldn't think of any trouble they could get into in the friendly space between Nordic and Egrin so they agreed to Jeonk's plan.

The Royal Cruiser descended on one of the new Capitals of Egrin with its umbrella of cruiser protectors fanned out overhead. Plask and Rakoup elected to remain with the cruisers. They said it was to maintain security for the rest of the party, but their real reason was: they didn't want to be involved in the diplomatic meetings with the Egrins. They considered the Egrins to be ordinary civilized people since an Argan space fleet helped them remove their former tyrants from high office. They didn't want to associate with Egrin's, or anyone else's, ordinary diplomats.

The royal party received the Egrin red carpet treatment from President Maltrik of the Republic of Rastluuk. The party hadn't arrived unannounced so there were leaders from other nations' anxious to meet them. The Egrins were especially happy to speak with Alice and Aslain, whom they knew, and had helped them form their new republics. The greetings went on for a long time. A band played as they exited the Royal Cruiser, and children gave the ladies flowers. Newly elected politicians cast their enthusiastic greetings at them from every direction. Jeonk thought it would never end.

In the midst of the diplomatic photo opportunity feast, Shok spied General Treast. He was the one Jeonk had talked with just before the war with Egrin got serious. Shok tapped Jeonk on the arm to point out the General's presence. Jeonk leaned over to Aslain and said, "You and Alice take care of the diplomatic work. You know more about it than Shok and I. We have some business to take care of."

Jeonk and Shok walked to where Gen. Treast was trying to disengage himself from the diplomatic melee. Shok asked, "How is everything going General? Are the new Republics doing all right?"

His enthusiasm was cautious, "Most of them are doing all right. We have two that seem to be going sour. The Planetary Forum is considering war with them. The two bad ones have turned their embassies into spy networks, and are trying to gain control of the most critical metals on Egrin. They are also using the news media to spread lies about political wrong doing in other nations. They are constantly accusing the other nations of being unfair to them. That is an old Veolsh trick. Most of us who are close to the government won't buy it.

"There are too many people on this planet who are not yet educated about the facts of liberty. The propaganda blitz is causing dissension for everyone by misleading those uneducated people. I'm surprised you came here at this time. One of their favorite accusations is that the rest of us have been bought off by the rich and powerful Argan imperial power. They are saying that only they, the accusers, are pure enough to bring true freedom to Egrin."

"Eject them from your Planetary Forum," Jeonk suggested, "or go to the Galactic Forum and accuse them of waging political and social war against the other nations on Egrin. In either case, they will be taken care of. They will have to back down or go to war. Maybe Shok and I can talk to them and show them the error of their ways. Can you arrange a meeting between them and us?"

"I can try," Gen. Treast replied, "but I doubt it. They probably won't come here to meet you. If you go there, the fifty Marines you brought for protection might not be enough. I can send my troops along to protect you, but I think it is unwise for you to meet with them on their home ground."

Shok suggested, "We can meet their representatives to the Egrin Planetary Forum in the Forum complex. A meeting there should be safe."

The General responded, "I can cover you there without any problem but their Forum representatives can't sneeze without prior approval. You can spend days having what should be a five minute conversation with them."

"We have an Embassy here in Rastluuk," Jeonk suggested, "I'll give a diplomatic dinner and invite the two top leaders from each of the problem republics. Do you think they will attend? We have to give a diplomatic dinner anyway, and you are invited. The three of us will manage a private meeting with them after the dinner."

Gen. Treast conceded, "I think they might. The dinner will give them an opportunity to increase their propaganda supply and allow them to use their personal association with Argan Royalty, and Admiral Shok, as proof of your lies. They have very consistently blamed King Jeonk and Admiral Shok for the downfall of Egrin society."

"I take it you think inviting them to dinner is a bad idea?" Shok asked.

The General replied, "We have had many meetings with them in many different settings. After each of the meetings, they spin whatever we have said in the meeting to support their own agenda. They are already calling Arga their opponent in the power struggle for the planet Egrin. They aren't looking for a resolution of their problems with the other nations; they, clearly, intend to take power over the entire planet for themselves. That's my opinion, but you may hear other opinions that disagree with mine."

"What kind of support do they have for taking over the planet?" Shok asked. "Two nations can't generally win against many nations and there are only two of them."

The General enlightened Shok. "When the nations were separated, Rastluuk inherited most of the banks due to our close proximity to the palace. We shared the money with the other nations so none would be left impoverished. The Egrin space fleet you fought in your war with the Veolsh on Egrin caused the loss of most of the spacecraft based in Rastluuk. Most of Egrins space power was based in Rastluuk and our neighboring two countries of Sompla and Crustpla. Two Argan cruisers, flying low ground support, effectively kept the ships based in those areas out of the battle. While Rastluuk lost most of our ships, the other two did not.

"When the countries were formed, Rastluuk shared the gold. Sompla and Crustpla didn't share their military power. Each of them is militarily more powerful than any of the other Egrin nations. The two of them working as allies are more powerful than all of the rest of us together. That is their power base. We could beat them easily in a ground war but we haven't a chance when they add their air support to their ground assault."

"We arrived here at just the right time." Jeonk said. "What's your plan Shok?"

The General laughed and Shok answered, "You might give me a couple of minutes to think it over but there's one thing for sure. We can't let this planet be taken over by two tyrants who expect to run it for themselves. It's our treaty obligation to the other members in the Galactic Forum to protect their sovereignty. What the General has told us, as a fellow Forum member, is sufficient for an official response from us.

"The first thing we need to do is notify the Rastluuk and Argan delegations to the Galactic Forum that there is a problem. They will bring it to the attention of the entire Forum. General Treast can do that immediately for Rastluuk, and King Jeonk for Arga, using the Forums communication network. That will take only a few minutes and can be done as soon as we stop talking.

"I can launch my fleet from Perlta and have it wander around the border of Rastluuk to make sure there are no ground battles to contend with in the near future. We need the General and President Maltric's permission for that. One of the cruisers will have to land occasionally so the commander can confer with Arga's delegation to Egrin's Forum. Doing that will make sure the fleet is noticed by the spies in the two embassies.

"We should invite the two want-to-be planet rulers to the diplomatic dinner. We'll make sure Plask and Rakoup are there. Just looking at those two old warriors might give our two pugnacious guests a more peaceful attitude. Jeonk, I think you should make a speech to inform the diplomats attending the dinner that Arga is always ready to honor its treaty obligation to protect the sovereignty of Rastluuk and the other nations in the Galactic Forum. You might wish to include how vigorously Arga will defend any who are threatened.

"What do you think General? Does that sound like the beginning of a safety net?"

Before the General could answer, Jeonk said, "We'll us Brak's fleet. I want yours kept close to home for a while. If the General wants some air support for his ground troops, Brak can use his cruiser-based fighters to help out. I think Brak's two hundred and forty fighters will be enough. What do you think General?"

The General was almost stunned as he replied, "I think it's a great plan. I didn't hope for anything more than some sympathetic sounding diplomatic rhetoric. You two move like a storm that covers everything in minutes. Alice told me the name Shok means 'quick' in the Argan language. What's the meaning for Jeonk, hurry up or you'll miss the ass kicking? I'll be at that dinner. I wouldn't miss seeing those two butt-heads faces when you make your speech, not for anything."

Jeonk laughed and said, "Then its set. I'll have to decide on a good time for the dinner. I'll see that you get an invitation and we'll talk again tomorrow. Shok and I have to arrange some things."

They met with Plask and Rakoup to set the plan in motion before they rejoined the ladies surrounded by the people they had in their notebooks from their last visit to Egrin.

Aslain informed Jeonk, "We, really, must have a diplomatic dinner for the leaders of the new Forum nations. Alice and Iliaska agree with me on that."

"We certainly must." Jeonk replied. "Shok and I will be looking forward to it. I think we should plan it for a few days from now. We want to be sure they can all attend."

"How thoughtful of you Jeonk." Alice agreed enthusiastically. "We certainly don't want any of them to miss it."

The day ended for the ladies with the thrill of meeting their friends after a long separation. The possibility of getting involved in some kind of action made the day for Jeonk and Shok. Even Plask and Rakoup were looking forward to the diplomatic dinner. For those two to look forward to a diplomatic dinner they had to attend, personally, was unusual but this one held the possibility of diplomatic fireworks. The Royal party retired, each looking forward to his different brands of future excitement.

Alice is a talking snuggler as she prepares for sleep. She talks as she snuggles to find just the right comfortable position, and Shok enjoys her talking and snuggling. As she did her nightly snuggling, She remarked, "One of my friends told me one of the Egrin presidents is a friend of Chokng Fould, that terrible Gamac king.

"Which president is that?" Shok asked.

"The president of Sompla," Alice replied. "You probably don't know about it but Sompla shares a border with Rastluuk."

Shok knew more about the Sompla border than Alice would have guessed but he had something else on his mind. He had been waiting for just the right moment to ask her about it for a long time. He asked, bluntly, blunt is as diplomatic as Shok can manage except for silence, "How did you and Iliaska dump that four hundred pound claw on Choking's castle?"

Alice put her arm across his chest, kissed Shok's cheek, then said, "Iliaska was really mad at the Gamacs for making me a slave, and selling me to the Mogs to be worked nearly to death in their rotten mine. I don't like the Mogs or the Gamacs any more than she does.

Iliaska said she bet she could position our repair module so one of its claws would hit Chokng's palace, if we released it just right. Iliaska positioned the repair module. I pushed the release button. We didn't believe we could really hit his palace, but we did. I'm not sorry about it either. I would have dumped both claws on him if I had believed we could hit his palace."

She raised herself on her elbows and looked at Shok as though she expected some kind of disapproval from him for dropping the claw on Chokng. Shok patted her bottom and said, "The next time, follow Rakoup's advice, call ahead to make sure he's home." Their mutual snuggling went ballistic after that.

The next day was interesting. The ladies spent part of the day showing the Royal Cruiser to their friends. Jeonk and Shok took Gen. Treast for a tour of Rakoup's flagship. The tour included a conference on how to best handle the problems with Sompla and Crustpla. The General had a meeting with President Maltrik during the previous evening and Maltrik was behind the General in whatever he wanted to do. Things are always easier when politicians are smart enough to get out of the way of the military after trouble starts.

They took Gen. Treast and some of his aides on a familiarization flight in Rakoup's cruiser, just a few hours. Plask and Rakoup liked the General and they became friends. In the middle of the cruiser tour, questions began coming from the Galactic Forum. The Forum members wanted Jeonk or Shok to explain the war danger and how they could help. Both spoke to different forum members, and gave the best explanation they could about Rastluuk's fluid situation.

They were careful to explain that they were trying to prevent a war--not start one. The Forum members agreed with the plan, but they wanted to get the approval from their home nations to decide what should be done to support their treaty obligation to a member nation threatened by war.

Jeonk and Shok spent the next two days being introduced to the people their wives knew from past associations, and the friends they were making in their present circumstances. The introductions were informal and the informality made the Argans difficult to protect. The frustration of the Marine bodyguards became apparent as they tried to keep them safe while a large number of people joined or left the crowd collecting around them. Gen. Treast had assigned some of his own guards that seemed more familiar with the people who approached. Shok noticed the Rastluuk guards occasionally taking someone aside as he approached, but there didn't seem to be any real promise of trouble.

The fourth day in Rastluuk became more interesting. Admiral Chosteel from the nation of Kristall on Paraca contacted Jeonk and Shok. He was chosen by the Galactic Forum to head up the Forum's effort to keep the planet Egrin and the nation of Rastluuk safe from war. Shok knew Chosteel well and had been friends with him for a long time. Chosteel looked tough and he was tough. He was the most successful guerrilla fighter in the galaxy. He knew more about his kind of war than anyone. If he and the Forum nations were getting into the Rastluuk situation, Shok didn't think there would be much for Arga to do. The Forum had grown to more than five hundred Forum nations, including Arga. Even though Arga would have to take a back seat, the sovereignty of Rastluuk was safe. Shok felt good about that.

A few days later, Chosteel arrived in a brand new cruiser with thirty fighters and corsairs from different nations. Shok was glad to see the cruiser. It meant Kristall was prosperous enough to build it and nobody builds just one cruiser.

Chosteel stepped out of his cruiser and looked around. Jeonk, Shok and General Treast stepped forward to meet him. Chosteel's chest was full of the medals he had won during the many years he fought the Veolsh Council. His uniform was new and his admiral epaulets were made of pure gold. Beneath the splendor, he still looked like the tough old bastard Shok had gotten to like. Shok stepped forward and said, "It's damn good to see you Chosteel."

Chosteel's greeting was as short as Shok's, "It's damn good to see you Shok. Where are the idiots who think they can start a war here? Hello Jeonk, General Treast, I think this situation will be cleared up quickly, one way or the other."

Jeonk offered, "We expect the idiots to attend a diplomatic dinner we are giving later this afternoon. The Argans, General Treast and you will be there with them. We'll fill you in on the situation between now and the dinner. I hope you will give a speech as the representative of the Forum nations. I'll be giving a speech for Arga. You can give yours right after mine, if that's all right with you?"

Chosteel answered, "Because you're the one who asked me, I'll give a speech, but speeches are usually made to start wars, not to stop them. I have one thousand spacecraft on hold if the idiots decide to go to war. If that isn't enough, there are thousands more if we need them. We aren't the down and out freedom fighters you and Shok met after the Veolsh War. We know the cost of liberty. We have become rich enough to pay our own way to keep it.

Chosteel and the antiwar party retired to the Royal Cruiser for a private discussion. It was a relaxing time for all of them. No new planning was necessary. They enjoyed their drinks and frittering away the time until the dinner was due to start. Shok had listened to Chosteel speak many times but he had never heard him make what anyone would call a speech. Shok thought it was going to be a humdinger.

President Maltrik had taken over the late King's palace for the presidential residence after the King's abrupt demise. Even though the dinning room was very large, there was barely room for all of the guests and their added protection in the huge room. Intermixed around the perimeter of the room were twenty-five Argan guards and twenty-five of Gen. Treast's, with an additional twenty-five of Chosteel's. That dinner would have been a bad place for someone to start trouble and there were even more guards on the outside.

Jeonk seated gen. Treast between Rakoup and Plask. Admiral Chosteel was between Plask and Shok. Alice was seated next to Shok. Jeonk and Aslain were seated at one end of the long banquet table. President Maltrik and his wife were seated at the other end. Directly across from Plask and Chosteel, Jeonk had seated the two idiots who wanted to start the war.

The dinner was all right but Shok thought they should have had some Cajun cooks to prepare it. The food wasn't his main interest anyway. As the dinner ended, Jeonk stood up and began his speech, "I'm glad so many of you could attend this international and interplanetary dinner. It is seldom we have the opportunity to meet so many friends.

"There is, however, a problem on Egrin. It seems that two of the nations are contemplating a takeover of the other nations, including the conquest of our dear friends in the nation of Rastluuk. The two nations contemplating the takeover have most of the military power on Egrin. Those two nations have neglected to recognize the awesome power of both the Galactic Forum and the treaty obligations between the Forum nations.

"Arga is giving its full support to Rastluuk and the other nations threatened on this planet. We will give the same support to any other Forum nation on any other planet that is so threatened. We are there friends. They are our friends, and if they were not, Arga would still honor its treaty obligation to the utmost of its ability. Admiral Chosteel of the nation of Kristall on Paraca is one of our friends. He has a few words to say to you. Admiral Chosteel, the floor is yours"

The Presidents of Sompla and Crustpla rose to leave before Chosteel could begin his speech. Rakoup and Plask stood up with them and said, "Sit down!" The two presidents looked a Plask and Rakoup for about a second before they accepted the double invitation and sat down.

Chosteel's speech was the one Shok and the Argans wanted to hear. Chosteel gave the two troublemakers a long hard look, and began, "Most of the nations in the Galactic Forum know what it is like to be under the thumb of a tyranny. All of us are willing to go to war to protect ourselves from new tyrants who think we have forgotten the lessons we learned from former tyrants. If the nations of Sompla and Crustpla haven't learned that lesson well enough to allow their own people to remain free, or, if they take the idiotic step needed to attempt the conquest of others, we will come down on them like a blanket of death.

"I have one thousand spaceships, of various types and sizes, from most of the Galactic Forum nations to back that promise. If the forum nations on Egrin need more than that, we will give them as much as they need. Sompla and Crustpla have been ejected from their membership in the galactic forum because of their belligerent attitudes and actions against their neighbors. The two nations dismissal from the Galactic Forum makes it easier for us to declare war on them.

"The nation of Arga made it possible for most of us to feel the fresh air of freedom. The Argans have frequently been accused, by these two rogue nations, of being the culprits who keep this planet from true freedom. There has been no bigger lie told anywhere on this planet. I am asking the Argans, who are always the first to defend the freedom of others, and asking nothing in return, to step aside--this one time. They have given enough of their lives, blood and pain for all of us. All of us sleep in safety because of them.

"I want the Forum nations to pull together, without the great power of Arga, and win this battle for freedom. I respect their obligation to abide by their treaty with the Forum nations. I will ask Arga for only two of its space fighters, and those two, only for the sake of Arga's treaty obligation."

The room remained in a stunned silence for a few seconds, suddenly the cheers started. Chosteel's speech loosened the lips of every nation on Egrin that was afraid of war with the two rogue nations. The two rogue presidents didn't wait for the after dinner dessert before they left. Aslain and Alice were quietly removing the tears from their eyes after Chosteel's speech. His praise for Arga had made them a little misty.

Shok was filled with admiration for the old warrior. Shok thought Chosteel might have just gotten up and beat hell out of the two presidents but he had, instead, made a great and forceful speech on the side of liberty. It was the first instant Shok realized the Galactic Forum had become a true success for liberty. He felt satisfaction for his part in forming the Forum.

Chosteel was mobbed by well wishers after the dinner, the after speech dessert was forgotten and the Argans stepped aside to let them pour out their appreciation for Chosteel's help, and his speech. The dinner and the defense of Egrin was a success, so the Argans thought. The two presidents would probably be finished in their own nations when word got out of their failure to establish a powerful presence at the dinner, and the loss of their nations membership in the Forum.

There was just one doubt in Shok's mind. Tyrants, on their home ground, can almost always come up with a pattern of lies to stay in power. They lie to themselves and they lie to their people. He would see in the coming days if Chosteel was right, speeches start wars, but they don't stop them.

Jeonk and Shok became busy with the business they came to Egrin to do, products and cargo. They spent weeks going between nations to establish the buying and purchasing needs they could supply. It seemed the Egrin King and Veolsh Council combination of government had concentrated on the political compliance of the people while leaving out the ordinary needs of the large population.

Egrin was short of the raw materials they should have gotten from mining their own planet, and short of the machinery to develop the raw materials. They were especially interested in purchasing mining equipment, factory machinery, technology, and high tech robotics machines. They needed manufactured goods to hold them over until their factories began producing the products their people were asking for. They also wanted cottonseeds, flax seeds and the equipment to plant and harvest both. Jeonk and Shok thought their wives, who were fond of cotton and linen clothing, had started the desire for those particular fabrics on Egrin.

Even though the Egrins had little to sell, there was a good future in developing their manufacturing potential. Jeonk and Shok invested heavily in that future potential and they both felt good about the probability for a profit on their deals. With the Galactic Forum protecting the borders of the Egrin nations, and the promise of future prosperity for their people, it was unlikely they would return to a tyrannical form of government.

The rhetoric in the news media from Sompla and Crustpla had changed dramatically. The Argans were now valued friends and the two nations return to membership in the Galactic Forum became an announced goal of both governments. The former belligerents at the head of those nations managed to stay in power but they seemed to have changed their tune. They expressed their interest in peace and friendship with the other nations as their only goal in life.

However, they made no offer to share their abundant supply of military armament. Shok expressed his doubts about their newfound love of peace to Chosteel. Chosteel gave Shok his pessimistic view of the idiots who had wanted war, "They're waiting for you and Jeonk to leave before they attack."

The Argans finished their business and decided their last day on Egrin would be spent in a beautiful village near the border of Rastluuk and Crustpla. The village stood in a lovely little valley that shared a narrow mountain pass connecting it with another valley in Crustpla. The mountains around it were filled with red leafed trees and there was a small but magnificent blue lake bordering one side of the village. The Argans decided to host a quiet farewell dinner attended by a few friends by the lakeside.

Jeonk sent a crew of people to the village a day early to prepare a mixed feast of Rastluuk and Argan dishes for the evening meal. Attending the dinner would be the Argans and their new friends. President Maltrik and his wife, Gen. Treast and his wife, Chosteel, Plask with Rakoup and Iliaska of course, Jeonk and Aslain with Alice and Shok rounded out the party.

There would, of course, be one hundred Argan Marines. The Oglaks who had come with Chosteel's small fleet insisted on being on guard duty because the party would continue after nightfall. There were thirty Oglaks and they would put themselves on sentry duty in the outlying area to make certain no one came near the dinner during the dark evening hours. General Treast supplied one hundred fifty of his ground troops.

The meal and the evening were superb until two of the Oglaks approached Chosteel to announce that the dinner party was about to be attacked by a large group of infantry coming across the border from Crustpla. Shok looked at Chosteel and said, "Your time table for the beginning of the attack is off by one day."

The Oglaks informed them that there were fifty heavily armed vehicles about the size of Argan command plaks and approximately two thousand infantry in heavy battle gear. The dinner guests had about five minutes before they were within the maximum firing range of the armed assault force. The invading troops included Mogs, Gamacs, Krexians, some who appeared to be from Prssk and others the Oglaks weren't familiar with.

The Oglaks were armed with the hard hitting machine-guns they usually carried. Each Oglak carried four bandoleers, each bandoleer was filled with several one hundred round clips for their weapons and they were good at using them.

Rakoup and Chosteel grabbed their radios to call in reinforcements. Jeonk, General Treast and Shok began positioning the guards to repel the attack. They had to stop the invaders before they got through the mountain pass at the other end of the village. If the two thousand advancing troops made it through the narrow cut, they would spread out and that would be the end of the after dinner battle.

SPACE LINE BY MARIVIN E. FOX

The Oglaks began setting up an ambush for the invaders on the Crustpla side of the narrow pass the invaders would have to use. The opening fire from the Oglak ambush could be heard at the same time the dinner guests and their guards prepared to join them. People who hadn't fought with, or against, the Oglaks had a hard lesson to learn about their nasty machine-guns. The metallic machine-gun rounds could pierce light armor and explode inside. Anyone hit by an Oglak machine-gun round was going down, no matter what kind of heavy battle gear he was wearing.

The Crustpla invaders hadn't planned against the Oglak magnificent night vision. They planned to be through the narrow mountain pass before they were detected. Oglak fighters are almost invisible at night. They pinned the enemy's forward troops down in the narrow valley, and kept them wondering who was shooting at them. The Crustpla attack vehicles were at a standstill in the rear of the column, unable to get to, or past, the pinned down troops in front of them.

The Rastluuk and Argan guards began their advance along the mountain slopes on each side of the cut, moving in a loose battle formation directly above the forward Crustpla troops that were pinned down by the Oglaks. The Crustpla troops began loosing more warriors from the Rastluuk and Argan lasers as they tried to break the Oglak hold on their advance.

The blazing lights from lasers piercing the night from the mountain slopes made better targets for the Crustpla troops than the invisible Oglaks machine-gun bursts. The Crustpla troops raised their sights, and fired up the slopes. The Argan and Rastluuk troops began catching heavy fire from the pinned down Crustpla invaders. Some of the defending troops went down from the enemy fire but the Oglaks on the leading edge of the battle had suffered no casualties so far.

The immobile armored vehicles commanders in the rear of the Crustpla column began firing on the mountainside with their heavy lasers but no one had advanced far enough to be hit yet. The bright bars of light were fearful to see but the armored vehicle commanders were firing in fear of a target that wasn't yet there. Their fear of the unavailable targets caused them to hit nothing worth shooting at.

Jeonk and Shok were on opposite hills looking down at the stymied attackers in the valley. They each signaled for two Oglaks to help, and quickly returned to a position near the front edge of the immobile column of armored vehicles.

The Crustpla invaders were using their armored vehicles like tanks. Each vehicle was smooth surfaced with turrets and gun ports enclosing its lasers. They were built to withstand laser hits but not Oglak machine-gun hits. They didn't look too tough to Shok.

Jeonk and Shok's Oglaks began spraying the lead vehicles with deadly machine-gun fire at the same time. The screams of the dying and injured troops inside scared the troops in the vehicles behind them and some of the ground troops near them.

The scared attackers from Crustpla still didn't know who they were fighting. They had come to kill surprised enemies who couldn't defend themselves. The Crustpla troops were not expecting to be killed by people who ambushed their surprise attack and couldn't be found in the dark.

The Oglaks blasted eight of the too lightly armored death machines. The screams of the injured and dying from those eight vehicles caused some of the ground troops to review their battle options and begin the fruitless trek back to where they came from.

The battle desertions by the Crustpla forward ground troops and the desertion of the troops in the nearby armored death machines allowed Jeonk, Shok and their Oglaks to advance on the targets that were still in the battle. They bypassed the armored vehicles with open hatches. Their crews had deserted and the vehicles were no longer in the battle.

By this time, the Argan and Gen. Treast's troops had advanced far enough to help Jeonk, Shok and their Oglaks. General Treast's troops and the Argan guards began positioning themselves in a line with Shok and Jeonk on the high ground, keeping the enemy ground troops between them pinned down with laser fire.

General Treast was worried that the Crustpla Army High Command would detect what was happening to its invasion force and send in reinforcements. He suggested to Shok, "We might be able to use our forces better if the Forum forces retreat to fortify the narrow entrance of this valley to Rastluuk. I can bring in a division of reinforcements from Rastluuk to secure the border. Nothing from Crustpla will be able to cross the border with my troops guarding it."

Shok answered, "According to the Oglak scouts, Crustpla doesn't have reinforcements in the area. General Chosteel and the Forum troops will probably begin flooding this area in minutes. Argans troops are even closer than the Forum troops, and are already on the way. Crustpla and Sompla are covered all the way. We need to keep doing what we are doing to control them until our troops arrive." The general seemed to be satisfied with Shok's statement.

Shok and the troops advanced on the next group of armored death traps. There were no personnel scanners in the newly encountered armored units, which was apparent because of their inaccurate firing patterns. There was still some of the two thousand-man Crustpla attack force seeking cover around the remaining armored vehicles. Those troops believed themselves to be surrounded by a superior force.

The Argans and those with them kept the Crustpla troops pinned down. The Rastluuk and Argan forces seemed to multiply as their troops coming from the rear caught up the Jeonk, Shok and the Oglaks.

They Crustpla troops fired up the surrounding hills at laser bursts without being able to see who fired the bursts. They were surrounded, in a confined space that was on the lowest ground. The enemy they couldn't see seemed to have access to reinforcements. The Crustpla infantry troops, and the troops still in the armored death traps were firing their lasers at the same phantoms.

Shok couldn't see Jeonk but he knew Jeonk and his two Oglaks were just opposite his position. The Argan and Treast's troops were making a slow advance behind Jeonk and Shok as they approached an area they could fire safely from without getting shot at by the crazy army in the valley.

The four Oglaks on both sides of the valley opened up at the same time. Their machine guns ripped the sides of the armored vehicles like hot rivet holes waiting to be filled. The troops who had just joined the Oglaks began firing into the melee of troops pinned down by the phantoms of the hills.

The Crustpla troops began a fear driven rout at the same time Chosteel's cruiser appeared in the direction they were retreating. An Argan cruiser, which had no need to respect their ground fire, descended into the center of the battle area crushing some of the enemy vehicles with its landing pods as it settled.

The two cruisers completed the battle perimeter bulwark in the valley. The Crustpla troops had nowhere to go, and no way to fight. They began dropping their guns. It was a satisfying sound to hear. With Chosteel's cruiser behind them, Arga's cruiser in the front of them, a bunch of Oglak machine-gunners on each side of them, and armed patrols they couldn't see surrounding them, the battle ended. The Oglaks had once again saved the Argan bacon, maybe for frying at some future time in a different battle.

Shok joined Jeonk on the stroll back to the civilized part of the valley. Their four Oglak sharpshooters kept a practiced eye out for any back-shooting stragglers someone might have missed collecting. Jeonk and Shok liked the Oglaks, Jeonk and he would have to think of something really nice to do for them.

They rejoined their wives who had emptied most of their laser clips in the battle. With the battle over and none of them dead--they were in a really good mood. Plask and Rakoup had supplied President and Mrs. Maltrik with the hand weapons they used in the battle. The President and his wife were in a good mood like everyone else. Not getting killed, when the odds against that appear to be overwhelming on the side of getting killed, is always a reason for warm feelings inside.

General Treast ordered five hundred of his oncoming troops to the Crustpla side of the valley to take the enemy of the day into custody. Jeonk decided to remain on Egrin, until he found the 'who' and 'why' of the gratuitous attack on The Argan's outdoor barbecue. Shok thought the polyglot crew of inept invaders represented more of an attack on Jeonk and himself by one, or another, of their longtime enemies than a serious invasion of Rastluuk.

"Alice told me the president of Sompla is friendly with Chokng Fould," Shok reported to the group. "Since the troops we fought came at us from Crustpla, it appears the president of Crustpla is also on old Chokng's very short list of good buddies. Chokng said he would take revenge on Jeonk and me for dropping a four hundred pound construction claw, he thought was a missile attack on his unsavory person, that fell on his palace. The attack from Crustpla may have been his revenge effort. Treast's interrogators will probably discover the truth of that mystery."

The Sompla and Crustpla news media carried early morning programs explaining the battle in detail. How they had gotten accurately detailed information about the battle so quickly was suspicious. Both denied the attack on Jeonk's barbecue had any national involvement, except to say some nationalistic military units from both nations had joined in the battle but without the permission of either government. Both governments blamed Jeonk and Shok for the attack on their own outdoor barbecue. The news report stated, "Choking Fould, while in his Imperial Castle on the planet Gamac, was the victim of a guided missile intended to kill him and all of the members of his family. The Gamac nation holds absolute proof of the Argan guilt in the cowardly attack. The Argans were, therefore, responsible for the attack against themselves while in the friendly nation of Rastluuk."

The real truth was discovered during the questioning by Gen. Treast's interrogators and it was a very interesting change from the media report. Old Chokng did want revenge on Jeonk and Shok for the claw dropping but his revenge included a certain amount of money from the two presidents. The off planet invasion participants had been in Crustpla for many months preparing for the general invasion of Rastluuk. Chokng's troops were on Egrin soil before the well-aimed claw tore its way through his bedroom.

The leaders of Crustpla and Sompla, who had expeditiously disowned their own army after its defeat, were guilty of previously rushing those troops to a nearby ground base in Crustpla. The motive for the quick change in military position occurred because their spies reported to the two governments of Sompla and Crustpla that President Maltrik and Gen. Treast would be present at the Argan party near the village.

The homegrown military units were supposed to get rid of President Maltrik and General Treast as their first priority. The troops from the pirate planets were supposed to take care of Jeonk and Shok as their first priority.

The invading troops were supposed to sneak unnoticed across the border as soon as it got dark. They would hit their surprised victims with deadly speed and disappear into the night. The speed, efficiency and terror of the attack would leave nothing but mystery and mourning behind it.

Sompla and Crustpla would have made extensive investigations of the matter, in due course, of course, as was their national duty. They would have sifted the area for clues with hand wringing ferocity. They would have mourned the loss of the galactic heroes for days. They would have put statues of them in one of their smaller parks. With unimaginable regret, they would have been unable to find a shred proof of who murdered the unfortunate victims at the party.

Unfortunately for both Crustpla and Sompla, the clues that would have been too difficult to find by Crustpla, ended up easy to find by Rastluuk. The clues were all talking to Treast's interrogators under the watchful, pissed off, eye of Admiral Sitak Rakoup. There is something about a pissed off Rakoup that makes people want to spill their guts. As it turned out, the original sneaky plan had two sneaky fallacies in it. They didn't sneak in far enough and they couldn't sneak out at all.

The sneaky murder attempt had given Admiral Chosteel enough information to invade Sompla and Crustpla--and he wasn't going to sneak in. He had already called for his one thousand spacecraft fleet. Rastluuk and the other countries had enough ground troops to invade and occupy Sompla and Crustpla after Chosteel's fleet pounded their military into submission.

Jeonk and Shok had done their second good deed for Egrin and survived both times. Jeonk knew his 'who' and 'why' of the attack. The planet hopping business venture was ready to move on. Chokng Fould would eventually discover what the people on Earth have known for a long time--if you try to kill the king, you better kill the king.

9

NOT SO PEACEFUL IKLUG

The royal party was welcomed on Iklug with a fanfare equal in fervor to its welcome on Egrin. The two planets are very much alike in more than one way. Both the Iklug and Egrin people are similar to Earth people in a general way. Alice and Aslain received most of the attention because they were well known by the leaders and diplomats of the Iklug nations. Neither Jeonk nor Shok had any personal friends on the planet. They couldn't escape the diplomats and prominent attendees at the arrival by sliding off to the side on some presumed important business.

Jeonk decided to meet all of the national leaders of the planet at one diplomatic dinner, similar to the diplomatic dinner on Egrin. However, the Iklug dinner held no promise of war on its menu. He intended for that one dinner to save Shok and himself the country hopping they would have to do to keep from slighting the other national leaders on the planet Iklug.

Plask and Rakoup insisted on staying on board Rakoup's flagship, busy taking care of fleet military matters, until Jeonk and Shok stirred up whatever trouble was available on the planet. They wanted no part of the dull diplomatic and business matters the two trouble magnets were visiting planet Iklug to take care of.

Jeonk and Shok were determined to disappoint both of them. The Iklugs didn't seem to have any problems requiring their trouble solving expertise. Bot trouble magnets were adamant about keeping it that way. Trouble was the last thing on their minds. A few mutually profitable business deals was their hearts' desire.

The diplomatic dinner was as dull as they expected, until the beginning of an interesting discussion among the different national leaders about an area on their planet. The leaders called the area, Shiska Frok, which means Abundant Trouble. The borders of Shiska Frok were closely guarded by the surrounding nations. None of bordering nations' inhabitants was allowed to enter Shiska Frok. None of the troublesome area's inhabitants were allowed to leave the Shiska Frok.

No nation would claim Shiska Frok for its own because it was too much trouble and expense to police it. Over time, the area became a kind of planetary no-mans-land. Shiska Frok was a large and generally uninhabited area during the planet's imperial days. Its first inhabitants were people who thought they would be tried and convicted for crimes committed during the Veolsh rule period of Iklug.

The fleeing dissidents flew from the nations of Iklug, and having flown, fled to Shiska Frok before the offended governments could arrest them for their various crimes.

No Iklug government had tried to take a census of Shiska Frok's inhabitants. No one knew, for sure, how many or what kind of people were in Shiska Frok. The various estimates ranged from one and one-half to two million people. Most of its present inhabitants were considered to be people wanted by the law. The most recent inhabitants had fled to Shiska Frok after Jeonk, Shok, and the Argans destroyed the Veolsh Council's power over the Iklug people.

Shiska Frok's population was increased further by those who wanted to get away from laws, although they were not wanted by the law. The remainder of Shiska Frok's population consisted of petty or serious criminals fleeing there to escape Iklug's various police forces. Evidently, Shiska Frok's closely guarded borders were less than impenetrable. If there is traffic one way, there is bound to be traffic both ways.

Later, on board the Royal Cruiser, Aslain and Alice brought up the subject of Shiska Frok. They were not happy about an untended caldron of crime somewhere on the Iklug planet, and its dangerous closeness to Jeonk and Shok. They didn't know where Shiska Frok was but everything is close if you have spaceships. Any trouble less than one solar system away is too close for the wives.

Shok knew Jeonk expected him to reassure their worried wives. Jeonk wants Shok to take care of things like that because it is less likely to work out if Jeonk does it. Jeonk thinks Alice is easier to explain things to than Aslain. If Shok can get Alice on their side, she will influence Aslain.

Shok stated their case, "We don't know where it is. We don't know anyone there. No power on this planet could drag us to it. We don't intend to go near it, through it, under it, over it, or in any other manner approach it. We could not care less about whoever, or whatever, is going on in Shiska Frok."

Rakoup was no help. He said, "If you two don't go there, Shiska Frok will attack you anyway."

Plask added his "amen" to Rakoup's statement and caused them a little more trouble.

"Kevin, how many pistols are you carrying?" Alice asked.

"In the first place," Shok answered, "you know I always carry three. In the second place, Jeonk always carries three. In the third place, that should be enough pistols for two guys who aren't going there in the first place."

Aslain gave them her worried opinion; "Shiska Frok is filled with people who blame the two of you for putting them there. Every one of them will be happy for a chance to shoot you on sight. I think you should take fifty Marines with you wherever you go.

Before either of them could answer, Iliaska jumped into the fray, "We've been on two other planets and we've had battles with people from five other planets. That's not a very good average for a business trip."

"We didn't send for anyone from those five planets and not fighting them was out of the question," Shok reasoned.

Jeonk decided it was necessary for him to enter into the battle of sugarcoated worries from wives, "It doesn't matter how many people from how many planets we have battles with. This business trip is going to remain a business trip. Shok and I cannot carry out our simple business chores and look like an invasion force at the same time. We aren't having fifty Marines tagging along behind us as we do business. We'll carry personal locators and an extra pistol in our briefcases. If we, God forbid, do get into Shiska Frok, you'll know about it the same time we do."

Jeonk didn't like family quarrels; he avoided them when he could but when he put his foot down, that was the end of it. The remainder of the evening was pleasant and there was no return bout with the Shiska Frok subject.

Jeonk and Shok had many business appointments in nearly every nation on the planet. They spent several untroubled days going from country to country using local transportation for many of the closer appointments. They both enjoyed becoming familiar with the ordinary people of Iklug and they could do that best with the personal contacts they made while traveling. They dressed as ordinary businessmen with their pistols out of sight. The Iklugs they met along the way seemed to enjoy talking about themselves and their planet with the two friendly strangers.

SPACE LINE BY MARIVIN E. FOX

They were flying on an inter-city shuttle from a city named Orklssk, only a few minutes from the city of Gaplit, where they had another business appointment. They had just gotten airborne when they heard a noise like, thud, in the forward part of the shuttle. The shuttle turned to the left as it descended. Shok didn't know what the thud meant. He knew that any time you hear one in the air; it, probably, is bad news.

The shuttle made a long, uncontrolled descent to a fifty-foot cliff above a fast running river. One side of the shuttle ripped open as it skidded to a stop at the cliff edge, dumping most of the passengers and luggage down the cliff and into the river.

Jeonk, the young lady they were talking to, and Shok, were the only live people left on the cliff. Both of them wished the passengers going down river the best of luck, because there was nothing they could do for them. Shok asked the young lady, "Where are we?"

The beautiful young lady, named Yonasa, answered, "Shiska Frok."

Jeonk looked over to where Shok was standing and said, "Rakoup was right, Shiska Frok has attacked us."

They checked the wreckage for their briefcases and concluded that the briefcases had gone down river with the luggage and passengers. Yonasa had no idea how to get to civilization. After all, she was as much of a stranger to Shiska Frok as Jeonk and Shok.

Jeonk and Shok's family would know they were down within minutes. They decided the best course of action or inaction in this case, was to stay put and wait for Plask and Rakoup.

After a few minutes of patient waiting, they noticed an armed party of about twenty people coming toward them from upriver. Jeonk and Shok knew the direction the shuttle had diverted from and the approximate location of Orklssk.

They didn't need a discussion before deciding not to wait and see if Plask and Rakoup could beat the armed party to the top of the cliff. They would find the best cover they could and head for Orklssk. The fifty Marines and two-dozen fighters Aslain would have looking for them would probably find them before they got very far.

They traveled five hundred yards on fairly level but rocky ground before they began the slow descent into a valley between two high hills. There was a trail of sorts on the next hill and it appeared to go in the right direction, toward Orklssk. Yonasa was having trouble walking in the low brush. Jeonk lifted her up and sat her on his shoulder so they could make better time. The three of them reached the trail on the next hill without any problem and Jeonk put Yonasa down so she could walk as much as possible.

As they topped the hill, they saw the Argan fighters turn from the crashed shuttle and head down stream following the briefcases with their personal locators inside. The fighter pilots wouldn't able to see them through the fat twisted trees on the hilltop. The trees were large and had spongy web-like structures hanging from their limbs. Shok supposed they were water collectors for the trees. The spongy webs did a good job of hiding them from the searching fighters and they had no way to attract the attention of the pilots.

The three of them continued on for several miles before coming to a small town at the base of a mountain that appeared to be one large rock. Some of the town's structures were cut into the base of the mountain. Those that weren't a part of the mountain were spread along the town's one street that followed the curve of the mountain.

They walked to the center of the town where they entered what appeared to be a bar and trading post. Shok and Jeonk carried voice translators and would have no problem communicating. Shok walked up to the only person in the place and ask for directions to Orklssk. Whatever function the man served in the place, he did tell them what Shok assumed to be the best route. It, at least, seemed to be in the right direction.

Shok asked the friendly seeming man if there was a place in town they could get something to eat. The man directed him to a place at the end of the street and it was one of the places cut into the mountain. They bought some water and canteens from the trading post, and proceeded on their way to what they all hoped would be a nice lunch. So far, Shiska Frok wasn't such a bad place to visit.

The two men and Yonasa entered the eatery and chose a table calculated to keep their backs to the wall, and at the same time give them a good view of anyone coming into the place. The food was as bland as mush, but Yonasa seemed to enjoy it. Jeonk conceded it was probably good fare considering the territory. At first, no one came into the place through the same door the three of them had entered, but several customers came in from the back of the place through a heavy stone door cut into the mountain. Shok decided there was more back there than just storage space.

Several armed men were in the place when they arrived but no women. The men looked at Yonasa with hungry eyes, but didn't try to approach her. Jeonk and Shok shifted their primary pistols to get to them fast if needed. After the quick shift the pistols could be easily seen. The sight of armed strangers, and one of them as big as Jeonk, reduced the men's ardor for Yonasa to a manageable level.

As the three of them finished their meal, eight armed men, coming from the street side, entered the eatery in a group, but didn't remain with the group. They spread out across the room, finding seats wherever there was a vacant chair. Suddenly, no one in the place was hungry anymore. The men who had been feeding their faces, began a race to leave through the back door they had entered. In their hurry, they left the uneaten parts of their meals on the tables. Shok glanced through the door to the street and saw another group of men approaching from a distance.

Jeonk and Shok have been in a lot of bad situations. This was one of them and they both knew what was coming. Jeonk threw a couple of gold coins on the table as Shok told Yonasa to head for the back door. Jeonk and Shok stood up to leave. They backed toward the rear exit with their hands near their pistols. Both hoped the men inside wouldn't try anything until the men outside arrived. It was a vain hope.

It wasn't a well-coordinated attack. Each of the men drew his pistol at a different time and from a different position in the room. The one in the far corner, on Shok's side, stood up and drew first. Shok hit him in the middle of the chest with his laser. Jeonk's first shot dropped the one nearest the door. They were pretty busy for the next second and a half. Both had their second pistols in their hands before the first two assailants hit the ground. The next four fell as each drew his weapon. The last two didn't make a try for it; they ran for the door and kept running toward the large party walking toward the eatery.

Jeonk and Shok might have held the place against the group coming toward the eatery, but they could have better weapons than the first eight. Shok watched the front to keep them back, if he could, while Jeonk checked out the rear entrance. Jeonk went through the heavy stone door and within seconds yelled, "Come on Shok, there's a river back here and some boats."

Shok hurried through the door to join Jeonk and Yonasa. Shok closed and blocked the heavy stone door as soon as he was through it. Jeonk untied a motorboat he found docked there, and was waiting for Shok to get in. The river had a fast current that carried them away from the underground river dock. Jeonk fumbled with the motor to get it going. The river was dark, but not totally dark. Every few hundred yards an opening was cut into the mountain to access the river. The people of Shiska Frok had cut the openings to get light and fishing boat access to the river.

The three tavern escapees had only been on the river for a few minutes when they noticed the water was rising. Jeonk said, "Shok shut down the motor for a minute."

With the noise of the motor quieted they could hear the rumble of rushing water behind. The river traveled through a mountain and its watershed was in some other mountains they didn't know about. It had been raining in the other mountains and the water was coming at them like a fast freight train down the river tunnel. Shok started the motor as fast as he could and yelled, "I'm heading for the next opening."

The water kept its rapid rise as they closed in on the opening cut into the mountain. During their quick trip, the water had risen so high Shok wasn't sure the boat could make it out of the opening if they could get to it. The roar of the water forcing itself along the roof of the tunnel behind them completely silenced the noise of the boat motor as they neared the opening. The boat moved faster with each passing second, forced ahead by the tremendous current of the swelling river. Shok had to fight the boat to keep it on the same side of the river as the next opening.

As the boat approached the opening, he turned the tiller toward it and gunned the motor as fast as it would go. They had to duck to stay below the roof of the tunnel, and they barely made it to the opening. The boat, pushed by the current, slammed into the far side of the opening to the outside. The boat motor stalled as the wall of water hit the opening.

The force of the water catapulted them to the outside. The boat fell out of the huge stream of water fifteen feet from the opening cut into the tunnel. All three of them sat in the water filled boat with the huge stream of water going over their heads.

Yonasa was stunned by the drop from the gargantuan stream of water, and too terrified to move. Jeonk reached toward her, grabbed her around the middle and carried her upside down like a sack of flour until they reached a dry spot that was high enough to keep her from drowning in the water streaming out of the mountain. Jeonk plopped her butt down on a rock until she could gather her terrified mind back to its original peace.

Shok and Jeonk checked their pistols and spare charge packs to make sure they hadn't lost anything important during the river ride. Both of them found they still had all of the necessities of life.

Yonasa had been pretty good so far. She traveled well, complained little and took orders quickly, but Shok could tell she wasn't in a very good mood; the adventure was taking its toll. She was soaked to the skin. Her hair looked like it had been put on backward. The river had washed her hair forward and it was going in all directions from there. Jeonk had carried her with her butt in the air, her feet and hands hanging down and then plopped her on a rock. Shok put on his very best, terrified, angry girl, conciliatory manner and said, "All things considered, you look pretty good."

She stammered, "You, you, pretty, pretty, we were nearly killed. I want to go home."

Jeonk could see Shok's sorry excuse for diplomacy wasn't doing very well with her. He said soothingly, "We'll take you there as soon as we find out where it is."

She stood up, looked at them with disbelief and pointed, "It's there! There! Over there! On the hill!"

Jeonk and Shok looked to where she was pointing and, sure enough, there was a city about a days march away on the top of a hill. Shok asked, "What's the name of the city you live in?"

"Orklssk," Yonasa answered, "I live there with my parents. I was going to Gaplit but I've changed my mind." Her shoulders lowered, and her eyes began to fill with tears, as she quietly repeated, "I want to go home!"

It wasn't easy to go around the water spewing out of the mountain but they finally found a wandering path toward Orklssk. Going around the water changed the one-day trek into two but the trail they followed seemed to be reasonably flat and it went through huge patches of succulent berries. The three of them had eaten only one meal since the crash and the berries tasted good.

The berries were easy to pick from the outside perimeter of the miserable brush like vines they were on. The vines sprouted four-inch thorns covering the thick intertwined vine growths with the berries on them. Yonasa called them dagger berries because of the long thorns on the vines. Some of the smaller berry patches were one hundred yards across.

The three of them covered ground at a pretty good clip for several hours and picked the easy to get berries as they walked. They were quietly ambling along a trail that moved along the bottom of a hill with the hill on one side and a particularly large berry patch on the other. They began hearing noises around them, animal growls and scuffing noises, but they didn't see anything immediately.

As they came to the middle of the berry patch, four animals that looked like very large saber toothed pit bulls came at them. The four animals stopped a few yards from them, two on the trail ahead of them and two behind. At the same time, several men charged over the hill brandishing clubs. The three were trapped on all sides by the attackers, the saber toothed pit bulls, and the impenetrable berry patch.

Jeonk grabbed Yonasa and pushed her between Shok and himself. Both of them whipped out their pistols and shot the big-toothed animals. The charging men were close enough to use their clubs, but were surprised by the laser pistols. Jeonk smacked the first one in the nose then hit another attacker with the attacker he had just smacked. He tossed the first attacker deep into the berry patch.

One of the attackers swung a club at Shok, but he missed. Shok hit him on the head with his pistol. He holstered his pistol as he grabbed the club arm of the second one and brought the club down on the club wielders head. By that time, Jeonk had thrown two more of them into the berry patch. Yonasa was screaming bloody murder as Shok drew his pistol and shot one of the attackers in his club-swinging arm.

The men going after Jeonk chickened out in their attack on him for some strange reason. Maybe it was because Jeonk was laughing at them for trying to beat him with a club. Instead of just running away to save their lives, the men came after Shok.

Jeonk grabbed the screaming Yonasa around the middle and shoved her backward to keep her out of the way so he could help Shok. Yonasa fell into a mud puddle beside one of the dead saber tooth pit bulls. Yonasa stopped screaming in fear so she could begin screaming in anger.

The remaining attackers turned their backs on Jeonk, as though he would go away if they ignored him. As Shok shot the front ones in their club arms, Jeonk picked up the rear ones and threw them into the berry patch. Within a minute or so from the beginning of the attack, Jeonk and Shok had all of them in the berry patch. Neither thought any of the attackers were dead but no one was going into the dagger berry patch to check their pulse, nor wait to see how they got out of the berry patch.

Yonasa was frustrated, angry, unhappy and in tears. All she wanted to do was visit her friends in Gaplit; she got Jeonk and Shok instead. She had been a cute girl, even with her messed up hair and dirty clothes, until Jeonk turned her into a mud-ball. That was the straw that broke the camels back for her. She walked silently ahead of both of them, but still within a safe distance to them, with determined strides in her squishy shoes. She refused to speak to either of them.

With Orklssk within easy, and a safe walking distance, one of the searching Argan fighters spotted them walking and landed only a few yards away. The pilot told them he had already notified the fleet that they had been found, and the shuttle would pick them up in a few minutes.

Aslain and Alice were on the shuttle piloted by Plask and Rakoup. The wives checked them over for new laser burns and knife cuts as they kissed them warmly and told them how glad they were they hadn't drowned in the river.

The two women turned to Yonasa before Shok or Jeonk had a chance to explain how insignificant their stroll through Shiska Frok had been. Yonasa spewed out her entire account of the adventure in Shiska Frok in a veritable explosion of words, "The shuttle crashed, then that big blue man and the little pink one took me to a town built inside a mountain. We were supposed to eat dinner and then leave but they got in a gunfight with a bunch of men in the restaurant.

"The big blue man found a river inside the mountain while the short pink man finished shooting the men in the restaurant. We had to leave the restaurant in a stolen boat they found inside the mountain. I thought we were going to drown because the water got so high and it piled up behind us like an avalanche."

She pointed to Shok and said, "That pink man ran the boat out of a hole in the side of mountain the water was going out of, and the motor stopped, but the river pushed us outside and dumped us on the ground.

"They both laughed, then that big blue one picked me up like a sack and dumped me on a rock. I was tired and wet and I was scared half to death but they made me walk and all we found to eat was dagger berries. While we were eating dagger berries, Shirskas with big teeth got in front of us and behind us. Those two shot the Shirskas and then men with clubs came over the hill.

"Those two laughed at the men with clubs and put their guns away. That big blue man hit some of the men and threw them in the dagger berry patch. That little pink one took clubs away from some others and hit them on their heads with their own clubs. Then the men with clubs ran away from the big blue one and all of them tried fighting with the little pink one.

"The big blue one put his hand on my stomach and shoved me backwards into a big mud puddle with a dead Shirska in it. The pink man drew his pistol and shot the men with clubs in the arms they were holding the clubs with, and the big blue man threw them all into the dagger berry patch." Yonasa stopped talking, her shoulders drooped, her lips trembled, and she said, "I look terrible, my new dress is ruined, and all I wanted to do was go home after the shuttle crash. I didn't want to go to those fights."

She ask Aslain and Alice if they would take her home before Jeonk and Shok could get her into any more trouble. Plask pacified her a little. He told her he would tell the king of Arga on them for being such high-level troublemakers.

Rakoup remarked, "I told you Shiska Frok would attack you if you didn't attack it first."

"You were right." Jeonk retorted. "Shiska Frok attacked us with its people, environment and animals. That's a pretty thorough attack."

Plask added, "And you pissed off one of the, otherwise, friendly inhabitants of Iklug. Its a good thing we're leaving soon."

Yonasa returned to the Royal Cruiser with them so Alice could help her clean up and give her some new clothing before they took her home. Supplying her with new clothing was no problem; she and Alice were about the same size. Alice gave her a tour of the Royal Cruiser so her trip to Gaplit wouldn't be a total loss. She seemed reasonably satisfied when she said good-bye and she was thrilled with her ride in the cruiser's shuttle that flew her to her parent's home. She's a cute girl and everyone hoped she would find a nice quiet husband someday.

10

THE VEOLSH PLANET

Their next stop was on the Veolsh planet. They would do the business they wanted to do with the nations of the planets of Oglak, Veolsh, Paraca, Nasti, Castu and Zopra from the Galactic Forum complex. Most of the nations on those planets were still rebuilding their societies after the Veolsh War. They might not have much to trade at the present but they would in the future. Chosteel said they were no longer the down and out freedom fighters they had first met, but it takes a long time to build new industries from destroyed industries or no industries. They would probably be looking for hardware to help them build. Shok and Jeonk would sound out their present needs and future trade possibilities from the Argan offices in the Forum Complex.

They put the Royal Cruiser into a holding orbit over the Veolsh planet with no plan to land and impress anyone. It, and they, had been there before. They didn't expect anyone to pay very much attention to them just because they had arrived. One of the Cruiser shuttles was used to travel to the planet's surface. The Shuttle could use the Forum Complex's landing area.

Jeonk and Shok did their diplomatic duty by going to the various offices of those they knew best, and gave their friendly greetings to everyone. The forum was humming with ordinary activities. None of the nations seemed to be having any unusual problems. There were no threats of war. The Forum staff was efficiently addressing the Forum's usual international contacts. Everything was pretty dull, but the dullness made an ideal atmosphere for them to conduct business.

Jeonk, Rakoup, Plask and Shok spent their days in the Forum's communication center talking to businessmen on the various planets. A pretty accurate picture of the area's business dealings was being built from those contacts. The new nations had a need for supplies the cargo line could supply them with, and there was an emerging picture of future manufactured products that would have a need for interplanetary cargo transportation. Jeonk and Shok were also getting a feel for future sales potential, and how they could fit themselves into that future. Many of the new businesses needed development money and Jeonk and Shok were entrepreneurs. They were frequent lenders of money to emerging businesses large and small.

They planned a one-time landing of the large cargo ship on each planet to give the businessmen an idea of how much cargo could be handled by one ship. After the show and tell landing, they would try to coordinate the incoming and outgoing cargo for the big ship at one port of entry on each planet until the cargo business increased enough to make a profit from more ports of entry. The different planets' businessmen were excited and eager for an interplanetary cargo line. They showed a great deal of interest in Jeonk and Shok's plans for future business.

Jeonk and Shok spent weeks receiving and answering questions from the six planets. The only interplanetary shipping done on any of the planets was for one time special order needs. The new cargo line was the first mass shipping of manufactured products on an interplanetary basis the businessmen would have an opportunity to use.

Shok was getting tired of the incessant explaining of cargo movement details, and Jeonk felt the same way. Fortunately, the dull stuff was about to end with the arrival of a spaceship from a planet named, Tuplej.

Tuplej was new to them. No one at the Forum had heard of it, but Tuplej had obviously heard of the Galactic Forum. Tuplej's location was more toward the center of the galaxy than the planets the Forum people were familiar with. They discovered the Veolsh Council had visited it on rare occasions. It was one of the planets Doskel had monitored in his search for the pirates.

They also discovered Tuplej was where the Veolsh Council had been given the fast corsair it used to outrun the Argan cruisers. The corsair Shok had shot down on the planet Nordic had come from Tuplej. The visitors in the spaceship from Tuplej were having trouble with the same government that supplied the Veolsh with the corsair. They had come to the Galactic Forum to petition for membership and protection from the same nation on their home planet.

Argan ears perked up pretty high at the news of a belligerent with a technology they couldn't match. Arga had their scientists working on the technology, but it would be a long time before they cracked the problem of super speed. Jeonk and Shok, with Plask and Rakoup, knew what they were going to do, but they had to go slowly and follow the standard Forum guidelines. The visitor had applied to the Forum for help.

It took another week for the Forum to convene, and two more days to conclude the discussions with the leader from the nation of Supek on the planet Tuplej. The Forum decided it didn't have enough information about the situation to act immediately. It appeared, at first glance, that Supek was a beleaguered nation that fulfilled the other requirements for membership in the Galactic Forum. The Galactic Forum decided to send an expeditionary fleet to Tuplej for the additional information they would need. The expeditionary fleet would consist of those nations willing to make the journey and return the information to the Forum.

Arga favored a large fleet due to the possibility of war with a nation using superior technology. Some of the members thought a large fleet might start the war instead of merely assess the situation on Tuplej. Shurs Coshti, the President of Supek, agreed with Arga. Jeonk immediately suggested that Arga could supply two of its fleets for the project. He would bring in Shok's fleet from Perlta; which, strangely, was already on its way to the Forum. Jeonk would add the remainder of Rakoup's fleet, presently flying, just as strangely, alongside of Shok's.

Chosteel had finished his war with the two idiots who had planned their takeover of the planet Egrin. Sompla and Crustpla had new leaders who were less inclined to be a bother to their neighbors and the planets spaceships were more evenly distributed. There were a lot fewer of them to distribute after Chosteel finished but those he didn't destroy were more evenly divided.

Chosteel, and the planet Paraca, wanted to put Chosteel's flagship cruiser and its fighters on the team. The Oglaks and a few of the Veolsh nations wanted some of their ships in the fleet. Some of the other Forum nations wanted a part of the action. President Coshti would be returning to Tuplej in the Royal Cruiser, escorted by thirty-two Argan cruisers and another fifty fighting ships of various sizes and nationalities. The spaceship Coshti arrived in would be tagging along behind the Royal Cruiser, if it could keep up.

On the flight to Tuplej, the Argans found President Coshti to be a serious and likable man. They expected the things he told them to be true to the best of his ability to express it. He said his nation wasn't capable of developing the technology his enemy was using. He knew the enemy nation, Pishtup, had given the Veolsh Council one of the fast ships the Argans were interested in, but he didn't know if the Veolsh Council gave anything in return.

The one Shok shot down on Nordic was the only one the Veolsh Council possessed. It was lucky for the Argans that the Veolsh Council didn't get it in time to incorporate its design into their space fleet. The Argans would have lost the Veolsh War if they had.

President Coshti told the Argans his nation had been friendly with the nation of Pishtup, his new enemy, for many generations. Suddenly and for some unknown reason, Pishtup had become belligerent. His nation of Supek was resisting the forceful suggestion that Supek and Pishtup would be better off if they became one nation under the leadership of Pishtup's King, Sot Pah.

Pishtup began increasing its already powerful military forces and Coshti thought they were building to attack. Coshti knew Supek couldn't beat Pishtup in a war and he knew the Galactic Forum's Charter was designed for the protection of sovereign member nations. He decided the best protection for his nation was membership in the Forum. He came to the Forum to petition for membership and that's where things stood, right now.

The Argans had many meetings with their Forum partners and President Coshti on board the Royal Cruiser. They were particularly interested in the military power of Pishtup. President Coshti couldn't tell them very much about the power of Pishtup's space fleet. Pishtup had become very secretive.

Pishtup's spaceship factories and fleet bases were in isolated areas where security was very intense and very little was known about them. The President thought they had a massive number of ships but none as large as Arga's cruisers. He thought the Pishtup military was depending on speed, superior numbers and standard weaponry to insure a victory against anyone they might have problems with.

The Forum plan for entering Supek was simple. They would keep their interplanetary fleet in low orbit over Supek as a warning to Pishtup, land a delegation, and carry on friendly relations with the Supek people. The Royal Cruiser would land and be available for tours by the people. The Forum delegation would get to know as much as possible about Supek and make their assessment of its qualifications for membership in the Forum.

If nothing happened, they would leave at the proper time, giving their assurances to Supek of its membership in and the protection of its Forum membership. If no war began while the Forum fleet was there, they would have no reason to start one and their suspicions would remain suspicions. Supek's Forum membership might be enough to cause Pishtup to back off and leave Supek free. If that happened, so much the better, President Coshti and the Forum's mission would be accomplished.

The Forum team was in Supek for several days enjoying the hospitality of a nation whose main worry was being invaded by its neighboring country. Supek was smaller than Pishtup but both nations were reasonably well off financially. Pishtup had formerly been a constitutional nation. It's many times re-elected leader, Sot Pah, seemed a very popular man.

Sot Pah had been friendly with Supek until two years prior to Supek's problems with him. He had become increasingly belligerent from the time he, suddenly, gained a great deal of power. After that time, Sot Pah had become the dictatorial ruler of Pishtup. No one in Supek understood the reason for his change in power and attitude, but they were receiving increasingly larger doses of its affects as time passed.

The Forum people who had come to help President Coshti and Supek didn't know how much Sot Pah knew about the Forum nations or Arga. The forum visitors to Supek were about to discover that dictator Sot Pah of Pishtup didn't consider them to be a serious threat to his war plans.

It was two hours before dawn when the battle stations alert sounded throughout the fleet. Pishtup had begun launching approximately one thousand corsair spaceships in attack formations. As they formed their squadrons, it became obvious that the Argan fleet was the target.

The Royal Cruiser was on the ground near the presidential residence. Jeonk immediately put it in the air to free the two Argan fleets from their protective formation and get them positioned for battle. The Argan cruisers were ordered to scan as much of Pishtup as they could while the battle was on and to destroy the incoming corsairs as they came into range.

The launch of the Forum and Arga s' five hundred and forty fighters, spread over a wide area around the fleet before the beginning of the battle. Pishtup's corsairs crossed the Supek border and the fighting quickly became fast and furious.

The Argan cruisers appeared almost stationary in their lower atmosphere positions compared to the speed of the corsairs. The Argans raised their fleet's altitude to one thousand miles above the surface. The fast little corsairs were too many and too fast for the cruisers to handle at low altitude. The cruisers needed more room to spread the fleet for better firing patterns. They left their fighters at the lower level to fight off the corsairs while the cruisers changed position.

Two hundred of the corsairs followed the fleet to the higher altitude. They became luminescent and faster in the upper atmosphere. The Argan cruisers did everything they could to hit the corsairs but they missed them frequently because of the corsairs' great speed. The cruisers computers were working at their maximum speed of acquisition or above the maximum in many cases. The fighters did better against the corsairs in the lower atmosphere.

The fleet commanders ordered the cruiser's computerized target acquisition systems off to see if their gunners could hit the corsairs with more affect using manually aimed lasers and pulse cannons. Amazingly, the gunners hit much more often using the manual-firing mode. The number of corsairs dwindled quickly as pulse cannons and lasers burned holes through their outer skin. Just when cruiser commanders thought they had the battle under their control, five hundred more corsairs launched from Pishtup.

The corsairs were equipped with very strong pulse cannons but no lasers. They caused damage to the fleet cruisers in the primary heat shield area of each cruiser and some cruisers suffered damage to their secondary heat shields. The Royal Cruiser, which had a thicker and different metal on its outer skin, received several hits but no penetration of its primary heat shields.

Jeonk gave the order to pull the two fleets out at flank speed. There were to many corsairs for the fleet to survive if they continued the fight using their present tactics. The Argan fleet needed its maximum speed to close the gap between its speed and the speed of the corsairs. At Arga's cruisers' maximum speed, their cruisers' computerized firing systems were able to hit the corsairs.

Since the Royal Cruiser could survive their fire, Jeonk used it to make a scanning run across Pishtup to see what and where their power was on the surface.

The Royal Cruiser went in low and fast across Pishtup. The corsairs returning from space and those coming up from the surface tried to knock it out. The dragon-spit effect they had as they entered space was missing at lower altitudes and their maximum speed was slower. The best Argan gunners were on the Royal Cruiser and they made good use of their talents.

The corsairs couldn't use their pulse cannons from behind the Royal Cruiser. Its thrusters burned too hot for their pulse cannons to be effective. They had to pull out to the side or above and below the Royal Cruiser to hit it with their pulse cannons. The Cruiser's gunners put them down at a rapid rate, but the Cruiser still received many hits before it cleared Pishtup. Jeonk had what he came for. The scan data would be valuable for the return engagement. Jeonk ordered the ship into outer space at maximum thrust.

The corsairs battled the Royal cruiser and the fleet into deep space, until they began losing too many corsairs as the fleet reached flank speed. The Argans discovered the corsair's firing systems were less reliable at the fleet's faster speeds. The corsairs began missing more often than they hit. The fleet downed approximately one hundred of the attacking corsairs before the corsairs broke off and returned to their bases in Pishtup.

SPACE LINE BY MARIVIN E. FOX

Arga's retreating fleets had lost most of their downed fighters over Supek. Jeonk talked by radio with President Coshti to make sure the downed fighters would be found and the survivors treated for their medical problems. He was careful to ask for the same treatment to be given to crews of spaceships from the Forum member nations. He, also, informed the President that the Argans and the Forum would return with a large enough fleet to take care of his Sot Pah problem.

Shok suggested the nation of Supek move enough troops to its common border with Pishtup to prevent a ground invasion while Supek waited for their return. He hoped the President would follow his suggestion.

Arga lost seventy fighters in the battle. Each of their thirty-six cruisers was damaged but they lost no cruisers. Half of the ships from the Forum nations were either destroyed or severely damaged. Chosteel's cruiser was badly damaged but still space worthy. The Royal Cruiser received some buckling on the outer heat shield from the corsairs pulse cannons but the ships battle integrity was intact. It would be thoroughly checked for damage that wasn't obvious.

Jeonk and Shok talked about the coming battle while they waited for the scan data to be piped from ship to ship, collated, and made ready for evaluation. Jeonk remarked, "Those Dragon Spit Corsairs are the best ships we've ever been up against. They have superior speed and an excellent armament system. We must deal with this new technology, whatever the cost."

Shok agreed, "If we had kept our cruisers in lower orbit and tried to fight them off, we would have lost the fleet. When we meet again, they'll know they can't beat us in open space, and we can't beat them in the lower atmosphere. I think we can bring in enough power to overwhelm them, unless Sot Pah has a very large supply of Dragon spit Corsairs. He thinks he has enough or he wouldn't have attacked."

"Our Black Hole fighters can probably handle them one on one," Jeonk added. They're tougher and nearly as fast but we don't have enough of them to win a war against a large number of Dragon Spit Corsairs. We can't afford to lose the cruisers it will cost us to beat them in a head to head war. We need a battle plan. The scan data should be ready by now. Lets see what we're up against."

The scan data collected from the fleet cruisers' data banks, including the Royal Cruiser's scan run, was alarming. The nation of Pishtup was one huge armament factory. They had amassed an armada of twelve thousand Dragon Spit Corsairs. All of their bases were in remote areas that were easy to secure from prying eyes. Their assembly factories were near a Pishtup border that was farthest from Supek and the factories seemed very busy. Pishtup might prove to be more of a problem than the Veolsh Imperial Cruisers in the Veolsh War. The Argans were very sure they could win with the help of the Galactic Forum, but the cost in personnel and spacecraft might bankrupt the Forum nations.

Jeonk said, "We need a plan."

Plask, Rakoup, Iliaska, Aslain, Alice, two Fleet Admirals, Chosteel, Jeonk and Shok were in a large conference compartment on the Royal Cruiser looking at the problem shown on the scan data displays. Rakoup asked, "Do you think Sot Pah will overrun Supek before we can get back?"

"I don't think so," Jeonk replied. "He wanted Supek as an intact present to drop in his hands. He intended to frighten them into a bloodless surrender by showing them they couldn't win. He wants more territory and financial power, not more ruin. What do you think Shok? You have a plan yet?"

"I think your right about Sot Pah and Supek," Shok responded. "I've been knocking this plan around in my head. I'll tell you about it and you help me iron out the details. We'll need to bring the Admiralty into it of course but much of it can be worked out for their approval before we land at Poshalla.

Sot Pah has a good tactical mind but it's obvious he's a new kid on the block when it comes to war. For instance, he has equipped his corsair fleet with pulse cannons but no lasers. If he were more experienced, his corsairs would have both. Pishtup's offensive weapons are good but we didn't scan anything looking into space for defensive purposes. He may not be aware of what we did to him when we scanned Pishtup during the battle.

"Jeonk and I have been doing some research on the original Black Cruiser at Meho. We've been working on a pulse cannon deflector grid for all of our cruisers. The deflectors worked fine on scale models. Our engineers went a step further and made the deflectors into pulse absorbers. The absorbers channel pulse cannon hits into a storage system that can be used as the power system for a Super Pulse Cannon. It's so efficient the SPC may need to be fired occasionally with no target acquired to prevent power surges from blowing out the absorber system. The engineers have the new system installed on the Black Cruiser and it's waiting for a chance to be tested. This is the chance.

"Next, we need to take the advice given by a Chinese General named Sun Tzu, 'Make a furor in the east; strike in the west'. Sot Pah put his corsair factories as far From Supek as he could get them. The factories are Sot Pah's East. We should make a fleet strike on them first. Arga will have to carry that part of the battle.

"The Forum fleets are closer than we are but, unfortunately, the Forum spacecraft are no match for the Dragon Spit Corsairs. Arga will have to carry the major load of the air battle with the Dragon spits. The Forum fleets will have to serve in support capacities.

"There are things we need to consider along with our commitment to a space war. Supek, and the Forum nations must occupy Pishtup. Sot Pah must be killed. If Sot Pah lives, he will keep his core of supporters for a later try and he'll do a better job the next time.

"The Forum's ground troops are the best fighters in the business. We need the Forum ground troops to help Supek invade Sot Pah's West, his border with Supek. The Forum troops and Supek's army will beat Pishtup on the ground with air cover provided by Arga and the Forum nations,"

"Your a long way from finishing off the Dragon Spits," Plask interjected. "What will they be doing while Pishtup is being invaded."

"The first thing to happen is the Black Cruiser dives on Pishtup," Shok explained. "It splatters a few factories in Pishtup's East. It also causes a few earthquakes with gravity pulses. That will disrupt their communications networks. We've done it before and we know it works.

"While the Black Ship is doing that, five hundred black hole fighters hit Pishtup's Dragon Spit bases on the eastern border and then head for space. When the black hole fighters clear the area, three fleets of cruisers, in three waves, make high speed, low level strafing runs on the factories and bases in Pishtup's East. The cruisers fly back into space as quickly as they can. That should draw most of Sot Pah's Dragon Spits out of their holes and after our cruisers.

"After the three fleets draw enough of Sot Pah's armada into space, a fourth Argan fleet will fly over central Pishtup at low level with all thrusters at one hundred percent, hitting bases we will select from the scan data. When the fleet finishes hitting the bases, it will immediately hit max thrust, leave the surface it has just creamed, and get into space behind the Dragon Spits following the other three fleets.

SPACE LINE BY MARIVIN E. FOX

"The fourth fleet will hit the Dragon Spits in space form the rear, immediately after the first three fleets hit them from the front. Our concentration of fire and destruction on Pishtup's farthest border will make Sot Pah think we are preparing to invade him from his East.

"Sot Pah will have to shift his mobile armament and his remaining Dragon Spit Corsairs to protect his East. The Black Cruiser will be unharmed, and maybe even unnoticed, at this point. I'll signal the Forum fleet from the Black Cruiser. The Forum fleet will be waiting in deep space on the Nordic side of Tuplej to come into Supek and Pishtup. The Forum fleet will download its troops, and immediately begin the invasion of Pishtup from the Supek border. That is Pishtup's West. The troops will have a spaceship umbrella made up from Argan and Forum fighters."

"If all of that works," Chosteel remarked, "and I was Sot Pah, I would surrender before you finished the fourth strafing run across Pishtup."

"Anyone with a better plan," Shok replied, "put it on the table. If you want changes, put them on the table."

Plask asked, "Shok, do you mind if we think it over for a while? All of this hit and run stuff sounds like a bunch of Oglaks hitting a Veolsh outpost."

"No it doesn't," Jeonk said. "It sounds like you and Rakoup hitting Prssk. I think Shok's plan is good but I want one change. Before the Black Ship goes in, I want Doskel's fleet to make one of their famous lights out raids. I want them to blow every circuit they can in one very quick low level run across Pishtup."

"If they do that," Shok objected, "the Dragon Spits will be following them before our Black Hole Fighters can engage them. The Black Ships Gravity Disrupters will take care of their communications. How about letting Doskel's fleet be the one going across Pishtup in the fourth strafing run? He can blow all its circuits I don't hit with the Black ship, as he passes, if there are any left to hit. It will give the invasion the same protection if Doskel goes first or last."

Jeonk thought it over, and said, "That sounds OK. You and I can direct the advance of the invasion from the Black Cruiser. Chosteel can help us if he doesn't have a different plan for himself; he's more familiar with the Forum battle formations than we are."

Aslain objected, "You have very competent Fleet Admirals who would welcome the chance to direct the invasion from your Black Ship. Admiral Brak knows as much about the Black Cruiser as either of you. Why do you and Shok need to be at ground zero every time something happens?"

Alice wasn't pleased either; "You and Shok would do better if you directed these multinational war activities from a location farther from the direct fire of Pishtup's pulse cannons."

Jeonk rubbed the top of his head and pretended he was considering a revision in the plan before he answered, "Shok and I are the only ones totally familiar with the Black Ships special equipment operations and inter-fleet communications setup. Admiral Brak knows as much as we do about using the Black ship as a weapon but he isn't that familiar with its special equipment. The ship kept us safe during the Veolsh war and it will keep us safe in this one. It's the only ship capable of doing what we need to be done. Shok and I need to be where we can handle critical situations fast. We need to be in the Black Ship to do that."

Before any more objections could surface, Chosteel asked, "You will need a about two hundred thousand ground troops for the invasion. How will you get them from the Forum planets to Supek? We can move troops but not fast enough for the lightning operation your planning."

"Arga has enough troop carriers for its part of the operation," Shok replied. "We can also use the large cargo ship we brought to the Forum. I'm sure you saw it. The cargo ship breaks into three sections and each section will handle more than one hundred thousand troops and their equipment on its sixty decks. The sections fly independently and we considered troop movements when they were built. Each section has a large galley and enough perishable food for the troops can be stored in its refrigerators. We can fly the separate sections to whatever staging areas are being used for troop buildups.

"The troops commanders will have to supply the food and comforts of life while the troops are in route and waiting for the invasion. They can live on the cargo ships until the invasion begins."

Chosteel had one more critical question, "How much time do we have for the preparation?"

"Ninety days," Shok answered, "from right now. I figure Sot Pah will be repairing the damage we did to him for that amount of time. He will be preparing for war while he repairs the damage. The ground invasion of Supek will happen when he feels his troops are battle ready. If my guess about the time for his preparations is correct, we have those ninety days to beat him to the draw."

Chosteel was leery of the timetable, "We may be able to put it together but it will be a sloppy operation. We need another month for a clean shot at it."

"Get as many Oglaks as you can on the operation, Shok advised. "The Oglaks have a standing army that's always ready. They like night fighting but they can fight in daylight when they must. Fill in with whoever is ready. We have ninety days. I don't think we have an extra thirty days. If Sot Pah doesn't invade Supek, we'll catch him by surprise. If he invades, it will be in ninety days."

Shok watched the old warrior change from a questioner to a planner. His face changed to a steel hardness before he spoke, "I'll put out a general call to arms in the Forum. Put your three cargo sections under my command. I want one of them sitting on Paraca, one on Oglak and one on Veolsh. The majority of the troops will be from those three planets. I need troops I understand and trust in this battle and those three fill that bill. Troops from the other planets will have to come to one of the three planets for transportation. If they can't make it on time, I'll have to leave without them but we'll have enough troops."

Jeonk said, "Our brand new cargo ships are under your command. They'll be where you want them to be before you need them. I can put a Fleet with each of them for protection."

"We can protect them using our own resources," Chosteel replied. "I better get back to my own ship and start moving things around to meet Shok's schedule."

Jeonk reminded him, "If you need anything at all, ask. If we have it, you'll get it."

Chosteel answered, "I know Jeonk, I know."

Plask and Rakoup had been pretty quiet so far. After Chosteel left, Plask opened up, "Someone will have to be with Coshti in Supek. He's the guy under the gun and he will need someone to coordinate activities for him and keep him from thinking we aren't coming if things get rough in his neighborhood. That someone can't be Jeonk and Shok for a change, it's my job."

Rakoup said, "My fleet is damaged and won't be battle ready in time for the attack. I'm going with Plask. Two of us will provide more certainty than one and Coshti knows both of us."

"You can't get to Supek without Sot Pah knowing your there," Iliaska remarked hotly. "We don't have a spaceship he wouldn't know is from Arga. He will shoot you down before you can land."

Plask answered, "We'll use that hopped up Paracan Corsair Shok has hid in the basement of his Lersta cottage. It looks different than any corsair Sot Pah has ever seen. We'll go in like rich tourist from Paraca."

Alice turned to Shok with a look of disbelief, "Kevin Kelly, you don't have a hopped up Paracan corsair hid in our basement! Do you?"

Shok responded as benignly as he could under the circumstances, "It's not exactly in the basement. It's in a cave hangar you can get to from a secret door in the basement, but it isn't, really, in the basement. I would have told you about it but you have a thing against fast corsairs. I thought we might need one sometime. It's better to have one around than to be sorry we don't have one around, when it's needed!"

"I guess I had better start checking under the beds for corsairs," Alice retorted. "I don't know where they'll turn up next. Aslain, you should begin a check for secret doors in the palace, you may find a few corsairs you don't know you have."

Rakoup finished laughing before he said; "Then it's settled. We'll use one of Shok's spare Paracan Corsairs from his private stock. I'm sure it's a vintage model he's been saving for some special emergency, and this is a special emergency. Alice will be glad to see the damn thing gone from the basement, where it's probably just gathering cobwebs."

Iliaska ended the corsair discussion with her adamant demand, "I'm going with you to Supek."

Plask spared Rakoup the argument, saying. "We're not taking a woman into a war zone. Anyway, you have to stay with Aslain; she needs you."

Iliaska wasn't so easily denied. She retorted, "We 'women' have already been in the war zone. We had to retreat to keep from being killed and the women didn't retreat first. The women retreated with the men, and there is no reason they can't advance with the men."

Plask took a more serious look at Iliaska before he replied, "Our women are brave enough, tough enough and smart enough to do most of the things we men do. Over the years they have died in many places for their God, Their families and their country. They make great sacrifices against monumental odds during their lives. You women are our treasures. Without you, we have nothing to win, and nothing to lose. If you are with us in a battle, our first priority becomes your safety, and we lose the battle because of it. When we know your safe, our attention is on the battle, and we win! We cannot have women in battle if we can prevent it--and we will not--if we can prevent it. You were here because we didn't know there would be a battle. You can not go with us to Supek."

That must have been the first time Iliaska, a very strong women, understood why Argan men didn't allow their women in battle. She walked over to Plask, hugged him and gave him a kiss on the cheek, then did the same to her husband Sitak Rakoup. She said, "You two have fun in Shok's corsair. I'll stay here with Aslain and Alice. Maybe I can help them find the other hidden corsairs."

The plan to help Supek was finished. All that remained was the uninteresting grunt work, logistics, studying scan maps, timing, coordination, landing sights, targets and a thousand other things one must consider in any big operation. Ninety days is never long enough for interplanetary war preparations but, somehow, fighting men manage to manage with the time they have.

11

THE SAVE SUPEK OPERATION

The ninety days passed with no insurmountable problems and the operation was on the move. The four Argan fleets came at Pishtup on its blind side. Chosteel's troops were ready for battle, and standing off on the Nordic side of Tuplej. Chosteel had fifty Paracan, fifty Oglak and fifty Veolsh corsairs protecting the three cargo ships.

The advancing fleets received word from Plask and Rakoup that Sot Pah was massing troops along the Supek border for an invasion. Shok's ninety-day projection was about right for Sot Pah's invasion.

Sot Pah seemed to think he had solved his problem of outside protection of Supek from his invasion. He was demanding a surrender from Supek before his invasion, and he had given President Coshti one week to reply. With the arrival of the Argan and Forum help, the battle to save Supek would begin one day before Supek's week was up.

Jeonk and Shok were in the Black Ship coming into Pishtup just ahead of the five hundred Black Hole Fighters. The Black Ship's scanners showed the Black Hole Fighters descending on Pishtup with a pounding attack on the targeted factories along Pishtup's eastern border. Burning buildings and explosions sent smoke skyward from dozens of locations along that border.

In minutes, a massive number of Sot Pah's corsairs were in the air to repel the attack. The Black Hole Fighters had hit hard. They lleft burning wreckage in their wake, then broke off the attack and retreated to outer space with the corsairs in hot pursuit.

Shok held the Black Cruiser low to keep it under the two incoming fleets as they passed overhead. The Black Cruiser was hardly noticed. The first Argan fleet of sixteen cruisers came into Pishtup low and fast from the southern border. The fleet was spread in a wide formation to give its cruisers the maximum firing platform to hit the targeted corsair bases as the fleet swept to the north.

Another fleet of Sot Pah's Dragon Spit Corsairs came in behind the fleet of cruisers to engage them but they were too late to prevent the massive damage to their bases. The second fleet of corsairs followed the first Argan Fleet into deep Space.

The Black Ship was still flying low and ignored as the Second Argan Fleet came on Scan from the South, with the third close behind it. Both fleets were spread in wide formations over virgin battle territory to cause the maximum damage on the ground targets. They, like the first, blasted their way across Pishtup; spreading exploding corsairs and burning military space equipment behind them as they passed.

More corsairs came after the two fleets but this time they came from the border near Supek. So far the plan was working; Pishtup had begun to pull the power of its invasion away from Supek.

The Black Ships holoscanners showed the Pishtup troops beginning to move away from Supek's border to the eastern border of Pishtup. At that moment, Rakoup came on the radio saying, "Jeonk, the Pishtup troops are beginning to pull away from the border." That was the moment they had been waiting for in the Black Ship.

"Do you have their communications center on target?" Jeonk asked.

"Twenty seconds to target." replied Shok.

Jeonk instructed the technician, "Set the Magnetic Field Disrupter for a force fifteen and prepare to fire."

"On target in five seconds." Shok warned.

"Fire now!" Jeonk ordered. "We're close enough."

The technician fired as Jeonk and Shok monitored the command holograph. The earthquake caused by the Disrupter's blast at low level put the communications center out of business. Its antennas swayed, then collapsed from the force of the quake and the main building lost one of its sides. Shok gave Doskel the OK to cross Pishtup and blow as many electrical circuits as he could.

Doskel was putting the Pishtup communication system out of business. The Galactic Forum battle commanders knew Sot Pah had already ordered his troops away from the invasion of Supek. The Pishtup army was regrouping to defend Pishtup's east border from the wrongly suspected ground invasion by the Forum nations. When Sot Pah discovered what a terrible mistake that was, the Argans didn't want him to have enough communications capability left to countermand his first order.

Doskel's fleet was supposed to clinch the communications deal by blowing Sot Pah's radios throughout the country. Even Sot Pah's hand held radios wouldn't be worth a damn. Doskel had been real good at that in the past and he would undoubtedly do a good job this time.

The Black Ship was no longer unnoticed. It had become an obnoxious earthquake machine and Sot Pah's troops intended to make it pay the price. Thirty Dragon Spits came directly at it. Shok had to move the Black Ship just as things were getting lively.

The Black Ship's holoscan showed Chosteel's one hundred fifty corsairs coming into Supek with the giant cargo ships behind them. Shok used the Black Ship to draw the thirty Dragon Spits to the east to keep them from noticing the incoming cargo ships and troops.

Doskel spaceships arrived like an electronic avalanche. His sixteen cruisers barreled across Pishtup at one hundred feet above ground with their thrusters at one hundred percent. While they shut down all of Pishtup's electrical systems, the ships thrusters were kicking up everything behind them that wasn't nailed down, and some that were nailed down. The landscape behind each of Doskel's sixteen cruisers looked like major tornado activity. The air was choked with flying debris.

Sot Pah's Dragon Spit Corsairs, that had been on a heading for the Forum's invasion troops, diverted to stop Doskel's fleet from rearranging Pishtup's life of conquest. Doskel' ground tearing attack had pissed off a major portion of Sot Pah's corsair invasion force. Doskel was forced to launch his fighters before he could climb into space. He had so many of Sot Pah's Dragon Spits attacking him, his maxed out cruiser fleet had to fight its way off the planet.

Jeonk and Shok had their own work to consider. They had drawn their very own thirty Dragon Spits to the east and were about to test the Black Ship's new Super Pulse Cannon absorption grids for the first time in battle. If it worked, the Dragon Spits wouldn't be able to hurt the Black Ship and the corsair attack would build up a super charge for the new Super Pulse Cannons.

The Black Ship kept low in the atmosphere as the corsairs made their attack. Jeonk and Shok hoped their low altitude would keep the corsairs from noticing their big, fat, expensive new cargo ships, which were landing as they fired.

The Dragon Spits were good formation fighters. They came at the Black Ship ten at a time, five on the port side, and five on the starboard side. The five on the port side fired and dived under the black Ship. The five on the starboard side fired and climbed over it. They did good work but the ship was undamaged after the first attempt and the pulse cannon chargers were full. The gunners on the Black Ship had to shoot something or vent the charges into the empty air and they chose to shoot something.

The next ten attackers lost six of the ten and the chargers didn't get enough power from the four they missed to fully recharge the cannons. The outer hull of the Dragon Spits was no match for the Super Pulse Cannon. When the Pishtup corsairs were hit with the Super Pulse Cannon, the Dragon Spits came apart like a paper lantern with a bomb going off inside. They made beautiful explosions and their exploding parts caused fatal damage to some of the other corsairs in the same formation.

Jeonk and Shok were proud of their engineers. They decided to let ten more corsairs hit the Black ship to build up the pulse chargers. They could have gotten some of them with the standard pulse cannons on board but they were testing new equipment and didn't want to ruin the test. Everything was fine as the incoming Dragon Spits formed their attack formation.

As the corsairs made their attack run, Shok looked at his global scanner and saw all fifty of the Oglak corsairs coming toward the Black Ship. The Oglaks assumed the Black Ship was in trouble and they were coming to help. Shok turned the gunners loose on the Dragon Spits, using the ship's standard lasers and pulse cannons, as the Oglaks engaged the Dragon Spits.

The Black Ship gunners downed five of the surprised Dragon Spits and the Oglaks took out the rest. The toughness and competence of the Oglak corsairs and their crews surprised Shok, and he and Jeonk didn't have a one of them hidden away. He knew the Oglaks were good on the ground but he had never fought in an air battle with them.

The Oglaks remained in formation as they zeroed in on the Dragon Spits. The Oglaks held their formation and fired on the Dragon Spits as one unit. The Dragon Spits could have outrun them but by the time they figured the Oglaks out, it was too late to run. The surprised Dragon Spits all splattered into the ground at about the same time.

The Oglak corsairs surrounded the Black Ship and escorted it into space for the battle between the Argan cruisers, the Black Hole Fighters and Sot Pah's Dragon Spits who thought they had chased them there.

Shok convinced the Oglaks the Black Ship was all right and the Oglaks should return to Supek to protect the ground troops. The battle the Black Ship was headed for had gotten far from Tuplej's and the Oglaks would be needed by the ground troops more than by the Black Ship. The Oglak pilots wheeled their corsairs and set their course for the ground battle as the space battle came on the Black Ship's scanner.

There were no missiles in this battle. The Dragon Spits didn't carry them and the battle was too close for the Argans to use them. They might target the fast moving Dragon Spits, miss the Spits and hit their own ships.

Shok could see wreckage on his scanners as they approached. Two Argan cruisers were destroyed and their wreckage was getting cold. They had been lost in the first moments of the battle. The Black Ship passed life pods from the cruisers and there were many destroyed Black Hole Fighters showing on the holoscan. They passed several more severely damaged Argan cruisers and many destroyed Dragon Spit corsairs. As the Black Ship flew closer to the battle, there were fewer destroyed Argan spacecraft and more destroyed Dragon Spits.

Shok put the scanner on a longer range to see how the main battle was going. The Dragon Spit's losses had forced the Spits to change their battle formation. Instead of attacking singly at their best battle speed, they were attacking the cruisers in the same formation they used on the Black Ship.

The Argan cruiser gunners and their protecting fighters had become more successful in breaking up the Dragon Spit formations. The Dragon Spits in the new formations became less able to get enough hits in the same place on the same cruiser to punch through their multiple layers of heat shielding. Still, Shok could see the cruisers' sides glowing red from taking hit after hit from the Dragon Spits. The Dragon Spits were slowly losing the battle but they were taking a heavy toll of Argan cruisers and fighters.

Jeonk suggested, "Let's bring the Black Ship into the center of the Dragon Spit formations and use our SPC to end it as quickly as possible."

Shok kicked the thrusters as hard as he could to get the last ounce of power from them while guiding the ship toward the largest concentration of Dragon Spits. The Dragon Spit pilots saw them coming, turned to engage them. Spit pilots pounded the Black Ship as it approached. The Black Ship no longer had a problem with getting enough of a charge for its Super Pulse Cannons. They were continually charged and continually firing. Their new worry was, can the new pulse cannons last with the intense pressure of continuous fire?

The Black Ship bolted through the formation, killing the Dragon Spits as it went. The intense destructive action against the Dragon Spit Corsairs, and the Spits inability to take Shok, Jeonk and their Black Ship out with repeated hits, gave the Dragon Spit pilots a real case of heart burn. More of them wheeled in the Black Ship's direction, giving the Argan cruiser commanders and fighter pilots the relief they needed to reposition.

The cruisers that had survived the Battle began spreading and stacking above and below each other across the center of the battle area. The Argan fighters were focused around the outer perimeter of the thousands of Dragon Spits. The fighters helped the cruiser commanders force the Dragon Spits into two killing zones. Jeonk and Shok watched the cruisers spread twelve wide and three deep across the battlefield. Jeonk boomed, "Shok, you better get us out of here quick; the cruisers are going to sweep this whole area with lasers and pulse cannons."

"I'm kicking it in the butt right now, "Shok boomed back. "Enough corsairs will follow us to keep our pulse cannons charged. I hope we leave enough of them behind so the cruiser sweep can take care of most of them. There must be three or four thousand corsairs in this fleet. We have to get one of these to take home. I have an empty hangar we can put it in."

They barely made it above the sweep before the cruisers began firing. There is nothing comparable to a cruiser sweep. Before every battle, the cruiser commanders hope they can position themselves for a sweep, but they seldom make it. It's a broadside from every ship in the fleet at the same time and it covers a broad area of space. A sweep is simultaneous continuous fire of all cruiser weapons and it is the deadliest concentration of firepower possible from a fleet of spacecraft.

Every ship in the Argan fleet began pounding Sot Pah's Dragon Spit Corsairs, at the same time, with continuous blasts of laser and pulse cannon fire. The blackness of space became daylight bright with the entire battle blazingly displayed. Lasers burned targets as they pierced space like a light show of death. Pulse cannons spewed balls of fire against crews who no longer knew where to fly to escape. Laser lances pierced the hearts of Dragon Spits breathing their last breaths. The eyes of the living watched the lives of the dying disappear. Explosion after explosion crisscrossed the battle area like flash bulbs appearing for a second, and then flinging their debris to join other flashes flinging their debris to graves in space.

The battle was over. The corsairs around the Black Ship and every Dragon Spit Corsair that could manage an escape, headed for home.

The fleets stopped firing and a comforting darkness returned to space, except for the thousands of fires still burning the defeated enemy spaceships. The Argan fleets would see to their wounded and rescue those in the escape pods still drifting desperately through space from Arga's destroyed cruisers. Jeonk and Shok turned the Black Ship's nose toward Supek and the ground war.

Chosteel, the old guerrilla warrior, was in command of the ground war. Jeonk and Shok weren't worried about the ultimate outcome. With Pishtup's space fleet in ruins, the outcome of the war was assured. The Supek side would win, but hundreds of Dragon Spit Corsairs had escaped the fleets' sweep. The Spits could return and support the Pishtup ground troops, and they could cause a massive number of casualties.

Jeonk ordered the undamaged Black Hole Fighters and the fleet fighters that could be spared, to return to Supek with the Black Ship. The four Argan fleets would follow as soon as they recovered their crewmen stranded in space.

Supek's fighter fleet was flimsy by comparison with the Forum's and there were only one hundred fifty ships from Paraca, Oglak and Veolsh to support the ground troops. No one knew how many Dragon Spits Sot Pah held back to attack Supek but they expected it to be more than the number of spaceships the Argans and the Forum had to fight them. Jeonk pushed the Black Ship and the fleet of fighters as hard as he could to bring relief to the ground troops as quickly as possible.

The fighters left the Black Ship high over Pishtup. The fighters would make a dive into the battle from the higher altitude and catch and Dragon Spits by surprise. Shok brought the Black Ship low across the Supek border, aiming for the heaviest concentration of Dragon Spits engaging the Forum's mechanized troops in Pishtup.

The first battle he saw was between a large group of Paracan and Oglak Corsta Ground Attack vehicles under bombardment from Dragon Spit pulse cannons.

The Corsta is a tough nut to crack. It is heavily armored and it can withstand hits from a pulse cannon as long as it doesn't get too many of them. From the top, the Corsta looks like a metal oval with weapons sticking out of it. It travels on six flexible legs attached to tracks that can move it in any direction over rough terrain.

Liquid fuel keeps the Corsta going and it can fly for short distances. Corsta crews try to keep them on the ground because the Corsta uses too much fuel to be kept in the air for long periods. A Corsta can move for days on the ground. In the air, it's good for about three hours. The Oglaks use them for armored personnel carriers and attack vehicles.

Shok saw the array of flashes from the Corstas' guns as he piloted the Black Ship closer to the battle. The Oglaks were hitting the Dragon Spits with steel projectiles from a standard cannon with the impact of a 105 mm artillery shell. The projectile is similar to their machine-gun rounds. It breaks into exploding shards after impact. Nothing lightly armored is likely to survive a hit from it. The Dragon Spits depend on speed and maneuverability; they have almost no armor.

The Corstas kept surprising the Dragon Spits with short jumps into the air followed by high-powered cannon blast that destroyed the Dragon Spit.

The Corstas' crews managed to keep the Pishtup ground troops in retreat by machine-gunning them if they didn't retreat. Causing the retreat of the ground troops was the Corsta crew's mission. Battling the Dragon Spits was just something they had to do while getting the mission completed. The Pishtup ground troops had nothing to counter the Corstas with but their Dragon Spit air cover, and the Dragon Spits were becoming increasingly fewer on the battlefield.

There were downed space ships from every nation strewn across the battlefield. Shok could see burning Corstas behind the front but the advance through Pishtup was slowly and relentlessly proceeding. The Pishtup troops were in a ragged retreat along their entire front, but Pishtup's Dragon Spits were keeping the battle alive for Sot Pah. Shok brought the Black Ship into a covering position for the Oglak Corstas as the Argan fighter fleet dived into the battle and engaged the Dragon spits near the ground.

The Black Ship's Super Pulse Cannons were still charged from the space battle. It's gunners brought down nine of the slow moving Dragon Spits before the others realized the Black Ship was back in the battle. The surviving Spits wheeled, and gained speed to disengage from their battle with the Oglaks, to attack the Black Ship.

Jeonk gave Shok a damage report, "Our primary heat shields have been penetrated on the aft section. We are losing the charge on the Super Pulse Cannons. You better start maneuvering for battle instead of letting them hit us to charge the cannons."

Shok popped the Black Ship up three hundred feet and spun it to take the next group of Dragon Spits head on to protect the damaged aft section. The laser and pulse cannon gunners threw out a field of fire to keep the unfriendly Dragon Spits from getting too close. The gunners downed a few more of the Spits before the Argan fighters and Forum Corsairs had destroyed enough Dragon Spits to force them to choose. It was obvious to the survivors that the only choice was between dead or gone. They chose to be gone but no one knew where they were going.

As the Dragon Spits deserted the Pishtup ground troops, the Black Ship received an information bulletin from Chosteel's command post at the center of the battle. Chosteel reported, "There are twenty Dragon Spit Corsairs leaving the planet and they seem to be heading into deep space. They won't be passing anywhere near the fleets you have heading in this direction. My guess is, it's Sot Pah and his best buddies. The ones who thought they could win this war."

Shok turned to Jeonk and said, "It's too late; we'll never be able to catch them."

"That means he has friends somewhere we don't know about," Jeonk replied. "Let's hope his friends are less inclined to wage war than Sot Pah."

Losing its air support made the Pishtup Army easy to polish off. Most of them surrendered as the Forum troops came into view. The Paracans are big, rust colored and mean looking. The Oglaks are even more dangerous looking, almost amphibian in appearance. With tens of thousands of Paracans and Oglaks coming at them, the Pishtup soldiers became very peaceful.

The Veolsh did a very good job in the battle but they are small and rather ordinary looking. Nobody is afraid of Veolsh foot soldiers because of the way they look. The Veolsh don't frighten anyone until they start shooting; then they're frightening. The Veolsh Corsairs are an old and reliable technology and they are tough; they downed many Dragon Spits in the air war and their Corsair losses were fewer than the Paracans and Oglaks.

Jeonk kept the Black Ship on station until it was obvious it wouldn't be needed to direct or support the ground activities. Shok wheeled the Black Ship and headed for Supek and a meeting with President Coshti.

The Argan fleets had returned and were hanging in a low orbit over Supek. Jeonk and Shok would have to decide which needed to return to Arga for immediate repairs and which would need to have repairs made at Supek before they could return to Arga. Some of the cruisers would have to remain at Supek until it was absolutely certain the war wouldn't get hot again. Sot Pah could return with help from his friends but that was a remote possibility. He lost most of his twelve thousand corsairs and his country. Few friends will face similar losses to be helpful to an old friend looking for a safe place to hide.

The Forum nations and the Argans remained on Tuplej for another six months after the war. President Coshti consented to take over Pishtup's problems and he had a big job on his hands. Doskel had done an exemplary job on the destruction of Pishtup's electrical systems. It would be several months before power could be restored throughout the country. The Black Ship's little earthquake did more damage than they expected. It caused earthquakes in other parts of Pishtup and some small ones in Supek. Jeonk and Shok apologized to Supek for putting out such a large charge from their Disrupter.

Jeonk brought several of Arga's damaged Cruisers to the surface of Supek so the people could get a feel for the space battle they couldn't see during the war. President Coshti and many of the people of Supek were shocked by the amount of damage the cruiser had suffered and they were even more amazed that the cruisers could still fly and fight. The cruisers they were shown suffered first through third degree hull damage.

The Argans couldn't show them the eight cruisers they lost in the space battle. If the cruiser sweep hadn't successfully destroyed so many of the Dragon Spit Corsairs, they calculated that Arga would have lost at least one fleet in the battle that would have followed a failed sweep.

Chosteel and the Forum nations agreed to keep troops in Pishtup until President Coshti felt secure in his ability to hold the country with his own troops. Chosteel and President Coshti calculated a probable two-year time frame to return the two nations to some kind of stability.

The damaged Argan cruisers were slowly replaced with undamaged ones from the fleets the Argans had left at home. When the Argans left, Jeonk assigned one fleet to remain over Supek. Sixteen cruisers hanging around in space and making frequent flights over Pishtup would be a powerful deterrent to renewed hostilities.

Jeonk and Shok reclaimed their Cargo ship and put the three sections back together. The cargo crews were delighted, not that they were in the air again and on course; each crew member would receive six months danger pay for setting on their butts and not getting one shot fired at them, that made them happy. Jeonk and Shok were happy about the not getting shot at part but not about the six months danger pay. They were being stuck with the six months danger pay.

Jeonk and Shok filled their cargo ship with war surplus Dragon Spit Corsairs. They didn't bother to count them as they put them in. No one knows how many Dragon Spits they have. A few of them may end up in one or another of their small spacecraft hideouts after they make a few structural improvements.

The Argan space engineers were charged with looking at the corsairs to improve the technology of Arga's space fleets. It's difficult to say how many will be ruined by the engineering effort. They stuffed enough of the Spits in the cargo ship for the engineers to have plenty of spares. They could wreck as many as it takes.

12

THE CHOKNG FOULD, KURSIT BALT PROBLEM

Jeonk and Shok were loafing along in the Black Ship, flying alongside their cargo ship loaded with their newly acquired Dragon Spit Corsairs. Jeonk ordered one fleet of cruisers to tag along behind them on the return flight to Arga. Jeonk sat in one of the command deck's reclining chairs with his hands behind his head and his feet on another chair. He seemed to be the picture of a man with nothing in particular on his mind. Shok knew him too well to buy that. When Jeonk looks like he has nothing on his mind, he has something on his mind.

Jeonk sat up, turned toward Shok, and said; "You know Shok, you and I have to do something about Chokng Fould and Kursit Balt, something without going to war. They've tried to kill us too many times for us to continue to ignore them. We're not very busy know. While we aren't doing anything, you think of a plan."

"The hardest part of any plan will be how we explain to our wives why we need a plan." Shok reminded him. "They think we're on our way home to live quiet peaceful lives, you as the King, me as a dedicated business man, and both of us as loving husbands who never again worry our wives half to death by getting shot at.

"We can probably pull off taking care of a couple of dictators without too much trouble but our wives are going to be trouble. They think we've gotten rid of our last enemy. Our wives won't be concerned about two tyrants, with dwindling power, who also live on separate planets."

Jeonk rubbed his chin and said, "You'll have to think of something. Those two won't stop trying to kill us just because our wives think we've turned over on a peaceful leaf."

Shok did a lot of his thinking out loud when he and Jeonk did their planning alone and Jeonk's really good at filling in the blanks. Shok started his speculations with the obvious, "We can't go in and blast them out of their holes, that's going to war. Another problem is, they don't like each other. They work together often enough but nearly always communicate with each other through their agents. They seldom meet face to face. Neither of them go anywhere, even on their home planets, without a large bodyguard and at least one mistress. They rarely leave their home planets. Most of the other planets want them dead for the things they've done in the past. Do you have any ideas?"

"They both love money," Jeonk replied, "and they live in fear of losing their power. They frequently change mistresses. They have large spy networks at home and on other planets. They both want to be considered legitimate leaders and members of civilized galactic society. They are never invited to interplanetary conferences or diplomatic events and they resent being treated like the criminals they are. I don't have any personal information about them, daily habits and stuff like that."

Shok continued his search for a plan, "We need to give them a reason to leave their home planets. We need a motivating crisis we can cause, and control well enough to get them in a face-to-face conference on some other planet. I'll look through their files in the black projects office. Maybe I can come up with something."

"I knew you would come up with a plan," Jeonk stated. "You've already got one started. We can flesh it out as we go along. I like the controlled crisis idea. It sounds a little too; Uh, Washington D.C. bureaucrat, but it might work.

"Chokng and Kursit are at their most dangerous right now. They've lost their financial base. Many of their best crooks are in prisons on several different planets. They blame you and me for all of their losses. Whatever their next target is, we'll be somewhere in the center of it. We have to take care of them before they take care of us.

"We may need to use a few of the Dragon Spit Corsairs we're carrying in the cargo ship's compartments. I'll have our engineers at Meho check them out and make whatever improvements they can as soon as we get home.

"The Dragon Spits are fast enough but they are flimsy; when they get one hit on their hull they are finished. They depend on speed to keep them safe. Sot Pah sacrificed structural strength to produce thousands of them in a short time. I think our engineers can improve them without driving the cost through the ceiling."

They dropped the subject of Chokng and Kursit during the rest of the trip home. Both of them wanted information of a specific nature before their planning could be considered useful. Arga was on scan and their wives had signaled the Black Ship to tell them the wives would be waiting at home. Shok and Jeonk expected their wives to have some kind of a homecoming party for them, and they were prepared for the usual bullet hole, laser burn, knife slash inspection. Their wives had been doing that ever since the battle with the pirates on the Veolsh planet.

Shok put the black Cruiser in the repair mode at Meho to fix the damage caused by the Dragon Spits at Pishtup. While Shok was doing that, Jeonk ordered their engineers to begin the Dragon Spit improvement project and ordered complete tests of its operating capabilities. Both of them had to move fast because their wives wouldn't understand a delay. The wives thought Jeonk and Shok had reduced their last enemy to ashes and would be in no hurry to start a new project. Both of them, very quickly, attended to the bare necessities of their coming projects and then took a command plak to the Royal Compound.

Their family and friends were waiting for them to land the command plak on the pad of the royal compound. Aslain and Jeonk's kids waited for him. Alice was waiting for Shok. Plask was there, Sitak Rakoup and Iliaska were there and they were all standing just a short distance from Shok's hideout Paracan corsair.

The family didn't give them much time for greetings. After one short kiss, they dragged both of them into Shok's Paracan Corsair for a trip to Plask's Lersta castle. The family was giving them a homecoming party and the party was at Plask's castle.

Plask piloted the corsair but his first stop wasn't his castle. He made a detour to the cliff behind Shok's Lersta cottage, pressed a button on the control column of Shok's Corsair; opened Shok's secret, camouflaged, automatic hangar door, flew the corsair inside and gave everyone a tour of Shok's secret hangar. Plask was especially proud of the way Shok had concealed the entrance from the basement to the hangar.

Shok felt the show and tell in his secret hangar could have been bypassed with just a little more understanding from Plask. Jeonk and Shok still had a few hidden corsairs no one knew about, but Jeonk and Shok. If they determined it was necessary to perform some discreet, off planet, business, they could still manage it.

Plask's castle was decorated for the occasion of the homecoming and it reminded Shok of Christmas on Earth. Emira's cooks had prepared a wonderful meal of mixed Argan and Cajun dishes for Jeonk and Shok. Alice had taught the cooks to make pan fried chicken, one of Shok's favorites. Iliaska cooked her Earth specialty, apple pan dowdy. They had barbecued brickle from Plask's lake and some fantastic wild game from the Lersta forest.

SPACE LINE BY MARIVIN E. FOX

After dinner, everyone retired to the verandah overlooking Lake Lersta. The men enjoyed some of Plask's Louisiana beer and cigars. If Shok ignored the show and tell in his secret hangar he thought it was a beautiful evening.

Sitak Rakoup's after dinner speech was the high light of the evening. He stood up, toasted Jeonk and Shok, and then said, "If there is trouble, get behind them. If you need help, find them. If you want the truth, ask them. If you want to be courageous, be like them. If you are wrong, you better get the hell out of their way. They are the first ones to recognize a threat and they have been at the center of every danger this nation has faced. Tyrants despise them and good people fight side by side with them.

"Whatever they have done has made life better for everyone else and I know they will continue to do good for God, family, and country. A king of Arga and a country boy from Earth have tamed the worst elements in our part of the galaxy. We have often been perplexed by what they were doing, and always proud when the job was done. They are known as strong and good men on every civilized planet. I am proud to have been a part of their lives and their plans. I'm proud to call them my friend."

Aslain, Alice and Emira had tears in their eyes. Iliaska looked at Sitak like she couldn't believe he had said that many words in a row. Jeonk and Shok felt guilty because they couldn't tell the family about their plan for Chokng Fould and Kursit Balt.

Plask added to Rakoup's speech, "It's easy for men with great power to compromise in the face of great difficulty. My son Jeonk is a man with great power who will not compromise no matter what the difficulty. That was my biggest worry when he became king. I thank God he found a friend with the intellect, the guts and the moral fiber, not only to back him up, but stand with him in every difficulty. I've thought of Shok as one of my sons for so long I have to measure him to make sure he isn't one of my sons. Something more than blood has made him a part of our family; his, and our souls are of the same family. God gave him to us. We thank God for the gift.

"Shok found another just like himself; he brought us Alice. We love them both. Everyone at this dinner is a part of the Shap family, body, blood and soul."

Alice was really crying after Plask's warm-hearted talk. She went to Plask, pulled his big shoulders down to her size and kissed both of his cheeks. Iliaska kissed him after Alice. Rakoup and Shok were always considered to be a part of the Shap family. Alice and Iliaska hadn't thought of themselves as part of the family before Plask spoke.

Alice turned the days at the castle into a second honeymoon for herself and Shok. She loved those big Argan beds and Shok loved her in them. Everyone had a great time. It was one of the most relaxing times Shok shared with the family. He knew Alice was very much the reason for that. Alice has a knack for making everyone around her as happy as she is. Plask and Emira didn't have a daughter and they treated Alice like a long lost daughter they had finally found. God help anyone who made Alice feel bad.

13

THE ASTOLIAN EMPIRE CRISIS

The warm days and cool nights stretched into months of pure family pleasure. Jeonk and Shok seemed to lose track of their Chokng and Kursit problem. Both were brought rudely back to reality by an official message to the King of Arga from a source neither had ever heard of. Jeonk and Shok hurried back to Poshalla to see what could be done about it.

The message itself was brutally to the point from someone calling himself, Astol, Emperor of the planets of the Astolian Empire. It was addressed to, His Majesty, King Jeonk Shap, Emperor of the Argan Empire. After the usual you are important and I am important baloney, the message got to the point, "You have extended your empire to many planets and you have become the most powerful person in your part of the galaxy. I admire your ability to carry your plans to completion. Under more friendly circumstances, I would welcome a fellow emperor as my friend. However, your drive to create a greater empire wherever you find planets to conquer has made enemies of the Astolian Empire and the Argan Empire.

"You have conquered most of the planets in your area of the galaxy and you have extended your empire into areas you were previously unaware of. You have brought an unfamiliar religion to the inner galaxy from the warlike planet Earth. This religion is now spreading throughout your empire.

"You have robbed my friend Sot Pah of his nation of Pishtup. You have annexed his planet, Tuplej, into your empire. We shall not fight a war over it. I have many planets and I shall select one for my friend to rule. I seek no trouble with you. I will tolerate no trouble from you. Any further adventures on the part of the Argan Empire that are close to the borders of the Astolian Empire will result in disaster for you.

"The Astolian Empire has drawn a line in space that you shall not cross without going to war with my empire. The line drawn around the Argan Empire includes your planet Okron, and the planets: Egrin, Iklug, Veolsh, Paraca, Oglak, Nasti, Castu, Mog, Krex, Nordic and Tuplej.

"Outside of the Astolian Space Line Boundary for the Argan Empire are the planets: Gamac, Prssk, Earth and all of other planets beyond the planet Tuplej.

"We will permit your cargo ships, now on Earth or traveling to Earth, to complete their journeys and return to Arga unharmed. When those journeys are completed, we will condone no further Argan commerce or Argan Empire travel to the planet Earth.

"Remain inside the boundaries the Astolian Empire has drawn for you and you will be safe. Your Empire may grow as it pleases you inside those boundaries. Outside of those boundaries, you will find only danger and war. I wish you long life and peace."

Jeonk read the incredible document in the Royal Headquarters of his palace. He finished reading it, then handed it to Shok. He said, before Shok could read it, "There will be an Admiralty meeting tomorrow. You read that piece of trash, and be ready to give your opinion on it at the meeting tomorrow. I would like to hear your opinion at the same time the Admiralty does. I need to give it some thought. There are some subliminal messages in it. I think you will want some time to think about it before you form your opinion."

The Admiralty meeting was full. All of the Admirals were on planet and in attendance. Jeonk made a special invitation to Plask to be there because his experience of many years and many problems might be very helpful in this meeting of national importance. Each of the Admirals had been given a copy of the message and immediately understood its importance to the nation of Arga.

The Astolian message had really angered Jeonk. When he was really angry, he didn't give his opinion first, he waited until everyone else gave an opinion before he gave his. He opened the meeting, "You have all read the message. I gave a copy of it to Admiral Shok yesterday and asked him to give his opinion of it at this meeting. Admiral, please proceed."

Shok stood up and began, "This message purports to be from an empire none of us are familiar with. We don't know if it actually exists. There are four major components in the message that are questionable. The Emperor, Astol himself, is questionable, and Astol mentions three others we are familiar with but have no respect for, Sot Pah, his friend, along with Gamac and Prssk. I checked my special projects office after his Majesty gave me the message. Chokng Fould and Kursit Balt have been missing from their home planets for at least the last sixteen weeks. They both disappeared at about the same time and haven't returned to Gamac or Prssk. Whoever Astol is, he knows those three. Astol is apparently being advised by them, if he wasn't invented by them. That's the first element.

"Next, the message insists that Arga is an empire in control of many planets. All three of Astol's friends and advisors know that to be a lie. If the Astolian Empire exists, its leader shows a weakness of mind to accept the word of three losers about another empire. No emperor can afford to be so poorly advised of the truth and hope to survive very long. We will, for the sake of argument, conclude that Astol is a real person. Since a real person in his position would have to know liars when he meets them, we must assume there lies suit his purpose. His purpose is to control everything outside of the Space Line he has drawn for Arga. Further, he fears Arga will defeat his purpose if Arga moves beyond those lines.

"Astol puts Gamac, Prssk, and Earth, outside of his Space Line Boundary. That boundary allows the Gamacs, Prsskians, and the Astolian Empire to be protected from Arga. It, also, controls Earth, if Arga remains inside its Space Line boundary. Following Astol's orders would also be an admission by Arga to acceptance of Earth and all other planets outside of the Space Line becoming Astolian Imperial property.

"You will notice, there are no rules for the conduct of the Astolian Empire outside of its Space Line. The only rule offered was for Arga to remain quietly inside the Space Line or go to war with the Astolian Empire.

"The reward for Arga's quiet acceptance of the Astolian Empire's free control of the planets, that are presently outside of the Emperor's self made boundary, is to allow the Argan Empire a free hand inside its Astolian arranged boundary. The planets inside the boundary are the Galactic Forum planets. One of Astol's advisors, Sot Pah, had a real bad experience with the Galactic Forum. I think that's the power they wish to control. Arga is the most powerful member in the Forum, and the one the Astolian Empire will most likely meet in space. If Astol and his criminal advisors can control Arga, they think the other members of the Galactic Forum will never bother them.

"There are two very surprising parts to the message. The first is the inclusion of Earth on the Astolian side of the Space Line. It is surprising only until you consider the closeness of planet Earth to Gamac and Prssk. We don't know if Earth has been singled out because of the amount of commerce it promises for the inner galaxy, or for its manufacturing potential, or because Chokng Fould and Kursit Balt, with the help of two new friends, hope to plunder it.

"The inclusion of Earth in the Astolian Empire nullifies Arga's cargo line. That cargo line is certain to grow and eventually seek broader markets throughout the galaxy. Earth would be a very rich plum for anyone who gains control of it. We have prevented that takeover before and I don't think we can accept it now.

SPACE LINE BY MARVIN E. FOX

"The second surprise can easily be called astounding. The message has no return address. We have no way to contact the sender, and there is no instruction for contacting a third party to begin diplomatic negotiations about boundaries. We are to accept what amounts to an ultimatum from one Empire to another without question or comment. Our future performance will be our only answer.

"I don't think the message is an outright fraud. His Majesty and I watched twenty Dragon Spit Corsairs leave Pishtup in a great hurry at the end of the war for Supek. Those twenty Dragon Spits had to be going somewhere. I think the somewhere is this, so called, Astolian Empire. How big and how powerful it is, I can't guess. It may be three losers, Gamac, Prssk and Sot Pah, trying to bluff their way to prosperity. It may be four losers trying to keep Arga and the Forum nations at home. I can guess with reasonable certainty that our old enemies, Chokng and Kursit, are there with our new enemies Sot Pah and Astol."

Jeonk said, "Anyone have a disagreement or anything to add to Shok's opinions about the message."

After a minute of thought, Plask reached out and slapped the table gently, saying, "I think Shok covered everything pretty thoroughly. What we are missing is what none of us know. Who in the hell Astol is or where the Astolian Empire is. The first order of business is to find out who we are dealing with. No one on Arga knows where to look."

Jeonk cleared his throat before he responded, "Actually, there are those on Arga who know where to begin the search. Shok and I, and most Admirals know a Veolsh navigator named Skish. He left our service and formed a Society of Veolsh Navigators after the fall of the Veolsh Council. His present residence is in the Veolsh capital of Pumg. If anyone knows where the Astolian Empire is located, he or one of his navigators will know. We can have that information for the asking. Does anyone else have a comment?"

Admiral Brak replied, "I think we need immediate protection for Arga and the space around us. The whole message is full of inaccuracies and it is weird. I think we should protect ourselves from any immediate danger. If the message was meant to send our fleets scurrying off in different directions to find a new enemy, it might be because the new enemy is waiting for us to do just that."

"Good point Brak," Jeonk answered. "We'll put four fleets in space immediately, and the four fleets will do their scurrying in Argan space."

Jeonk adjourned the meeting after the other comments were heard. Jeonk, Plask, Rakoup and Shok took a command Plak and were on their way to Plask's castle to rejoin their families. Jeonk said, "Dad, I want you and Sitak to take over Shok's job in the Office of Special Military Projects for a while. Shok and I are going to be too busy for him to handle it and I think you and Sitak are the only ones who can understand everything that goes on there."

Plask replied, "Sure, we can do that, can't we Sitak?"

Rakoup nodded yes and said, "Shok has almost cornered the market on secret projects. Plask and I have wanted to get inside his offices on many occasions but we didn't want to appear to be snooping."

Then Jeonk turned to Shok, "Is your fleet ready to fly. You and I have some places to go and we'll need a battle ready fleet to get there."

"I have two cruisers in the repair docks but if we need a full fleet we can borrow two from Rakoup or Brak," Shok replied.

Jeonk thought for a few minutes before he spoke, "Fourteen will be enough. If we need more than that, two more fleets probably won't be enough. Our first stop will be at Pumg on the Veolsh planet; we need to talk to Skish."

As soon as Jeonk finished speaking, Shok knew they were going to cross the Astolian Empire's Space Line to see if Astol was real, or some old enemies invented a new scam. Shok reminded him, "Most of my fleet has the new pulse cannon system installed. It's the first fleet to be fitted with it. I think Arga may need more cruisers with the same system. Before we leave, how about ordering all of the fleets to be refitted on an emergency schedule."

Jeonk shook his head yes and said, "Dad, you and Rakoup take care of that. Put Brak in charge of the refitting. He's the fastest and the best we have. He'll get it done in half the time anyone else would."

They arrived at the castle and explained the situation to their wives and families. There was no discussion about Jeonk and Shok being careful or letting someone else do the job. The situation was beyond careful and everyone knew it. They were going to do whatever they had to and that was that.

Alice was especially quiet as she snuggled close to Shok that night. He held her very close for a long time before he noticed the tears in her eyes. She didn't say anything about it but Shok knew how worried she was for him. He didn't know how long he would be gone and she would be worried for as long as he was gone. Shok thought in the quiet of his mind as Alice clung to him, "Sometimes, the most difficult thing we do is leave the ones we love so we can protect them from people who have no love for them."

The fleet was in space before the sun rose over the Lersta Mountains. Shok pushed it at flank speed on a track for the Veolsh planet and the meeting with Skish. Shok felt better about leaving when Rakoup put two of his cruisers on special assignment to protect the family and Plask ordered General Sokeasel's troops to protect the castle.

Their arrival on the Veolsh planet was routine. They met with Skish and a few of his navigators in the Galactic Forum complex. The question was simple. They wanted to know if Skish or any of the other navigators were familiar with the Astolian Empire. Skish was the first to answer, "I know of a planet named Kashtool, beyond Tuplej about fifteen light years. Its leader's name is Astol. There are two other inhabited planets near Kashtool. The two planets are about as technologically advanced as the planets in this area. Astol wasn't ruling them at the time.

"The Veolsh Council invited Astol to join the Veolsh Council system of planets but he refused. I don't know how strong he has become since that time but his empire, if one could really call it that, wasn't strong enough to resist if the Council wanted to go to war to make him join. The Veolsh Council didn't consider him much of a threat. Kashtool was too far away for them to bother annexing it by war. The Veolsh Council thought of Astol in the same way you think of Prssk or Gamac. They considered Astol to be a man of great pretensions but little substance."

"What of his space fleet?" Jeonk asked. "We think he supplied the design for Sot Pah's Dragon Spit Corsairs. The Dragon Spits are very fast but they are structurally weak. They are formidable in battle because they are fast and can be produced quickly in large numbers."

Skish replied, "I don't know for certain that Astol gave the Dragon Spit design to Sot Pah but he would if he thought Sot Pah would make him a greater man.

"We navigators studied your battle with the Dragon Spits in the war for Supek. We think they have a fatal flaw. Their technology is based on high intensity light generators inside the ship and the same generators are used to power the ships. Your cruiser sweep put so much light around them that their power systems were immobilized and the Dragon Spits became easy targets. Their light based systems are made primarily for deep space but they can be operated more slowly at the surface level.

"If a pulse cannon burst is aimed in front of them, their guidance, flight control and armament systems malfunction for several seconds. The pulse cannon burst need not hit them directly to be effective. A close miss will force them to reset everything before they can return to a functional mode of operation. A few seconds is a death trap for them if their enemy knows how to use those few seconds. For your Argan gunners, the Dragon Spits will become sitting targets."

Shok thought the pulse cannon information needed to be fleshed out, "The only weapon the Dragon Spits carry is a pulse cannon. How do they maintain control when they fire their own pulse cannons?"

Skish surmised, "There are two ways they may do it. They may use a controlled narrow spectrum for their own pulse cannon discharges or they may use a synchronized override for their discharges. We couldn't be certain from the information we have but we favor the synchronized override theory. Your engineers will be able to tell you when they finish their tests on the Dragon Spits. For now, we know a way to defeat them and that's enough.

"When I received the notice of your intention to stop here, and telling me what you wanted. I took the liberty to gather some Veolsh navigators to go with you on your emperor hunt. We are available if you want us.

"I also notified the Paracans, Oglaks and the Veolsh nations. They have been working on their own systems to fight the Dragon Spits and they are pretty sure you will find some to fight. Jeonk, all of them have great confidence in your, and Shok's, ability to find the problem and face it. They think the Galactic Forum has an interest in making sure no dictator, strong or weak, surrounds us. What do you say?"

Jeonk had the look of a man who was trying to find a way to refuse but Shok knew he couldn't. Finally, he said, "Glad to have all of you on board but we are trying to find out who we're dealing with, not punch him out. Anyone in the Galactic Forum who has the speed to stay with our cruisers is welcome to come along. I'm especially pleased to have you and your navigators with us. Skish, you will, of course, fly with Shok and me. It will be like old times."

Shok thought his cruisers would leave the Forum spacecraft behind when his reached cruising speed but they didn't. Their spacecraft weren't the fighters they used in the Supek war. The Forum ships were cruisers, smaller than the Argans but fast and trim. Each of the nations traveling with them launched twenty of their newest. The largest of them, from Paraca, could launch four fighters. The smaller Veolsh and Oglak cruisers could launch three and all of their cruisers were as fast as the Argan Cruisers.

Space flight is the technological system used to bore people half to death while they go some place that's terrifying. The space fleet was in the boring part but the terrifying part was just over the horizon. The fleet scanners were punching holes in deep space to find any trace of incoming space traffic. They had no idea what Astol had in his box of tricks.

It wasn't unreasonable to assume Chokng and Kursit informed Astol of Arga's propensity for hunting down and dealing with troublemakers. They might also have kept their mouths shut in some vain hope the Argans would think the whole thing was a hoax and not bother on this one occasion. The fleet kept safe, all scanners were on long range.

SPACE LINE BY MARIVIN E. FOX

The fleet shortened its scan range as it approached Kashtool. It seemed Kashtool was asleep as they approached the planet. They received no greetings, and no threats of bodily harm from its puffed up Emperor. The Argans were beginning to think they were at the wrong address. That was just before things began lifting off the surface of Kashtool, very fast. The Astolians came at them from four positions on the planet. Their ships lit up as they entered deep space.

Shok ordered the fleet to position for a sweep. He had already briefed the fleet about the Dragon Spit's fatal flaw. It was going to be an interesting little battle. Their Forum partners were breaking right and left to avoid the Argan sweep and begin their training on whatever the Argans missed, couldn't or didn't hit. The Dragon Spits were grouping for a full frontal assault That isn't a good tactic when the assault force is about to face a previously prepared cruiser sweep, but the Astolians could be in a cruiser sweep-learning mode.

Shok waited for the Dragon Spits to fire their first pulse cannon rounds before he gave the order for synchronized fleet fire. The space between the Argan fleet and the Astolian Dragon Spits lit up like a June noon in Arizona, as the pulse cannons from fourteen cruisers fired simultaneously. Skish was right; the surviving Dragon Spits appeared to be lost in the field of light. The seconds it took for the Spits to reset as the light dwindled was more than enough time for the fleet gunners to target the Spits that hadn't been destroyed in the sweep, and finish the first wave off individually.

The second wave was smarter than the first. They fanned out and came from the sides to put the Forum cruisers between the Dragon Spits and the Argan fleet. Shok ordered the fleet to break in two directions. Seven cruisers would go over the top of the Forum ships to the right; seven more would do the same for the left. Shok's fleet of cruisers would have to fly over the Forum fleet, break to the center of the Dragon Spits, and depend on their new pulse cannon technology to blast hell out of them.

The Forum cruisers had launched their fighters at the beginning of the battle. The Argans hadn't launched theirs yet. The cruiser commanders could do that at their own discretion if Shok didn't give the order but none of them chose to do so. They were waiting for the real battle and they didn't want their fighters out there zooming around spoiling their aim during a small battle.

Ten of the Dragon Spits ganged up on a Paracan Cruiser. The Paracan Commander fired all of his pulse cannons in front of them in one broadside, and then let his gunners take them out one by one. Ten more Dragon Spits were right behind the first ten. They broke and cleared the Paracan cruiser's area rather than go down fighting. Forum fleet gunners and fighters took most of them out as they wheeled to escape. The Dragon Spits ten on one firing pattern was broken and a one on one battle with a cruiser was insanity. Shok wondered what they would come up with next.

The surviving Dragon Spits cleared the area and headed for home. The mixed Argan and Forum fleet was still intact after the first engagement. Shok immediately ordered the fleet to scan the surface for ground based pulse cannon and lasers batteries. They also looked for Dragon Spit launch sites they could hit from space. They quickly identified some of all of the above and began punching pulse cannon and laser holes in them from their position in space.

The fires and explosions were nice to see but they apparently raised the Imperial hackles of Astol the Magnificent. Shok could tell Astol had finally concluded the foreign fleet was here for some serious business. Floods of Dragon Spit Corsairs began lifting off of the surface from places the fleet hadn't gotten around to blowing up. There were so many Spits no one could count them.

Shok ordered the fleet to launch fighters. Two hundred ten Argan fighters and two hundred Forum fighters is a small flood in its own right if the pilots know how to fight Dragon Spits. All of them knew.

Shok ordered the fleet to regroup for another sweep as the fighters spread out to flank the incoming Dragon Spits and attempt to force them into the sweep area. It appeared on the holoscanners that most of the Dragon Spits would be in the sweep area without fighter urgings. The fighters were ordered to stay out of the sweep area and take care of the tardy Dragon Spits and those to shy to accommodate the fleets sweeping intentions.

The Forum cruisers formed up with the Argans on this sweep. Their commanders had seen how well the last sweep had worked and decided it was the best tactic. The flood of Dragon Spits seemed overwhelming if only their raw numbers were considered. It was hard to believe Sot Pah could launch that many. If Skish hadn't given them a tactic to beat the Spits, or if his tactic had been wrong, Shok would have ordered the cruisers to pull out to save the fleet. There was no way to defeat such a large number of the Spits in a head on battle ship to ship. Fortunately, Shok and the other commanders knew that most of the Spits were dead meat.

The cruisers were stacked and spread one above the other at two-mile intervals and ten cruisers wide at two-mile intervals. They would sweep everything from twenty miles wide at the cruisers' hulls to a minimum of five hundred miles at surface level.

They were closer to Kashtool on this sweep than they were on the last one. The surface could expect some collateral damage. Shok hoped it wouldn't be civilian damage but he would have to wait and see. For people who came to Kashtool to find out who they were dealing with, and not to punch anyone out, they were sure raising hell.

Why an enemy fleet would advance into a cruiser sweep twice in the same day was anyone's guess. Shok's one guess was, "They didn't understand what happened the first time, couldn't see the tactical error they were making the second time, and compounded both errors by putting everything they had in the second battle. Still, there they are in numbers our computers are too busy to count."

Shok watched them light up us as they reached the edge of their own atmosphere and entered deep space, rows of them, one row behind the other. The light affect was tremendous. Thousands of lights streaming up from the planets surface in one brilliantly beautiful, but doomed array.

The Dragon Spit leaders reached their maximum firing range as Shok ordered the fleet sweep. With seventy-four cruisers firing at once, space no longer looked like Arizona at noon, it looked more like Arizona, burning, at noon. They repeated the altered firing pattern for thirty seconds at one-second intervals. When they stopped firing, there was nothing in the sweep area for individual gunners to fire at. The Dragon Spit fleet had been pummeled so hard most of it was falling back to the surface instead of finding the usual repose of destroyed space ships and crews in the bleak peace of space.

Twenty-five hundred square miles of the planets surface displayed the results of the pulse cannon discharges that weren't dissipated in space. Everything in the square seemed to be on fire. Anyone inside the burning square would need a lot of luck to stay alive. Shok hoped it was raw countryside.

Shok broke the Argan fleet into seven divisions of two cruisers each. The pairs of cruisers were positioned to cover the planet from all angles. He ordered his cruisers to make surface scans for Dragon Spits Astol could have held out of the battle, and to report any evidence of Gamac or Prssk spacecraft of any kind. The surface scans would show if Astol had saved bases to be used in an effort to hide a last-ditch threat to the fleet.

It was time to find the erring emperor, Astol the Defeated. Chokng and Kursit would certainly inform Astol and Sot Pah that the Argans wouldn't be giving up on them just because the Argans won the battle. All four of the losing despots would be hunted and found someplace they hoped they couldn't be found. An ersatz imperial team would certainly have provided itself with a good place to hide, in case someone real showed up to challenge their crowns.

After an hour on station, a small spacecraft the size of a shuttle appeared below the flag cruiser Jeonk and Shok were in. The flagship's gunners targeted it but held their fire because the small ship was flying erratically. Shok ordered them to continue to hold their fire and told his communications officer to try to contact it. The communications officer wasn't having much luck until Shok told him to broadband one of the receivers to see if the shuttle was trying to contact the flagship.

They received an English speaking female voice and she was saying, "This bloody damned airplane won't fly right and those bleeding space ships won't answer. I'll get killed here for sure. If any of you bastards here my voice, say something! Tell me how to fly this thing. I'm escaping and you are the only place I can go."

Shok transmitted to her receiver channel and said, "Lady, this is Admiral Kelly. I'm an American and I will help you. I'm in the cruiser that is directly above you. I can see you directly below me. Calm down as much as you can so I can give you instructions."

She came back, "I saw Astol and those three ugly pieces of dingo dung light out so I stole this thing they fly around in. I was in it a few times before and watched how they flew it but it doesn't do the same thing for me it did for them. I can't get it to go straight and I don't know how to land it."

Shok tried a soothing approach, "You have done just great so far. I don't want you to be frightened so I'll tell you how we can bring you aboard this spaceship. Take your hands away from the controls. That will make it go in the same direction all of the time and it doesn't matter which direction. We have you and we will not lose you. You are safe. When your bloody airplane is going in the same direction all of the time, I will bring this spaceship close to your airplane. When I get this spaceship close to your airplane, I will use what I call a tractor beam to pull your airplane into this spaceship. It may get a little warm inside your airplane when that happens. That is normal and you are not to worry. When you are inside this spaceship, I will come to your airplane and let you out of it. You and I will have a cup of coffee and something to eat together."

Her shuttle stabilized immediately and she replied, "For a cup of coffee, I'll do anything you want."

Shok kept talking to her as the crew tractor beamed her shuttle aboard. As soon as the tractor beam began pulling the shuttle inside, Jeonk and Shok went aft to get the mystery girl from Earth out of the shuttle to see who they found on an unsure escape course in space. One thing they both agreed on, "She's one desperate and gutsy girl."

Shok could see how to open the shuttle's hatch but he didn't want to scare her. He knocked before he began to open the hatch. She opened the hatch before he could. She stood in the opening looking at Jeonk and Shok like she expected to see monsters. They stared back, wordlessly. She wore a pair of skin clinging, gold colored pants with a gold jacket designed to show off her beautiful breasts. She had blond hair, blue eyes and she was five feet eight inches tall. To say she was stunning was small praise. Shok gathered his senses, offered her his hand for the small step out of the shuttle and said, "I'm Kelly, would you like to have that cup of coffee with Jeonk and me?"

She took his hand and replied, "I would almost die for a cup of coffee or anything else anyone on Earth drinks."

They took her to the galley instead of a conference compartment. They wanted her to be comfortable and not to feel threatened by two strange men taking her into a secluded area. Shok guessed she had already been forced into too many secluded areas since her arrival on Kashtool. They had questions to ask her about Astol and Kashtool but didn't want her to feel threatened if she chose not to answer them. Shok ordered three cups of coffee and pastry for the three of them from the cook.

The beautiful girl kept staring at Jeonk as though she couldn't figure out what he was. Shok thought it was better if he gave her his information before he asked for any from her. He told her about his association with Jeonk and the Argans and why they had come to Kashtool with blood in their eyes. Shok was being careful so she wouldn't think they were just more crooks taking what the Kashtool crooks had accumulated for themselves. He told her about Alice and their lives on Arga. Shok talked for several minutes while she finished her coffee. He asked her if she would like another cup of coffee and she said, "yes."

When she appeared more relaxed, Shok asked her, "What's your name and where are you from?"

She answered, "My name is Sherril Strang and I'm from Australia."

Shok laughed and said, "Not from Gunder Guy, where a dog shit in the tucker box?"

She started to laugh a little but she didn't quit make it. The fact that she was actually safe hit her then. Tears welled up in her eyes and her lips quivered a little. She couldn't say anything. Jeonk reached over and gave her a big, blue-handed, pat on the back. Shok took her hand and said, "You're really safe Sherril. No one in this galaxy, including the dingo dung that has been bothering you can take you off of this ship.

When we finish here, we'll take you to Arga. After we reach Arga, you can go home on the first ship going to Earth. We have a shuttle going between Arga and the Argan Embassy in New Orleans, Louisiana. From New Orleans our embassy will arrange your first class passage to Australia. You'll be back home soon."

She gained control of her emotions and said, "Thanks, but you need to know there are thirty more Earth girls down there. The guy with the ugly red skin and the one with the big flat nose brought them several weeks ago for that miserable scum, Astol. I saw some of them but they talk funny and I couldn't understand much of what they said. They kept pointing at themselves and saying Nordic. That ugly little Astol likes Earth girls. They brought the girls as a gift for him."

"Sherril, Do you know where they are now?" Jeonk asked. "Is there some place in particular he would keep them?"

She thought before she spoke, "Probably in a place called The Young Ladies Imperial Service Academy." Before Astol will have anything to do with girls, they have to learn the language, and be taught his brand of palace etiquette. All the inside help are taught there before they go to work. All of the help inside Astol's palace are girls.

"The special girls, like me, are kept in a separate building. After we learn the language, we are trained to please Astol in special ways. I'm sure you know what I mean. The Earth girls they just brought in are probably still being taught the language. They won't have gotten into the rough part yet. You'll spare them a lot of pain and humiliation if you can get them out of there right now,"

"Can you tell us where the Academy is," Shok asked, "and how best to approach it to keep them safe while we're getting them out?"

She drew a map showing the location. The Academy consisted of six buildings on Astol's palace grounds. The academy was only a few hundred yards from the palace. One building stood alone in the complex, away from the cluster of the other five. That was the building Astol kept his foreign girls in. Its isolation made it easy to hit but they wanted to keep the girls safe while they hit it.

Shok hated to ask her to return to the place she had risked so much to leave, but her familiarity with the insides of the buildings in the palace complex made her the ideal person to help them get the other girls to safety.

Shok said, "Sherril, you don't have to do this if you don't want to, but it would be a big help for us to have someone along who can speak the Astolian language. We intend to free those girls and any others we find who want to be free. We can do it without you but you will know where to look if they try to hide them anywhere on the property, including the palace.

"We also want Astol and the dingo dung with him. Our cruisers are scanning this entire planet for them right now. I will give you some of the strangest looking and most competent bodyguards, you have ever seen in your life, for your protection, if you go with us."

She gave him her first smile before she replied, "I'll go with you. You just give me two pistols and a knife like the one your carrying, and tell those strange looking guards not to get in front of me when the shooting starts."

Shok began to appreciate how this beautiful girl could steal a shuttle she could barely get off the ground and aim it toward an unfamiliar spacecraft filled with people she didn't know. He smiled and gave her an admiring pat on the arm before he said; "You've got it kid. We have a practice simulator you can take a few shots on to get familiar with the laser pistols. I'll give you three pistols just in case you have to shoot a few more times than you're planning."

By the time Sherril finished with the simulator, Jeonk had finished briefing the Argans, Paracans, Oglaks, and Veolsh who were going with them on the raid. They were going to attack the palace but before the palace attack, they intended to free the Nordic girls.

Fifty fighters landed on the palace grounds to let out as many troops as they could. Fifty more fighters were overhead for support. After the first wave let their troops out and lifted off, the second wave landed and did the same thing. There were two hundred troops on the ground and one hundred fighters overhead before the air to ground transfer stopped.

Jeonk, Sherril and Shok landed in one of Shok's fleet fighters and left the fighter on the ground. It was a dark night and the lights from the palace were to far away to spoil the operations protective darkness. The Oglaks hurried to make sure the three of them were protected as fifty troops surrounded the building Sherril said the girls were in.

They didn't bother to knock; the Veolsh put small charges on the entrance door and blew the locks. After Jeonk kicked the door in, an interplanetary mix of troops pushed him out of the way to go in first. Everyone wanted to be the first to rescue the girls.

Shok heard yelling behind him. The palace guards had heard the noise made when the locks were blown and the door was kicked in. Shok could hear the palace guards behind him yelling for backup support. Before Shok could say anything, the Argans in the rear of the invading party turned their lasers on the noisy guards and terminated that noise. The Oglaks, who had helped to push Jeonk out of the way, began firing short bursts from their machine-guns inside the building the girls were in. Over the Oglak machine gun noise Sherril Strang yelled, "Stop firing, you Ugliks might hit the girls. They're in the back rooms or the basement."

The Oglaks couldn't understand her but she needn't have worried. Shok explained, "The Oglaks are professionals. They are holding their machine-guns low and firing high for head shots on those they see. Their missed rounds will hit high on the walls and go outside the building." The ground floor of the building was quickly cleared of Astolian guards and Sherril began checking the sleeping rooms for the girls.

She found the girls, still in their sleeping quarters, a little shook up but unhurt. Shok quickly explained the situation to the captive girls and some of them recognized Jeonk and Shok from the times they were on Nordic. The girls were easy to work with and were quickly gotten out of the building and on their way to Shok's flagship.

Sherril remarked, "I'm glad we didn't find any of them in the basement. That usually comes after they learn the language. It did with me."

Jeonk and Shok had her show them to the basement to see what she was talking about. The place had the appearance of a medieval torture chamber with high tech improvements. Everything in it looked like it was made to hurt someone. Shok had the Oglaks clear the building while he let Sherril have some fun breaking the stuff up.

After she had worked off some of her anger, he let her torch the building. The three of them watched the fire for a few minutes before Jeonk said, "People who do that sort of thing will find some way to do it but not in this building." Jeonk and Shok were more determined than ever to find Astol and his accompanying dingo dung pals.

The Argan troops had stormed the palace while the others were in Astol's Academy of Horrors. They had Astol's staff of good-looking girls from the Academy assembled on the main floor of the palace. Everyone working there was young, pretty and female. Sherril translated as Shok asked if there were any Earth girls or foreigners in the group. There were none. Shok asked if any of them would like to be free of palace duty. He explained that Astol would not be returning if his hiding place could be found. Most of the girls were glad to be free of the place and asked if they could go home to their families. Sherril told them, "There's the door; go when you please."

The exodus was quick and none of them asked if they could gather their things before they left. Maybe they didn't have any personal things worth taking with them.

One of the girls stayed behind after the others had gone. She told Sherril she thought she knew where Astol was hiding. She heard Astol tell three important strangers that they should go to his underground palace. She said she wasn't sure of its location, but she knew it was in a big mountain. She thought the big mountain was the one they would be able to see from the front of the palace when it was daylight. The girl gave Sherril her message then hurried after the others who had already gone.

Shok asked one of the Oglaks if he could see the mountain clearly. The Oglak said he could but he couldn't see any lights showing around it. Jeonk radioed one of the Oglak cruisers and asked to have a crew land and make an inspection of the mountain. A hidden entrance is only hidden if no one knows where to look for it. The Oglaks would find it at night even if Astol hid the entrance at the bottom of coal pit. If Astol and his friendly dingo dung were in that mountain; they were as good as found.

Jeonk turned to Sherril and said, "Your job is finished. You've done very well and we appreciate your help. I'll have someone take you back to the cruiser. You'll be safe there with the other girls."

SPACE LINE BY MARIVIN E. FOX

Sherril's reply was less than tactful, "Look you big blue, person, I've been waiting five years to cause that dirty little rat trouble. I'm not leaving until I get him. I didn't get one shot at his bloody guards because those Ugliks got all of them first. I'm going with you. Tell those Ugliks to keep out of my way."

Shok turned away to keep from laughing, but Jeonk was trapped. He rumbled a few notes of laughter as he said, "Maybe we'll need an interpreter. You've come this far. You can ride with Shok and me."

"Who the hell is Shok?" she retorted.

Shok said, "I'm Shok. The people in the cruisers call me Shok instead of Kelly."

She replied, "Oh! That's OK. I thought a Shok would take my three pistols and knife away from me."

It didn't take the Oglaks long to find the imperial Astol's hidden entrance. They had it staked out and were putting explosive charges on it as Jeonk and Shok put the combative Australian beauty into the fighter for a quick trip to Astol's hideout in the mountain.

Shok assured her the Oglaks wouldn't blow the door off the place and kill Astol before they arrived. She had two pistols in her hands and one in the belt of the cute pants she was wearing. The knife Shok gave her was in its scabbard. she had pushed the scabbard down her back between her clothing and her skin. She could make a quick grab for it from where it stuck up over her left shoulder. Sherril had a five-year grudge to settle with Astol and company. She was armed, primed, and ready to settle it with finality.

The three of them landed their fighter near the Oglaks. Shok quietly told two of the Oglaks to stay with Sherril but let her do the shooting, if they thought she could shoot without hurting herself. Jeonk and Shok would stay close so they could take out the ones she might be slow to take care of herself.

Tyrants usually keep their hideouts well guarded on the inside and they expected a pretty good battle. Outside guards would have given away its hidden position and the troops treated the outside with less caution than the inside. Two cruisers swung into position overhead and landed Argan Marines to help in the surprise opening of Astol's palace away from palace.

Shok had to move Sherril away from the entrance before the Oglaks blew it open. He thought she was so eager to be the first one inside that she didn't think about the explosion going both ways. Shok told her, "We actually have experienced warriors to go first. Girls have to go second." The Oglaks blew the entrance open but the interior was well lighted. The Oglaks moved out of the way to let the Argans and Paracans take out the interior guards.

Astol was expected to have other exits he could leave from at the first sign of trouble but there were two cruisers, fifty or sixty fighters and plenty of guards surrounding the mountain. Astol would probably think twice and then decide not to use one of his other entrances. Astol was trapped and he would understand that after some serious consideration of the problem. A quick look at the guns pointing at him from outside would help him solidify his decision.

After some jockeying for position, Shok managed to get ahead of the beautiful fire breathing Aussie. With Jeonk and Shok ahead of her and the Oglaks troops around her, Shok thought she would be safe. She still had a pistol in each hand and she obviously intended to use them. Jeonk was worried she might shoot Astol and his empire building partners before he could ask them a few questions.

They cautiously navigated the labyrinth of passages, moving toward the sound of the heaviest fighting. Sherril tried to get ahead of everyone, but Jeonk, Shok, her two Oglak bodyguards or some of the troops, filled the passage ahead of her. She couldn't shoot any of the bad guys from where she was but she couldn't get shot either.

The passages ended in a large room. There, in all of their imperial glory, was Astol, Kursit Balt and Sot Pah. Shok turned to Sherril and said, "Don't shoot anyone. We have some important questions to ask and dead men can't answer questions. Keep your pistols handy. We haven't secured this place yet. Astol or one of the others may have bodyguards crazy enough to try a rescue. If you need to shoot, shoot then."

Shok asked Kursit Balt, "Where is Chokng Fould? He should be with you and our intelligence said he was here. Where is he hiding?"

Kursit replied, "Fould left after the first attack on your fleet failed. He said he wasn't hanging around to see how you kicked our Asses. He left while you were preparing to meet the second attack. Choking told me, 'I know it's that bastard Shok and that damned blue King out there. If their tactics don't get you, their blind luck will.' The coward took his fleet with him."

"We know where Astol's fleet is," Shok continued, "but we don't know where yours is. I assume you didn't hitch hike with Chokng to get here. Where is your fleet and where are the twenty corsairs Sot Pah arrived in?"

Astol broke his silence to answer for Kursit and Sot Pah, "Their small fleets are far from here on another part of the planet. They are unimportant. Great destroyers like yourselves shouldn't be worried about such small matters."

Any time a rotten little tyrant like Astol tells you not to worry, it's time to worry. Jeonk and Shok gave each other a quick look. They realized the three dingo dungs weren't scared enough for the situation they were in. Shok knew they expected to be rescued and he was sure it would be soon.

Jeonk ordered the fleet to converge on the area and launch their fighters for cover from the outside. Shok organized the troops on the inside of Astol's hideout, positioning them to defend the large room they were holding.

While the troops were shifting to defensive positions, Sherril had quietly worked her way to within good shooting range of Astol and his accompanying dingo dung. Shok noticed her and shoved her between two big Paracans. He told them to keep her down low. Sherril didn't know what was going on and she got mad. Shok heard her yelling at the two Paracans, "Stop shoving me around. I can't shoot my pistols." Without explanation, Shok let her fight it out with the two Paracans. He knew hot action was a heartbeat away.

Sherril was still yelling at the Paracans on Shok's left. The Paracan, Argan, Oglak, and Veolsh troops began coming into the room from different passages. None of them knew where the danger would come from but they all knew it was coming.

Panels in the walls around the room suddenly flipped up. Astol's troops began entering the room from behind the flipping panels. Sherril and the others were surrounded, but Astol's troops had a handicap. They didn't know where Astol and his fellow escapees were in the room. In the seconds it took Astol's troops to locate him, Shok's troops began firing. The Astolians began answering their fire immediately.

The Paracans guarding Sherril were too busy staying alive to keep her under control. Sherril squeezed out from between the two Paracans, took careful aim and put four lethal laser rounds into Astol the deceased. He dropped like a rock. Jeonk was watching Shok's back and Shok watched his. Shok's troops dropped Astol's troops as fast as they took aim. The room looked like a light show at a Rock festival. Lasers crisscrossed the room in so many directions it looked like no one could survive, friend or foe. Oglak machine-guns were the only weapons making any loud noises. Their bup-bup-bup sounds could be heard above the low sizzle of the lasers hitting both sides.

Kursit Balt and Sot Pah began working their way out of the room to Shok's left, but he was too busy to stop them. Shok's troops couldn't waste their time with someone who wasn't trying to kill them. The two dung piles were plainly in an escape mode, they weren't shooting at anyone.

Sherril, now free of anyone who could keep her from shooting, eyed the two imperial escapees from her crouched position as they slithered behind a few Astolian troops who were in front of one of the flip up panels. She dropped four of the troops before she had a clear shot at the two escapees. She didn't hit Kursit but she pumped so many laser rounds into Sot Pah, he crumpled in a smoking heap. Kursit realized he was next on her priority to shoot list. He made a quick dive into one of the newly opened flip up passageways and disappeared.

The Astolian troops realized they no longer had anyone to rescue and it was damned dangerous in there. They made a speedy exit back into their flip up passageways. Shok's troops kept firing until there was no one left to shoot at. The Oglaks jumped into the darkened passages behind the fleeing Astolians. Shok could hear their machine-guns as they took out some of the fleeing Astolian troops. Jeonk hoped the Oglaks would find Kursit Balt and get rid of him, but his speedy exit picked up even more speed when he no longer had to duck Sherril's very accurate laser fire.

Shok made a quick assessment of the damage to his troops. He had seventeen down but only five of them were dead. Nearly all of the forty-three Astolian troops in the room were dead. The thermal protection suits Shok's troops wore were better than theirs. Shok had received some minor laser burns and Jeonk had three or four.

Sherril's excellent marksmanship removed any hope of getting information from Astol and Sot Pah. Jeonk and Shok found no relief from their Chokng Fould and Kursit Balt problem. They would salute the solution to that problem in due time.

The troops would have to remain in Astol's hideout until the fleet medics took care of the dead and wounded. Shok walked over to Sherril, who was still checking things out to make sure all of the live people in the room were friendly. One of her pistols was empty but the other one still had two rounds left in it. Shok put new power packs in the pistols for her and said, "Nice shooting. You did good! Where did you learn to shoot like that?"

"My father taught me to shoot when I was a little girl," she replied.

"I wish I could shake his hand," Shok remarked. "He does fine work. Let's see how Jeonk is making out." They walked to where Jeonk was talking to the Oglaks who had just returned from the chase in the passageways. None of the Oglaks reported finding Kursit Balt. The Oglaks said there were many hidden exits in the passageways and the Astolian troops who had survived disappeared into them.

Jeonk put his hand on Sherril's shoulder and said, "Some of the Paracan and Veolsh troops noticed your courage during the battle. You have a half dozen marriage proposals so far. Before you get married, I want to give you this." He picked her up by the waist, lifted her up to his level, kissed her right cheek and then kissed her left cheek.

He put her down before he said, "Thanks! Those were beautiful shots you hit Astol and Sot Pah with. It took a cool head and some real courage to make them. If you need a job, Shok and I always have room in our businesses for someone like you. We have a job for you in Australia if you don't want to stay with us in Arga but we'll talk about that later."

Sherril was misty eyed again. It had been a long time since anyone was nice to her and it was easy for her to see Jeonk really liked her as a person. That's the first time Shok had seen him do anything like picking Sherril up and kissing her. Shok remarked, "It looks like your five years in hell will turn out to have a golden lining. I thought of trying to hire you for the Australian operation before but I didn't want you to think we were pressuring you to take it.

"I want you to know that your ticket home has nothing to do with anything else. If you want a job in Arga, you can still go home and return. If you don't want a job anywhere in the inner galaxy, you'll still get home just as fast. If you take the job in Australia or not, you will get home just as fast. We both want you for the job but it's not our call. Your decision is the only important one."

Sherril began to worry about what they might want her to do. She dried her eyes, and then said, "I worked in an auto parts store. That's all I have done. How can I work for people from another planet?"

"Don't sell yourself short," Shok replied. "You're obviously very intelligent. You survived being kidnapped and taken to a strange planet. You survived five years with one of the galaxy's lest known but worst tyrants. You volunteered to help free thirty other girls when you could have said, 'no, I'm afraid to help.' Believe me, we would have understood if you said no. We would have thought no less of you for it. You shot down one rotten king who had recently lost a war, and was here looking for a new start. You also ended the shaky career of a little rat that called himself an emperor. You did all of that in less than one day after you escaped from them.

You have a cool nerve and a courageous mind. We can find herds of people better trained than you are but finding one with your courage and brains is a real problem. We can give anyone the training they need, but we can't give a one of them your ability and courage. You will do just fine. I approve of Jeonk's offer and I would have made the same one but at a different time."

Jeonk interrupted Shok's pep talk with, "We have to go Shok. Kursit and about fifty Dragon Spits have left the planet. We'll take two cruisers and follow them. The Galactic Forum will bring people in to sort this mess out and find out what kind of governments these people want. Sherril, you can stay here and leave on the first homeward bound cruiser. Shok and I may have some fighting to do."

Sherril retorted, "I'm not staying here with all of these stranger. I want to go with you and Shok. I'm not afraid, and I know you will win if you have a fight."

Jeonk took a long look at her, shook his head and laughed. Then he said, "You don't have to prove to me that you are not afraid. I wish you would stay here where it's safe, but I can't leave you with a bunch of people you don't know. You can come along and live dangerously with us. If you get killed it's your own fault."

Sherril perked up as she walked with Shok and Jeonk toward their fighter. Several prospective grooms from three very different planets were sorry to see her go.

They caught the cruisers in route, landed on Shok's flagship and made their way to the command deck. The corsairs had a long head start and were eating up space far ahead of them. The corsairs seemed to be on a course to reach Prssk.

SPACE LINE BY MARIVIN E. FOX

Shok didn't believe Prssk was their real destination. He thought Kursit and his corsairs were leading them toward Prssk to put them on the wrong course, then change course and try to hide on some uninhabited part of Nordic. He remarked, "They could be trying to make Gamac. They would be too vulnerable on Prssk. Kursit knows there is nowhere on Prssk one of the Argan fleets can't find and destroy his fleet. Kursit might know somewhere to hide on Nordic, or he might think Chokng Fould will hide him and his corsairs on Gamac." Jeonk and Shok were sure of one thing about Kursit; wherever he was going, he was too savvy a thief not to have prepared a place to hide before he arrived.

The cruisers were too slow to catch Kursit in his corsairs. The Argans had to out think him. Shok ordered a course change to Nordic. He thought Kursit would be trying to hide on Nordic, and Kursit was eating up time hoping to lead the Argans away from it.

The Argans decided to fly the shorter course to Nordic, arrive ahead of Kursit's fleet of Dragon Spits and intercept him before he could land. Jeonk decided to order an Argan fleet to patrol Gamac just in case Kursit and his fast fifty had fooled them about Nordic. If Kursit's fleet made it to Gamac, Jeonk's patrol would have them on scan and Kursit would have to divert from Gamac or fight.

Kursit was too smart to fight a losing battle he could run from. His retreat from the battle would force him to Nordic. If Jeonk and Shok were wrong, Kursit might lay in a course for Prssk. If Kursit knew of an unfamiliar planet he could hide on, and he was headed for that planet, he was home free for the moment.

Jeonk ordered Doskel's fleet to make flank speed to Gamac and cover Chokng Fould and the Gamacs. They were Kursit's helpful partners in the thieves trade. Jeonk ordered Rakoup's fleet to join him and Shok at Nordic. Two cruisers couldn't cover fifty Dragon Spit Corsairs intent on getting lost. At this moment, Kursit and his fleet of fifty corsairs were the most desperate, get lost, fleet in the galaxy.

Shok put one cruiser in celestial orbit near each of the Nordic planet's polar regions. He let the planet spin below them as they scanned for the Dragon Spits. If Kursit had headed his fleet directly for Nordic they would find them in the scan data.

Shok's cruisers didn't find the corsairs while scanning the planet, so Shok ordered the cruisers to hold position and remain silent. The corsairs would be easy to detect on the cruisers receiving sensors aimed toward Gamac and Prssk. The cruisers held their positions until Rakoup and his fleet arrived.

Rakoup brought his fleet's scanners on line and made a more thorough search of the planet Nordic just in case Shok's two cruisers had missed the corsairs. He found no Corsairs on Nordic. Shok and Jeonk put their heads together and decided Kursit and his corsairs either went to Gamac or did what they thought was unthinkable, and decided to hide on Prssk.

Shok contacted Doskel on patrol over Gamac. Doskel reported he had seen nothing but he was getting a lot of bad mouth from Chokng Fould. Chokng was trying to act innocent, as though he didn't know why Fleet Admiral Doskel would be looking for criminals on his planet of galactic do-gooders.

Rakoup had brought his entire fleet with him so Jeonk and Shok decided it would be better if they continued the search with Rakoup on the command deck of his flagship. They took Sherril with them--she still didn't want to be left with strangers.

Rakoup is as tough looking as it gets and Sherril was a little afraid of him. She hung back, hiding behind Shok for a while. She decided Shok wasn't big enough, so she got behind Jeonk. Rakoup noticed her anyway. He said, "Jeonk, bring that pretty girl here and introduce me to her? You and Shok have a knack for finding pretty Earth girls."

Shok took Sherril by the arm and told her Rakoup was a very good friend of his and he was only as fierce as he looked if someone happened to be one of his enemies. She reached her hand toward Rakoup and gave him one of the prettiest cardboard smiles Shok had ever seen. Rakoup noticed her discomfort as he took her hand. He said, "No one as pretty as you need have any worries on one of my ships. This is the safest place in the galaxy for you. Your welcome here."

Shok translated Rakoup's greeting to her and she relaxed quickly. She stayed on the command deck and after a while became more comfortable among the big blue strangers.

After a short conference, all three of them agreed it would be a good idea to take the fleet to Prssk. Kursit might have prepared someplace on the planet for just such an emergency. If he did, it would take some serious scanning to find it. Shok didn't think it was likely for Kursit to have prepared a big enough hideout for himself and a fleet of fifty corsairs. He thought they would find the corsairs before they found Kursit.

Sherril made friends with Rakoup on the way to Prssk. She spent part of her time sitting on his command pedestal where she could see what was happening on the outside of the ship as well as the inside.

Shok knew how she felt. He recalled the days when he first went into space with Jeonk. Space was a different world and it was exciting to be with friendly people who whizzed through space. Everyone could see she felt very good about it. Shok lost his doubts about her willingness to take the job Jeonk had offered her. The job would give her a chance to spend some time whizzing around like the rest of them.

Prssk appeared on the scanners and Rakoup spread the fleet for the search. The cruisers came in fast and took stationary orbits around the planet. They had no idea where Kursit might be hiding, or if he was hiding on Prssk. They were sure he would be found underground if they found him on Prssk. Rakoup's fleet had only a limited capability for underground detection and that meant they would need some good detective work to find Kursit.

The preliminary scans of the planet showed no corsairs above ground. There was no sign of any unusual activity on Prssk. They didn't detect any suspicious activities in the outlying areas. Prssk seemed to be going about its usual unsavory activities quietly. They continued making the scans, hoping to uncover anything that would give them a clue to the Dragon Spits whereabouts. The scan data updates continued coming into Rakoup's command holoscanner and being displayed to show the topography and population activities of the Prssk planet.

Sherril kept looking at one area of the display and Shok asked her what she was looking at. She said, "If I could build something to hide in, I would build it right here." She pointed to series of canyons on the smallest continent and the canyons joined near the center. She continued, "There must be big caves somewhere in those canyons. Hiding in them would be a matter of making them livable."

Jeonk told Rakoup what she had said. Rakoup stared at the holograph of the canyons for a long time. Shok expanded that section of Prssk to see if a more extensive look at the canyons would show anything more. The bigger Shok made it, the more it looked like there might have been some excavation done in that area. Rakoup smiled, slapped Sherril on the back; and said; "I think she may have found them for us. I'll put two cruisers in the canyons. We'll stay overhead in case they decide to try an escape."

The cruisers lowered quietly into the canyons. Their scanners at close range would be able to detect manmade structures inside the canyon cliffs. One of the cruiser Commanders reported that his scanners were detecting mine structures in the cliff side where the canyons converged. His scan data indicated that neither the cruiser's pulse cannons or lasers could be used to clear the inside area of the excavations. The cruiser couldn't be sure of its targets and the Commander still wasn't certain who or what he was dealing with. It could be something as innocent as a mining operation.

They hoped those inside would be Kursit and his fellow escapees. If it were, they had to know the Argans were outside and preparing to go in. Kursit and his crews would be preparing to use an exit in another part of the canyon, or getting ready to repel the Marines as they entered.

Rakoup ordered the cruisers that weren't engaged directly in the canyon activity to disperse and cover the possible exits outside of the canyon. The two cruisers inside the canyon would unload their Marines and prepare for an assault. Rakoup decided to shuttle his flagship's Marines to the surface in his fighters before the assault. He would keep his flag cruiser above the main canyon to give whatever assistance was needed to the ground troops. The cruisers positioned around the canyon's perimeter would prevent the Dragon Spit Corsairs from getting away.

Sherril realized what they were going to do. She asked Shok if she could go along. Shok gave her a flat no and told her it was too dangerous. She was safe where she was and she would have to stay on board Rakoup's cruiser. She didn't fuss with him about it. Shok thought she had accepted his decision.

Jeonk, Rakoup, and Shok became busy with the troop placements in the canyons and the problem of setting explosive charges to blast an entrance for the assault. Rakoup ordered his cruiser's Marines to join the other Marines on the ground. When they were all shuttled to the canyon floor, Jeonk and Shok would join them for the opening ceremony. Rakoup would stay on board to take care of problems if any arose. When the troop transfers from the air to the ground were completed, Jeonk looked around the command deck and said, "Where's Sherril? She was here a few minutes ago."

"I don't know." Shok answered. "I told her she couldn't go with us. That's the last time I saw her. Being forced to stay here didn't seem to be upset her."

Rakoup offered, "I saw her moving toward the fighter bays when the Marines were getting ready. She couldn't have gone with the Marines. They wouldn't let her--or would they? I'll see if she's with them."

Rakoup called his commanders on the ship's radio and found her with his Marines. He asked how she got there. A very unfortunate Lieutenant replied, "She got in the fighter with me. I couldn't understand what she said. She made hand signals and said, 'Rakoup', like you told her to go to the canyon floor. Then she made more hand signals and said, 'Jeonk, Shok,' like they would join her later. There was no seat for her on the fighter. She climbed on my lap and pointed toward the canyon. I thought you wanted her to go for some reason. I can send her back if you like."

"Rakoup," Jeonk suggested, "ask the lieutenant how she is armed?"

Rakoup asked, and the Lieutenant replied, "She has three laser pistols, one combat knife, a laser rifle and a bandoleer of charges for the rifle. Do you want me to send her back?"

Shok remarked, "I'm not sure we have enough Marines in the canyon to get her back on board a fighter. She's after Kursit. I don't know what he did to her on Kashtool but it was pretty bad. She only missed taking him out because she was too busy ending Astol and Sot Pah's careers as sex slave masters. We'd better get down there and make sure she lives long enough to get past that part of her life. I can't go home and tell Alice we let her get killed in some insignificant battle with Kursit Balt."

Jeonk added, "If we make our wives miss shopping for new clothes with her because we let her get killed, we'll have no peace from now until kingdom come."

" All three of our wives have been informed she's with us," Rakoup reported. "What do you think Iliaska will say? Sherril stole a laser rifle from my cruiser, and then talked one of my Marine Lieutenants into taking her off of 'my cruiser' with him. I'm going with the two of you. I'm turning over command of this cruiser to my Vice. I wouldn't miss this girl going after Kursit for a one on one cruiser battle."

The three of them grabbed a fighter and joined Sherril, who apparently intended to lead the assault on Kursit's hideout. Jeonk asked Sherril, "Do you know how to shoot that laser rifle?"

"My father taught me to shoot rifles," she replied. "One of the big blue guys showed me how to shoot this one. It works just like a laser pistol. It's bigger and it either hits harder or burns bigger. That's all I needed to know."

Rakoup signaled his troops to blow the entrance to Kursit's hideout. One Argan king and two Argan Admirals stayed between Sherril and the exploding entrance. She tried to go around Rakoup as soon as the dust cleared but he put his arm around her waist and held her back. The Marines took prone positions outside the tunnel and began firing inside. Laser and pulse cannon fire poured from the cavern they had just opened but it was too high to hit the Marines.

The Marines at each side of the entrance launched explosive charge to land inside the cavern. The explosions were loud but it wasn't possible to tell how much damage they did. It was still too early in the battle for the Marines to enter the cavern.

Rakoup ordered the Marines away from the entrance. He ordered three of his fighters to take static positions in the canyon leading to the cavern entrance. The fighters were to concentrate their pulse cannon fire into the cavern at different angles to destroy the pulse cannons firing from inside. After some intense firing from the fighters, there was a large explosion from inside the cavern.

Rakoup pushed Sherril to Shok and ordered the Marines inside. Rakoup followed the Marines. Jeonk, Sherril and Shok followed Rakoup. The large explosion was caused when a pulse cannon burst from one of the fighters hit one of the Dragon Spits. Several of the other Dragon Spits were damaged when the first one exploded but none of them were on fire. The Marines found only ten Dragon Spits in the first cavern. That meant they had other caverns but where the caverns were was still a guess.

The Marines found passageways leading to other parts of the cavern system. Shok thought they were probably booby-trapped. He handed Sherril to Jeonk, had the Marines clear the debris from the explosion, and move one of the Dragon Spits so he could fire its pulse cannon into the passageways. The Dragon Spit's pulse cannon would destroy the booby traps if Shok was right about them being there.

Shok fired into all four of the passageways. Only one of them exploded when he fired into it. Shok thought that was the way to go. They didn't have enough time to booby-trap all of them. Shok explained, philosophically, "There are times when we don't have enough time to do all of the things we would like to for unexpected guests. I'm sure Kursit and his friends would liked to have booby trapped all of the passageways but time was on our side."

Rakoup ordered the Marines into the blown passageway. Sherril walked calmly beside Jeonk as he and Shok followed Rakoup and the Marines farther into the cavern system. The explosion from Shok's pulse cannon shot had occurred on the far end of the passageway and there was debris to be cleared before they could proceed. As the Marines cleared the debris in front of them, they heard lasers firing behind them.

Sherril heard the same lasers, turned and ran toward the sound of the fighting. Shok turned and ran toward Sherril. Jeonk and Rakoup followed behind him. Shok caught up with Sherril at the end of the passageway. Her laser rifle was trained on another passageway and she was blasting away with it.

Two groups of Astolian troops were fighting the Marines in an attempt to get to the operational Dragon Spits near the cavern entrance. One bunch of Astolians were firing from behind a large piece of the destroyed Dragon Spit, using it to protect themselves from the Marine lasers. The second group of Astolians was firing from the entrance of a passageway to the right. Sherril had the second Group pinned down and was keeping them from coming out of the passageway to support the first group.

Between the Marines holding the front of the cavern and Sherril firing from the back of the cavern, the Astolians were in the crossfire. They couldn't move forward to the operational Dragon Spits. Jeonk, Rakoup and Shok added their laser fire to Sherril's in the crossfire and forced the second group of Astolians to retreat back into the passageways.

After Sherril and her high level backup helped the Marines force the Astolians out of the main cavern, Rakoup ordered his Marines to advance down all of the passageways and secure the other ends. The Marines in the booby-trapped passageway had finished clearing the debris and were fighting the Astolian Troops at the other end. The Marines, having passed through the other three passageways, were near enough to the first group to support them in the battle. The Astolians, who couldn't escape and were no longer in a position to fight, surrendered.

Jeonk pressed Sherril into duty as his interpreter to the Astolians. She spoke with the Astolian troops for a while then turned to Jeonk and said. "Kursit left right after they got here. He told the Astolians that they would be safe here. He told them no one could possibly find this place. Kursit told them to stay here until he was sure the Argans weren't around anymore. After that, he would arrange for them to stay on Prssk or go back to their home planet." Then she added, "We'll have to attack Prssk to get rid of Kursit. He's hiding among his own people where he thinks we can't find him."

Jeonk studied her for a minute, and then asked, "Is your revenge important enough to attack an entire planet to get him?"

"Revenge hasn't anything to do with it," Sherril replied. "He's been hurting girls like me for so long he thinks it is his right. I don't want to let him continue to hurt other girls the way he did me. I have a responsibility to them. I want him stopped. If it costs my life, I want him stopped."

Shok asked, "Is that why you risked so much to take out Astol and Sot Pah?"

She turned to him and just said, "Yes."

"What about Chokng Fouled," Shok asked, "the one with the strange red skin? You haven't said much about him except you called him dingo dung."

"He didn't hurt anyone." She replied. "He brought two girls of his own kind with him. They didn't look beat up or anything. They acted like they liked him. He did help Kursit bring the thirty girls for Astol. For that, I would shoot him if I could but I don't think he's in the same class with the other three. The other three were filthy beasts. Anyone who lets them get away is to blame for what they do in the future. I don't want to be the one to blame."

"We don't want to be blamed for letting Kursit go," Jeonk assured her, "but he's deep underground by now and it will take time to dig him out. We have people who know how to do the digging and they'll find him. You don't know much about Chokng Fould but Shok and I do, and we aren't going to take the blame for letting him go either. He may not be a filthy beast but he's a murdering pirate and his end is just as certain as Kursit Balt.

There is nothing more we can do here. We'll be leaving for Arga on Rakoup's cruiser. He'll leave people behind to clean up this mess and get the Astolians back to whatever fate awaits them on Kashtool. The entire nation of Arga is probably waiting for you by now. My wife, Aslain, Shok's wife, Alice, and Rakoup's wife, Iliaska, are all waiting for you. We had better put Rakoup's cruiser in space on a heading for Arga, or our wives will be mad at us for taking so long to bring you to meet them."

As they left the cavern, every Marine who could get close enough patted Sherril on the shoulder or grabbed her hand to say good-bye. She made a lot of friends that day. Rakoup's Marines had been told about her courage in the battle on Kashtool, and they watched her in action on Prssk. They wanted to rename one of their Century Units after her but that became such a popular idea they had to name Rakoup's Marine Division after her to satisfy the demands of his troops. Shok remarked, "One thing is certain, three wives and all of the Argans are going to love that girl."

Rakoup pushed his flagship flat out, to reach Arga quickly, out of his respect for three impatient wives. Jeonk and Shok not only wanted to get Sherril into the hands of their wives, they wanted to begin the search for Kursit and their business with Chokng Fould boiling in the pot of necessary activities.

They planned the tactics for the Office of Special Military Projects while in route to Arga. Shok would have to give the plans to Plask. Jeonk had left Plask in charge of the Special Military Projects office. Jeonk and Shok would have time to enjoy the company of their wives while Plask handled the search.

Shok had two regrets for the trip. He regretted missing Kursit Balt and Chokng Fould on Kashtool. The second regret was yet to come. He regretted that he wouldn't get to hear Rakoup explain to Iliaska how one small girl taking her first ride on a cruiser, could steal a rifle from his cruiser armory, and talk an Argan lieutenant she didn't know and couldn't actually talk to into taking her into an Argan battle. The real interesting part of his explanation would be after Iliaska reminded him that Argan men will not allow Argan women in battle. Iliaska thinks some Argan women should be allowed in battle; like, Iliaska, for instance.

Rakoup brought his flagship into Shok's base at Perlta. Perlta is close to Poshalla and also close to Plask's Lersta castle, where all three of them thought their wives were anxiously waiting for them to put Sherril under their personal care.

Cruiser landings are generally uneventful. Cruisers come and go all of the time and they are frequently seen landing, taking off or in some holding pattern over Poshalla. Argans are a low key people when the want to be and that's most of the time. Once in a great while they drag out the red carpet for returning heroes who have done a great job in protecting their nation.

There was a large crowd and a Marine band waiting for Rakoup's cruiser to land at Shok's Perlta base. King Plask and the three wives were waiting at the front of the crowd. Jeonk, Rakoup, Shok and Sherril stepped out of the cruiser to the strains of the Argan National Anthem. A twenty-foot long banner just behind the royal party said in English, "ARGA WELCOMES SHERRIL STRANG."

Jeonk said to Shok, in Argan, "It's lucky we found her or no one would know we came home."

Rakoup was trying to keep from laughing as he said, "All you two did was destroy twenty thousand Dragon Spit Corsairs and protect Arga from a few tyrants trying to become the galaxies next emperors. She's the one who actually shot the emperors.

Sherril asked, "How do they know my name?"

"Half the galaxy knows your name by now," Shok answered. "News travels fast in the inner galaxy. Kursit will have told his friends about the death of his galaxy-grabbing partners, Astol and Sot Pah, and of his own narrow escape from your well-aimed pistols. Sot Pah's spies on Kashtool will have informed his friends in the nations of Pishtup and Supek on the planet Tuplej of the several shots you took Sot Pah down with. The warriors of the Galactic Forum nations, who were with us in the battle on Kashtool, will have passed the good news to the nations of eight other planets in the Galactic Forum. You are the only girl who has ever shot down two filthy dingo-dung beasts that were also royal tyrants in one day. Added to that, you picked up your weapons and went after his partners, the two most wanted royal thieves in the galaxy. Everyone who knows about you will be telling your story to everyone who doesn't. You are one of the most well known people in the galaxy."

Plask and the three wives came forward as Shok finished his explanation. The wives gave their husbands a quick public kiss and whisked Sherril toward a command plak waiting in front of Shok's Marine band playing "The Hero Returns" for all it was worth.

After Aslain made a short speech of praise for the courage and marksmanship of Sherril, Aslain, Alice and Iliaska got into the command plak with Sherril. They stopped the command plak in front of their husbands for a brief instant as they left. Alice said out of the window, "We'll see you at the castle. Emira wants to meet Sherril."

Plask exclaimed, "That's my command plak and they just left me standing here!"

Rakoup exclaimed, "That's our wives and they just left us standing here!"

Jeonk exclaimed, "I've never seen anything like that in my entire life!"

Shok exclaimed, "Wait until we see the bills for the shopping sprees they'll take her on. We will have never seen anything like that in our entire lives either!"

They all started laughing at Shok's cost analysis. Plask saved the day for them. He said, "Shok, this is your base; do you think you can arrange a command plak that will make it to the castle? I'm anxious to see what will happen next. The three of you can tell me about the battle on Kashtool and Prssk on the way."

"Sure," Shok replied, "but we need to get to the OSMP offices in Poshalla before we go to the castle, if you don't mind. Jeonk and I need to brief the office on the search for Kursit Balt and Chokng Fould. The last we heard of Chokng, he was still on Gamac. Kursit is probably hiding out somewhere on Prssk but we can't be sure where they are. Our intelligence network will have to find them. We can't leave them running around loose, they've become too dangerous."

Plask and Rakoup agreed that was the thing to do. Shok briefed the OSMP in Poshalla then headed the command plak toward Plask's castle.

The ladies were in Emira's kitchen having coffee when they arrived at the castle. Sherril had her hair done and she was wearing one of Alice's dresses. She looked very pretty in the light blue dress with her blond waves pouring down to her shoulders. She had finished telling the other women about her adventures and the ladies were asking her questions.

As the men entered Emira's kitchen, Aslain turned to Jeonk and asked, "Jeonk, how could you and Shok let this poor defenseless girl get into those battles? She could have been killed."

"I don't know about the poor part," Jeonk defended, "but she sure as heck isn't defenseless. She can shoot as straight as anyone else. We needed an interpreter on Kashtool and she was the only one available. We had bodyguards with her all of the time. Shok and I kept her with us most of the time. She's a lady with a mission and she doesn't let anything she can move out of the way interfere with her mission. She did very well. We have no need to apologize for her or ourselves."

Shok broke in at that point to bring their search for Chokng and Kursit into perspective, "We've just come from Poshalla and the search for Kursit and Chokng has already begun. We should be able to locate them within the next few days. When we know where they are, we'll take care of them, wherever that is."

Alice and the ladies weren't quit satisfied with such a nebulous plan for the two galactic thieves, kidnappers and sex maniacs. Alice spoke for the group, "Sherril told us some of the terrible things Kursit did to her--things women don't tell to men. We want you to let us help you go after him. We want to make sure he can't do those things to any other woman."

Since Alice was Shok's wife, he answered her, "You will remember what Kursit and Chokng tried to do to this family. Whatever they have done to anyone else is dead-ended, and dead is what they will be. We've been after both of them for a long time. It's an Argan Military duty to keep the royal family and all other people on Arga safe from them. The Argans' assigned to that duty are trained to perform it without any help. None of you have that kind of training.

"As Sherril can tell you, we lost men on Kashtool, and on Prssk. They were well-trained men but we still lost a few of them. We don't intend to lose any of you and that includes Sherril."

Plask added, "We have an organization working on the problem and they are good at what they do. Shok is right. He and Jeonk are the best people I know to take care of it. Those two crooks aren't hiding from Argan women, they are hiding from Shok and Jeonk. They didn't run from Kashtool because of you ladies and Sherril, they ran from Jeonk and Shok. Let them handle it, as they have handled every other threat any of us know about."

Rakoup put his thoughts into the discussion, "We love our wives. When they are in danger, we stop fighting with precision and begin fighting with anger. We lose our precision, and the fine line that sometimes makes the difference between life and death. We need to know you are safe."

Jeonk ended the discussion amicably, "Mother, do you have anything to eat in the castle, we're hungry."

Emira responded with a kiss on his cheek and said, "We expected you hours ago. We haven't eaten because we waited for you. The food is probably not as good as it could be. The cook will serve it immediately and you'll just have to eat it the way it is."

SPACE LINE BY MARIVIN E. FOX

The dinner was still tasty. There was no more talk of the women going after Kursit and Chokng. The battle weary men slept in the castle that night and had pleasant private reunions with their wives. Shok's final thoughts were of Sherril. He hoped she wasn't having bad dreams about her time on Kashtool. She had sympathetic friends around her and that would be a big help.

14

THE ARGAN WOMEN ATTACK CHOKNG AND KURSIT

Jeonk and Shok sat killing time in Jeonk's military office, mourning their lack of success. They couldn't find the two most wanted crooks in the galaxy. Shok's spies were searching constantly for Kursit and Chokng. Months passed with little to show for their efforts except false trails.

The Galactic Forum nations were searching for them as seriously as the Argans. Most of Forum nations wanted the two as badly as the Argans. Every nation had promised to give the Argans any information they found. Shok thought he had every civilized planet in the galaxy locked down so well that neither of the bad guys could hide on them. The Argan spies on Gamac and Prssk assured Shok that Kursit and Chokng were somewhere else, but where else, no one knew.

The women were beginning to get impatient with the ineffective search. They wanted the two best examples of dingo dung, this side of Australia, out of the inner galaxy criminal life. Anyone who could put them that way was okay with them.

Jeonk couldn't let Sherril go home to Australia because Kursit and Chokng had put a half million gold skirb price on her head to be paid to anyone who killed her. Kursit and Chokng didn't like it because she killed, with malice aforethought and a few well-aimed laser shots, the most promising meal ticket they had seen in their lives.

Jeonk took his feet off of his desk, plopped them on the floor and said, "Shok, we have to get out of our dingy offices and look for those two ourselves. Everyone is missing something and we won't find out what they're missing sitting around our offices. Let's take one of the Dragon Spit Corsairs and find them. Being out in space will clear our minds so we can think. Where do you think we should go first?"

He was right about the thinking. If the plushest office on the planet looked dingy to him, it was time they got to the job of finding them. Shok replied, "The only planet that isn't completely locked down is Nordic. Nordic is almost uninhabited except for a few thousand Earth people. We can stay at our hunting lodge while we search. We haven't had a chance to use it yet.

Have you thought of a way to go without telling our wives? They'll insist on coming along if they find out. If they come, we won't be able to follow Kursit and Chokng's trail if we find it."

Jeonk thought for a minute before he spoke, "I think we should tell them we need a break. We'll say we're just going to Nordic for a few of days hunting. We'll tell them we need to go alone to clear our minds and to get a better perspective on Kursit and Chokng. They'll buy that."

"All right but you have to tell them," Shok cautioned. "Everyone thinks I'm some kind of planning machine. A machine doesn't need a clear mind; it keeps going no matter what. I'll tell Alice it was your idea, and I'll tell her tonight. Tomorrow morning Alice will tell Aslain we need a break, and Aslain will agree because Alice told her. You tell Aslain we want to do a little hunting but don't tell her until after Alice talks with her. Maybe you and I can get a line on Kursit and Chokng on Nordic. We'll ask Rakoup to mind the office while we're gone."

Jeonk's plan, with Shok's timing, worked without a hitch. They were on their way in one beauty of a hot rod Dragon Spit, alone. They both felt good about pulling it off. Flying the Dragon spit was great. It handled easy and it was the fastest ship either of them had ever flown.

The Argan engineers had solved the problem of it shutting down for a few seconds if something as bright as a pulse cannon fired in front of it. If the late Astol had the engineering skill to match his ambition, the Argan fleet would have been torn to bits on Kashtool, and Astol might have had a chance for his criminal empire.

They landed at the hunting lodge on Nordic and began checking with the Nordics for reports of strangers. The Nordics were happy to see them. It was the first time the Nordics had a chance to thank them personally for the return of their thirty women. Between the many thanks, they managed to ask questions about strangers visiting the planet. The Nordics had seen no one. They had seen no strange spacecraft going to or from the uninhabited parts of the planet. The only visitors they had were the occasional Argan supply ship bringing in equipment or trading for the farm products the Nordics grew.

Both of them knew the Nordics could only see a small portion of their planet. It would be easy for someone in hiding to avoid being seen. They checked the places they knew the Gamacs had used before, but they came up dry. They flew the Dragon Spit around the planet for three days, scanning the planet as they went. They thought Nordic was the only planet Kursit and Chokng could go where the two crooks and their fleet could avoid detection by the planet's population. They became increasingly disappointed at not finding them and Nordic was turning out to be as depressing as their offices.

The following day Jeonk received a report from Rakoup, who informed them, "The Iklugs used the Galactic Forum communications system to relay some very interesting information to our Poshalla office. The Iklugs reported a buildup of strangers in Shiska Frok. The Iklugs say the increase has been occurring for the past few months. They have identified Gamacs and Prsskians as the major groups of strangers. They say Shiska Frok has been very quiet since the strangers arrived. The usual criminal activity coming from the area has diminished to an unbelievable point.

"The Iklugs think someone is organizing the criminal elements of Shiska Frok, and they are worried about it. They think it may be the Kursit Balt and Chokng Fould you warned them about. The Iklugs have refused to move on Shiska Frok unless criminal activities begin happening, and are clearly coming from Shiska Frok. They will allow us to go into the area if Arga brings enough troops to handle the situation, whatever it is. I suggest you return to Arga immediately to handle the situation."

Jeonk replied, "We're leaving Nordic immediately. Both of us hope Kursit and Chokng are actually surfacing in Shiska Frok. Shiska Frok means abundant trouble in Iklug There isn't anyone closer to the meaning of the words than Chokng and Kursit." He turned to Shok and said, "I hope they're there. We can blast hell out of Shiska Frok and receive nothing but praise from the people of Iklug. I can't think of a more natural habitat for Kursit and Chokng."

Shok was ahead of him with a plan, "We'll need to land Marines and mount a search for them. They won't give up without a fight, and they won't come out of hiding to join in the fight. It will be almost like a house-to-house attack.

I expect the normal population of Shiska Frok to get out of our way if they can. We can allow them to get out of the way, but we can't let them get behind us. Some of them will probably be able to tell us where Kursit and Chokng are hiding but not until they are sure it's to their advantage to give them up.

We should keep enough cruisers overhead to keep the Gamac and Prsskian spacecraft on the ground. We can trap them in Shiska Frok and keep them from leaving if we make our attack in one well coordinated air and ground move."

Jeonk added, "Shiska Frok is a pretty big place. I think we should bring in ten thousand of General Sokeasel's ground troops just to be safe. We'll use two fleets of cruisers to cover the area. The fleet Marines and the ground troops can work together to find Kursit, Chokng and their pirates. Does that sound about right to you?"

"Sure does," Shok replied. "No matter how many rag tag pirates we have to fight, they can't face Arga's professional soldiers and Marines. The best they can do is become a target rich environment. I think we have them cold. We have to get there fast, before some friendly spy on Iklug tells them we know where they are. They'll be out of there quick if they find out we're coming after them."

They were still a few hours from Arga when Rakoup called them again. Rakoup seemed in a hurry. He reported, "Our wives and Sherril Strang have taken sixty Dragon Spit Corsairs from the base at Yadki. They apparently intend to go after Kursit and Chokng at Shiska Frok."

"How did they get sixty Dragon Spits in the air?" Jeonk interrupted, "Who are the pilots and how do they know Kursit and Chokng are at Shiska Frok?"

"Plask and I have been teaching Aslain, Alice and Iliaska how to fly the Dragon Spits," Rakoup confessed. "They became proficient in the Dragon Spits I have at my base and the Spits Shok has at Perlta. We thought they were just giving rides to the women in the fleet, but they were teaching them how to fly the Dragon Spits. There are three hundred Dragon Spits at Yadki.

"Aslain took a large party of women to Yadki. Alice, Iliaska and Sherril Strang were with her. The other women were from the fleet. Aslain ordered the base commander to let her party have sixty Dragon Spits. She told the Base Commander they were going to make a surprise visit to you and Shok while you were on your hunting trip.

"I found out about it three hours ago from a routine message I just happened to see from Yadki. There wasn't much I could do about it until I received an urgent message from the Veolsh planet. The message said a fleet of sixty Dragon Spits passed through their area, and they thought it might be Kursit and Chokng. Your sixty Dragon Spits, our wives, and a large group of fleet women are on a course for Shiska Frok.

"I'm the one who told them about the location of Kursit and Chokng. I knew how anxious they were to rid the galaxy of those two. It never occurred to me that the women would go after Kursit and Chokng by themselves. I have two fleets in the air and they are in hot pursuit. The ladies have a few hours head start on us and they are in the fastest spacecraft we have. Plask and I have one of the Dragon Spits waiting. We'll be in the air in five minutes."

"We've already vectored for Iklug," Shok reported. "Put another fleet in the air with all the Marines it can carry. We won't need the extra fleet but we will probably need the fleet's Marines. We'll meet you at Shiska Frok."

"Damn it!" Jeonk said. "Do you think we should get the Iklug's involved?"

"I don't think so," Shok answered. "The Iklugs were afraid to go into Shiska Frok to take care of the problem themselves, and the women should be arriving on Iklug soon. If we ask the Iklugs for help, we may be warning Kursit and Chokng that our wives are gunning for them. The Iklugs may refuse to help even if we ask. I don't think anyone can help. There isn't enough time for anyone to organize the help before we get there. The women have to survive on their own for a few hours. We're the only help they have and we're moving as fast as we can."

Jeonk gave the problem his simple logic treatment, "Their Dragon Spits take a minimum crew of four. There are at least two hundred and forty women in the fleet of sixty. None of them know where anything is in Shiska Frok. It may take them hours of scanning to locate anything they think is a target.

"The operation is a ground operation and none of them know anything about ground offensives. They will have to get together and plan an attack on the ground target--or targets, after they identify something they can shoot. That will take more time.

"I don't think Kursit and Chokng will launch their corsairs to face fifty Dragon Spits because neither of them will know the Spits are being flown by inexperienced crews. I think those facts will give us a chance to get to Shiska Frok before the women make their attack."

Shok added his own simple logic to the equation, "Rakoup and Plask will be right behind us. If we can keep the women from landing; you and I, with Rakoup, and Plask, can organize the women to keep Kursit and Chokng on the ground. We can use the women's scan data to hit the spacecraft on the ground. Maybe we can save the day. With luck, we can keep our wives and their crews alive, and still capture Kursit and Chokng."

Coming into Shiska Frok's airspace was a study in how simple logic can get it all wrong. The Argan women and their fleet of dragon Spits were in a major air battle over Shiska Frok. It was easy for Shok and Jeonk to identify the women's side; they were flying the Dragon Spits. It wasn't difficult for them to identify Kursit and Chokng's ships. They were flying everything else, and they easily outnumbered the Dragon Spits.

The neighboring Iklug nations had launched their own fighters to protect their borders from the several different kinds of spacecraft fighting above Shiska Frok. The Iklugs weren't sure who was fighting in the battle, and they didn't know which to shoot, even if they decided to shoot.

Jeonk and Shok dived into the middle of the fray, taking out a couple of Gamac corsairs as they dived. Jeonk ordered the women's Dragon Spits to climb high and fast enough to get them out of the battle but none of them paid any attention to him.

The women were doing a damn fine job of dog fighting. When a bogey got on their tail, they out climbed it or outran it and then whipped their Dragon Spit around and returned to the attack.

The women flew the Dragon Spits in formations of three. Each of the Spits in the formation protected the other two as much as it could, and that seemed to be pretty successful plan of attack. Shok saw very few downed Dragon Spits but there were many enemy ships downed. Jeonk and Shok listened as their radio filled with the women talking to each other. They had a handle on the battle; that was for sure.

Jeonk began to notice how good they were. He said, "Shok, they must have read the manual you wrote on Dragon Spit tactics. They must have been practicing in the simulators to do as well as they're doing. They are beating hell out of Kursit and Chokng's fleet.

They listened to Rakoup's voice as he entered the area. He ordered, "Iliaska where--Plask take that guy out with the port pulse cannon--Iliaska, where are you? You and the other women get out of that mess now! We'll take it from here."

Iliaska didn't answer. She was probably busy trying to get a bead on somebody. When she was little less busy she answered, "Sitak, we're busy, either shut up and shoot or just shut up. We don't need any help."

They listened intently as Aslain gave the order, "Prepare for a sweep."

In one quick maneuver, the entire Dragon Spit fleet bolted from the battle. Jeonk and Shok in their Spit, Plask and Rakoup in theirs; were alone in the middle of the battle. Jeonk signaled Rakoup to climb out. Rakoup began his climb even before he got Jeonk's signal.

Kursit and Chokng's ships thought they had won the battle. The Dragon Spits appeared to them to be trying to escape from the battle. The pirate ships wheeled to give pursuit. They followed the Dragon Spits to kill as many as they could before the Spits disappeared. Jeonk and Shok joined Rakoup and Plask above the battle to get out of the way of the sweep. They had a very good view of the operation but there was nothing they could do to help until the women finished the sweep.

On Aslain's signal, The Dragon Spits wheeled from their fake retreat. They stacked six high and nine across with a few empty spaces; they had lost a few ships. The two opposing fleets were head to head. The Dragon Spit sweep began as they gained speed. The pulse cannons of the Dragon Spit fleet all fired at the same time, filling the space between them and the pirates with deadly fire. The fury of their fire matched the fury of their disgust for Kursit and Chokng.

The oncoming enemy fleet had no time to maneuver out of the way. Most of the pirate ships showered the debris of their destruction across Shiska Frok. It seemed everything that could burn on Shiska Frock was set on fire by a downed and burning pirate spacecraft. The few pirates who escaped the deadly sweep turned tail and ran from the battle.

The battle was over but the Kursit, Chokng problem wasn't solved with its winning. Kursit and Chokng were still below them in Shiska Frok. Jeonk and Shok agreed, those two weren't the kind to risk their own skins in a battle they could get others to fight.

Jeonk and Shok knew the two pirates well enough to know they would have many men around them to put up a fight when they were found. The two pervert potentates would still be able to leave in one of their reserve spaceships if they could find enough empty sky to fly in.

Jeonk grabbed his radio to talk with the women in the Dragon Spit fleet, "You have won a fine battle, and all of you did well in the battle. However, you did not take care of the Kursit Balt, Chokng Fould problem. They aren't dead and you did not fight them. They are almost certainly still below us in Shiska Frok. With your help, we will keep them on the ground until the fleet arrives. We, and the fleet will take care of them when the fleet gets here.

"Until then, I want you to follow my orders to the letter. Spread your fleet so each ship can cover a large enough scan area to cover Shiska Frok. If anything leaves the ground, a ship of any kind, you must shoot it down. Shok and I in this ship, Rakoup and Plask in their ship, will be above you to cover the entire area. If a ship of any kind gets above your ships on an escape course, you must not follow it. We will take care of it. You must remain in your positions to cover your area. One of us will take care of a bogey that gets above you. I'm asking the Iklugs to cover the entire Shiska Frok border to take care of anything we can't from our internal positions.

"It will be two days before the fleets arrive. We must remain on station, and alert during that time. Make sure crew rests are covered by other crewmembers. Your ships must be battle ready at all times. Any deviation from this order will be a matter for military discipline. You did well in the part of the operation you planned. I admire your skill and courage but your plan was not comprehensive enough to meet the objectives of the operation. Kursit Balt and Chokng Fould are nearly as much of a problem now as they were before you arrived. If they have escaped while the battle was going on, they will be even more of a problem.

"I have asked the Iklugs to send in rescue squads to recover our downed personnel and rescue is on the way for the downed crews. I hope they all survived. I would like your commanders report on the downed ships including the names of the downed crew members."

Jeonk was an angered king. He thought the women had messed up a military operation He and Shok were about to pull off with clinical precision. Shok didn't think it was a good time to remind him that the commander's report he was waiting to hear would be from his wife. Shok let him simmer as he watched the scanner to see how well the female fleet covered Shiska Frok.

The Dragon Spits rose to fifty thousand feet, spread across Shiska Frok and held their positions. It was a good maneuver. Anything coming off of Shiska Frok was going to have a difficult time getting away from them. Jeonk remarked, "They have it covered like a blanket. I'd like to know how and when they learned so much about fleet maneuvers."

Shok thought he had simmered long enough. He said, "Do you remember when Rakoup told us he was teaching Alice about fleet maneuvers? He was probably teaching Iliaska at the same time but he didn't tell us about that. Alice and Iliaska must have taught Aslain what they learned. Plask and Rakoup are always happy to explain a past winning battle in minor detail to a bunch of amazed women. I'm sure each of the amazed women paid close attention to every cruiser maneuvering word.

"The women in the military have always been encouraged to use the simulators so they will understand the problems men face in battle, and no one would have paid any attention when they used them. There are training videos on every battle we've been in and the tactics and the logic of the tactics are in those videos. How they gained the proficiency they showed today is a guess but the basic information is available to any of them who wish to look."

Jeonk had cooled down quit a bit, He said, "That sweep was a sweet maneuver. They took it from cruiser tactics and adapted it to the Dragon Spits. The women in that fleet have been practicing somewhere for a long time. I think I'll let that be their little secret. You and I are going to find out but without asking any of them.

"You don't get mad at Alice and I won't get mad at Aslain. When I talk to Rakoup, I'll ask him not to get mad at Iliaska. I know Alice and Iliaska helped Aslain plan the battle. If we keep quiet about it, they'll eventually tell us everything. I'll have to give some medals for valor to the women in this battle. I can't give medals and be mad at them at the same time."

The Dragon Spit fleet held its position and nothing came off the floor of Shiska Frok. The Argan cruiser fleets arrived, landed their Marines and took positions to control the airspace over Shiska Frok and Iklug. The arriving Argan fleets left no chance for the pirates to escape. The women in their fleet had effectively closed out the possibility of another air battle. The incoming cruiser fleets hadn't bothered to launch their fighters.

Jeonk set up a command post in central Shiska Frok and spread the Marines throughout the Shiska Frok area. Shok doesn't like calling it a country but it's as large as one; it just isn't organized like one. Jeonk had the three Dragon Spits flown by Aslain, Iliaska and Alice land at the command post. He wanted them to be in on the planning of the search for Kursit and Chokng. He told Shok, "If they ever sneak off and do something like this again, I want them to know enough about it to do it right or not at all."

Sherril Strang flew as a gunner with Alice in her Dragon Spit. Alice told Shok, "Sherril shoots as straight from a Spit as she does on the ground." The four women wore the same thermal suits the fighter pilots wear. They each had three pistols and a knife just like Jeonk and Shok carry. Jeonk and Shok used to be the only one's who carried three pistols and a knife. Now, almost everyone does, and the women were no exception.

The command post began receiving reports of Marine skirmishes at various places in Shiska Frok. The skirmishes were with the regular inhabitants of Shiska Frok and ended quickly without loss of life. Many of the regular Shiska Frok inhabitants were captured and questioned. Most of them had at some time been in contact with the Kursit and Chokng crowd but they didn't know where they were now.

The nearby wives, who had become Spit Commanders, said the enemy spacecraft came at them from various locations in Shiska Frok but the largest number came from a canyon area that began fifty miles from the command post.

Jeonk ordered a cruiser to make scans of that part of Shiska Frok. If there were a large groups of people in the area, the cruiser would find them. The most promising area was in rough country. Rivers and canyons ran the length of the search area in the bad lands of Shiska Frok. The cruiser scans showed signs of mining activity that was apparently in progress, but there were no people working the mines. The scans also indicated there were many large cave entrances in the area around the mines. The cruiser sent its fighters down for a visual but they found nothing and were not fired upon.

Shok had a gut feeling Kursit and Chokng were there somewhere. Jeonk had the same gut feeling as Shok. He said, "Shok, they were underground on Kashtool and they were underground on Prssk. I'll bet they are underground here. We can find them."

Sherril Strang demanded; "I'm going with you."

Alice put her hand on Sherril's shoulder, leaned close to her and quietly said, "Not a good time."

Jeonk and Shok walked to their Dragon Spit, talking with Rakoup and Plask as they headed for theirs. Jeonk and Shok would begin their half of the search from one end of the canyon system, Plask and Rakoup would begin from the other. They decided to work toward the center as a team. Rakoup ordered his fleet fighters to hang overhead but not to interfere unless they received specific orders.

Rakoup and Shok piloted the Spits. Plask and Jeonk handled the radios to keep the pilots updated on each other's progress. The Spits' scanners were difficult to use because of the large deposits of natural metal ore in the canyons The scanners couldn't see through the metal. The main canyon was about a hundred miles long and it was honeycombed with caves. Finding the pirates was going to be a dangerous, tiresome job.

Each cave was a different matter. The Spits could scan inside from the entrances, but the scanning Spit had to cross directly in front of the entrances to do the scanning. That was the dangerous part. The discovering Dragon Spit would find someone waiting inside, waiting to shoot. Shok thought Kursit and Chokng would hold their fire unless they were convinced they had been discovered. Jeonk passed Shok's personal logic on the subject to Rakoup and Plask.

The searchers decided to keep going when they discovered the hiding place. Whoever made the discovery would remain in the best position, out of the line of fire, until the other Spit arrived to assist the discoverers. Shok's logic was pretty good if all of the pirates or the main body of them were in the same cave.

Jeonk and Shok were about half way down the canyon when they came slowly into the area with the most caves. Shok and Jeonk could see Rakoup and Plask ahead, swinging their Spit back and forth across the floor of the canyon and checking the caves. Both Spits held the same altitude, maybe ten feet above the floor of the canyon.

Plask and Rakoup began crossing the mouth of a large cave very near the place Jeonk and Shok were searching. Plask cautioned, "I've got something here." Rakoup brought his Dragon Spit to the other side of the entrance and spun it to cover the mouth of the cave from the other side.

Shok piloted his Spit across the mouth of the cave's brother, or maybe another entrance to the same cave, a short distance away. Jeonk reported, "There are more of them in here and it looks like a large party."

Shok tried to spur the Dragon spit to the other side of the mouth of the cave. It was no go. Just as he thought they had it made, a blast from a laser hit the Spit in the right rear section. The Dragon Spit hit the deck hard and skidded to a halt about thirty yards from where Rakoup and Plask were hanging low.

Rakoup spun his Spit to cover them. His Spit was hit directly in its aft section as he finished his spin. The laser came from a small cave directly across the canyon. The same cave Jeonk and Shok were hit from. Rakoup's Dragon Spit came down with its nose on top of the nose of Shok's downed Spit. The two Spits looked like a head on fender bender with a fire at both ends.

Plask and Rakoup came bounding out of their Spit, as Jeonk and Shok leaped out of theirs. They were safe from the large cave entrances, but the guy across the canyon kept firing. They had nowhere to go. There was no cover they could get to without being shot down by the pirates in the caves on both sides of them, or the guy directly across the canyon. The four of them were pinned down tight. The downed Dragon Spits were their only cover, and the cover kept disappearing as the gunner across the canyon chewed the Spits into smaller and smaller pieces with each burst from his laser.

The heat from the burning Dragon Spits became intense. The Spits were getting too small for protection. The constant pounding by the laser hits were reducing them to nothing. Time was running out. Rakoup's radio transmission was quick and urgent; "You fighters, get down here fast, and clear the cave across the canyon with your pulse cannons.

Four fighters dived down, one split second after the other, firing into the cave entrance before each fighter thrusted out. Suddenly, there was one hell of an explosion inside the cave. Fire, filled with the remains of whatever they were storing in the cave, came shooting across the canyon floor like a freight train from hell coming right at them. The four of them dived away from the center of the oncoming stream of fire to the paltry cover they found behind the fiery remains of their chewed up Dragon Spits.

The fire burned out before it swallowed them. The Dragon Spits gave them some cover from the cave spewed debris. All four of them were covered with the dirt carried by the explosion, but none were hurt. Jeonk remarked, "There were at least two men in the cave across the canyon."

Shok looked up at him from his dirt filled refuge and asked, "How do you know; did you take roll call before the explosion?" Jeonk pointed behind him and there, stuck against the canyon wall, were two burned up bodies.

Plask shook the dirt off of his shoulders, wiped the dust off of his baldhead and said, "They didn't kill us, and we didn't kill us. I think, all things considered, we will win this battle."

Rakoup retorted, "It's been a hell of a day. Those dead guys against the wall of the canyon are the only ones who have ever shot me out of a spacecraft. I think I'll wait until all things are finally considered before I give my opinion about who is going to win this battle."

They still had the problem of the pirates in the caves. Rakoup shook the dirt out of his radio and called for the fleet Marines to deploy for an assault on the caves. Rakoup didn't think that would be much of a fight for his Marines but finding Chokng and Kursit wouldn't be easy. The two master culprits could be expected to sacrifice everyone else as they tried to escape. Losing the top two guys on the galaxies most wanted list would make the entire operation an exercise in futility.

The fleet cruisers were positioned to cover every possible escape route. With three fleets in the air, all of Shiska Frok was locked down tighter than a rusted bolt. The two crooks couldn't go anywhere, but if they weren't inside the caves, they were going to be real tough to find.

The Marines put mobile scanners in front of the caves to get as much of a picture of the interior as they could. The scanners showed a very extensive cave system. The two caves were connected and the pirates inside had already retreated beyond the range of the scanners.

The Marines advanced into the caves using their scanners to warn them when they approached the area where retreat would be impossible for the pirates. The Marines remained in control of the areas as they were cleared. As they advanced deeper into the cave system, each area was lighted to maintain security.

The inside of the cave system was weird. Metallic outcroppings were everywhere. Large green crystalline structures protruded from the walls of the caves and bright metallic looking crystals rose from the floor. Shok broke some of the crystals off and put them in his pocket as they proceeded through the cave. He also found metal that looked like Gold mixed with some grayish looking stuff. He put some of that in his pocket with the crystals.

The Marines cautiously entered a large chamber where their scanners became useless. The scanners received stronger return signal than they were transmitting and the returns were coming from everywhere. The scanner's viewing screens blossomed until nothing could be seen on them.

Shok thought they were in the area the pirates would most likely use for a final battle. The cave was covered with outcroppings of the strange crystals on its ceiling, walls and floor. The metallic stuff was sticking out of the floor of the chamber everywhere they looked. The pirates could be hiding all over the chamber without being seen until they began shooting. Rakoup decided it was too risky to proceed under these conditions.

Jeonk, Shok, Plask and Rakoup held a quick conference to decide on a safe assault. They decided to douse all of their lights and spread the marines for a field of fire. Rakoup could talk to the entire troop through their helmet radios, and he positioned them for maximum safety. The Marines would be ordered to fire across the chamber for effect. If there were no pirates in the chamber, the Marines would receive no return fire when they fired their lasers. They could assume the chamber was empty if there was no return fire and the search could go forward from that point.

They doused all lights but the chamber didn't go completely dark. There was still a green haze from the crystals. None of them could see very much from it and it slowly dimmed but it was still there.

Rakoup had put the Marines in the prone position along one side of the chamber. For some reason, their night vision glasses didn't seem to do them very much good. The green haze made the use of night vision glasses questionable. Most of the Marines decided to remove their night vision glasses.

SPACE LINE BY MARIVIN E. FOX

Rakoup gave the order to fire and the Marines laid down a blanket of fire. Lasers crossed the chamber in a continuously shifting pattern beginning across the floor of the chamber and climbing higher in the chamber with each order to elevate fire. The Marines fired a few salvos before they began receiving return fire from the pirates. The chamber was filled with Chokng and Kursit's pirates who had been holding their fire in the hope of ambushing the Marines as they crossed the chamber.

When the firing began, the Marines intentionally tried to miss the outcroppings because the outcroppings would block their lasers and make them ineffective. The pirates were less careful with their return fire and began hitting the crystals. The laser hit crystals lit up like light bulbs showing the positions of the pirates.

The Marines in the prone positions around the wall of the cave were difficult for the pirates to see. That position put the Marines outside of the immediate light of the crystals, but the pirates in the center of the cave became highlighted by the crystals' glow.

Most of the pirates had chosen to wear night vision glasses in the week haze of the crystal light. The sudden explosion of lights blinded the pirates wearing night vision glasses when the lasers hit the crystals.

The Marines shifted their laser fire to the pirates they could now see in the light of the green crystals. The Pirates tore off their night vision glasses and tried to get behind the outcroppings as they blindly returned the Marines fire. The Marines quickly discovered that hitting the metal outcropping spread their lasers in weird patterns around the outcroppings. Hitting the metal outcroppings caused the ricocheted laser light to scatter in short multicolored arrows of fire. Laser beams are only one color. Why hitting the stuff in the cave caused the laser light to scatter in different colors was a mystery caused by something in the metal or the crystals.

The multicolored laser scatter bouncing off of the metal still had enough power to cause injuries. The green crystals lighted up even more as they gained power from the laser scatter hitting them. The Marines stopped targeting the pirates and began firing rapid laser bursts at the outcroppings. Lasers hitting the crystals caused the whole chamber to explode with laser arrows surrounding, and hitting the pirates.

The screams of the pirates hit by the multicolored laser arrows were quickly drowned out by the screams of pirates trying to surrender. The fight was the most spectacular anyone in the cave had ever seen, and one of the shortest. The pirates began throwing their weapons in the direction of the Marines to prove they were getting out of the fight.

There were nearly two hundred pirates and eighty Argan Marines in the cave at the beginning of the battle. Many of the pirates were killed but Rakoup lost none of his Marines. The Marines were outfitted with protective thermal clothing that effectively protected them from the laser scatter from the crystals. The pirates, who weren't dressed for a battle they hadn't expected to fight, had no laser protection.

The surrender wasn't total. The two pervert-potentates the Marines had gone into the cave to find were not among the surrendered pirates. Most of the pirates spoke Argan, and getting information from them was no problem.

The pirates were no longer interested in protecting the engineers of their defeat. They took the Argans to the entrance of a small chamber in the back of the ambush cave. The defeated pirates said Chokng and Kursit had chosen the safety of their private hiding place while waiting for the outcome of the battle.

No one wanted to go into a darkened chamber from a lighted one to get them. The Marines brought in a few of their portable lights and illuminated the inside of the small chamber. There, standing in the center, as the lights brightened the chamber, were the long lost Kursit and Chokng. The kings of two planets, pardon me, Chokng calls himself the Emperor of the Gamac Kingdom, with their hands in the air. Their final retreat had no exit, no place to hide and had left them no place to run. Jeonk and Shok finally had them trapped.

Jeonk and Shok walked into the chamber for a satisfying close look at the two who tried to murderer them and their families, kidnapped women and made them sex slaves, and had tried to control the galaxy for their own criminal profit. They were a part of every serious problem Jeonk and Shok had faced for years. It was comforting just to get an up close look at the two most wanted master criminals in the galaxy, standing in worried defeat.

Chokng was the first to break the spell of Jeonk and Shok's silent enjoyment, "You can take our pistols. We won't resist."

Jeonk replied, coolly, "You can keep them. We don't want you two running around half dressed. It would damage your royal reputations."

Kursit added his own uncomfortable opinion, "We know you want to kill us. You and Shok are going to act like your not paying any attention to us. When we try to use our pistols, one or both of you will shoot us. We've heard about that trick. You might as well take our pistols. We aren't going to use them even if we get a chance to shoot both of you in the back at the same time."

Chokng added, "We know Plask and Rakoup are waiting for us in the big chamber. They will have no mercy on us if we kill either of you. We know we're trapped; let us give you the pistols."

Kursit growled, "Don't touch your pistols Chokng. That's what they're waiting for. They have to take the pistols from us."

Jeonk grabbed Kursit and Shok grabbed Chokng. They yanked them out of their little cave chamber and paraded them past their fellow pirates on the way to the outside of the cave. Kursit and Chokng were still wearing their pistols for the parade. There were a few unkind comments from their fellow pirates about their lack of courage as the two super pirates were propelled toward the light of day. Some of the Gamacs spit on the ground behind them as they passed. That's the cruelest, non-lethal, insult a Gamac can make.

Plask and Rakoup fell in right behind Jeonk and Shok in the parade. Rakoup said, "It would be easy for me to let a couple of their former admirers escape to spread the word about how tough the most feared tough guys on their planets were at the end."

Plask agreed, "Good idea Sitak but let four of them go. Two might not make it back to their own planets. This Shiska Frok is a tough place."

Jeonk kept silent; Shok knew there would be no escapes to mar a perfect capture but he didn't know the perfect capture would be marred by other considerations. They exited the cavern to find a crowd of people waiting for them. A few of the Argan women had arrived. Shiska Frok bordered on three Iklug nations and waiting outside was one King, one President and one National Manager with their accompanying generals, seconds in command and various nationally important fellow dignitaries in tow.

The Argan women, the national leaders and everyone else wanted Chokng and Kursit on charges ranging from the most lethal to the most disgusting. They all wanted them really bad. Most of them immediately began complaining because Jeonk and Shok hadn't removed the culprit's pistols.

SPACE LINE BY MARIVIN E. FOX

Sherril Strang didn't complain about the pistols. Shok thought she had some last hope of Chokng or Kursit going for their pistols so she could end her quest to finish them off.

Jeonk refused to give the two up. After all, the Argans captured them. They were under Argan control. Jeonk and Shok had plenty of evidence against them, and they had followed them across the galaxy to capture them. However high level the accusers from Iklug were, each of them amounted to just one more Johnny come lately, outside of their own jurisdictions, trying to horn in on the capture.

The king in the group of prisoner purloiners had made a call to the Galactic Forum about the capture. He called well before the capture because he was sure the famous Jeonk and Shok would get it done. A call from the Galactic forum came to Rakoup's flagship as Jeonk stonewalled the intruding dignitaries. The Manager of the Galactic Forum complex on the Veolsh planet wanted to speak with his Majesty Jeonk Shap.

Word had traveled fast on that high speed Galactic Forum communications system Shok had gotten them to install at great expense. The number of nations already bringing charges against Chokng and Kursit had reached large proportions. Jeonk knew a majority of the Galactic Forum nations wanted Chokng and Kursit for high crimes and higher crimes.

The Galactic Forum Manager had received many requests for Jeonk to bring the two captured kings to the Galactic Forum. All of the interested nations in the Forum could find some satisfaction by helping to do whatever would be done to the two most disreputable crooks in the galaxy.

Jeonk advised the Forum Manager that he would think it over and let the Manager know when he made his decision. Jeonk handed the two prisoners over to Rakoup, saying, "Watch them, if they make a move to escape, or anything else, let Sherril shoot them. She's standing there just waiting for them to try. She deserves to have the first shot. She'll go for Kursit first. Watch Chokng a little closer."

Jeonk signaled to Shok and both of them walked to where they could speak privately. Shok looked back to see Sherril standing about fifteen paces from Chokng and Kursit. She stood easy, almost nonchalantly. Sherril didn't know what Jeonk said to Rakoup in the Argan language but Shok knew she was waiting like a coiled spring. Chokng and Kursit put half a million gold skirbs on her lovely head and both of them knew they were in immediate danger--even before Rakoup walked off a few paces.

Rakoup doesn't like to be too close to the target when he draws his pistol. Kursit and Chokng guessed something lethal might happen to them. They slowly raised their hands above their shoulders.

Jeonk asked Shok, "How can we get out of giving Kursit and Chokng to the Galactic Forum nations--if Rakoup or Sherril don't shoot them? Every planet in the Forum will want to make them prisoners. The Forum will agree to each nation imprisoning them for a given period of time. The Forum will want Chokng and Kursit to be shifted from one nation's prison to the next nation's prison for the rest of their lives. Somewhere in shifting from one prison to another, they'll manage to escape. We'll have to hunt them down again." You know the Galactic Forum better than anyone else. So, how do we keep from having to give up Kursit and Chokng to them?"

Shok drafted the original rules for the Galactic Forum. He didn't have to guess about his answer; he knew the answer. Shok replied, "The Galactic Forum has no judiciary system, has no police force and has no sovereign powers. It's only a meeting place for nations to inform each other of matters they wish each other to know. The only reason they know we're here is because of that great communications system we had them install. The Galactic Forum can't force us to give up Kursit and Chokng. I know you know all of that and being forced to give them up isn't what you want me tell you.

"Let's start with Iklug's claim on them. Shiska Frok is a no-man's-land on Iklug. The Iklugs were afraid to go after them in Shiska Frok so they called us. We came to Iklug and did their job for them. No nation on Iklug has a legitimate claim to Kursit and Chokng. They want them to increase their own prestige on Iklug and in the Forum. That's why the Iklug king called on the Galactic Forum. He hoped the Forum would champion his cause because we captured them near his kingdom.

"The other two Iklug nations' bureaucrats want the same thing for the same reason. Many of the Forum nations want Chokng and Kursit on criminal charge of their own. They will not champion the Iklug's hope to take them.

"None of the Forum nations have a legitimate claim on them, and they have no way to establish a claim using the Forum Charter. We have extradition treaties with many of the Forum nations but we have the only legal claim on Chokng and Kursit because we captured them in a no-man's-land, not in any of their countries. No nation in the galaxy has a legal claim on them and they won't try to make one.

"The Forum nations are hoping we will remember our friendship with them and give them a share of our responsibility for these two criminals. There is our real problem and you want me to find a way for us to take care of the Chokng and Kursit problem without offending those friendships.

"Our real problem is with the nations on Paraca, Oglak and Veolsh. They have fought on our side in every battle and are the first ones to back us when there is trouble of any kind. We are so close to those three that we might as well be blood brothers. Chokng and Kursit aren't worth risking those friendships. I think we have to maintain our friendship with those three in this matter with as much enthusiasm as they have given us in more dangerous times.

"What I'm going to suggest is in the national interest of Arga, not what I personally want done with Chokng and Kursit. First, we can't execute them as we want and they deserve. We must keep both of them as prisoners on Arga for a long period of time, perhaps ten years. We have the first claim, and as a point of our national honor, we must respect our own claim. We can allow the other countries to imprison them afterword, and the Forum nations will understand when we insist on our priority for the nations that imprison them.

"When we finish with Chokng and Kursit, we will insist the Paracan nations imprison them next. No one escapes from a Paracan prison and all of the pirates on Gamac and Prssk working together couldn't break them out. After the Paracan nations finish imprisoning them, we insist on Kursit and Chokng being imprisoned by the Oglak nations. The Oglaks live mostly underground and their prisons are underground.

"Chokng's and Kursit's pirates won't take a chance on facing the Oglak machine-guns even if they figure out which underground prison they are in. Next, we insist on the Veolsh imprisoning them. The Veolsh prisons are as dry as the Oglak prisons are wet. If those two live through the Paracan, Oglak and Veolsh prisons, they'll be the oldest prisoners in the galaxy and everyone else will still be waiting their turn to imprison them."

SPACE LINE BY MARIVIN E. FOX

Jeonk was thoughtful for a moment, before he began to laugh. He said, "Pardon me, I was thinking of Kursit and Chokng in an Oglak prison. I visited one of them one time. I would give them to the Oglaks right now, except for our national honor. Maybe we can insist on turning them over to the Oglaks after Arga. I think you have a good plan but how can we get all of the Forum nations to try them. If Kursit and Chokng have to be present for trail their trails alone could take years."

"I don't think we'll have a problem with that,' Shok stated. "We'll insist on the other nations trying them in absentia and make them guarantee to imprison them for the agreed on time. They will be convicted in every nation before we hand them over to the first nation on our priority list. Those two cowards have too many accomplices to allow them to be transferred around the galaxy for trial. The organizations they headed are still there. We didn't wipe them out."

Jeonk asked, "What was your personal preference in taking care of Kursit and Chokng?"

"I wanted Sherril and the women take care of them," Shok answered. "The problem would be finished in two shots; although, Sherril tends to keep on shooting until her pistols are empty. She, our wives and a large part of the Argan Women fleet Officers want to make sure those two don't have an opportunity to do whatever they did to Sherril and a lot of other women. They know Kursit and Chokng would have done the same things to them if they had the chance."

Jeonk had his own first preference, "I wanted to take them to Arga and hang them in the Royal Compound. They tried to blow it up and kill all of us. That would be my way of telling people it's dangerous to try to kill us, but hanging them has become too complicated. We can't shut the rest of the Galaxy out. We'll give your plan a try. Like they say in your Republic, fly it from the flag pole and see if it gets saluted."

They returned to the waiting assemblage of people wanting to find out what the fate of Chokng and Kursit would be. None of them were happy. The King, the President and the National Manager wanted them pretty bad, but Jeonk stonewalled their arguments as the two captured potentate pirates were shifted to Rakoup's flagship. Once Chokng and Kursit were on board the cruiser, the various national entities shut up. They knew it was a done deal.

The Argan women were another problem. They were mad at Jeonk, Shok, Rakoup, and Plask for not finishing off Chokng and Kursit. The names of the husbands were given in the order of which they were maddest at.

The wives and the women warriors refused to fly their Dragon Spit Corsairs back to Arga with the men and the three Argan fleets. They said, almost in unison, "We got here without you and we can get home without you. The four of you said you would get rid of those perverts. You didn't!"

The four masculine causes of the women's dissatisfaction didn't have happy homes for a long time after that. Taking care of Sherril Strang's problem, and getting her back to Australia, was one of the lest of their worries. They made Kursit and Chokng tell them where the half million gold skirb bounty on her head was being held. A special bank on Gamac was holding the gold, and honors for anyone who killed Sherril.

Rakoup took three cruisers and some Marines to Chokng's rotten excuse for a capital to take care of that little problem. Jeonk, Shok and Plask went along with Rakoup. All four of them were on the receiving end of hourly cold shoulders at home and they thought a small battle fought to save Sherril's life might help their wives warm up a little.

Gamac is a miserable excuse for a planet. It's full of rocks, ridges, deep canyons, high mountains and almost nothing is level on it. Gamac is so dry you would have to search for water to find any. The whole planet looks like it should have a sign hung on it saying, danger, falling rocks!

The special bank holding the Sherril Strang bounty was perched on top of the capital city's highest rocks that hadn't fallen yet. The only building sitting higher than the bank in the capital was Chokng's palace.

As they descended, everyone checked to see if Chokng's roof had been repaired where Iliaska and Alice dropped the claw through it. There was no hole in the roof so they thought Chokng had finished the repairs before he and Kursit headed for Shiska Frok.

The bank was a remarkable edifice that displayed the Gamac distrust of its own people. It was four stories of thick walls with sharp rocks sticking out everywhere on the outside. It was difficult to tell if the sharp stones were set that way on purpose, for reasons having to do with protection, or just sloppy stone work. The roof of the bank had one pulse cannon and one laser to protect it from airborne attack. There were guards on top of the bank, guards on the ground around the bank, and guard posts from the bottom to the top of the mountain. Anyone using the bank was well inspected before he made it all of the way to a teller.

The three cruisers went in fast and took stations even with the roof of the bank. The surprised shooters on the roof began deserting their posts as soon as the cruisers appeared. The Gamac guards chucked their guns over the side of the building so no one would think they were about to use them. It took all of two minutes for the entire compliment of Gamac defenders of ill-gotten wealth to make it far enough down the mountain to insure their safety.

Whenever an Argan cruiser is seen on Gamac or Prssk, everyone assumes it's Rakoup and they are usually right. There are no arguments about who is in charge, everyone agrees, its Rakoup.

Rakoup put his Marines on the ground and immediately had them inside the bank chasing the guards out. Their were no windows in the bank for the customers to see what was going on outside. The vanishing guards hadn't bothered wasting their valuable time telling the customers inside about the foreign invasion. While the Marines were going inside the bank, Jeonk, Shok, Rakoup and Plask followed behind to see what kind of customers would climb so high to do their banking.

Most of the customers had shiny clothing on, like Gamac's pirates, smugglers and slavers wear. Shok noticed Veolsh Imperial coins among the money they had, and he thought it was part of the Veolsh financing for the pirate trade. He made sure all of the customers made deposits even though each one of them said he was making a withdrawal

The four husbands forced the bank manager to show them where the deposits were stored for safekeeping. The bank manager, after a quick discussion, showed them the banks super strength vault. The super strength master of all Gamac vaults was sunk beneath the bank in the rock of the mountain. It would be next to impossible to get to the vault from the outside of the bank, but the four cold-shouldered husband were on the inside.

The four of them robbed the bank. They didn't just take the half million gold skirbs meant to pay Sherril Strang's killer. They took everything in the bank. It took several hours to shuttle all of the gold, silver, jewels and stolen goods from the bank to a shuttle, and then into Rakoup's cruisers. Rakoup's Marines were busy with the job right up to the time Rakoup decided he should blow up the vault.

Plask was all for it but Jeonk and Shok didn't care if Rakoup blew up the vault or not. Rakoup felt his reputation was at risk. He had to do something worthy of himself to keep the Gamac's respect. If he didn't blow up the vault, the Gamac's might think he had gone soft and his next raid on Gamac's Pirates might be a problem. Besides that, it was the challenge. Here was a deep vault sunk in a stone mountain and he felt his experts could put shaped charges in the walls of the stone vault to bust it open. Unfortunately, the charges would also bring the entire bank down.

As per instructions, Rakoup's demolition experts converged on the bank and put their shaped charges in the vault. After clearing the area of Gamacs to insure there was no collateral damage, Rakoup set off the charges. The loose rocks on the mountain flew outward and surrounded the mountain in a neat circle with a dust cloud covering the top of the mountain.

When the dust cleared the mountain looked a little weakened but sitting on top of it, just a little worse for wear, was the bank. It was a little tilted to one side, and there were a few cracks in the walls, but it was still, mostly, intact. Plask said, "Rakoup, the bank is still there, and the vault is still under it."

Rakoup isn't one to accept a small glitch in his original plan as a major defect in the final result. He still had plenty of shaped charges. Rakoup promised, "This time you will see how an explosion can be a work of art." Rakoup wouldn't tell the other three what he intended to do. He took his explosive experts and their shaped charges back into the bank, damaged though it certainly was. Jeonk noticed two of his Marines carrying a medical stretcher with a big ball of something on it into the bank.

Jeonk asked Shok, "What do you think that ball of stuff is on Rakoup's stretcher?"

"I don't think Rakoup is one of those who saves big balls of twine," Shok remarked. "It's probably part of his art supplies."

"It's been a hell of a day," Plask added. "I wouldn't have missed this for Emira's promise to quit serving me cold meat because we didn't kill Chokng and Kursit."

Rakoup and his experts finally returned to his flagship after they finished decorating the bank with their artwork. Rakoup remarked, "We're all set except for repositioning the cruisers."

Plask asked, "Why do we have to reposition the cruisers? Nothing can hurt a cruiser except another cruiser."

"That bank can," Rakoup replied." He turned to his pilot and said, "Order all three cruisers up a thousand feet and back away from the bank another five hundred feet" After the cruisers were positioned, Rakoup announced, "This is real art. You'll have to see it to believe it."

The people in the Gamac capital knew something big was going to happen and they didn't want to miss it. Very few of them had ever had enough money to put it in the bank and they didn't care what happened to the bank. Some of them pointed at the bank and others clapped their hands. None of the cold meat husbands thought the Gamac hand clapping was necessarily meant to applaud Rakoup's efforts.

The Gamacs knew Rakoup was in their capital and that meant fireworks. Fireworks are always good crowd drawers, no matter who supplies them, or why. Hundreds lined the streets below the mountain the bank was on, waiting to view the handiwork of Rakoup, the most feared and famous man who ever came to Gamac.

Rakoup's three command decks were filled with the Marines who laid the charges in the bank. None of them wanted to miss their most artistic endeavor. The four husbands commanded one view port on Rakoup's flagship and a few dozen Marines stared out of the others. Rakoup gave the nod to his Chief in Charge of Blowing Things Up.

The four vertical corners of the bank blew out a split second before Rakoup's stretcher full of art supplies went off. The bank roof came off and vented skyward as the walls of the bank, still partially intact, surf boarded outward and crashed to a hard landing halfway down the mountain.

Chunks of the exploding bank bounced off of the cruisers circled around it to watch Rakoup's handiwork in motion. Jeonk said, "Damn, Rakoup, you could have killed us all."

A few bouncing chunks of the Gamac bank didn't worry Plask. He congratulated Rakoup and his team of bank exploders, "You have to admit it, that was one of the finest explosions any of us have ever seen. Rakoup deserves the credit! Cruisers are made tough. You can't bring a cruiser down--with a bank."

"I apologize," Jeonk, responded, "Rakoup did a beautiful job on the bank. I'm glad I saw it with my own eyes."

Rakoup gave Jeonk a quiet clinical response, "The next time someone asks a bank to hold money for killing an Argan, the proposition will be given more thought. I made Sherril an honorary Argan when I saw how she went after Kursit and Chokng."

Plask added, "And I'll make her a real Argan citizen anytime she wants."

They made it back to Arga and their disgruntled wives without further incident. The Gamacs' capital wasn't hurt very much and they could probably find something else to build on the shortened mountaintop Rakoup's artistic work had left in the capital city. The wives were no less cold to them just because they blew up the bank. Chokng and Kursit were still pounding rocks in one of Arga's prison compounds. That left the two super perverts too close and too lively to suit the women.

Sherril was finally put on the road to Australia after Rakoup had reduced the money on her head to one blown up bank. She took the job Jeonk offered her and what amounted to three hundred thousand dollars a year in American money was more than she expected to be paid. If Jeonk and Shok's business with Australia worked out, and it probably would, she would become a rich young lady with the percentage they offered her for being its manager.

They were still worried that some of the killers looking for her might not have gotten the word about Rakoup taking the money for killing her. Jeonk sent her and about half a ton of stuff from the ladies shopping sprees, on a cruiser to Australia. Her welcome home would be a big one.

Aslain, Alice and Iliaska finally told Jeonk and Shok how a pirate fleet had found enough guts to come up and fight an Argan fleet. The impatient and disgusted women had waited for the pirates to come out of their caves and fight, but the pirates wouldn't come out of hiding and give it a try. The ladies kept their fleet in plain view over Shiska Frok to entice the pirates but pirates didn't know the crews were all women.

Aslain, as per the duties of an outraged woman and Fleet Commander, challenged them with, "You two perverts who like to torture women haven't the courage to come out and fight women who can fight back. There are no men in this fleet, just women. We will beat the filthy life out of you and your fellow perverts. Show us how brave you are, you filthy cowards."

Chokng and Kursit thought it would be an easy battle. They knew Argan women didn't go into combat. Argan women couldn't be expected to have enough battle experience to put up a good fight. Kursit and Chokng thought the Argan women were weak and didn't know how to fight. A few women, and some Dragon Spit Corsairs would be fun to play with while they were being killed. Killing the Argan women would sweeten the revenge pounded into the blue King and the rotten Earthman.

The ladies taught the combined pirate fleets the tactics it wouldn't be able to pass on to the rest of the pirates in the galaxy. The Argan women put the spacecraft form both of the fleets belonging to the royal pirate perverts in little burning piles all over Shiska Frok.

The wives refused to moth ball the fleet of Dragon Spit Corsairs they stole from Jeonk and Shok's personal stock. Jeonk and Shok had three hundred of their war surplus Dragon Spits hidden at Yadki that weren't in use, and they thought, far from prying wives eyes. Alice and Iliaska found them. They also told Aslain and a few hundred Argan women fleet officers and enlisted personnel about the hidden Spits.

Aslain, Alice and Iliaska kept their brand new purloined female fleet active, by the authority of the Queen, to make Jeonk and Shok suffer for not properly getting rid of Kursit and Chokng the way the women wanted.

Jeonk and Shok moved their Yadki Dragon Spits to a new hiding place, possibly a more secure one, to make sure the women's new Dragon Spit fleet didn't take on a larger dimension. Both wanted to maintain some control over the size of the women's fleet, and their own, which was two parts of the same fleet, as Jeonk and Shok saw it.

Jeonk and Shok wanted the Dragon Spits for commercial reasons. They intended to use them to form a private civilian police force to protect their far-flung business interest. Shok and Jeonk vowed, "Our two hundred and forty, along with the women's fifty four Dragon Spits, will be back in our private fleet--one of these days."

It took the four lonely hearts, two kings and two Fleet Admirals, nearly a year to get back on the good side of their wives. That's how long it took Kursit and Chokng to figure out a way to escape from the Argan prison.

Kursit and Chokng managed to get some weapons, somehow, somewhere, and tried to shoot their way out of the prison. They were killed in the attempt. A Gamac corsair was waiting for them outside the prison compound, but they didn't live long enough to reach the corsair.

No one has been able to explain how a Gamac corsair landed close enough to the prison to pick up Kursit and Chokng. The wives believe Jeonk, Shok, Rakoup, and Plask, names given in the order of which the women were maddest at, planned the whole thing to keep their promise to their wives, 'to take care of the Kursit, Chokng problem.'

Jeonk and Shok headed a military investigation into the event but found no evidence of how the strange breech of Argan security occurred. They found no evidence pointing to the actual course the Gamac corsair flew to land on Arga. None of Kursit and Chokng's accomplices were captured in the strange escape.

Jeonk and Shok are both known as interplanetary corsair fanciers, but there is no record of them ever having owned a Gamac corsair, which they consider to be an inferior piece of equipment. That's the story the two of them are giving to the three hundred and seventeen Galactic Forum nations patiently waiting for their turn to imprison Chokng and Kursit.

The husbands were, once again, enjoying the warm shoulders and sweet nights of wifely companionship. Both nights were a lot of fun but the women were bursting with the need to share the good news of Chokng and Kursit's demise.

The wives and their fleet of fifty-four Dragon Spit Corsairs, with all female crews, are flying to Australia. The women want to, personally, give Sherril Strang the good news of Chokng Fould and Kursit Balt's mysterious but sudden and certain demise.

Shok and Jeonk both know there are a few perverts in Australia, and they don't want the women starting a war because they accidentally encounter some of them. Shok, because he is from Earth and Jeonk still believes the myth that Alice is the easy one of the two wives to convince of anything, had the job of instructing the three women Fleet Commanders and their fleet crews about the husbandly concerns for their safety.

Shok instructed them in the following manner, "Don't go anyplace alone. You are big enough to be safe if you stay in a group. If you are assaulted, pound the guys who are trying to assault you into the ground. Call the local authorities if you are only insulted or upset by unsavory types. Jeonk and I like the Aussies and we plan to do a lot of business with them. We have big money riding on those Aussies and we are a little tired of war.

The End

www.ingramcontent.com/pod-product-compliance
Lightning Source LLC
Chambersburg PA
CBHW080019130626
46556CB00016B/3234